Praise for

Pages from the Book of Broken Dreams

Kat Jackson possesses a remarkable ability to forge emotional connections with her readers, setting her apart as a storyteller. By delving into shared human experiences with vivid and tangible details, she crafts narratives that leave a profound and enduring impact. Readers are drawn into her tales because they become emotionally invested in the struggles, triumphs and sorrows of her characters. Through skillful storytelling, she seamlessly integrates poignant moments that resonate with her audience, allowing them to truly feel the depth of the emotions portrayed in her well-crafted scenes. Whether exploring themes of love, loss, or happiness, these emotions imbue her stories with a sense of authenticity and relatability that lingers long after the final page is turned. This unique quality is what sets her apart as a writer, and it is why I eagerly accept any opportunity to read and review her work.

Storytelling exposes a vulnerability within writers, and I love the way Jackson is willing to take risks with hers. *Pages from the Book of Broken Dreams* captures themes of vulnerability, fear, self-doubt, courage and love with a heartfelt and youthful insight that's so relatable one can almost reach out and touch it. It's tagged as a romance, but it's more than that really. It's a reminder that dreams fuel passion. Without them, life loses its shine.

-Women Using Words

I really enjoyed the descriptive writing style this author has. From places, streets, buildings, baked goods, and emotions. I was there, I saw, smelt, tasted, and felt it all and got lost in the world Jackson built.

-The Lesbian Review

In Bloom

In Bloom delves into profound themes with a level of artistry that deserves commendation. Jackson's narrative skillfully unravels the intricacies of the heart, emphasizing its enduring capacity for hope and resilience. The thoughtful construction of this narrative is marked by compassionate grace. It is raw, tender and remarkable in every way.

-Women Using Words

All the emotions the author explores are very powerful, full of grief and regret, but I never felt overwhelmed. The author gives a reader two women who are finally beginning to feel a need for some kind of relationship after years of emotional pain, making the story about that and not the falling happily into bed as the end goal. There is understated complexity in the plot and an often gorgeously crafted prose that drew me in.

-The Lesbian Review

The Missing Piece

…What I enjoy most about Kat Jackson's writing is she doesn't feel the need to follow the formula. Her characters are just as unconventional as their creator. Her writing is intelligent, and her characters show tremendous growth as the novel progresses. Jackson is a unique voice in the sapphic community and one who seems to improve with every book.

-Laura G., *NetGalley*

Another good read by Kat Jackson! She's becoming one of my favourite authors and I certainly look forward to future releases. I love her writing style, her enjoyable characters that always have that chemistry needed from the onset and her great storylines that capture you from the start.

-Jo R., *NetGalley*

Golden Hour

Kat Jackson has written another excellent book! If you've not already, check some of her other books out. *Golden Hour* is no exception, I love her writing style and her books have "drawn" me in.

-Jo R., *NetGalley*

Rapidly becoming one of my favourite lesbian authors, she writes intelligent books that explore more than just a romance.

-Claire E., *NetGalley*

I am coming to find that I really love books by Kat Jackson, she manages to pull me in on an emotional level and I enjoyed the pairing between Lina and Regan very much. The way Lina's PTSD was handled and described gave the book more depth than the average romance novel and when it's done in the way Jackson does it, it's very much lifting the book to a next level. *Golden Hour* can be read as a standalone, yet Lina was first introduced in an earlier book (*Across the Hall*) and that couple has a role in this one as Lina's best friends. Highly recommended!

-Dominique V., *NetGalley*

The Roads Left Behind Us

The writing is beautifully filled with so much emotion and intelligent dialogue, I was sad when it ended. The environment is academia which makes the content of many conversations slightly elevated over other romance novels. Yet very understandable and warm. The characters are real, interesting, and distinct. I liked all of them. I highly recommend this story.

-Cheryl S., *NetGalley*

That was some marvelous writing; the vocabulary alone was spellbinding. The two MCs and every single supporting character are so well fleshed out that you feel as if you stepped into a room full of your friends and are catching up on all the gossip. The "will they, won't they" makes quite a pull at your heartstrings, but the end result makes the shipwreck all the more survivable. Their love story is charming, it's refreshing, it's as stormy as it is placid, and you will find yourself smiling hard at the MCs' antics throughout. A play at the Student/Professor fantasy, but you'll find these two are on equal footing in the PhD program where a delicious age-gap and big, beautiful brains war to find shelter.

-Alice G., *NetGalley*

Across the Hall

I loved Kat Jackson's first book, *Begin Again*, and I've been not-very-patiently awaiting the release of her second. I was not in any way disappointed! If you're looking for a layered tale of wonderfully flawed people, look no further. What enchanted me so much about *Begin Again*, and what runs through *Across the Hall* is one of the things that makes humans so interesting is that we are not perfect.

Mallory and Caitlin are complex characters with great depth, who I alternately wanted to hug and shake. Their stories are carefully crafted, and I am so thrilled to hear that Lina is getting her own book!

-Orlando J., *NetGalley*

Kat Jackson's *Begin Again* was an incredible debut and she became my favorite new author of 2020. Needless to say I was really looking forward to this sophomore effort. It didn't disappoint.

It's a workplace romance featuring two mains with a lot of baggage to bring to a fledging relationship. This story is really told in third person from Caitlin's POV, so we don't really know what's going on in Mallory's head. I really enjoyed following the ups and downs of the relationship and it was hard to tell where it was going. I started reading and next thing I knew, I was finished. That's what I love about a book.

-Karen R., NetGalley

Begin Again

Begin Again is one of the most beautiful, heartrending, and thought-provoking books I've read. Kat Jackson manages the rare feat of making a lesfic novel that toys with infidelity meaningful and elegant. While this all might sound a bit grim, it does have plenty of lighthearted moments too.

-Orlando J., NetGalley

Begin Again is one of the most thought-provoking, honest, emotional and heartrending books I've ever read. How the author managed to get the real, raw emotions (that I could believe and feel) down on paper and into words is amazing. If you read the blurb you will know, sort of what this story is about. But it's much more than that. As other reviewers have stated, it's not a comfy read but was totally riveting. I read it in a day, I just couldn't put it down. Definitely one of the best books I've read and if I could give it more stars I would for sure! Superbly written. Totally recommend.

-Anja S., NetGalley

Deck the Palms

Other Bella Books by Kat Jackson

About the Author

Kat Jackson is a collector of feelings, words, and typewriters. She's an educator living in Pennsylvania, where she enjoys all four seasons in the span of a single week. Kat's been consumed with words and language for essentially her whole life, and continues to spend entirely too much time overthinking anything that's ever been said to her (this is a joke, kind of, but not completely). Running is her #1 coping mechanism followed closely by sitting in the sun with a good book and/or losing herself in a true crime podcast. Contrary to popular belief, Kat does (somewhat) believe in the potential of happily ever after. Most days, anyway.

First Edition - 2024

Editor: Alissa McGowan

ISBN: 978-1-64247-618-7

Acknowledgements

First and foremost, thank you to everyone at Bella for providing the space and opportunity for writers like me to bring their dream stories to life. I'm grateful and still a little stunned that I get to do this.

Alissa: Thank you, as always, for working with me through this process. I think we reached a new "lol" count on this one.

This one took a village, so buckle up, y'all.

JJ: My incredible, supportive, hilarious, fiery, justice-loving codependent long-distance writing partner. I honestly don't know if this book would exist without you. Granted, we both know I was always up for sprints because I am a quick tippy-tapper and kicked your ass every round. Suffice it to say, you came into my life at the exact moment I needed you to. (I'm getting emotional while I'm typing this so I'm documenting that as proof of how important you are to me.) Not only did you get me through this book, you also helped get me through That Other Stuff. Amazingly, I still like you even though you question my taste in women. You're forever my favorite fake-date (gross, is that a trope?), and I cannot wait to see what kind of writing adventures we get into. I love you big, bro. PB&J 4ever.

Laura: My darling friend, I adore you more than words can say. Thank you for always being there whenever I need you, whether for the most ab-crushing of laughs or for a solid reality check. I love every adventure we've been on so far, and can't wait to see what kinds of trouble we get into as time goes on. Also, don't get mad that JJ got a longer note here; I love you both equally. (Hi Deb!! Love you!)

KL: Listen, I am not okay with the fact that you beat me in a couple writing sprints. Like, NOT OKAY WITH IT. Whatever… At least we finished writing our books. Thank you for being a damn solid human. Woodchippers forever.

K.V.: My OG alpha reader. Your love for my characters truly keeps me going. Thank you, thank you, thank you for being in my corner and cheering me on even when I'm being an absolute avoidant pain in the ass. You are my Canva Queen and I so appreciate everything you help me with.

Ga9: There are lots of places I could go with this cute little acknowledgement. AI, squirrels, Jessica Rabbit, ripped jeans, The Mini, science (lots of science!). I feel honored to be the first customer of All Star BFS, and I'm eternally grateful for all the services your company has efficiently provided for me, especially while writing this book. Dare I say your company has gone above and beyond several times? I do dare. And I appreciate it all immensely.

T.B. aka Mrs. Turner: My dude, I would be remiss if I didn't nudge you onto this list, and it's not just because of your "calm, soothing voice." Thank you for engaging in this weird and wonderful long-distance friendship we have. Say hi to Trea for me.

Hot Stacy: I just love you guys. Thank you for being in my world.

And to my readers, thank you for taking a chance on my books. I know they're not "standard romance" (yes, I'm making a typical Kat Jackson facial expression whilst typing that), but they represent something important to me. Parts of myself break through into every book I write, and most of the time, I'm not willing to admit what those pieces are. Just know they're there, and know that they've been tucked away for various lengths of time, waiting to get their moment in the light. Thank you for taking in my words, and unknowingly holding those pieces as you read.

Because each time I finish writing a book, I'm lighter.

Dedication

"She is a little explosion of hope…"
-Foy Vance, "She Burns"

Deck the Palms

Kat Jackson

BELLA
BOOKS

CHAPTER ONE

Sand had never felt so soft. It was strange, unnerving, and delicious all at once. For someone accustomed to the gritty, pebbly, sometimes stabby sand of the upper east coast, the nearly white expanse covering the beach that butted against the Gulf of Mexico felt wrong—and criminally right. It didn't feel like *sand* at all. More like flour. No, confectioner's sugar.

Whatever the proper comparison, oh, it was decadent, and the tension in Allison's shoulders began to unknot as she continued digging her bare toes into the piles she'd shoved together with her heels. She shifted her gaze from her feet—toes recently painted the bright pink of her childhood dreams—to the elderly couple walking slowly in the gentle lap of the surf. One man kept his hand steady on the other's lower back. Their heads were bent close together, each covered in a faded baseball hat, and every few steps, one man would throw his head back in laughter while the other looked on, clearly pleased he still had that effect on his partner.

A dying ember of hope flickered deep within Allison. She smiled, caught herself, and scowled. Within the space of a breath, the ember was extinguished.

It was nearing 5:15 p.m. and the sun was beginning to sink lower in the cloud-streaked sky. By instinct, Allison rubbed her bare arms, then laughed. Shaking off the habits of "real" winters would take time. Colliding thoughts of time and habits tied a quick ribbon around her lungs, its bow punctuating her breath with a stinging gasp.

So many habits to break, and all the time in the world to create new ones.

She pushed her feet deeper into the sand and locked her gaze on the horizon, now glowing gold. She'd prefer not to create new habits—well, scratch that. New good habits were fine. New bad habits, ones she would need to strike out, scrub away, scour off: those she could do without. It seemed to Allison, however, that she was an expert at forming new bad habits. She'd made a list of them, a slightly mad, bulleted rundown of all her failings from the age of twenty. She was in her mid-thirties when she'd created that list, fully in the embrace of a terrible breakup alongside the reappearance of an ex she had no business even speaking to. (Naturally, they'd done more than speak, which had summoned six new bolded items to the list.) Now that she was nearing forty-two, The List required several pages.

It was so long and so horrible that she'd been tempted to leave it in Portland when she'd packed up to move across the country. She'd held it with the tips of her fingers, even dangled it over a half-full industrial-strength black trash bag. The moment her fingertips released the sheets of poison, her heart had done one of those weird trip-hop-skip things and she'd gasped, dug deep to pull up coordination she'd never known she had, and managed to grab The List before it plopped into the sea of trash it, frankly, belonged in.

But mistakes, for Allison, were not trash. They were points of reference, reminders of What Not To Do Ever Again.

Did she follow her own rules? Of course not; she was a Libra. But still. She wanted the proof, the full measure of everything she'd done wrong, *in hopes* she would never (or at least infrequently) do it again.

A shriek from the water's edge pulled Allison from her mental prison. She squinted at the water, her vision blocky and dark around the edges from gazing a bit too long at a point near the sun. A handful of children had arrived, breaking the relative calm and quiet of the beach. A frown tugged the edges of her lips—once a curmudgeon, always a curmudgeon, it seemed.

Kids were fine! Plenty of her friends back in Portland had kids, and she'd been a more-than-decent Aunt Alli. But right now? Their presence was not...preferable. She'd just wanted a chill sunset moment at the beach before—

As another playful scream erupted from the incredibly healthy lungs of a toddling child, Allison rolled her head back and shook it. Her hair fell back into place as she righted her neck and avoided looking at the army of kids now littering the water's edge. She tucked an errant piece of hair behind her ear, then tugged the bill of her baseball hat lower. Probably not her best move, shoving a hat onto her head before meeting her not-quite-girlfriend for dinner at a restaurant with a dress code.

Allison stood, brushing the fine sand from the back of her jeans. Her fingers grazed the spot where her back pocket was slowly ripping itself away. She'd have to go home before dinner anyway; this outfit would be frowned upon not only by the host, but also by Holly. She could fix her hair, or at least try to.

"You need to make an effort," she muttered as she walked toward the water, pausing to roll her jeans an extra time—another ritual from summers spent at Jersey beaches where the ocean was unpredictably splashy. Here, there didn't seem to be any rogue waves at all.

What there was, however, was a group of twenty-somethings setting up camp a few yards away. As Allison neared them, she groaned in tune with the jarringly loud music. She fought the urge to shoot the group her—if she must say so herself—rather refined eye daggers as she passed. She did glance at them, as surreptitiously as possible beneath the cover of her hat, feeling both strings of rage for their thoughtless disruption of the chill beach atmosphere and jealousy for the laughing, easy camaraderie among them.

With the water lapping at her ankles, Allison walked down the beach, away from the little children and the older children. She pulled off her hat, wanting to feel what was left of the sun on her face. All she'd wanted was to watch the sunset in peace. To regroup and steady her jangling nerves. To, maybe, come to a decision that would feel right instead of just make sense.

But no! The universe clearly was not interested in giving her space to commune with nature, to settle her racing mind. It was, instead, rife with disruptions and agitations. Just like—

"No. No, no, no." Allison stopped in her tracks. It couldn't be. There was no way.

Slowly, with trepidation and certainty that she wished was a little less certain, she raised her arm and touched the crown of her head. Her hand yanked away upon contact and she shut her eyes briefly, not wanting to see what she already knew was smeared on the tip of her middle finger.

Had she had tears left to cry, they would have spilled out upon sight of the bird shit coating her fingertip. Alas, she'd cried herself dry before leaving Portland and all she had left in her was a feral scream that was pushing the limits of social acceptability. She squelched it, leaving it spiking in her throat, but just barely.

Miserably, Allison looked at her other hand. The very one, yes, holding the baseball hat an ex had given her years and years ago. It was old, faded, perfectly broken in, and the ultimate protector from a runny pile of bird excrement landing atop her freshly washed hair.

Perhaps this shit show was another sign from the universe, but its meaning was lost on her. With a final glance at the sinking sun, she turned to walk up the beach. Now she had no choice but to shower again, and if she was going to be on time for this date, she had to head home before the sun took its bow.

Just as well, Allison thought as she trudged toward the sidewalk. She considered putting the hat back on but didn't want the memory of the poop stuck to the inside of the hat.

Besides, she knew close to no one around here, so if she fostered a reputation as Bird Shit Lady, so be it.

As she waited to cross the street, her eyes landed on something foreign yet beautiful. She blinked, trying to right the image in her head. Christmas lights? Methodically and artistically wrapped around the trunk of a palm tree? She tilted her head as though that would bring clarity. Sure, it was November, and the holiday season was rapidly approaching. But shouldn't there be fake Christmas trees lining the streets? Something more traditionally festive?

She was jostled from her confusion by an older woman trying to cross the now carless street. Allison fell in step behind her, still gazing at the cheery trunk of the palm tree.

"When in Florida," she mumbled, shaking her head and cringing at the feeling of dried aviary crap clinging to her scalp.

Palm trees decked with Christmas lights, fine. Feces flung from flying feathered creatures? That she could do without.

CHAPTER TWO

The walk from the beach to the rental tiny home was short, less than ten minutes, and largely spent on side streets. It was part of the appeal of the rental and in the three weeks she'd been living there, Allison had made the walk every day. She didn't know yet if her Clearwater stay was permanent, hence the week-to-week rental agreement, so she was absolutely not going to take this incredible proximity to the beach for granted.

Home, or at least temporarily so, Allison unlocked the door and stepped into the compact quarters she was still working on making feel like they belonged to her. As far as tiny homes went—not that she had much exposure beyond HGTV—it was a comfortable one. Since it was built on a lot and not the kind that came on a trailer, there was real plumbing and electricity, all connected to the systems already in place for the larger home on the lot. The house itself was small, because of course it was, but Allison didn't need much space. She was accustomed to apartment living anyway, and found a certain freedom in no longer sharing walls with neighbors.

The walk from the entrance through the living area to the bathroom was a mere ten steps (yes, she'd counted on her first day there). After stripping off her jeans and T-shirt, Allison stepped into the turquoise tile-and-glass shower, wasting no time in ducking her head under the hot stream of water. She scrubbed hard, to rid herself of both the literal defecation and the mental shit-pile clouding the vision of her semirelationship. One she was beginning to think she had no business being in. But maybe she did! Maybe it was just too early to tell.

It wasn't that she'd been single for so long that she was clamoring for a new relationship. It was more that, despite all her attempts to break the cycle, she'd been in a parade of long-term commitments (admittedly, of varying levels of actual commitment) that didn't work, or didn't fit—but she'd stayed. Way, way past all the points she should have left. It was possible (as more than one friend had gently and not so gently pointed out over time) that Allison didn't know how to be alone. But she'd felt entirely alone in so many of her relationships that she feared the opposite was actually true: She didn't know how to be in a relationship and *not* feel alone.

This new dating situation, a mere two weeks in, was doing little to contradict that unhealthy but comfortable narrative.

It was five steps from the bathroom to the bedroom—a room that was, by tiny home standards, spacious. A queen-sized bed fit with room to spare for a nice sized closet and a bureau that looked like it had been salvaged from a flea market. And she meant that in a nice way; someone had obviously taken the time and effort to restore the hulking piece to nearly pristine quality. And it smelled heavenly, like wood and varnish with the edges of the fumes sanded off.

Allison gently tugged open the drawer that held her underwear. She paused, eyeing the assortment, wondering if tonight was the night. She bit the side of her lower lip. Did she even *want* tonight to be the night? What if she did, and it didn't happen? Or what if she was ambivalent, and it did happen, and she was happy about it? It could also happen and be terrible, which felt frustratingly likely. She blew out a breath and grabbed a pair of mids, the "fine if someone sees them, and not a waste of someone doesn't" underwear.

The rest of her outfit came together in a flash: dark jeans with no holes, a white button-up with the sleeves carefully rolled to her elbows, and a pair of brown Adidas Sambas that Allison wasn't sure were even hers but had somehow traveled across the country with her. As she slid her feet into the mystery shoes, she looked longingly at the assortment of flip-flops and Birkenstocks lining the floor of her closet. Wearing closed-toe shoes at the beach felt like a crime. Alas, the damn dress code.

A glance at the clock made her grunt. She rushed back to the bathroom, raked a comb through her hair, and hoped it would air dry enough to look presentable before she got to the restaurant. Which she had to drive to. *Which* she was annoyed by. Because, hello, highly walkable beach town? A literal dream for someone who hated driving?

"This better be worth it," Allison muttered as she hurried through rubbing on some moisturizer followed by a few spritzes of perfume. She shook her head as she walked down the stone path to the parking pad where her dark-blue Toyota Prius sat. She heard herself, loud and clear. And Holly was fine! She was fine.

It was Allison's attitude that was not at all fine.

Right. That was the problem.

Definitely.

Holly was waiting at the entrance of the restaurant when Allison arrived. She could tell Holly was doing her best to look nonchalant, like she *wasn't* waiting for someone. She was standing stock straight, her long, bare legs glowing with what appeared to be a fresh spray tan. The short pale-pink dress she wore was tight, leaving little to the imagination. Her arms, nicely toned from excessive amounts of group exercise classes, were crossed firmly over her torso, giving a nice—if unnecessary— lift to her impressive chest. Large round sunglasses hid her almost certainly darting eyes, but her lips were pasted into a friendly smile.

Allison kept her eyes locked on Holly as she approached, taking her in, surveying her for something familiar. There wasn't anything; she already knew that. Holly was the complete antithesis of every woman Allison had ever dated.

And that was the point, of course. Here, she would do *everything* differently. And in doing so, she wouldn't add a single item to The List.

"There you are!" Holly exclaimed when Allison was a few steps from her. It was for show, the exclamation. They both knew Holly had tracked her every move from the moment her car pulled into the parking lot.

"Hey," Allison said, coming to an awkward stop. Her hesitation must have shown because Holly blew out a tiny sigh before leaning in to hug her.

Holly held on to Allison's hand as she pulled back from their brief embrace. She eyed her up and down, smiling appreciatively if a bit wickedly, and a sizzle zipped through Allison's body. This was why she'd continued seeing Holly: She felt desired by her, and dammit, it had been far too long since she'd felt desired by someone this attractive.

Holly's brow wrinkled as she finished her overview of Allison. "This is the nicest outfit you have?"

The sizzle dead-dropped into a puddle of shame, extinguishing Allison's excitement. She looked down, trying to see herself through Holly's eyes. There was…nothing wrong with her outfit? No, no question mark. There was nothing wrong with her outfit. It followed the stupid ass dress code and it looked classy enough. Allison cleared her throat, the button-up suddenly feeling like a straightjacket. She'd been certain she'd nailed "casually not trying too hard but trying hard enough in a casual way."

Holly obviously felt differently. She sighed again, this one not as tiny as the previous. "It's okay. We'll go shopping this weekend." She flicked her blond-highlighted but otherwise dull-brown hair over her shoulder. "Come on, we're almost late for our reservation."

She waited for Allison to open the door for her, and after a fumble, Allison did. She trailed after Holly as she strode to the host, air-kissing him like they were old friends. Which they probably were, considering Holly was a lifelong Clearwater resident and knew at least three people wherever she went.

As they settled at a table right in the middle of the bustling restaurant, Allison tried to loosen up. She liked Holly! She did. Holly was attractive—no, she was hot. Absolutely hot. And kind! She was very nice to Allison, always complimenting her—well, hang on. That whole comment about her outfit couldn't exactly be filed under "nice." Okay, no worries. It was a slip. Allison looked down at her lap. She could have made more of an effort.

"I'm *so* hungry," Holly said, her words flecked with a whine. "I had a protein shake after Pilates this morning but work was so busy, I didn't have time for anything else."

Allison opened her mouth to agree that she was also hungry, but before she could, Holly was off and running.

"I literally walked into a list of eight missed calls at the office." She placed the menu on the table and leaned forward, her manicured nails grazing her jaw before clenching into fists to hold her chin up. "I had a showing at ten, right? And everyone knew I had another two showings this afternoon, so I had no time for phone calls today. But did anyone at the office take calls for me? Did anyone look at my calendar and slide buyers into slots for showings?"

Again, Allison attempted to reply, but not even a letter slipped out before Holly went on.

"No. They didn't. So not only was I totally booked and so, so busy with showings, but I also had to find time to return phone calls and schedule appointments." She shuddered, as though connecting with people who would potentially buy a home from her was a horrible, unsightly thing far beneath her.

Holly's recap of A Day in the Life of an In-Demand Realtor continued, interrupted only by the waiter appearing to take their order. Allison found her voice, opting for the chopped salad with blackened chicken. She also ordered a bottle of pinot grigio for them, which earned her a sultry smile from her date.

"I love that wine," Holly purred. "I love when you do things like that."

Allison, gifted with an opportunity to speak, found herself wordless. She searched her brain for the right response. Or a good response. A flirty response, even! Anything!

Seconds passed as her brain flipped through possible replies. Nothing.

Undeterred by Allison's inability to flirt back, Holly picked up right where she'd left off. She monologued as the wine was delivered and poured, through the space of waiting for their meals to be served, around bites of her food before pushing the plate—still three-quarters full—away and refilling her wineglass. She maintained eye contact and gestured in ways that implied she knew she was not alone at the table, but not once did she provide an opening for Allison to enter the conversation.

Until the check arrived, that is. With a bat of her eyelashes, Holly effortlessly nudged the black folder toward Allison's side of the table.

"Oh," Allison said, then cleared her throat. "This one's on me?"

"Well, yeah, baby. This was your idea!"

Baffled and mildly concerned regarding Holly's understanding of who had suggested coming to a restaurant with, that's right, *a fucking dress code*, Allison didn't argue. She slid her credit card into the folder and propped it up to signify it was ready to be taken.

Because she was beyond ready to go.

Holly immediately reached over and flattened the folder. "So, baby, what did you do today?"

A quick wash of shame spread over Allison when she realized how quickly she lit up by being asked such a simple question, and this far into the date. The shame spread when she realized she didn't have much of an answer.

"The usual," she said. "Looked over some paperwork, walked to the beach."

The interest in Holly's eyes flickered. "That's it?" She smiled, but it was rimmed with plastic. "I love how relaxed you are. Aren't you ready to get moving on everything, though?"

It had only been just shy of three weeks, because yes, Allison had started dating Holly mere days after she'd moved to town. But in that short amount of time, she'd picked up on Holly's number one skill: pairing something that sounded like a compliment with a passive dig. Unfortunately, that was not something Allison was experiencing for the first time.

And despite all sorts of therapeutic conversations with her friends and taking time for herself and blah blah blah, she still, *still*, fell victim to familiarity breeds contentment. At least she knew it. That had to count for something.

"Kind of." Allison shrugged. She didn't want to talk about all of that, not now. Not here. Not—and she tried to relax her shoulders—in this outfit that felt like it was glued to her skin. "It's just, uh, you know. A lot of work. It's a little overwhelming."

The bill folder was whisked away. Allison watched, forlorn, wishing the waiter could make her disappear just as quickly. Her wish was semigranted minutes later as she and Holly walked out of the restaurant, which, Allison had to admit, was very good despite its absurd wardrobe requirements.

"I love spending time with you," Holly said, sliding her arm through Allison's. "We have such great conversations."

Allison coughed, her throat chafing against what she wanted to say but refused to for the sake of politeness. "We do?" came out anyway, but it seemed the question mark only registered to Allison's ears, given the next words from Holly's mouth.

"So, my house or yours?"

Allison squirmed in her mind. This was the first time *that* particular subject had come up. And, if she was honest, she wanted to have sex. She was mostly comfortable with Holly, and found her attractive, but she wasn't sure yet if she was attracted *to* her…and this would be a good diagnostic tool for that.

The List flashed in her mind. Somewhere on there was a warning against this exact kind of thing: Do not sleep with someone unless you are truly into them and want to continue dating them.

She should probably add: Don't use sex as a diagnostic tool for level of attraction because if you don't already know that you're attracted to someone, sex isn't going to solve the equation.

But The List was far away, tucked into a notebook in her bedside table in the tiny home. And Holly was right there, right next to her, asking whose house they should go to.

"Yours," Allison said, the single word sounding much more confident than she felt.

Holly emitted a noise that sounded like a squeal, but Allison had a hard time believing a woman nearing forty would squeal.

"I was hoping you'd say that! You're going to *love* my house!"

Allison smiled gamely, allowing herself to be pulled toward the parking lot where they shared a semi gratifying kiss before getting into their cars and driving toward a night that would be memorable in some way.

At least Allison hoped so.

CHAPTER THREE

The shriek of a whistle pierced through Drew Kingsley's repetitive thoughts about the best tiles to use for a kitchen backsplash, jerking her away from work-think and back to the soccer game. She sat up, scooting to the edge of her seat, and scanned the field. It looked like they were finally getting ready to begin. She resisted the urge to look at her watch for easily the twentieth time since she'd set up her chair and parked her ass on the sidelines. She could have sworn the start time was 2:30, but it was almost three and—

Whatever. It's not like she had anything pressing on her schedule that was nudging up against this timing error.

Drew blew out a breath and eased back into her chair, wiggling till she found the sweet spot. No one was running around the field yet, so she let her mind drift back to tiles. She was getting tired of customers requesting the same old subway tiles, time and time again. It was trendy, yeah, but Drew typically strayed from trendy. The white-on-white-on-white kitchen phenomenon was sucking her creativity dry, and she was desperate for a client who actually liked color. Or patterns. Anything, *anything* other than white subway tile butting up against white cabinets and a white farmhouse sink.

It could be worse. How exactly, she wasn't sure, but she'd been in the home renovation business for long enough to know that it could always be worse.

A commotion rose across the field, a mixture of loud talking and excessively amused laughter. Drew tilted her head, resting her cheek in her hand, and watched. A large group of people was setting up camp, seeming not to care if they were blocking someone else's view. A canopy popped out, its limbs snapping into place. Next, a canary-yellow umbrella spread its wings and was planted in the ground at an angle. Chairs were unfolded and blankets billowed before being spread over the grass. Amused and a bit mortified, Drew watched as a golf cart rolled to a stop next to the canopy, a cooler the size of a mini fridge strapped into the back. Cheers erupted as though the king had arrived to deliver refreshments to his thirsting peasants.

"Unbelievable." She looked away, focusing on the field, but couldn't stop herself from glancing back at the show her family was putting on.

With a flash of secondary embarrassment, Drew watched as one of her brothers, dressed in Florida-dad requisite khaki shorts and a golf polo, carefully strung lights around the edge of the canopy. She braced herself, hoping they were simple white lights—still absolutely ridiculous for a midafternoon kid's soccer game—instead of—

She groaned loudly as the lights lit up. Red and green. *Blinking* red and green. Her mom, standing a few feet from the canopy, clapped excitedly and Drew's heart pinged in that familiar soft place. Okay, fine, there was something…cute… about the display. Overtly festive, yes. Unapologetically in the face of all the people attending the soccer game regardless of their preferred holiday traditions, yes. Completely out of place but somehow still bringing joy, yes. A little festive spirit never hurt anyone.

Even Drew Kingsley, bona fide year-round Grinch, could attest to that.

She tore her eyes, somewhat begrudgingly, from the enthusiastic noise across the field and looked at her phone.

I see you.

Drew grinned then immediately pulled her baseball hat lower to try to hide her face. She wasn't trying not to be seen. She wasn't hiding behind an umbrella or an oversized, gaudy canopy, after all. She was just sitting in her damn chair on the sidelines, like a normal person trying to watch a damn soccer game that still hadn't started.

Her phone buzzed again and she hesitated only a moment before glancing down at it.

It's not even baseball season, you weirdo.

Drew didn't hesitate to quickly flash her middle finger. As she lowered her arm, she gestured toward her hat, which happened to be her favorite Phillies hat. It was perfectly worn in, faded and frayed in all the right ways. Over the years she'd accumulated an impressive (to her) collection of Phillies hats, but she saved the nicer ones for… Well, okay, she didn't wear them. Maybe one or two if she was feeling fancy. She just liked having them.

"Drew!"

She dropped her head against the back of her chair and stared at the sky. She counted the seconds aimlessly, estimating about twenty-three would pass before—

"*Drew!*"

Oh, that had to be a new record. In response, Drew simply raised her arm and waved, this time with all her fingers. That would suffice. Surely.

Instead of a third summoning, the opening notes of "Little Saint Nick" blasted across the field.

That did it. Drew huffed angrily as she jumped from her chair, snapped said chair back to its over-the-shoulder-carrying option, grabbed her always-present water bottle, and stomped directly across the field. She paused only to kick an incoming ball with more force than was warranted, which earned her gleeful screams from the five-year-olds swarming the field for imminent play.

Drew made it to the bedazzled canopy without injury or too much disruption just as The Beach Boys reached the line "And a real famous cat all dressed up in red," which meant she was in time to see her mom executing the mildly embarrassing choreography she'd come up with back when Drew was a little kid. The hand gestures got weirder and more concerning by the year.

No hellos were exchanged as Drew headed directly to the speaker and turned the volume down. Her mom merely continued dancing. She may have waved but the gesture could have also been part of her snazzy moves.

"Apologize to your brother for disrupting the warm-up."

Drew looked over her shoulder and scanned the field for her younger brother, Van, who had zero soccer experience but had somehow landed a gig as a soccer coach. He caught her eye and shook his head, but he was laughing.

"He's fine," Drew retorted, opening her chair and sitting down. She made sure to stay about four feet away from the edge of the canopy, lest anyone think she was actually related to these people. She also avoided eye contact with her father, who, despite Drew being forty-four years old, still believed he had the power to tell her what to do.

For a few sacred moments, Drew sat silently as her family bustled around her. Snacks were handed out to the tagalong kids. The adults, all seven of them, slowly settled into their preferred places with their preferred beverages (nonalcoholic only; even her family respected the laws of school property). As though the coaches had been waiting for the Kingsley family to settle in, whistles blared and the game began.

The window for familial calm and quiet was closing rapidly. For now, all the adults were focused on the chaotic flurry of short-legged activity on the field. The Kingsley grandkids, too, appeared to be watching as they talked amongst themselves. But Drew knew she had limited time before someone tried to talk to her. She tried to make herself as small as possible—something she had never excelled at, despite being a woman of few words.

She tugged her Phillies hat down again, this time so she could dart her eyes around and assess the situation she had mostly unwillingly walked into. Her dad was sitting in the most elite lawn chair one could buy, sunglasses hiding his eyes, but Drew knew he was focused on the game. For all Greg Kingsley's faults, he was devoted to his grandchildren and would put work aside (for an hour) for them. Drew's mom was already up and moving around, checking on the handful of grandkids who were hanging out—some by choice, some by family obligation. Ava and Kit, both fourteen and therefore smarter than everyone in the family, were lying just behind the canopy, soaking in the sun while whispering middle school gossip. Eleven-year-old Blair was entertaining her cousin Remi, who was four and utterly enamored with her. And Jett, seven and the sweetest of Drew's ever-growing crew of nieces and nephews, was sitting next to his dad. Both appeared completely absorbed in the game, though considering both teams were composed of overly energetic and highly distractible five-year-olds, there wasn't much of a "game" happening.

A cloud of expensive perfume puffed around Drew as Natasha lugged over a chair and sat down next to her.

"So, was it our darling younger sister screaming your name, or the dreaded Christmas Is Upon Us soundtrack that got you over here?"

Drew rolled her head to the side and looked at her older sister. "You know it was the song."

Natasha laughed, not taking her eyes from the field. Specifically, not taking her eyes from her five-year-old daughter, Fiona, who had perhaps one athletic bone in her tiny body. "Yoli knows how to get what she wants."

It was the truest statement anyone could make about their mother. And it wasn't that Yolanda Kingsley was conniving or manipulative. She couldn't be farther from it. What she was was a ball of sparkling congeniality, a tiny half-Cuban woman packed with too much power for one person. She was, in a word, enigmatic. No one ever said it aloud, but the Kingsley family business would never have become what it was had Yolanda not been steering the ship alongside her husband. And much to everyone's surprise—and in some cases, misery—Yolanda didn't bother to pass down any of that critical personality DNA to a single one of her six children.

Drew felt neither misery nor surprise, for the record. She didn't aspire to be like either of her parents. She was perfectly fine with having inherited only the visual marks of their genetics, graced with her mother's dark-brown hair and equally dark-brown eyes, plus the cherry on top of thick eyebrows that gave her a perennially brooding appearance. She was equally pleased that, unlike her three shorter and much curvier sisters, she'd received her dad's genetics when it came to height (on the tall side) and physique (lean and slim-hipped).

"Where's the sign?"

Natasha gestured to the canopy. "Behold, the new and improved Kingsley advertisement strategy."

Sure enough, the logo for Kingsley Properties was emblazoned on the side of the canopy. It was somehow less obnoxious than the 4x4 sign their father typically propped up in front of their chairs. Drew was sure the logo was on the opposite side of the canopy as well, providing soccer game attendees on both sides the opportunity to wonder if they needed a new home, and gosh! How convenient if they did! A whole family was here to service whatever selling, buying, and building needs they had!

Drew swallowed, throat burning with the acid that always accompanied thinking about her family's business. *Their* business. Not hers. Two very, very different businesses.

Whistles and cheers erupted from the field, and Drew sat up, scanning the grass for three familiar forms. If she'd missed a goal, she would never hear the end of it—from the players, or their parents. Natasha jumped to her feet, clapping and yelling.

Drew stood too, half-worried and half-impressed at the idea of Fiona having scored a goal. Alas, false alarm: Within seconds,

Drew spotted her curly-haired niece kneeling on the opposite side of the field with another tiny human, both petting the grass.

Natasha snorted, having also caught sight of her daughter. Her older child, Ashley, was in college and a star lacrosse player. The sixteen-year gap between pregnancies seemed to have annihilated any chance of Fiona receiving athletic inclination from her mom, who had been a decent athlete in high school.

The gap also explained why Natasha's husband had left her, seeing as he'd had a vasectomy four years before Fiona arrived. The fact that Fiona had the same exact coloring and hooked nose as one of the construction workers who frequently worked with the Kingsleys also helped explain the divorce.

It was one of many familial missteps that the family, at large, didn't talk about.

"It wasn't any of them," Natasha said as she sat back down. "But it was Fiona's team. At least I think it was? Do they even have teams?"

Drew shrugged. As the only childless sibling in the family, she tended to rely on everyone else to know about kid things.

"So what's new with you? I haven't seen you in, what, a couple of weeks?"

More like a month, but Drew wasn't counting. "Nothing. The usual."

"The usual," Natasha mocked. Four years sat between the sisters, and it had always been enough to rouse competition, and irritation when Drew refused to engage with said competition. Natasha forever believed she had some kind of authority over Drew. They got along for the most part, but it was a superficial relationship. The only sibling Drew considered herself close to was her younger sister Celeste and truthfully, not even she knew much about Drew.

And Drew preferred to keep it that way.

The game sped along, Natasha happily chatting away about her daughters. Drew half-listened, half-watched the game, and kept one ear trained toward whatever was being said under the canopy. From what she could tell, Celeste was giving unsolicited parenting advice to their sister-in-law, Amaya, who was weeks away from delivering her third child. Drew's youngest sister, Mae, was buzzing between her children and husband, making sure everyone was hydrated and protected from the November sun. Yolanda (only called Yoli by her children, never to her face, and usually only when she was doing something outlandish… which was often) had settled next to her husband, who— miraculously—still appeared to be focused on the game and not his phone.

Drew was itching to sprint from the familial closeness, and nearly did so as soon as the game ended. She stood, packed up her chair, and shifted from foot to foot, wanting to see her three nieces before she left. She may not have been the kind of daughter her parents (still) wanted her to be, but she was a devoted aunt.

Grass clippings and flecks of mud accompanied Fiona, Noa, and Margot as they sped over to join the family. Van was further down the sidelines, cleaning up the mess of a post-game snack.

"Aunt Drew!" All three girls beelined to her, ponytails and pigtails sweaty and messy.

Drew dropped to her knees and opened her arms, grinning as three squirmy, overheated bodies fought for the best position in her hug. Their voices overlapped, giving Drew a rundown of their game. She got in a few words, but mostly listened to their hyper chatter.

Fiona and Noa soon raced off to find their moms, leaving Margot reaching for another hug. Drew scooped her up and held her close.

"I love you, Aunt Drew."

"Love you more, Go-Go."

The little girl giggled and kicked her legs, ready to be released from Drew's tight hug. Once on the ground, she grinned up at her aunt before heading to her mom, Mae, who gave Drew a little smile and wave.

The miniature hole in Drew's heart sealed up once again. She surveyed her family, making sure everyone was occupied, before picking up her things and heading back across the field. On her way, she clapped her younger brother on the back. Van looked up long enough to thank her for coming and Drew nodded in response.

She walked faster as her truck came into sight and wasted no time in throwing her chair into the back and climbing into the driver's seat. There, alone and surrounded by quiet, Drew exhaled a long held-in breath, letting the stress of being around her family slowly leak out.

CHAPTER FOUR

The intimidatingly thick file folder fell with a hollow thud to the dust-covered countertop. Allison pushed it away from the edge, as much to save it from spilling to the dirty floor as to remove it from her field of vision. The weight—both literal and metaphorical—of its contents brought her a feeling she hadn't experienced in a long time. It was something like anxiety. Excitement bordering on terror with a side of uncertainty. All layering together, dripping into one another and making a new emotion that could not be contained in one word.

Mostly, she was clueless, but that was more of a circumstantial status than it was a feeling.

Slowly, Allison walked through the desolate space. It was dim and musty, but still held a charm beneath the darkness. It was small but not too small; it had old character from beach days gone by, and a massive potential for becoming modern while still holding on to the success of its past.

When she reached the wall of floor-to-ceiling windows on the far side of the space, Allison ran her finger through the filth clouding the panes. It was granular, like sand was caught between the clumpy strings of dust motes. She couldn't help but smile. Sand here was inescapable, something that might have irritated her at another point in her life. But now, somehow, it felt comforting.

Realizing the end window was actually a door, she twisted the handle and swung it open, allowing a gentle sea breeze to filter into the space. She placed her hand on the casing of the window to her left and jumped back when it wiggled beneath her touch.

"Wait a minute." Perplexed, she scanned the metal frame and grinned when she found the handle, camouflaged with black paint to match the casing. The doors begrudgingly slid along the track, the noise ear-splitting, but the end result was worth it. Sunlight and fresh air flooded the room. Dust clumps and decades-old piles of dirt swirled, spinning into a mini tornado in the middle of the empty room.

As the tangible filth danced around the room, the smeared mess of emotions inside of Allison began to settle, leaving a sense of contentment settling low in her chest. She stood in the open wall of windows and leaned out into the sunny day. This she could work with. *This* she could have never done back in Oregon.

This, she thought, was why she was here.

Two hours later, Allison was lying on the floor in the center of the room, wondering exactly what the hell she'd been thinking when she'd decided to make a go of it and move here instead of at least planning a visit first. She had a feeling that's what normal people did: survey the options before committing to a gigantic, slightly uninformed leap across the country.

While it was true she could go back to Portland—she could go anywhere, really, whenever—there was something about *here* that felt right. Even if her surroundings weren't quite...up to par.

She'd cleaned the floors to the best of her ability, but that wasn't saying much since she'd arrived at the building with just a broom and a Swiffer. Still, she could actually see the floor now…which meant she could also see that it definitely needed to be replaced. And sooner rather than later.

And then, because why not, she'd used the broom to sweep the debris off the countertops hulking in one corner of the room. It was not her best cleaning decision, but it mostly did what she wanted it to do, and she had also learned that the counters and cabinets needed to be replaced. She added that to her mental checklist, which she was not yet willing to transfer onto paper.

In a move that not even she would repeat, she'd used the Swiffer to…yes…clean the walls. That had actually not been her worst decision of the morning. The effect was mediocre—there was a lifetime of accumulated dirt clinging to the walls—but the Swiffering had delivered a delightful surprise. The walls did *not* need to be replaced! It had been a concern voiced by Holly, of course, who had Experience with These Things: Any property so close to the beach, a.k.a the water and the weather elements that accompany the water, is likely to suffer more damage as a result. The inside seemed fine. Fine-ish, at least. Allison was hoping there wasn't an external issue, but she had a feeling she wasn't going to get that lucky, especially after noticing the rust on the window casings.

With the space relatively clean, or at least cleaner, Allison had grabbed the hulking file folder and sat down on the floor, ready to sift through the endless parade of papers. She still didn't have a plan, truthfully. She had an idea. She had a thought. She had a maybe. But a plan? No. Nothing of the sort.

And yet, as she rifled through the papers, making piles that made sense to her, a bubble of potential floated through her. She could do this. She knew she could because she'd technically done it before. With her former business partner, Neil, she'd built their coffee shop, Perk, from the ground up. Neil had the money; Allison had the ideas. Once they got Perk up and running to a success neither of them had anticipated, Neil had left Allison to manage everything while he tended to various other commercial properties.

Creating Perk had been a team, then a group, effort. Then, she'd had a business partner and said business partner had a ridiculous amount of money. Allison, here in Florida without a partner, did not have access to endless funds. But she did have some funds, courtesy of having sold her half of Perk before leaping across the country.

And she had this perfect property, a sidewalk away from the beach, which was—if she accepted it—going to be handed to her for free. It was a parting gift from her grandfather, as outlined in his will, that Allison and Allison alone would have rights to the property. It was her decision; she could sell it, or she could make it her own. The possibilities were actually, for once, endless. The ideas, unfortunately, currently were not.

The only idea taking root in her brain was: another damn coffee shop.

Allison pushed her damp hair behind her ears and continued staring at the ceiling. Which, to be fair, was in great shape. It was sloped and needed to be painted, but that was no surprise. The exposed wooden beams looked to be secure. They weren't in pristine shape, but she liked the lived-in look. More than that, she believed that a comfortably worn-in, casual style befitted a business so close to the beach.

What this place really needed was a gigantic ceiling fan. Or maybe multiple ceiling fans. Because even with those windows open and perfectly temperate early winter Florida temperatures, it was warm and sticky inside.

With a slow exhale, Allison sat up. She pulled her knees to her chest and looked straight ahead, marveling at the pristine view the window wall provided. The ocean glittered like a soothing beacon. She could definitely get used to coming to work every day if this was what she got to gaze at between customers.

She shook her head, knowing it wasn't that easy. None of this would be easy, if she chose to do it.

The thing was, if she really sat with it, the choice felt like the easiest "yes" she'd ever said.

She grunted and dropped her chin to her knees. Her indecision felt like a too-tight jacket that she continually took off then put back on, thinking *this time it will fit*. The longer she sat there and overthought all the reasons this could be the worst decision she could make at this very moment, the tighter the jacket felt, and the more often she took it off…only to reach for it moments later.

"Enough." Allison pushed herself off the ground. She grabbed her phone from the counter closest to her and walked through the open wall of windows, grinning as she did. She couldn't help but picture a few refurbished cafe tables right outside. Even as she was enjoying that image, she was shaking her head and pressing a button on her phone—a button that would bring her much needed clarity.

Moments later, Emery's face filled the screen. "Hey!" she said, genuine excitement in both her tone and her expression. Allison grinned back reflexively, then felt the corner of her mouth slide down. If her best friend was that happy to see her, shouldn't her sort-of-girlfriend be even more so? She certainly hadn't been last night. Unwilling to travel down that problematic path, Allison shook the truth from her head.

"Help me," she said, her voice plaintive and near a whine.

Emery squinted. "Help you? Correct me if I'm wrong, but aren't you standing less than twenty feet from the beach? Everyone knows salt water solves all problems, Allison."

"Not this kind of problem."

"Oh," Emery said slowly. "You're moping."

With a petulant groan, Allison kicked the toe of her shoe against the worn wood of the deck. "Maybe. But for a good reason."

On her side of the phone, Emery looked relaxed and composed, the picture of Mature Life Decisions. And she'd gotten there, to that blissful point of advancing through an excellent career and marrying the woman of her dreams. The path to that point, Allison knew because she'd been a passenger for the ride, was riddled with potholes and dead ends. Even a yield onto a one-way highway. In the wrong direction. But Emery had made it through all her wrong turns and near head-on collisions, landing happily in New York City with her wife.

Allison peered at the screen, trying to figure out where her best friend was. "Are you traveling?"

"No." Emery shifted a bit so the wall of her bedroom appeared. "I'm home getting over the flu."

"New wallpaper?"

"Yeah, you like it?"

Allison nodded side to side, her body language as uncertain as her gut response to said wallpaper. It was a splattered mash-up of dark greens and darker blues. Very moody. Very Emery. "It's...different."

"That's what Burke said." Emery smiled, a dreaminess settling over her features. "I think she secretly hates it, but—"

"She's so in love with you that she'd never say if she did," Allison finished, knowing the script. And it was true. The way Burke loved Emery was the stuff romance books were made of.

Allison scowled as a notification from Holly appeared. She swiped it away.

"So why are we moping?"

Leaning against the counter, Allison held up a finger. "Let me turn you around." She flipped her camera so Emery could take in the scene. "So. This is it."

She was silent for a moment, but attentive. "Okay. Walk me around."

So Allison did. Patiently and purposefully. She ran a commentary as she walked, pointing out the positives and negatives as she saw them. She heard the soft excitement in her own voice, the tentative hope that flickered around the edges of her words. She tried to flatten it but found she couldn't.

The tour ended at the wall of windows, easily Allison's favorite part of the storefront. Or back, as it was. Or front? Considering it faced the ocean? She shook her head. Semantics.

"And this," she said to Emery, gesturing for effect before realizing only the tips of her fingers appeared on the screen, "is the best part of it all."

"Oh, Allison," Emery said quietly. "This place is amazing."

She flipped the camera back and shot Emery a look. "Really? You don't think I'd be in way over my head with"—she gestured again, this time her arm entirely visible—"everything?"

"Well, it's definitely an undertaking." Another text from Holly appeared and Allison swiped it away too. "But you wouldn't be doing all the work on your own, would you?"

"God, no. My expertise in this area is limited to being a pretty okay painter. I've been researching local renovation and design companies." The words slipped out, the secret now in the open.

"So you *are* serious about this." Emery grinned. "I knew it."

"No, I'm still thinking about whether or not I want to sell it. I haven't made any decisions."

"Yeah, okay. I know you. You've probably spent the last week compiling a spreadsheet with information about these companies. Name three off the top of your head."

"Smith Restoration, Southern Magnolia Designs, Kingsley Properties." Allison gave a half-smile. "I have eight total."

"Of course you do." Emery laughed, then dropped the phone when she started coughing. "Hang on," she managed before giving in to the coughing fit.

Allison waited her out, sending two more text notifications to the graveyard before Emery came back, her cheeks splotched red but utterly pale beneath.

"Who's sending all those texts?" Emery leaned closer to the phone. She cleared her throat and reached for a glass of water on the table next to the bed.

"My latest mistake," Allison retorted. She cringed immediately. Holly wasn't that bad. She just wasn't… She wasn't the right fit.

"That realtor? I thought you were going to end it."

Allison stepped out into the sunshine, her back to the accordion windows. "I was, and I should have. But I, um…Yeah."

"Oh. You slept with her."

Double cringe, if such a thing existed. External and internal cringe, perhaps. "I may have."

Emery snorted, which only made her cough again. Moments later, she took a deep breath that sounded a little rattly. "And?"

"And nothing," Allison said with a shrug. "I don't regret it but it wasn't the best decision I've made in the last ten years." She paused and looked toward the sky. "Also not the worst decision I've made in the last ten years."

"I can vouch for that."

"I know you can." Allison sighed and looked Emery in the eye. "I needed to feel something. I know that sounds horrible and shitty and like I used her, but I didn't. We've been dating. People who are dating sleep together. So we did, and..." She trailed off, knowing Emery would say what she didn't care to admit.

"And you didn't feel what you wanted to feel."

Allison nodded. "So, now I know."

"Have you broken up with her?" Emery rolled her eyes. "Never mind, I guess she wouldn't be bombarding you with texts if you had."

"Not yet," Allison admitted. "I mean, I know I'm probably going to. I just...It's nice having someone here." Her stomach coiled in on itself. "Shit. Am I using her?"

"You could maybe just be friends? Instead of sending her a message you clearly don't want to send."

"Right." She turned to go back inside, but before she did, she flipped the camera again. "This is the exterior. The side facing the ocean."

"I can tell."

"I know," Allison said. "It needs work. Not as much as I feared, though."

Emery was quiet as Allison walked back inside and leaned against the counter, then slid till she was sitting on the floor. She angled the camera back to her face and waited for Emery to drop whatever truth bomb she was building.

"Here's what I'm thinking," Emery began, and Allison immediately relaxed. She and Emery had been friends since college, going on twenty plus years now, and she was truly the calm to Allison's storms. As they'd gotten older, the storms had changed but Emery had remained the constant soothing force in her life. Allison valued her thoughts and opinions more than anyone else she'd ever met. And truthfully, Emery wasn't the beacon of Good Choices; she'd made her share of homewrecking mistakes. But her self-awareness and way of communicating was a buoy in Allison's sometimes turbulent seas.

TL;DR: She wanted to be Emery when she grew up.

"You worked so hard at Perk," Emery went on. "You made that business what it was, and probably still is. You *can* do this, Allison. We both know that."

"Right," she murmured.

"And this property, while it needs a lot of TLC and a lot of help from people who know how to do these things, is incredible. The location is awesome, too. It reeks of potential, even over the phone."

"Hang on," Allison said. "You are forever telling me not to get hooked on potential."

Emery nodded approvingly. "Yeah. Potential in people. Not business opportunities, especially one like this."

"Fair."

"This is being handed to you, Allison. Just passed right into your lap." Emery widened her eyes and shook her head. "Honestly, I'd think you were crazy if you didn't take this opportunity and run with it."

"Really? You don't think it's, I don't know, irrational?" She jabbed at yet another notification from Holly.

"Not at all. I think it's going to be a lot of work, but I also think you're finally at a point where you can put the tools you've acquired over the years into this work and get something outstanding out of it."

"Therapy speak."

Emery shrugged. "Comes with the territory."

Allison looked around the space, trying to see it with the newest eyes possible. "Maybe I should call those top three companies."

"Good. I'm hanging up before you change your mind."

"Probably a wise choice," Allison said through a laugh.

"But before I do," Emery said, "I think this is the best good decision you've made in a long, long time."

Emotion pricked at Allison's eyes, a golf ball bobbing in her throat. "Thank you, Em. Seriously."

"Anytime, always. Text me later and let me know how your breakup goes."

Before Allison could fire back, Emery had hung up.

CHAPTER FIVE

Two days later, Allison was drowning in information about restorations, design, and general building improvements. Oh, and code. She'd forgotten all about codes. She'd been so overwhelmed and mentally tapped out by all the business *stuff* that she'd agreed to meet up with Holly.

Because of course she hadn't broken up with her after talking to Emery, or the day after. Or even after the totally abysmal date they'd just had.

It had started well enough. Allison had picked Holly up from her office, and they'd gone for lunch at a bistro on the outskirts of town. No dress code, thankfully, so Allison was safe in her torn jeans and flip-flops. She'd debated wearing a hat but decided that would be pushing it a tad too much if she wanted to continue dating Holly.

Which, hello, red flag. But Allison merely saw it as yellow.

Her seesawing indecision about continuing to date Holly? *That* was the bigger red flag but it wasn't flying high enough on the pole yet.

Lunch had become a bit boozy. And then a lot flirty. They'd left Allison's car in the parking lot and taken an Uber to Holly's house. Thus commenced part two of their terrible date—really, the only terrible part. Lunch was fine. But the sex? Not fine. Sexual chemistry simply did not exist between them. At least Allison thought so; she couldn't get a read on whether Holly was genuinely into it and enjoying herself or if she was faking it.

Another red flag, waving gaily. That one Allison saw clear as day.

The first time they'd had sex, she'd chalked it up to first-time/new-person nerves. It wasn't off the charts terrible, it just wasn't good. And Allison had had good sex. She'd also had decent sex, mediocre sex, so-drunk-you're-not-sure-who's-touching-whom sex. She'd had… Okay, fine. She'd had a lot of sex. Not a ton of partners, but a ton of sex.

So with the first time out of the way, Allison was sure (kind of) that they'd settle in and the second time would definitely be better.

Alas, no. It was not better. It was, in a word, horrible. Every kiss rolled through her with a kind of dread. Every touch felt heavy with a promise Allison couldn't keep. Halfway through, she realized she was still fully dressed and didn't want to undress. Like, at all. But Holly, after selfishly enjoying the hell out of Allison's willingness to put her pleasure aside (or appearing to? Allison truly was not sure), eventually decided that wouldn't do, and took off Allison's shirt. And bra. But that was it. She may have slid her hand down the front of Allison's jeans and done something that she seemed to think was very elegant and sexy, but Allison found it all troubling and deeply unsatisfying.

And the worst part was: she realized she didn't care.

When the very first opportunity arose, she made an excuse and ordered an Uber back to the bistro. By the time she got home, she was worn out and annoyed with herself. All she wanted was a long shower and to lie on her bed and stare at the ceiling, wondering where exactly she'd got it all so wrong.

She cringed as she pulled her car to a stop beside her rental. The List would tell her in no uncertain terms where she'd got it wrong. Repeatedly.

Her plan for moping, with or without the pointy-fingered lessons on The List, was interrupted the moment she stepped out of her car. Her feet hit the ground, she slammed the door behind her, and the next sound she heard was—

"Allison! How are you, girlfriend?"

The voice and the silly term of absolutely unfathomable endearment broke through the invisible scarf of melancholy around Allison's face. She smiled and looked up and across the yard to the tiny-statured woman who'd called to her.

"Hey there, Carol," she said, waving. "I'm doing okay. How are you?"

As an answer, Carol gestured to the impressive mound of weeds next to her. "Would you take a look at this pile of yard trash? All growing in my garden!"

"You'd never know by the looks of the yard." And that was an understatement. The entire lot was punctuated with gardens that flowed throughout the lawn. Carol owned the main house on the lot and rented out the tiny home as an Airbnb. She'd been delighted when Allison contacted her and requested an indefinite stay. As she said, "It'll be so nice to have a gal around to gab with." They'd gabbed a few times, never for too long as Carol was an incredibly busy seventy-eight-year-old childless widow. Her social life far exceeded any that Allison had ever had.

"Thanks, doll." Carol tossed another weed onto the pile. "I'm making lasagna for dinner. Come over at six."

An excuse formed on Allison's lips, dying before it became a spoken sound. She had nothing to do and no one to talk to, and maybe, just maybe, moping all night wasn't her best bet. Especially since moping about Holly would spiral into moping about her looming decisions about the property, which would dovetail into a pile of moping about life that would rival Carol's weed heap in size.

"Okay," she heard herself say. "I'll be over at six."

After showering and giving herself a strictly timed period of moping (no List involved), Allison found she was looking forward to having dinner with Carol. She'd done it twice before, and never had to say much. Carol was a conversationalist, and an entertaining one at that. She had stories about everything and everyone.

Tonight's topic, begun before Allison even knocked on the back door, was the Thanksgiving potluck dinner to be held at Sunset Dunes. Carol, who was chattering away on the phone as she waved Allison into the kitchen, volunteered at the local assisted living facility she often referred to as the Dunes. From what Allison could piece together from one side of the conversation, there was uncertainty regarding who was bringing what, despite a well-organized sign-up sheet that had been posted in both the dining area and the main gathering area since the beginning of October.

Allison sat at the kitchen table as Carol buzzed around the kitchen. The smell coming from the oven was otherworldly. She knew from previous visits that Carol preferred Italian food over anything else. Allison shared the penchant for carbs and cheese and sauce, and lucky for both of them, Carol was a fantastic cook. She cooked with love, talked with spice.

"Sorry about that, girlfriend," Carol said as she turned from the oven, her wiry but strong arms flexing with the weight of the baking pan. "That Blanche, she can talk an ear off."

Allison snickered behind her hand, knowing Carol was just as guilty. "Sounds like Thanksgiving's gonna get messy," she said.

"Oh my Lord, you have no idea." Carol sat down with a huff and immediately reached for her wineglass. After a long sip of red wine, she smacked her lips and shook her head. "I told Blanche we should only put up one sign-in sheet. Having two? Stupid, foolish. Half the dishes are repeats! No one needs four servings of sweet potato casserole!"

Her mouth full of steaming lasagna, Allison could only nod compassionately, if one could nod with compassion while trying not to scald off the roof of their mouth. It would be a worthy loss; the lasagna was *that* good.

"And would you believe no one is bringing a turkey?"

Actually, she could believe that. She hadn't been to Sunset Dunes but Carol had shown her the website, including virtual tours of the apartments. None looked conducive to roasting a Thanksgiving turkey that could feed the nearly one hundred and fifty residents.

"You could just do a side dish extravaganza," Allison said, half-joking. "Who needs turkey, anyway? Everyone knows the best part of Thanksgiving is everything else on the plate."

Carol nodded, her fork frozen in front of her mouth. "I like the way you think."

They chewed in silence for a moment, Carol soon breaking it with the question Allison had really hoped she wouldn't ask.

"What are your Thanksgiving plans?"

The truth was, she had none. Her mom lived in Georgia and had already informed Allison that she would be working on the holiday. Allison hadn't spoken to her dad since she was a teenager, so no dice there. The only other family option was her younger brother, Matt, who was all the way up in Jersey City. He had his own life and didn't care about holidays. No one in the family did, come to think of it. The Bradleys just weren't festive people.

"I'm not sure," Allison said slowly, choosing her words carefully. The last thing she wanted was to make Carol feel like she had to take care of her. She hated the idea of making anyone feel that way, truthfully, but it felt especially horrible to put that task on a seventy-eight-year-old woman. "I think I'll crash my"—she nearly choked on the word she couldn't bring herself to say—"friend's family gathering."

She wouldn't, of course, because Thanksgiving was eight days away and if she didn't get it together and end it with Holly before then… Well. She would be gravely disappointed in herself.

And not for the first time.

"Well, if that doesn't work out, you can always come spend it at the Dunes," Carol said, utterly nonchalant about Allison's weird response. "Hey, speaking of that." She narrowed her eyes. "Didn't you used to work at a coffee shop?"

A swell of pride ribboned through Allison's heart—a sensation she imagined would never go away. Perk was, to date, her greatest achievement with the least amount of bad habits attached to it. "I did. Co-owned one, matter of fact."

"So you're pretty handy with making those fancy coffee drinks, huh?"

She hid a grin behind another forkful of lasagna, now less steamy but still beautifully stringy with melty cheese. "I sure am."

"Great. The Dunes' cafe is in need of some help." Carol knocked the butt of her fork on the worn Formica table. "And you are just what we need."

This time Allison really did almost choke. "What?" she sputtered, then reached for her glass of wine.

"The girls working there don't know what they're doing. You do. Problem solved."

How the problem was solved was beyond Allison's available cognition, but she was not in a position to let Carol down, so she nodded, agreeing to swing by and check things out.

Before Carol could expand—and Allison knew she wouldn't—there was a light knock at the back door. Both women turned as it opened.

For the third and hopefully final time, the choking felt like a real threat. Allison grabbed her wineglass and took an unrecommended swig.

"Well, look what the cat dragged in," Carol said gaily, clapping at the sight of the mystery visitor.

Mysteriously *hot* visitor was more like it. Allison's face flamed with both agony over nearly choking and a landslide of instant attraction. She gripped the sides of her chair and stared at her half-eaten plate, wondering if she could look up at this person without totally losing her cool.

"Sorry." The voice was just gruff enough to carry a toughness that sounded like it was dying to be softened. "Didn't realize you had company."

"Oh, it's just my friendly backyard neighbor," Carol said, standing up. "You hungry, kiddo?"

"No. Thanks, though. I better go."

And with that, the mysteriously gorgeous visitor evaporated from the room. Or they probably backed out of the door they hadn't even closed when they'd come in, keeping one foot outside in case of a need to run.

It didn't matter. The image of the visitor's face was imprinted on the inside of Allison's eyelids. That short, shaggy dark hair, hanging with just enough nonchalance over soulful, dark-brown eyes. The tanned skin that looked like it didn't ever have to see the sun to maintain that beautiful burnish. And that jaw. Oh, that jaw. It could cut glass and rain the shards over Allison's body, and she would willingly bleed.

"Get a grip," she whispered, then jerked her head up, having forgotten she wasn't alone. But seriously, Allison. One look at a hot stranger and you're ready to bleed out for her? A grip is the first on a long list of things you need.

Carol was yammering on about something, but Allison hadn't caught the beginning of it and was now totally lost. She waited till Carol sat back down with a refilled glass of wine before asking the only question she could think of.

"Do they come here often?"

Carol gave her a strange look. "Does who what?"

Allison gestured toward the door.

"Oh, you mean Drew? Not so much anymore. She checks in every so often." Carol smiled, a gentleness radiating from her. It was clear she cared for Drew, whoever Drew was, and Allison suddenly needed to know *exactly* who Drew was. "She's a good girl."

"She…lives around here?" Oh, she was bad at this.

"Sure does," Carol said. "Born and raised. So, hey, what kind of fancy coffee drinks do you make? Anything with a Thanksgiving theme?"

Allison cleared her throat, trying to clear her mind at the same time. Whoever Drew was, she would remain a mystery (a *hot* mystery) for the time being. And that was probably for the best. For many reasons.

"Well," she began, "I do have a talent for drawing fall leaves in foam."

CHAPTER SIX

Drew emitted some strangled combination of a grunt-sigh, and not one of pleasure, as she pulled up to the building on Eldorado Avenue. Jacqueline Smith was not one of her favorite people to run into at a potential jobsite. She wasn't the most offensive of the other designers in Clearwater Beach, but her ego was three times the size of her body.

Another grumble escaped Drew's lips as she got out of her truck and leaned back in for her notebook. She wasn't even supposed to be here. The whole meet-and-greet, let's walk through and craft an estimate thing was the entire reason why she'd hired Kelly, her estimator. Drew could do it, and had for years. But, as had been pointed out to her on more than one occasion, her personality was sometimes the deciding factor when dealing with an estimate. It could seal the deal, or break it.

The odds hadn't been much in her favor there.

So, Kelly. And Kelly was great, very effective and clients loved her. Kelly was also out of town due to Thanksgiving creeping up in two days. She'd taken down the info and passed it to Drew as she left the office last night.

"This one needs to be done ASAP," she said, shooting Drew a look that meant she was not fucking around.

Drew knew the look but couldn't resist trying to get out of the one thing she hated about her own business. "It can't wait till you're back?"

"No." Kelly's tone said it all, and Drew nodded, a silent promise to keep.

She resisted the urge to kick the tires of Smith Restoration's ugly-ass neon-green work van. It was eye-catching, all right. And hideous.

Alas, Drew Kingsley was a mature, professional businesswoman, and the only thing she kicked on her way into the slightly run-down storefront was a single rock that ricocheted off the jagged edge of the sidewalk and hurtled itself back into Drew's foot.

She could have stomped on it but she didn't, instead turning and walking up a short set of stairs that would definitely need to be replaced if this place had any intention of being up to code.

Once inside, Drew took a slow look around. It was a decent sized space with plenty of light. She'd done her research and knew the building was built in the seventies, so not too old, but also not young. Her quick perusal let her know that it had good bones, judging from the way the walls had held up over the years. No noticeable cracks in the floor, either. A good start.

As she continued looking around, a conversation spilled out from the back area of the space. Drew did a double-take as two women walked into her line of vision. There was Jacqueline Smith, to be expected, and next to her, laughing as though she'd known Jacqueline for years, was the friendly backyard neighbor.

Drew looked away as quickly as she'd taken her second glance, doing her best to appear to be inspecting the ceiling beams and not eavesdropping. The conversation halted quickly, likely because they'd noticed her awkwardly gazing skyward into the abyss of the vaulted ceiling. Well, she couldn't help that it was an odd feature for a 1970s' beachfront former sandwich shop.

"Just checking for holes," Drew said.

"That's Drew for you," Jacqueline said, her voice saturated with false sweetness. "Always looking for something extra to charge you for."

The old Drew of twenty years ago would have fired something equally shitty back. This Drew, knowing both her skill and the finely honed power of silence, merely smiled. Let sinking ships scrape the bottom of the ocean, her grandmother always said.

"Well, it was great meeting you, Allison," Jacqueline said. Her voice had lost some of its saturation. Drew gave herself a mental high five. "I'll get this estimate back to you tomorrow. Feel free to call me if any other questions come up."

"I will, thank you."

Drew darted a look over at the blond woman, the friendly backyard neighbor. Her voice was huskier than expected. She didn't look like she sounded. Drew, usually a master at pairing voices with faces, was perplexed.

She was even more confused to find them alone. But of course Jacqueline couldn't be bothered to say goodbye. She was probably busy kicking the tires of Drew's truck.

Oh well. Drew was here to do a job, not worry about her lame-ass competition. She banished all thoughts of Jacqueline from her mind and focused on the woman standing in front of her.

"Hi," she said. "I'm Drew."

"I know," the woman said. She shook her head as an embarrassed smile crept across her lips. "Only because Carol said your name. After you left. Last night?" The questioning chagrin shifted into confusion. "Wait. Are you from—"

"Southern Magnolia," Drew finished. "Kelly is my estimator but she had to go out of town, so you get me instead."

That puzzlement slid right back into red-cheeked awkwardness. Drew sighed, but made sure it didn't escape her mouth. She had a problem with accidentally sounding flirtatious and it got her into more trouble than she cared to admit.

"Anyway," Drew said. "You're Allison?"

"Oh, God," she said, shaking her head. "Sorry. Yes. I'm Allison. Potential owner."

"Potential?" Drew reached for the slip of paper Kelly had given her. She was sure that hadn't been written down.

"Yeah, I wanted to assess the situation before I took it on."

Drew raised her eyebrows. She'd assumed this woman, who hadn't spoken a word in the thirty seconds Drew had spent in Carol's kitchen last night, was meek. Or maybe just…shy. Definitely easily thrown off her game by the presence of Drew, which meant absolutely nothing to Drew. It was just something she observed. But that statement was firm, to the point, and admirable. This wasn't someone who jumped without looking over the edge.

"Sounds good," Drew said, trying not to sound impressed. "Show me around." She'd meant to form that as a question but the period snuck right in there, proving yet again how her personality tended to make or break these meetings.

Allison, to her credit, didn't miss a beat. "Might as well start right here."

And so they did. Allison walked Drew through the space, pointing out things she'd noticed (again, impressive and surprising knowledge of what needed fixing) and asking a few questions. She was subdued, not oozing with the excitement Drew tended to see in potential clients. Another point for Allison—as a business owner. She seemed to be level-headed about this venture.

Drew pointed to the accordion doors. "You'll want to seal those up."

"What? No." Allison gaped at her. "Seal them up? Like knock out the windows and put up a wall? No way."

"No," Drew said patiently. "And they're doors, not windows. Resealing the connection points so your air-conditioning stays inside." She hesitated, unsure of how much to toss onto Allison's plate. "Actually, it might be best to add tinting, too. Otherwise, the direct sun will roast everyone in here."

"Oh. Right. Got it." A faint blush swooped over Allison's cheeks, giving her an innocence that made Drew's stomach do something uncharacteristically weird.

"There's a small kitchen back here," Allison continued, leading them in that direction. "I'm not sure if I'll want to keep it."

"What's your plan?"

"Just coffee," she said quickly. "I don't want the hassle of food. At least, not food that has to be prepared here."

Again, a smart decision. This woman must have some experience or at least had read some books to know that getting food involved was a whole other level of complication for a business.

"Oh shit," Drew said abruptly as she walked into the kitchen.

"Yeah. Bit of a problem area."

An understatement. Drew was careful not to touch anything as she toured the space. She was conscious of Allison watching her and shrugged off the feeling that came with it. Plus, she needed to concentrate on her tentative steps to make sure she didn't fall through the floor.

It would have to go. The entire space, everything in it. Drew moved to the outside walls, trying to gauge if they were salvageable. The space itself could be turned into a decent storage area, or a small office. But it was going to take a lot of work.

"Bathroom," Drew said as she walked toward Allison.

She wrinkled her nose and shrugged apologetically. "No running water yet."

"I don't need to use it," Drew said pointedly.

"Oh, right. Duh." Again, the pink flush across Allison's cheeks. "Over here."

She led Drew toward the back of the space, and Drew kept her eyes trained on her surroundings, not on Allison. She reached up, put a finger against her chin, and turned her own face away when her eyes betrayed her and latched on to the way

Allison's ass perfectly curved into her baggy jeans. (They were not, somehow, baggy on her ass. They were very, very nice on her very, very shapely ass.)

Drew needed this estimation to end immediately.

Her wish was granted, as the bathrooms (both single stalls) were in fixable shape, and thus ended the tour. Drew jotted down a note about the kitchen potentially becoming an office. She'd have Kelly deal with all of that when she sent the estimate to Allison.

"You'll hear from us—" Drew cut herself off, then sighed. Fucking Jacqueline was going to have the estimate to Allison tomorrow. And Kelly was out of town for four more days. Drew gritted her teeth, hating what she was about to say. "Soon," she finished.

"That's vague," Allison said, leaning against the counter and looking around the room instead of at Drew. "Is that a Florida way of life kind of thing?"

Drew bristled. She hated holidays for myriad reasons, but vacations were right up at the top of the list. They jammed everything up, from estimates to work progress. Don't even get her started on supply issues.

"It is not a *Florida way of life kind of thing*," Drew said, trying to keep her mocking tone not so mocky but likely failing. "I told you, my estimator—"

"Is out of town," Allison finished, finally looking at Drew. Her eyes were striking, a green-blue color that leaned more toward blue but also looked a hell of a lot like the ocean that was visible through those stunning accordion doors. "I remember."

Drew shifted from one foot to the other, suddenly feeling like she was on a chopping block and Allison was hovering above her, wielding a knife. "She might want to come see the space," she said, furious at herself for saying that. "She doesn't always trust me to do this part of the job." She exhaled loudly. "She's much better at it than I am." *Shut* up, *Drew.*

She did. Finally.

Allison was still watching her carefully. They stayed in silence for less than ten seconds, but time stretched to an eternity within that hush.

"Okay," Allison said. "I get it. I'll wait to hear from your estimator. I have one more company coming tomorrow anyway. I'll wait till I have all three estimates to make a decision." She raised one corner of her mouth. It looked like she wanted to smile but just didn't have the strength (or desire) to do so. "Either way, I'll make a decision."

"You could sell this place for a good amount."

"I know." Something flashed over Allison's face. Irritation? Or maybe frustration. "So I've been told. Repeatedly."

Well, Drew was in no frame of mind to play therapist, so she reached out her hand and waited for Allison to take it. After a beat of staring at it with eyes that seemed to have never seen an outstretched hand waiting for a shake before, she did, gripping Drew's hand with just enough force to show she knew how to shake a hand.

Drew yanked her hand back as though she'd touched a hot stove. Allison, her hand still extended, tilted her head and assessed Drew before slowly lowering her arm.

"Are you—"

"Who's the other company?" Drew interrupted. She knew what word was coming next and she hated being asked that question. Also, obviously, she was fine. "The one coming tomorrow?"

Allison wrinkled her nose again, and Drew could see how that could become an endearing gesture. She erased the thought immediately. "King something? Kings…"

Drew swallowed, her saliva filled with drywall nails. "Kingsley Properties."

Allison snapped her fingers. "That's it! You know them?"

As she turned to leave, Drew shook her head. "Never heard of them."

Try as she did, Drew could not stay away from her family on Thanksgiving. She had lobbed thirteen different excuses at her mom and oldest sister. They batted them back with swift agility, reminding her that as a member of the Kingsley family, she had duties to "show face" at holiday events. No one specified for how long Drew had to show said face, however, and she kept that tucked in her back pocket as she walked into her parents' sprawling home late Thursday afternoon.

It was easy to get lost in the madness of the massive Kingsley family, and Drew did that as soon as she could. Everyone was there—everyone was required to show face, after all—and though the house was obnoxiously and unnecessarily large, it still felt like the rooms were teeming with people. Drew's five siblings, two older and three younger, all came with spouses except for one (Natasha swore she would never marry again but Drew didn't buy that). And with the siblings and spouses came children. Many, many children: fourteen, in fact. Their ages ranged from twenty-one to four, plus number fifteen currently in utero.

The younger kids swarmed their Aunt Drew as soon as they laid eyes on her. And Drew, never one to deny the love she had for those kids, soaked up every moment of it. Her siblings were too cool and sophisticated to spend time with the kids; they preferred to hobnob with each other and their parents, Drew's least favorite family bonding activity.

And that's how she found herself caught up in a lively game of indoor soccer in the basement with seven of her nieces and nephews. They were playing in socks, which was a safety risk (one of Drew's sisters had broken her ankle in high school while playing sock-soccer on wrestling mats), but they were having a shriekingly fun time, so who was Drew to stop them?

She did receive quite the stink eye from her oldest brother, Derek, when he came down to gather everyone for dinner. Ironic, too, since his kids were too old for sock-soccer and had spent the last two hours on their phones in one of the living rooms.

"Hello, darling." Yolanda air-kissed Drew when she made her way into the spacious dining room. "So nice of you to join us."

"You didn't give me much of a choice," Drew muttered, giving her mother a real kiss on the cheek.

Yolanda's eyes sparkled as she smiled up at her daughter. "And why would I?"

Before Drew could retort or engage in a normal "how are you, what's new?" conversation, Yoli was off, circling the enormous table to ensure everyone was moving toward their assigned seats.

Relief washed over Drew when she found hers, clear on the other end of the table from her father. Maybe she could get through this dinner unscathed after all.

"Everything looks splendid, Yolanda," Afton, one of Drew's various suck-up brothers-in-law said as he sat down across from Drew. "You've outdone yourself!"

But she hadn't, although everyone would carry on pretending that she had. Yolanda hadn't so much as turned the oven on; the spread on the table was courtesy of the two chefs permanently employed by the Kingsley family. Why no one outright acknowledged that, Drew had no idea, but she made a note to be sure to sneak into the kitchen and thank the chefs before she left.

As the seats filled, plates began to weigh down with food. Drew kept quiet as she passed bowls and platters, taking only her three favorites: turkey, creamed corn, and stuffing, which was her grandmother's recipe. Remembering that brought a lump into Drew's throat. She hated that her grandmother wasn't here, but she hadn't been able to convince her to come. She'd take that up with June the next time she saw her, and like hell would her grandmother skip out on Christmas dinner. If Drew had to be here, so did she.

It was a Thanksgiving miracle that Drew had been seated by her college-aged nephews and niece. She'd once been their favorite aunt, too, and even though they were older and no longer wanted endless piggyback rides or to kick her ass in Wii Bowling, they still tolerated her enough to include her in conversations about things Drew felt woefully out of touch with. She tried to keep up, but eventually shifted her focus to her plate and the mental countdown of when she could leave.

She was only half-listening to the conversations at the other end of the table. Her father held court there with Derek, Celeste, and Peter, Celeste's husband. They were Greg Kingsley's best soldiers, always ready to do whatever needed to be done with the ever-growing business. Drew picked up on a few key words like "excavation" and "prime land." Her stomach churned and her fists clenched around her knife and fork. Growing up, she'd enjoyed the fruits of her family's labor as most clueless wealthy kids would. She'd never had to ask for anything and enjoyed every single privilege that came with being a Kingsley. But once Drew decided to ditch college in favor of working for a local construction company, she hadn't been able to get behind the way her family did business, their hunger for money and willingness to destroy in order to "rebuild." Not to mention her family made it clear they didn't approve of Drew skipping out on college, which began the slow rift between her and her father.

For many real estate and design professionals in the Clearwater area, being handed a career with Kingsley Properties was a dream, but as an adult, Drew realized it felt more like her nightmare. So, after learning the trade of construction, she got her real estate license and struck out on her own. Southern Magnolia Designs was in its twelfth year and was doing better than Drew had expected, or even wanted. Having grown up with money, Drew sought success in the form of personal gratification, not dollar bills. But she loved what she did, even if it butted up right against everything her family stood for. Perhaps she loved it a little more *because* of that.

The tryptophan worked its magic and the intense work conversation lulled after dinner. Drew moved through the rooms like an agitated ghost trying to find a resting place. She knew she wouldn't find one there, though. She was simply biding time until she could disappear and reclaim her peace far away (well, not exactly, as a mere one point five miles sat between her house and her parents' house) from the ceaseless noise and activity of twenty-five people spread throughout the rooms of a bayfront mansion.

As Drew moved from the third living room toward the kitchen, she remembered she had an out. That damn estimate for Allison. She could work on it, at least, and have something to go over with Kelly. Maybe even something to send to Allison, a "preliminary" or "working" estimate. She hated the idea of even one more day passing by without getting those numbers to her, especially knowing her own damn family's company had been there yesterday and undoubtedly churned out a robotic estimate before the end of the business day.

After thanking the chefs and being rewarded with a bag brimming with leftovers—including extra stuffing for her grandmother—Drew bobbed and dodged her way to the front door. Her hand on the ornate knob, she breathed a sigh of relief too soon.

"There she goes," Yolanda sang, her voice echoing through the two-story foyer. "Without even saying goodbye."

"Sorry, Mamá." Drew turned and waited for her mother to approach. Another round of air kiss-real kiss was exchanged, this time with a quick hug thrown in for the holiday. "I have work to do."

"On Thanksgiving?" Yolanda tsked as she shook her head, her dyed rich-brown bob barely moving. "You have one hell of a mean boss, Drew."

She grinned at her mom. "Sure do."

"Let's have lunch soon, okay? You tell me when you're free." Yolanda squeezed Drew's upper arm. "Make time for me, okay?"

Drew cleared her throat against the welling of unexpected emotion. Her relationship with her father may have been outright contentious, but her mom would always be her mom, and even as one of six kids, Drew had grown up feeling nothing but endless, unconditional love. She cherished that feeling even when she purposely avoided her family.

"Always, Ma." Drew leaned down for one more cheek kiss before opening the door and walking into the cool night.

CHAPTER SEVEN

The volume of numbers swirling through Allison's brain was enough to make her want to dip her head, repeatedly, in the ocean. Except it wasn't cold enough—she knew from her walk earlier that morning—to numb the way she desperately needed it to.

It wasn't that she'd assumed this move and this potential enormous project would be easy. She knew it wouldn't be, but she hadn't been fully prepared for how heavy it weighed on her, nudging and poking her to make a decision she didn't feel qualified to make.

What she *should* be doing was making a concentrated effort to go over the three estimates she'd received. That last one, from Southern Magnolia, was the least professional of the three, but somehow the most authentic in its lack of professionalism. Allison couldn't put her finger on it but the night before, she'd kept coming back to it, tracing her fingers over the screen of her iPad. The estimate itself was great, the perfect middle ground between the other two. It came with a note, however, that said it was "an estimate of an estimate," words that gave Allison a little laugh.

Instead of hanging out with numbers and details and lofty ideas, oh my, Allison was on her way to Sunset Dunes to meet Carol. She hadn't relented on the whole "come check out the coffee shop at the senior home" thing, and Allison figured it was the least she could do for the woman who had dropped off a week's worth of potluck leftovers (heavy on the sides, low on the mains) late Thanksgiving evening.

Not only dropped it off, but also did so without asking a single question about why Allison was home and not with her supposed friend and their family. Subtlety wasn't Carol's forte, so Allison knew the older woman had restrained herself.

As she approached the assisted living facility, Allison squinted. That couldn't be right. As she got closer to the sprawling nest of buildings, she shook her head half in wonder, half in amusement.

Every single palm tree lining the front of the building (and there were many, almost acting as a shield from the street) was strung with blinking white lights. It was early afternoon but overcast, so the lights were putting on an eye-catching show. Closer to the building was an elaborate display of blow-up snow globes, each with a unique internal setting. One featured a doll perched atop a rocking horse, another held the Grinch captive. Allison trailed her fingers over the one that contained a giant vibrating yellow star draped with sparkling green garland.

The path from the sidewalk to the main entrance of Sunset Dunes was dotted with—wait for it—snowflakes. Allison crouched down, trying to figure out the mechanics behind them. They looked spray-painted, but that would be a wild gesture for a seasonal decoration. She was running her finger over a particularly huge flake when she heard a familiar voice.

"Waterproof chalk," Carol said as she walked up to Allison. "Isn't it gorgeous?"

"It's very pretty," she conceded, still eyeing the designs with suspicion. "Does that mean it's permanent?"

"Oh, of course not. They'll wash away with the next hard rain." Both women glanced skyward. "Someone will draw them again the next day."

"Seems kind of sadistic," Allison muttered as they walked into the building.

"Keeps 'em busy," Carol said gaily, waving at several nurses. "Now, do you want a tour? Or shall we go straight to the problem?"

Allison paused in the hallway and looked around. Before she could respond, Carol took the words from her mouth.

"That's right, doll. You've been here before! Silly old me." She tugged on Allison's sleeve. "Not much has changed. Come this way."

She led Allison down the hall, past the hallway that led to the eastern wing of living quarters. Sunset Dunes housed two wings of apartments—the eastern side for able-bodied elderly folk and the western wing for elders who needed a bit more assistance, but not to the point of needing nursing home level care. Most of the west wingers, where Allison's grandfather had spent his final four years, used canes or wheelchairs. A few had more internal concerns, like mild dementia, and required proximity to caring professionals.

Though Allison had only visited her grandfather a handful of times at Sunset Dunes, she didn't have any recollection of the facility being quite so...festive. And she was pretty certain she'd visited over Christmas at least once. The decorations lining the halls were something she would have remembered. It looked like the holiday section in Target had thrown up, and more than once.

"This is a lot," Allison remarked as she trailed Carol down the hall. For a tiny old lady, she was quite the speedy walker.

"Oh this? This is nothing, girlfriend. Wait till you see—" Carol cut herself off, throwing a devilish grin over her shoulder. "We'll talk about that later."

Allison, too consumed with the explosion of winter holidays hanging from the walls, caught the edge of the grin but didn't think much of it.

"And here we are!" Carol announced with a flourish. "The Cafe at Sunset Dunes. Clunky, isn't it, that name? I keep telling them they should rebrand but they brush me off."

The familiar scent of coffee cocooned the women like a worn blanket. It was usually a comforting scent, but for some reason, Allison felt like it could suffocate her if she took too deep of a breath. She bit the inside of her cheek to keep herself grounded, to push off the worry that had been hanging over her like a puffy storm cloud. It had been there since the moment she said "coffee" without thinking when Drew the non-estimator half-asked what she was planning to do with the commercial building. She'd have to sort through those feelings soon, but now was not the time to crack open that potential torrential downpour.

As Carol tottered around saying hello to the residents who were enjoying a midday cup of caffeine, Allison took in the space. It was small and homey, inviting in a way that made Allison feel like she had stepped into an old friend's home.

"Over here!" Carol called, waving her to the area that housed an old espresso machine and a guy in his early twenties who looked like he was asleep standing up.

"Donny, meet my friend Allison," Carol said. "She's here to help you."

He sighed heavily, barely containing an eye roll. "How many times do I have to tell you that I don't work here?"

Carol waved him off. "You're here every day. That's working."

"No, it's *volunteering*." Donny gestured to the hulking machine next to him, which looked to be about as old as one of the women sitting nearby. "I don't even know how to use this thing. The residents make their own drinks."

Allison gawked at Donny, then at Carol. "Is—what? Seriously? Is that true?" She narrowed her eyes. "I thought you said some girls work here."

Another wave off from Carol, this time in Allison's direction. "I meant the residents. Sometimes they like to pretend they're working here. They know what they're doing. It's fine!"

"They burn the milk every time," Donny said, his voice flat. "And when I try to help them, I get hit."

Both Carol and Allison turned to him. "Hit?" Allison said. "Like a punch?"

"No," Carol said immediately. "He means a friendly swat. Nobody gets whacked too hard around here." She leaned in closer and dropped her voice. "These people like to do things for themselves. We let them be as independent as possible. And they love coffee! So why wouldn't they make their own drinks? Donny here sometimes polices them a little too much, you know?"

All three turned at the sound of loud laughter from the corner of the room. Allison's stomach dropped, then flipped.

There stood Drew. Well, more accurately, there bent Drew. She was right-angled at the waist, leaning down to talk to a very small old woman with a head full of stunning white curls. The laughter was coming from the two other women at the table. A man, stooped and handsome, was wobbling his way over to join the group, a big smile pressed over his thin lips. It seemed that corner table was the place to be, and Allison was *certain* Drew hadn't been there when they'd walked in.

Another explosion of laughter burst forth as the man sat down. Allison turned and scanned the counter, eyeing the cabinets with scrutiny, wondering if there was booze hidden for the residents to give a little boost to their lattes. That kind of laughter didn't come from a jolt of caffeine.

"Oh, the comedy club is here," Carol said. "They—"

"Burn their milk just like the rest of 'em," Donny grumbled before walking away.

Allison watched as he picked up some cups and napkins that had been left behind. "He's a delight," she said.

"I try to get him to joke around with the residents, get him a little less grumpy, but no dice." Carol picked up a bottle of milk and sniffed it before putting it back into the mini-fridge. "He's on probation. Wrote some bad checks. But he's a good boy. Anyway! Show me what you got, doll!"

Between the chaotic bounce of the conversation and the knowledge that Drew was here—and *why* was Drew here, exactly?—Allison had forgotten what it was she was supposed to show she got. Or had. Whatever.

"The coffee!" Carol said when Allison didn't move. "Make me something fancy. I'll be over there."

And with that, she scurried off to the corner of the room, right to the so-called comedy club. Allison cut a quick look toward Drew. She had turned a chair backward and was sitting on it with her arms hanging over the back (now front) of the chair. She looked completely at ease. In fact, it was the most relaxed Allison had seen her.

Allison cleared her throat and turned so her back was to Drew. A stranger, she reminded herself. A woman she had seen exactly two times prior and knew subzero about, so who was she to say she looked relaxed?

"Shut up," Allison muttered. Drew was a nonissue; this espresso machine, however? A total issue.

She inspected the hunk of steel before her, taking in its age and potential. It smelled like it had made approximately one hundred shots of espresso past its prime. And the fact that the residents made their own drinks had Allison in a near-panic. There was no way this machine had been properly cleaned in years.

So, like any seasoned barista, she pushed up her metaphorical sleeves and got to cleaning. As she worked, trickles of conversation and laughter floated around her. So too did Donny, who hovered at times, stood at a pensive distance at others. Allison kept her focus on her task, doing her best to ignore the other person in the room who had a strange and inexplicable presence that she simply could not fully ignore.

Satisfied with having gotten the espresso machine as clean as it was going to be, Allison set about making a few shots, just to test the waters. They poured more smoothly than she thought they would, and after a sniff test, she dared to sip the third one. "Not bad," she said quietly before tossing it, just as she had the two before.

As the fourth shot dripped into the ceramic cup, Allison poured whole milk into a steel pitcher and stuck it under the steam wand. She didn't have to watch the milk or use the thermometer; the sound was enough to tell her when she'd hit the sweet spot. The shot went into a paper cup, followed by the milk. Then, with care and practice, Allison poured in just enough micro foam and went to work. Moments later, she smiled approvingly at the Christmas tree drawn into the top of the latte.

She waited for the familiar spread of satisfaction, the "job well done," the "this is what you were made for" sensation that had forever accompanied her completion of espresso drinks. Nothing. Instead, that storm cloud hovered closer, sucking the air from her lungs and leaving her under a warning shower of muddled confusion.

There was nothing to do in that moment, so Allison turned and walked toward the comedy club, now whittled down to Carol, the man, and the woman with the wild white curls. She blinked, wondering where Drew had escaped to.

"Perfect timing!" Carol said, clapping once. "I was just telling June and Charlie about how you're going to save the cafe!"

Allison's hand trembled and she watched the foamy Christmas tree quiver. "Save it?" she asked, setting the drink down before she shook the design away. "I don't know about that. I think Donny has everything under control."

"But can Donny do *this*?" Carol said, showing the drink to June and Charlie. "I don't think so, girlfriend! You're hired!"

This time, panic punched through Allison's entire body. She gripped the back of the empty chair she stood behind. She was terrible, *terrible* at saying no, especially to people who were relentlessly kind to her. Yes, she would eventually need a job, but she had that whole…other thing…going on, and was this even a real job? She wasn't on probation, no offense to Donny; she—

"She's kidding, honey," the woman with the white curls said, patting Allison's cold hand. "No one works here."

Allison wanted to feel relieved but that was impossible, given her internal organs had clenched together and, God, she needed fresh air.

"But if they did, you'd be hired!" Carol set down the cup, having taken a delicate sip. "This is the best drink I've ever had here."

No one but Allison looked up when movement at the doorway shifted the air in the room. Drew was back, head angled down, eyes focused on her phone. She was texting somewhat furiously, but her face gave away zero emotion. Allison, still mired in her new and conflicting coffee-related emotions, couldn't take her eyes off Drew. Her hair was hanging in her face, blocking Allison's view of her eyes. Why this was important, she didn't know. It didn't make any sense. Again, Drew was a *stranger*. And Allison had a girlfriend! Kind of.

Okay, not really, and just the thought of Holly made her feel worse instead of better. Allison closed her eyes briefly, long enough to force herself to angle her gaze away from Drew.

She had so many things she needed to figure out, and immediately.

"I have to get going."

Oh, that voice. Allison opened her eyes and saw that Drew had come back to the table. She was crouched down next to June, she of the wild white curls, and gazing at her with utter tenderness.

"So soon?" June reached out and touched Drew's arm. "You just got here!"

"I know, and I'm sorry. It's wo—"

"Work, I know." June leaned over and hugged her. "You'll come tomorrow?"

"Always." Drew stood up and only then did she meet Allison's eyes. Again, the air shifted, like a warm breeze edged with the first touch of winter had swept through the room. With barely a nod of recognition, Drew turned and left.

Allison watched her until she realized Carol was watching her watch Drew. She brushed her hair out of her eyes and fumbled for something to say, finally settling on the truth.

"I should go too," she said, standing up straight. "I have a lot to look over."

"Of course," Carol said easily. "You've got big decisions to make!"

"The biggest." Allison held in the sigh dying to escape her lungs. "I'll make a point to come by every few days and make sure the machine is clean."

"Oh, we would appreciate that," June said. "Wouldn't we, Charlie?"

The old man merely grunted in response.

Carol stood up and took Allison's arm, steering her toward the door. "Thanks for coming in. It's nice to have young faces around here."

"I really don't mind coming in to check on the machine," Allison said. "I wasn't just saying that."

"I know. You don't say things you don't mean."

Allison glanced at Carol, wondering how she'd picked up on that tidbit of her personality. It was strange and comforting. But mostly strange.

"And don't take Drew personally, girlfriend," Carol went on. "She's a walking, rarely talking salt lick of a human being. She's got a good heart in there but only shows it to June."

"I didn't—" Allison stopped just outside the doorway. "She's—she's fine. I don't know her."

"You will." A grin that sparkled with mischief lit up Carol's face. "We'll talk soon, girlfriend. I have big plans. Big plans!"

Allison could only watch as Carol careened back toward her friends, a new pep in her step that made Allison wonder what in the hell she'd gotten herself into.

CHAPTER EIGHT

Allison's phone, still face up for reasons she could not explain, lit up yet again. She stared at it with mild disgust before nudging it further down the bar top away from her. For all she cared, the dude next to her with the torn-up Marlins hat could steal it. She would not grieve its loss for a moment at this point.

On second thought, a stolen phone wouldn't be the best outcome for the evening. Allison tapped the side of it with her pointer finger, pushing it closer to herself and out of Mr. Marlins' grasp. She continued to ignore the notifications mounting on the screen, however. The texts could wait; they were undoubtedly the same as the four earlier messages that remained unread.

She turned her attention back to the wall of liquors facing her. It was a dusty, rag-tag collection of spirits that looked like a very lopsided age-gap relationship. Some were sparkling with newness and other bottles had to be over fifty years old. Allison wrinkled her nose and looked down at her glass, still half full of a local IPA. She'd be sticking to beer, thank you very much.

Speaking of… She shifted on the ripped barstool, testing her balance. The room didn't shift with her, so she was still in the realm of Have Another Beer. As her phone lit up yet again, she chugged the remaining hazy liquid in her glass. The moment the empty thudded down onto the worn bar top, the bartender arrived and whisked it away, only to return it, full, moments later.

Allison nodded her thanks and took a sip of her fresh beer. She was old enough to know that drinking away her problems—well, *problem* in this case—wouldn't help, nor do anything near solving said problem. Well, wait. She'd solved the problem last night. Or so she hoped.

As the opening strains of "The Twelve Days of Christmas" rocked out into the bar, Allison picked up her phone and took a steadying breath. Ten texts. All from Holly.

She opened their thread and scrolled past the pleas for reconsideration. Yes, there. She'd made it perfectly clear that she wanted to end their relationship. Holly had said *Okay, I understand.* Ah, but she did not, as evidenced by the deluge of variations on *Can we talk?* and *Allison, we were so good together!!! I don't understand!* Ending their little almost-relationship via text was not the most mature thing Allison had ever done (once she'd broken up with someone via email, which was definitely worse), but she simply had not had the energy to face Holly the previous night.

Or ever again, really.

With a furtive glance over both shoulders, Allison reached into her pocket and pulled out a thickly folded collection of papers. The List, rarely seen in public, had made it out from the privacy of bedside tables and could breathe fresh (or centuries old) air right there in The Hideout, the dive bar Allison had discovered just last week. It was within *walking distance* of her rental, which was the most amazing thing ever.

Carefully, with a delicate touch reserved for lovers and enemies alike, Allison unfolded The List. She skimmed over the first page and resisted the urge to hang her head in something that felt like shame but didn't quite meet the dictionary definition.

She flipped to the last page, the one with space waiting for additions. She should have thrown it out back in Portland. But she'd suspected she'd need it here in Florida, and the knowledge of that made the beer in her stomach slosh angrily.

The pen scratched across the paper, leaving nothing behind. Allison drew tight circles on the top margin. Still nothing. Reverting to middle school techniques, she drew the pen across her palm, hoping the warm moisture would reinvigorate the dead Bic. No luck. She threw the pen onto the bar top and watched as it bounced joyfully off the scuffed wood and ricocheted into the wall of booze.

Mr. Marlins laughed loudly, pointing toward the bottles, which showed no harm other than a single red bow having popped off to the floor. The bartender nodded approvingly, as though he had been dying to throw writing utensils at the glass decanters. He'd also strung garland around his neck like a boa. A dog barked, high and yappy, and from somewhere close by. It was then that Allison realized the song blaring into their eardrums was not the standard version of the gift-giving Christmas song, but rather John Denver and The Muppets crooning away about lords leaping and pipers piping.

Slowly, Allison looked around, wondering what vortex she'd accidentally stepped through and where in the world she'd ended up.

"Florida," the woman a few stools down said. The very woman Allison had not even realized was sitting there. Whoever she was, she looked like she'd just gotten off a yacht and also had the ability to read minds, which made the already uncanny sensation even more intense.

"I'd say you get used to it, but you never do." The woman cackled with delight at her own joke that wasn't even a joke and tossed back one of the three shots of Jack lined up before her.

As Miss Piggy warbled on about five golden rings, Allison weighed her options. She needed to add to The List, right now, before the urge passed. She doubted Mr. Marlins had a pen. The bartender should, but he was occupied at the other end of the bar, talking animatedly with a customer. That left Yacht Lady who, now that Allison looked more closely, had a small black-and-white dog sitting in her tote bag. One paw was hanging over the edge, its toe fur tufted like the Grinch. The dog was wearing a Santa hat. Because of course.

Because Florida.

Allison looked back at The List. She could see the imprint of the dead pen's furious attempt to write "Holly." That would have to be enough for now. She'd darken it when she got home.

When she folded The List back into its portable form, Allison's eyes caught the name she so often tried to avoid seeing, let alone think about. Considering it was in block letters that took up the entire second page of The List, it was purposely hard to avoid.

Sidney.

Yes, Sidney. The plight, in female form, of too many years of Allison's past. The love that wasn't love at all, just misguided obsession and crackling chemistry that never quite burst into flames. A fire tempered and doused, time and time again, by Sidney's inability to and disinterest in committing to a relationship with one woman. Allison, specifically.

There were dates beneath her block-lettered name, but there was no need to look at them. Her knowledge of how much time she had wasted on Sidney was acute and exact. It was time she would never get back, time clipped with lessons she'd had to learn countless times before they stuck. Time that seemed so far away but always silently brushing against the present.

Allison shoved The List into the pocket of her cargo pants and put both hands on her beer glass. She would drink Sidney away. She would drink Holly away. She would also drink this godforsaken ridiculous Christmas song away, because Miss Piggy was *not* an impressive vocalist.

It wasn't until her glass was empty once again that Allison looked up. She caught the bartender's eye just as he was walking away from the opposite end of the bar, and as he moved toward her, she was gifted with a vision of someone who was becoming oddly familiar.

Drew was seated at the end of the bar, turned so her back was against the wall. She had a clear view of Allison but all her focus was concentrated on the Megatouch in front of her. Her eyes, darker in the dim light, were squinting, and the corner of her bottom lip was pulled between her teeth. Allison swallowed, the heaviness in her stomach giving way to a flutter of lightness. She swallowed again, having no desire or need for that feeling. Not now, not ever. Never again. Nope. She was done with women.

Once her newly full glass was in front of her once again, however, Allison's eyes skipped their way down the bar and landed once again on Drew. It was just that her concentrating face was unbearably cute. Like, okay, a little intimidating. But so, so cute. No, sexy. Unbelievably sexy. That bottom lip—oh, that *lip*.

Her staring must have been a tad too intense because a moment later, Allison found herself not staring at Drew's mouth but rather directly into her deep, dark eyes. Drew made a face, one that echoed loving sentiments of "What the fuck are you looking at?" before offering the quickest half-smile Allison had ever seen come and go. It was so fast she wasn't certain it had appeared at all, but Drew's eyes were back on the Megatouch before Allison could offer a return smile.

Or something like a smile. Allison was drunk, of that she was certain. The bottles of alcohol across from her had started bobbing with the music, which thankfully was no longer the caroling of The Muppets but—oh, God. No. Fucking Alvin and the Chipmunks?

"Who's controlling the damn juke?" Mr. Marlins yelled.

"Relax, Tommy. The song's almost over."

"Fuckin' singin' rodents," Tommy Marlins muttered. "That shit ain't right."

Allison caught Drew's eye long enough to be graced with a smirk before her attention returned to her screen.

"Aw, come on, Tommy." The bartender thunked a fresh glass of Miller Lite in front of him. "You got some merry-happy in ya, I know it."

Tommy opened his mouth and embarked on a long-winded explanation of exactly how much "merry-happy" he resolutely did not have, even in a place that "looks like the elves took a giant Christmas crap in here."

Allison laughed into her beer glass. Tommy Marlins was not wrong on that account. The Hideout had gone to the extremes with the festive spirit, even more so than the innovative decorations at Sunset Dunes. The inside of the building was bedazzled with at least six four-foot-tall fake Christmas trees, all of which had a different theme of decorations. Allison was privy to the one that was nautical, figuring it was a nod to the bayside residence of the bar. One of the trees was a hot mess of red and gold. She could not figure out what was what on that tree. Cranberries? A vomit of gold tinsel? No idea. It was hideous, and somehow perfect.

Beyond the trees, the bar top itself was dotted with Santa figurines. They were ethnically diverse and all painted with enormous smiles, dimples shining in the glowing light of multiple strands of multicolored lights that hung haphazardly from the rafters above. There was a jolly blow-up snowman positioned behind the bar, waving gently each time the bartender walked past it.

As the Chipmunks faded out and something Allison had never heard before began to play, Tommy Marlins thumped his fist against the bar top.

"Not this shit again. I did not come here to listen to the country's worst Christmas songs." The last couple of words slurred together.

"Give it a rest, Tommy," said Yacht Lady, who was nonchalantly holding her dog on her lap. The Santa hat was askew and in the dog's mouth was a stuffed pickle, also donning a Santa hat. Allison stared. Was the dog smirking? No. Did dogs smirk? Seriously, where *was* she?

"Give it a rest, Tommy," Marlins mocked, pretending his right hand was a chattering mouth and clapping his fingers together with each word. "How about you and your dog give it a rest, Ivy."

Allison leaned back to let the jabs fly past her as Lou Monte sang his way through "Dominick the Donkey." She stole a quick glance over at Drew, who was definitely smiling now despite still being laser-focused on the Megatouch. As Ivy and Tommy continued their drunken back-and-forth, Allison sucked in a breath, grabbed her beer (her *last* beer), and eased off her stool. Seconds later, she was standing next to the empty stool beside Drew.

She waited for an invitation. None came. Drew didn't even look up, and now that Allison had a clear view of the Megatouch's screen, she understood why.

Through laughter tainted with hops and barley, Allison managed to say, "You've been staring at naked women this whole time?"

Drew held up her free hand to shush Allison, who complied, stifling her giggles to the best of her intoxicated ability. She waited patiently as Drew raced through two more rounds. Allison reached in to point out the left boob that was definitely bigger on the right side of the screen, but Drew swatted her hand away, and then time ran out. The high score screen popped up and Allison's jaw dropped. The initials DK were next to every single score on the screen.

"That's all you," she said.

"No shit."

"What is this, your second job?"

Drew snorted, still not suggesting Allison sit down with her. "It's a hobby. I'm sure you think it's vulgar."

"I mean, I'm sure you could be looking at real naked women if you wanted to. Instead of weird pictures of naked women from the eighties on a computer in the middle of a dive bar that has definitely seen better days."

That made Drew turn around and look at her. Her face was a smooth stone of inexpression, but a hot flicker of anger danced in her eyes. "What do you want?"

Allison shrugged, the motion lopsided. Okay, yeah, she was feeling the alcohol. "Can I sit?"

"No."

She sat anyway and tried not to be offended when Drew shifted on her stool, angling her body away. "Do you come here often?"

"Seriously?"

"What? That's a normal question to ask."

Drew narrowed her eyes. "That's a pickup line."

"I'm not trying to pick you up, I promise." Well, kind of promised. The idea of Drew… It was not unappealing. Even through the fog of her alcohol-addled mind, Allison couldn't help but notice the way her body was trying to lean closer to Drew, who seemed to have moved even further toward the edge of her stool.

"Don't. It would be a waste of your time."

Drew's sly grin, even paired with a cold steel wall of boundaries, did not cool Allison's system. She knew that grin. It had been used on her many a time. She may have even used it once or twice herself. But Drew slid it away as abruptly as it had arrived, composing herself back into an impenetrable force.

"Can I buy you a drink?"

"That's also a waste of your time." Drew gestured to the glass of water next to the Megatouch.

Water. Okay. A curveball Allison hadn't expected, not that she expected everyone to drink. And she hadn't even meant to flirt—not on purpose, anyway. She was in no place to flirt. Part of her whole fresh start in Florida thing was to avoid flirting, avoid women, avoid all things relationships.

Or, just, maybe to stop making the same mistakes that were littered throughout The List. Allison patted her pocket. Safe and sound, heavy with regret.

Just like her heart.

Oh, okay, she really needed to stop drinking. Immediately.

Though her glass was still three-quarters full, Allison set it on the bar and pushed it toward the far edge. Her eyes caught Drew's hand moving quickly over her phone, and as "Dominick the Donkey" ended, "We're a Couple of Misfits" began. Allison waited for an outburst from Tommy Marlins, but he was quiet.

Not quiet. Just flirting. With Ivy. With the dog—a papillon, Allison was pretty sure—between them.

And Tommy was wearing said dog's little furry Santa hat as a miniature red-and-white cone on his forehead as though it was the most normal thing he'd done all day.

"Yeah," Drew said, seeing Allison's revelation. "Happens every time."

"Those two?"

"Yeah," she repeated. "The fighting is how they flirt."

Allison rooted around in her beery brain for a funny retort but got distracted by her phone. Ringing this time, not just a text. She yanked it out of her pocket and gasped as The List tried to flee the scene with her phone. In her haste to secure the papers back in her pocket, she dropped the phone.

Drew, with unexpectedly catlike reflexes, caught it before it hit the sticky floor. She placed it gently on the bar then side-eyed Allison.

"How do you know her?"

A glance at the phone, blazing with the first and last name of her latest mistake, confirmed Allison's suspicions. "Holly? Oh. Uh." She couldn't form the words to explain the thing she couldn't fully explain and didn't want to admit. And why she didn't want to admit it to Drew was a mistranslated message she didn't have the patience to decode.

"None of my business," Drew said lightly, firing up another round of naked ladies with impressive…hairstyles.

"Yeah, of course, I know." Allison shoved her phone back in her pocket, snuggling it against The List. "It's just—"

Drew stood abruptly, her own phone in her hand. Without so much as a glance in Allison's direction let alone an actual parting sentiment, she left the bar, leaving Allison staring after her, dumbfounded. And, admittedly, a bit hurt.

Allison leaned forward and curled her hand around her discarded beer, suddenly thankful the bartender hadn't whisked it away.

CHAPTER NINE

Drew jogged over the misshapen white blobs on her way into Sunset Dunes. She stopped briefly to crouch down and inspect one that was particularly unsettling. She was pretty sure they'd looked more like snowflakes the last time she'd been here, but now, they were closer to haunted clouds, eerily similar to the cluster that lived over Drew's heart.

She made her way inside, waving hello to the staff members as she walked through the halls. Since her grandmother June had moved into the Dunes five years ago, Drew had become an accidental celebrity amongst both the staff and the residents. For the life of her, she didn't understand why. Spunky niceness was not her thing, never had been. Sometimes a few days stretched past without her so much as cracking a full smile. June swore up and down it was because Drew's curmudgeonly personality rivaled the most acerbic of the residents'. Though likely an insult, Drew was strangely proud of her grandmother's assessment.

But she was nice enough to acknowledge everyone she passed, something a crab-ass would not do. Did she smile with each wave? No. No reason to. The wave was enough.

"Well, well, well. You finally made it."

Drew rolled her eyes as she slipped into the chair next to Carol. "I'm on time."

"You're usually early."

She shook her head. There was no point in arguing with Carol. Drew had tried many times, all to disastrous results. The woman was as headstrong as the longest living running bull in Spain.

Drew glanced around the cafe. It looked no different from when she'd been there a few days ago and been somewhat sidelined by running into Allison, who looked as surprised and unnerved as Drew had felt. That woman could not hide a single emotion on her face. Drew bit the inside of her lip, holding back a stupid smile that held no meaning and had no reason to illuminate the room. Allison had hidden absolutely nothing the night before. She'd been drunk, of course, which Drew noticed immediately. But between the awkward attempts at flirting, there was something that had radiated off her. Something Drew innately understood and wanted nothing to do with, because it was the root of all her inner haunted clouds.

"You look a little rough around the edges, Drew."

She scoffed, brushing her hair off her face. She'd seen the bags under her eyes that morning and tried to ice them out with a couple of cold gel packs. "Long night."

"Oh yeah? Got yourself a lady finally?"

"Hardly."

Carol tsked and shook her head. "I'll never understand why you keep that good heart locked up so tightly. People are missing out on you, Drew Kingsley."

"No one is missing out on me," she said firmly. "There's nothing to miss out on."

"Oh, Lordy Lord. I didn't sign up for the pity party parade today."

Drew tipped her chair back, letting her toes keep her anchored to the floor. "I was working last night, if you must know."

At that tidbit, Carol's bright blue eyes lit up. She'd had cataract surgery and loved to show everyone the new sparkle in her irises. Right then, both eyes were glowing with a hunger for information.

"Where? What happ—"

Saved by the scuff of lazy feet entering the room, Carol's questions died in the stale coffee-scented air as she and Drew both turned toward the doorway. Drew's stomach sank, just enough to annoy her, when she caught sight of Allison, who had halted and was staring at them with a mixture of curiosity and apprehension.

Again, Drew had to bite her lower lip to prevent both it and its upstairs friend from turning upward. That was a new one; she couldn't remember the last time she'd been greeted with a look of pure, uninhibited dread.

"Hey, girlfriend!" Carol exclaimed, waving Allison over to their table. "Come! Sit! Let's chat. We have so much to talk about!"

"We do?" Drew mumbled, side-eyeing Carol. She hadn't bothered to ask for specifics when Carol had asked her to be at the Dunes to "chat." She figured it had something to do with—

Oh, fuck. Shit mother fuck. No.

Drew slowly tilted her head to look at the table. The dark-green binder appointed with puffy silver snowflakes waved a silent, smiling hello, daring her to run away.

She contemplated accepting the dare but knew she'd disappoint her grandmother if she did. As a rule, that was something Drew tried never to do. So she sat and waited, her stomach dropping more with each passing second that Allison and Carol chattered on about dirt and plants and flowers and other earthy bullshit.

"Okay!" Carol clapped a few times, a quiet sound muffled by the soft wrinkles of her hands. "Let's get down to business, shall we?"

Allison darted a look at Drew, who happened to be accidentally staring at her. But only because Allison looked like she'd been run over by a semi sometime between Drew leaving the bar and Allison shuffling into the cafe. The bags under her eyes had literal pounds on Drew's, and her skin—normally tinged with a healthy tan and pinkish cheeks—was sallow. And her smile was gone. Erased. Vanished.

That, for some inexplicable reason, made Drew shift uncomfortably in her chair.

"Business?" Allison croaked, then cleared her throat. "I thought we got this whole cafe thing figured out."

"Oh, that. Of course we did! This"—Carol patted the dark-green binder lovingly—"is a different kind of business."

Drew groaned and tipped her chair back further. Falling would be a saving grace at this point. Hell, a concussion sounded like a great excuse for a vacation and a get out of jail free card for Carol's imminent announcement.

"And what is that?" Allison asked. Poor thing, she was clueless. Drew wished she could send her some kind of signal that would get them both out of what was about to be thrown into their laps.

"This, doll, is the holy grail." Carol waited for them to laugh, and when they didn't, she supplied the amusement instead. "Oh, lighten up you two. This is going to be the most fun you've had in ages!"

"Define fun," Drew deadpanned.

"Okay, okay," Allison said, holding up both hands. "Can you please stop speaking in riddles and just say what's going on?" She pressed one hand against her forehead. "And does anyone have Advil?"

"I do, sweetheart."

All three turned to the soft voice coming through the doorway. Drew smiled instantly, the real smile that only June inspired. Her grandmother made her way into the room, each step taken with caution and the assistance of her cane. She put her ever-present giant purse down on a chair and rooted through it, coming up with a bottle of Advil.

Allison breathed a sigh of relief and accepted a few pills from the bottle. "Thank you so much," she said, her voice as quiet and calm as the sunrise.

Drew shivered. That voice had to go and never return.

Advil swallowed and Drew resolved to never be in a situation to hear that tone from Allison's mouth ever again, Carol brought them back to attention. June settled in next to Drew, patting her thigh.

"As you know, Drew, Sunset Dunes holds a yearly Winter Wonderfest." Carol raised her eyes to the ceiling, likely trying to avoid fully rolling them. "We have to be very careful about the holidays here. Everyone needs to be included, and winter is for everyone, so we don't do anything Christmas-y." She looked directly at Drew. "Your mother is not allowed to DJ the party."

Drew snorted. "Noted."

At Allison's look of confusion, June stepped in. "Drew's mother has an affinity for Christmas songs."

"Obsession is more apropos," Drew said drily.

"We'll need secular music," Carol went on. "But it has to be upbeat. Last year it was all those funny technological songs. No one could dance to them, so everyone sat in their chairs and got sleepy!"

"So sleepy," June agreed, nodding sagely.

Allison looked at Drew, mouthing "technological" with an implied question mark. Drew hesitated, not ready to build any kind of alliance with this near stranger who also happened to have shockingly beautiful eyes (even with the punching bags hanging below them), then mouthed back: "techno." Allison nodded, swiping her shaggy blond hair behind her ears.

Drew cleared her throat to avoid choking on the inhale that didn't make it to her lungs. She wished Allison hadn't taken that damn Advil because she looked alive again. Alive, and undeniably beautiful. Her face, now fully exposed with its color coming back, was a landscape painting of soft tanned skin. Her cheeks, full and topped with a pale smattering of freckles, framed both sides of a full-lipped mouth. Drew was certain she wasn't wearing make-up and the natural pink of her lips was a color women probably dreamed of finding in a lipstick. Framed by lashes that were darker than they had any right being, her eyes, though striking in their ocean-blue hue, held a halo of sadness Drew couldn't help but feel drawn to.

And that—that right there, the sadness and the yearning to move closer to it, to extinguish it—was enough for all the sirens in Drew's body to set off at once. She hurried to recalibrate herself, to erase the visual of the woman sitting across from her, the damn woman she had a feeling she—

"Drew?"

"Yup." Drew swung her gaze to Carol. "What's up?"

"You think you two can take it from here?"

She dropped her chair legs to the floor, slamming into gravity with them. "Take what?"

"Weren't you listening, honey?" June's hand pressed against her arm, the touch soothing as it had always been. "You and Allison are going to plan Winter Wonderfest."

"And you've got nineteen days to do it!" Carol said, the words loud enough to be considered an overly enthusiastic yell.

Drew looked at Allison again, finding her hands braced against the edge of the table. Her expression, for once, was difficult to read.

"We're what?" Drew said.

"Look, Drew," Carol said, employing her former teacher's voice. "I'll help you. And June will too." June nodded. "But we need some fresh eyes and ears and decisions for this year, and who better than the two of you?"

"We don't even know each other," Allison finally said. "How are we supposed to plan this in nineteen days? I—" She paused, her teeth visibly clenched. "I have a lot going on right now."

Drew nodded in solidarity. "And I'm running a business."

"We know, we know. Like I said, we'll help!" Carol shook her head. "You're going to be fine. Who knows! Maybe you'll become friends!"

"Carol, it's almost time for indoor cornhole." June began to stand and Drew jumped to action as she always did, helping her grandmother find her footing.

"Look at that! We've got to go." Carol sprung to her feet, the picture of elderly agility. "June and I are holding tight in second place. I think we can take down those old farts today."

As the two older women walked toward the door, Allison and Drew found themselves locked in an awkward stare across the table. Before either could make a sound or a move, Carol called back to them.

"And if you lose that binder, there will be hell to pay!" The door to the cafe shut on her exclamation point.

Silence bit down on them, nipping their ears with a sullen urgency. Drew shook out her shoulders, trying to displace the odd feeling that had overcome her. Allison remained seated at the table. Her eyes were glued to the binder.

"She's serious," Allison said finally.

"Did you mean to have a question mark at the end of that statement?"

"No." Allison shook her head. "My only question is what the hell are we going to do?" She looked up at Drew, who took a steadying breath against the electric zip that zagged through her body when their eyes met. She ignored the curious look Allison gave her as she shifted her gaze to the wall behind her. What an incredibly ugly painting that was. Huh.

"Drew?"

"Yeah," she said automatically. She stuffed her hands into the pockets of her work pants. The dirty ones, of course, because she was leaving here and going directly to a job site that was in the midst of deconstruction. "So. We're going to plan Winter Wonderfest."

"*How?*" The panic in Allison's voice rang loud and clear, so loud Drew heard her own eardrum crackle.

"We just will." Drew backed away from the table. "But I gotta go now."

Allison scrambled out of her chair, grabbing the binder as she followed Drew. "You're just leaving? Now?"

"I have to," she grumbled, walking speedily through the halls. She was impressed Allison was matching her step for step. "I have a job."

"Yeah, and I will soon too." Allison hesitated. "I hope so, anyway."

Drew said nothing, because what was there to say? (Plenty, obviously, but she stuffed it all in the back pocket of her pants, hoping that once she sat down in her truck, all the words would flatten and flutter away. She'd be sure to keep her windows open.)

"I'm meeting your estimator later today," Allison added.

"Right."

"For what it's worth, I'm very happy with the estimate you drew up."

"Well, hopefully Kelly agrees with it," Drew said.

"Yeah."

A riveting conversation, one Drew could not wait to get away from.

"Drew, I'm—look, I'm sorry about last night."

They were outside now, stepping over the deranged sidewalk snowflakes. Allison slowed as she crossed the formerly wintry path, and Drew took advantage of that to speed up and hightail it to her truck.

Unfortunately, she underestimated the quickness of Allison's step and found her right next to the driver's side door as Drew unlocked it.

"Hello? I said I was sorry."

"Yeah, great." No, that didn't feel good. Drew sucked in a breath. With one leg in the truck and the other pushing off the ground, she looked at Allison. "It's okay."

"You totally ran away from me."

Had she? Drew thought back, and then—right. "It wasn't about you."

Allison opened her mouth but must have rethought her response because she shut it without making a sound. Her lips pressed together, she nodded. "So, how are we going to do this? Plan?"

Drew pulled the other half of her body into her truck and cautiously shut the door, then leaned into the open window. Allison looked up at her, determination written across her face.

"We'll figure it out." What she didn't say was that she would never let her grandmother down, and June happened to love Winter Wonderfest more than everything—except for Drew, that is.

"Um, how? We don't—how?" Allison rolled her eyes, clearly frustrated. "Should we exchange phone numbers?"

"No," Drew said, her tone short and without room for discussion. "I'll see you around."

She didn't wait for Allison's response, and as she pulled away and chanced a look in her rearview mirror, she felt the slightest ruffle of shame.

CHAPTER TEN

Allison was absolutely certain that she had never had such vicious hangovers prior to moving to Florida. Something about the alcohol down here made for easier drinking and harder consequences. Or maybe it was her, and not the state. She'd heard rumors about hangovers amplifying in rude and incalculable ways once a person entered their forties. Allison, just one year into that smashing decade, had been battling a headache for forty-eight straight hours following her misguided glasses of beer at The Hideout. It had eased with whatever powerful dose of Advil June had given her on Monday, but today, Wednesday, that fucker was back with a vengeance.

The banging and commotion of demo workers in the building wasn't helping, either.

She pressed her fingertips against her temple as she moved outside and into the hazy sunshine. "Oh, God." She winced as her eyes tried to roll back into the darker side of her head then reached around and yanked her baseball hat out of her back pocket and jammed it onto her head. Not great, but it helped a little.

Yes, she was standing outside *her* building. After weighing pros and cons that never assembled into the game of tug-of-war she'd been expecting, she'd officially decided to keep it. Things had moved faster than she could have imagined, especially in seemingly low and slow Clearwater Beach. When she'd met with Drew's official estimator on Monday afternoon, Kelly had been enthusiastic about the space. She'd approved Drew's estimate, making just a few jokes at her expense, and explained that the demo crew would be available on Wednesday morning, so Allison would need to start selecting materials as soon as possible.

"Wait," Allison had said, shocked. "That soon? How is that even possible?"

"Perfect timing, that's how." Kelly, a short brunette with oversized glasses, grinned, exposing a slight gap between her two front teeth. "We finished a project early and usually have extra downtime between the holidays. It's not a terribly busy time for us."

Allison had nodded as she tried to take in that not only was she absolutely going to do this, she was going to do it now. Like, immediately. And maybe that was for the best—she didn't have time to second-guess her decision.

An even nicer bonus was that Southern Magnolia had ended up with leftover materials from their last job, so some of the demolition that was taking place now was going to be patched up in no time. That former job had ended due to the business running out of money for their renovations, which wasn't the best omen.

The speed with which the project came underway was either kismet or a disaster waiting to happen. Allison wasn't sold on either option.

"Allison?"

She turned toward the unfamiliar voice, shielding her eyes against the cloudy glare that had settled over the beach. "That's me."

"Hey, I'm Cam from Southern Magnolia. I'm here to start walking through ideas and materials with you."

Again, the sheer speed of everything. Maybe it wasn't a hangover after all; maybe it was whiplash from launching herself into a project she'd thought would take months to begin.

"Right," Allison said. A loud thud boomed from inside the building and she shut her eyes against the noise.

"We can hang out here if you want." Cam's voice was gentle and steady, a balm against the backdrop of cacophonous construction.

She took Cam in, an absolutely adorable human wearing custom coveralls with a name tag embroidered with *Cam* and *he/him*. Allison smiled, feeling the surreality of pronoun coveralls in Florida. She'd expect that back in Portland. Here? Not so much.

"That would be great." She tilted her head toward the building. "The noise is a lot."

"Are you okay? We can do this another day."

A twine of emotion ribboned through Allison. Empathy, but she was on the receiving end. That was something she hadn't experienced in a while.

"I'm okay," she assured Cam, hoping her voice didn't give away her sudden burst of feeling. "Just fending off a massive headache."

"Migraine?" Cam gestured to Allison's face. "You have the look."

"There's a migraine look?" She wanted to laugh but knew it would make the pain worse. "I think it might be a migraine, yeah."

Cam held up one finger. He twisted his messenger bag around and opened the flap. Seconds later, a bottle of Excedrin hovered in front of Allison along with a bottle of water. She gave him a curious look, then decided not to look a gift horse in the mouth and accepted both items.

"I also have a migraine stick," Cam said. "Some people aren't into oils and stuff, but I swear it always helps me."

Allison held out her hand and received a roll-on stick. Cam directed her to roll it over her temples and on the back of her neck. The soothing scent of peppermint eclipsed the ever-present scent of the beach, and she breathed deeply.

"Thank you. Are you always this prepared?"

"For migraines, yes. Chronic sufferer." Cam returned the Excedrin and the stick to his bag. "Are you sure you don't want to do this another time? We could meet tomorrow."

Allison shook her head, then shrugged. "Honestly? Migraine aside, I'm overwhelmed with how fast everything is happening."

Cam nodded. "I totally get that."

They stood in silence for a few moments. Allison closed her eyes, willing the pills to work quickly. Her neck felt looser, at least.

"Let's at least look over some basic stuff," she suggested as she opened her eyes. "Maybe nothing I have to think too hard about?"

Cam's face split into a wide grin. "Yes! Let's do it. I'm so excited about this project."

The two sat at the lone table that remained outside of the building. It had surely seen better days, but buying outdoor furniture was far down on Allison's list.

"So, what kind of aesthetic are we going for?" Cam palmed his forehead. "Wait, sorry. What kind of business is this going to be? That information seems to be a big secret."

It remained a secret to Allison, too. She'd been sure she was going to continue her Perk lifestyle and open a beachside coffee shop. It was what she knew, what she was comfortable with. It was also what she was good at. But at some point, something had shifted. She thought back to the way her body had responded to being in the vicinity of an espresso machine. No, she wasn't sure what kind of business she was going to open. Not anymore.

"Is it crazy to say that I don't know yet?"

Cam leaned forward, his chin resting on his closed fist. Excitement sparkled in his bright green eyes. "Yes. Completely. But I love it."

Relief and a lessening of brain pain settled over Allison. She knew she'd figure out her plan sometime, and likely soon, but for now, she just wanted to get some of the boring, standard design stuff out of the way.

"Good. Then you'll be the first to know once I figure it out."

"No! Let me be the last. It's much more exciting that way."

Allison laughed. "Okay, we can do that. I have a totally clear image of the flooring I want, regardless of what happens with the rest of the space, so maybe we can start there?"

"Absolutely." Cam pulled out his iPad and scooted his chair closer. "Let's dive in."

Sooner than she'd thought possible, Allison's migraine was gone and she'd selected flooring for the main space as well as the bathrooms. A thin line of excitement was beginning to run through her, but she pushed it down, not wanting to get ahead of herself.

"I love the color of the luxury vinyl tile," Cam said, jotting notes on his iPad. "It's perfect for a beachside business of mystery."

"I want the overall look to be clean." Allison leaned back in her chair. "I'm obsessed with these windows and want my customers to be able to focus on the view, not a bunch of random shit cluttering the space." She thought back to Perk, and how it was the complete opposite of uncluttered. She'd wanted the space to be homey and inviting, mismatched and quirky. It was the ambience she loved then. Now, she wanted something new.

No, she *needed* something new.

Cam nodded appreciatively as though Allison had spoken all those thoughts aloud. He looked up suddenly, peered inside the building, then dropped his eyes back to the iPad. "Oh, Drew's here. Weird."

Allison fought very hard to avoid turning around. She did not need to see Drew. Well, actually, wait. She *did* need to see Drew because they had a lot to discuss. And plan, apparently.

"Are you thinking white walls?" Cam continued, seemingly unfazed by his boss showing up unexpectedly. "They'll look killer with those dark floors you picked out."

"Um, yeah, I think so. Maybe just the slightest bit off-white? I want it to be warm but chill. Inviting."

Another sage nod, more notes jotted down. Allison continued to avoid turning around, figuring that if Drew came here to see her about this Winter Wonderfest situation, she could come out here. Allison would not be running to her. In any capacity.

The embarrassment of trying to buy Drew a drink as a friendly gesture but having it kind of misread as something more curdled in the bottom of Allison's throat. So, too, did all the beer she'd drank after that to try to wipe away the fact that maybe she had wanted it to be something more and knowing she had absolutely no business doing that.

To shove herself out of those cyclical thoughts, Allison cleared her throat and looked at Cam. "Have you worked for Drew for a long time?"

"Yeah, pretty much since she started the business."

Allison waited for a natural continuation of the conversation, but Cam was focused on the iPad. Okay. Fine. She'd try again.

"Is she, uh, a good boss?"

"The best."

Another dead end. Well, that's what Allison got for asking questions that didn't demand much of an elaborated answer. As she thought about other routes she could take to get some information about this virtual stranger she was suddenly tasked with planning an entire event with, Cam continued tapping away, making small noises of approval.

"Are you leaning more toward beachy or refined?" Cam asked, holding up the iPad for Allison.

She looked at the images of renovated spaces, taking her time swiping through them. Nothing was jumping out at her. All she knew was that she wanted more clean lines, less dingy darkness.

"This one looks good," she said, handing it back to Cam.

He grinned and gave her a thumbs-up. "Beachy-refined. Perfect."

A noise from inside made Allison finally turn around, though she loathed to do it, lest Drew see her and think she was scoping her out. Through the windows, she saw Drew standing in the middle of the room, arms crossed firmly over her chest, talking with one of the construction crew. She had a Phillies hat pulled low, making it difficult to see if her face was showing any indication of her mood.

"Drew's a Phillies fan?" Allison said accidentally but perhaps slightly on purpose. It was a perfectly appropriate question, given Drew's choice in hats.

"She is," Cam said lightly. "Goes to all their spring training games."

"Has she always lived down here?"

Instead of answering, Cam held up the iPad yet again. "What do you think about these toilets?"

An hour later, toilets were selected, along with sinks and toilet paper dispensers, the latter a thing Allison hadn't even considered having to pick out. Cam had mapped out an image of the bathrooms—two single stalls, both gender neutral—and Allison was in love. Had she ever imagined she'd fall in love with a bathroom? No. Definitely not. Alas, here she was. Enamored with toilets.

"You're in luck," Cam said as they walked back into the space, which was quieter now. Two guys from the construction crew were inspecting a wall near the former kitchen. Drew was nowhere in sight. "We should be able to get the toilets in by next week."

"That fast?" Allison shook her head, still grappling with how quickly everything was unfolding. "When we opened the cafe back in Portland, I feel like it took a really long time for orders to arrive."

Cam tilted his head from side to side, a confident smile on his face. "You've never worked with Drew before."

Okay, that had to be an opening—for what, Allison didn't know, but she wasn't going to let it slide. "And by that you mean…"

"Drew has a way." Cam motioned toward the former kitchen, where suddenly, Drew appeared. Her brow was furrowed in concentration, and it did not help Allison's silly little flicker of "oh, she's cute" that she did not care to have. Not one bit. "She's really well-connected and people respect her."

That was good information, though Allison wasn't sure what she could do with it. She liked knowing that Drew was well-respected; she had felt that was the case, and was happy to have her gut instinct validated, especially since her instincts (or what she thought were gut feelings—maybe they'd come from another organ after all) were sometimes a bit—

"Wow! You're not wasting any time."

The fine hairs on the back of Allison's neck stood to attention. She squinted, disbelieving the sound of the voice that had entered the room.

"And that's my cue to leave," Cam said in a low voice. He darted a look toward Drew before resting his hand on Allison's shoulder. "I'll be in touch."

The magnitude of Holly's presence filled the room almost to the corners, leaving a tiny tunnel for Cam's escape, which he jogged through without looking back. Allison blinked, still bewildered by the unexpected and unwelcome drop-in. She waited for Holly to meet her eyes, to offer some kind of clarity as to what the fuck she was doing here.

But Holly wasn't looking at her. No, her eyes were laser-focused on Drew, who was giving Allison a look that clearly implied she was not enjoying this visit either.

The three women stood in silence, a strange triangle of eye contact and avoidance. Drew widened her eyes at Allison, sending a message that could not be translated. Allison glanced between her and Holly, stunned and little irritated that Holly couldn't be bothered to rip her locked eyes from Drew to the woman she'd recently been dumped by.

Well. All right. Allison shrugged it off. She could be the bigger person, no problem.

"Hi—" Her attempt to initiate conversation was immediately cut off.

"So good to see you, Drew." Holly's voice was coated with a sickening film of sugar that Allison, in her admittedly limited experience with her, had never heard. It was stomach-turning.

Drew, wordless, held up a hammer.

A deranged cackle flew from the depths of Holly's lungs. Allison took a step back, unsure if the laugh or the hammer would do more harm.

"I always did love your sense of humor," Holly said, still laughing. She threw her hand against her hip, jutting her best assets into prominent view. "So how did you two meet?"

At that, Drew walked off, shaking her head. When she disappeared from view, Holly stopped laughing and emitted something similar to a sigh, then looked at Allison for the first time.

"Hey," she said, voice flat, all her previous enthusiasm gone.

"Um, hello?" Allison crossed her arms. "What are you doing here?"

"I was in the area and I saw Drew's truck outside." Holly looked around the space, either searching for Drew or plainly avoiding looking at Allison. Either option gave Allison a queasy sensation. "I figured you had made a decision so I thought I'd stop in and see what's going on."

Low lying clouds of Allison's past rumbled into a new storm overhead, the wind and thunder harsh and familiar. "Did we agree to be friends?"

If Holly was struck by the pithy remark, she didn't show it. In fact, she ignored it altogether. "I'll be sure to stop by next week and check your progress." She glanced at Allison. "How did you find Drew, by the way?"

"Same way anyone who needed renovation services would find her," Allison said, her voice tight. "Holly, there's no reason for you to stop by next week. Or ever."

She smiled, a winning gesture that likely worked on many people, but not Allison. "Oh, Allison, I won't be stopping by to see you." With that, she flicked a wave with her manicured fingers and spun, leaving Allison stunned and irritated yet again, this time with a side order of embarrassment.

She didn't have long to drown in the overlapping feelings. Drew reappeared as soon as Holly stepped out of the building. Her face was contorted, her eyes ablaze.

"I have one sheet left to hang," Drew said. Not a single emotion that was on her face reflected in her voice. Allison marveled at the talent. "Then I'll be out of your way."

"You're not in my way," she said automatically, suddenly hating the idea of Drew leaving. Especially now, *even* now, with her own emotions circling around her like Pigpen's cloud of dust.

"Looks like you and Cam got a good start on picking materials," Drew went on. "The faster you make decisions, the faster we put in orders."

"I understand how this—"

"I work closely with local suppliers. Turnaround time is faster than you would expect."

"It's fine, Drew, I—"

"I like to keep projects moving. I don't like unexpected delays." The comments were paired with Drew taking off her Phillies hat and running her hands through her dark hair. She jammed the hat back down.

"Neither do I, but—"

This time, Drew interrupted with her hammer, bashing through a sheet of drywall with impressive speed and grace. Allison knew there was a less messy way to handle that, but she let Drew go, sensing she needed the release. When Drew didn't say anything, Allison barged in.

"Will you let me finish a sentence now?"

She wasn't sure because Drew was standing in the shadows, but she could have sworn a smile flickered across her lips. "Sure."

Now that she could speak, Allison wasn't sure what to say. She settled on, "There's really no—"

"So, I was thinking—"

"Oh, fuck you."

To Allison's surprise, Drew burst into laughter. It was a sound that would follow her home, tuck in around her for the night. It was not at all the way Allison had imagined Drew's laugh would sound, and it did terrible warm things to her. Things she immediately doused with the reminder that Drew was kind of an asshole.

Or not an asshole. Just…difficult.

"As I was saying," Allison said, as much to distract herself from the uncomfortable thoughts and feelings bouncing through her as to finish her damn thought, "you don't have to rush. I don't have a timeline in mind."

"It's how I run my business," Drew said, lifting a sheet of beat-up drywall. "It's not personal."

"I didn't think it was." Had she? Maybe. A tiny bit, if she was willing to admit that much. But the thought floated off—no, it was bashed off the sweet spot of Kyle Schwarber's bat with Drew's succinct comment.

"Yet."

Allison could have sworn she'd heard that single word muttered from Drew's lips, but the noise of the drywall being thrown into a garbage can rang louder than her voice.

It wasn't until much later, when Allison was lying face down on the sofa in her rental, that she remembered seeing Drew's mouth move as she tossed the drywall, the "yet" hanging between them like a dream catcher caught in a sudden gust of wind, unsure of which way to swing, which hope to hold on to.

CHAPTER ELEVEN

Of all the strange and random things Allison had gotten herself involved in throughout her adult years, planning a Winter Wonderfest for a community of elderly people was not on the list. (She was hoping, for the record, this wouldn't have to be added to *The* List.)

There were a few years at Perk that she had decided to do more community outreach around the holidays. Mostly that meant she and a few of her coworkers set up coffee stations at homeless shelters. One year she decided to "coffee cater" a breakfast for Emery's company, and while it was a success, it also involved a ton of work that Allison was ill prepared for.

But this was different. As she sat on the beach late Thursday morning, she wondered, again, what she'd gotten herself into and how she'd gotten herself into it. Carol hadn't given her or Drew an opportunity to say no, not that Allison would have. She already felt indebted to the older woman and had a lingering emotional attachment to Sunset Dunes that actually made her feel good about being involved in the event.

When her grandfather had lived there, Allison had been living across the country. She'd always been close to him growing up, despite rarely living in the same area. Perhaps it was because of that—their established communication habits—that she was able to feel connected to him even when they were separated by a long stretch of states. They talked on the phone at least three times a week, though Mack Bradley could be difficult to get a hold of; he was apparently quite a popular resident at the Dunes.

Despite knowing that she'd been able to sustain a loving relationship with her grandfather, Allison felt a bit of shame over not having been able to see him more often. So, when Carol sprung the Winter Wonderfest directly into her chagrined lap, she wouldn't have said no even if given the opportunity.

Her coplanner, however… Allison shook her head as she pulled her knees to her chest and looked out over the Gulf. She'd missed a prime opportunity the previous day to corner Drew about needing to get to work on, well, everything. Something had shifted in the air between them before they both left the building, and just like Drew's surprisingly heartfelt laugh, it had followed Allison home and poked at her throughout the night. She was avoiding her own building today, at least for the moment. Whatever had transpired, whatever wires had crossed and zapped yesterday fell into an inexplicable category for Allison. And she hated that more than anything. So, avoidance was a game she was happy to play.

For the moment. Because there was no way she was going to do everything for this winter party explosion herself.

Sitting at home and using her laptop for research would have been the more practical decision, but the longer Allison stayed in Clearwater, the more she understood the subtle pull of the water. She felt infinitely calmer while sitting on the beach. And so, there she sat, her phone in one hand, a notebook on her lap, and a pen lost somewhere in the sand at her feet.

It turned out there were plenty of options for wintry activities. The snag was revealing itself as what was and wasn't conducive for a crowd well over the age of seventy. Allison had a running list (before the loss of her pen, of course) and was going over her favorites. The longer she stared at her phone, however, the more annoyed she became that Drew wasn't sitting next to her, providing her salty opinions.

A smile flitted over Allison's lips before she bit it down. She'd known her share of grumpy human beings, but Drew had pulled into the front of the pack and was darting ahead, the first-place trophy within her grasp.

But that laugh. It remained in Allison's head, drifting and ebbing with the slow waves brushing against the shoreline. She wanted to hear it again, and again, and was terribly annoyed with herself that that was a thought her mind had even created.

With an exasperated sigh, Allison flopped back onto the sand, not caring about the fine particles sure to make their way into her hair. She had no business thinking about Drew. In fact, Drew *was* business—the owner of the business Allison had hired to renovate her still undeclared business, but yes, she did have an idea, it just didn't quite make sense yet—and that was all the more reason for Allison not to think about her ever. Or her stupid amazing laugh that was all at odds with the curmudgeonly persona Drew projected.

"Okay, enough." She stood up and brushed the sand off. Turned out she'd been sitting on the pen—no time to figure out how that had happened.

If she didn't have the guts to drag Drew into the debacle they had sitting in front of them, she would seek out another source.

"Oh, doll, relax. Everything will come together." Carol swooshed away Allison's ramble of worries with a single swipe of her hand. "You have the binder?"

Allison gingerly set the binder on the table between them. Thankfully, Carol had chosen to sit in the atrium of the Dunes and not in the cafe. The more Allison went in there, the worse the stench of coffee became, which disrupted everything she thought she knew about herself.

And frankly, she was not in the mood for an existential crisis.

"Wonderful." Carol paged through the binder until she landed on a very well-organized spreadsheet. "These are the activities that have been done over the last three years. We try not to repeat." She wiggled her pencil-thin white eyebrows, only visible because her skin was perennially tanned. "Most residents wouldn't remember if we did the same thing every year, but I like to spice it up when we can."

Spicing things up was not high on Allison's Winter Wonderfest brainstorming list. She avoided wrinkling her nose but couldn't help a few unfortunate images that came to mind.

"They do love to role-play," Carol said, her tone a tad too dreamy for Allison's liking. "You know, Santa, the elves, Mrs. Claus. You get the idea."

"I'd rather not," she said, trying to avoid bringing in additional upsetting mental images. "I think maybe I'd like to try a different angle. Preferably one that doesn't involve the word 'role-play.'"

Carol laughed and patted Allison's hand. "Oh, doll, don't be afraid to live on the edge for a bit. You'd get a kick out of—"

"I was thinking about putting people into groups of three and having them make one person into a snowperson," Allison interrupted loudly. "You know, toilet paper, some supplies for hats and a carrot nose."

"Snowperson," Carol repeated, chuckling. "I love it. Let's do it."

Relieved, both with the approval and the dodging of more role-play discussion, Allison put a check mark next to "snowperson" on her list.

Carol leaned over to get a better look at the list, which had a grand total of six ideas. "You're gonna need more than that, doll."

"I know. I'm working on it."

"And Drew? Has she been helping you?"

Allison paused. The temptation to get Drew in trouble with this take-no-shit woman was high. Like, ridiculously high. She also had a feeling that if Carol told June about Drew's continuing difficulty, that would not go well for Drew.

"Drew's…busy," Allison settled on.

"She is not too busy for this," Carol said emphatically, rapping her knuckles on the table. "You have to boss her around a bit. Make her know she's gotta pull her weight."

Allison shifted in her chair, royally annoyed with liking the idea of bossing Drew around.

"What's she so busy with?" Carol scoffed. "She has plenty of time."

"Well, she's doing the renovations for my…my soon to be business," Allison said, tripping only slightly over her indecision.

"No, girlfriend, her company is doing the renovations. Drew's very hands off with projects these days."

The image of Drew showing up unexpectedly and surveying the work for longer than a visit from the boss would require, then bashing her hammer through the drywall flashed through Allison's mind. Quite the opposite of hands off. Hands very much on, in fact. Sexily so.

Allison gritted her teeth against the image, then said, "She was there yesterday. Working."

When Carol didn't immediately reply, Allison looked over at her, expecting her to be distracted by the binder and its plethora of spreadsheets. But no. She was looking straight at Allison, a curious wisdom in her stare.

"Well, isn't that interesting," Carol said, each word slowly following the next. She made measured pauses an art form.

"Is it?" Allison leaned in, suddenly ready to engage. Maybe she'd get more info out of Carol than she had from Cam.

"Hmm," was all that came next. After another measured beat, Carol nodded once, then flipped to a new page in the binder. "Let's talk food and drinks." She must have noticed the look of shock on Allison's face because she patted her arm reassuringly. "Most of that work is done, of course, but I want to see if your young brain has any exciting last-minute additions."

Allison started to say something, anything to return to the topic of Drew, but All Business Carol had come back to the table, and was off and running in a one-sided discussion about the merits of sherbet punch.

"I hope this is helping you get a better idea of Winter Wonderfest," Carol said sometime later, interrupting her own analysis of pigs in blankets. "June said I dumped this on you and didn't explain enough." Her eyebrows knitted together. "I tend to do that, it seems. Anyway, Drew knows all about it so she can fill in any blanks I don't cover. All the other information is right here"—she tapped the binder—"so all you and Drew need to do is get together and figure out the entertainment."

A mighty feat, apparently. Allison was tired from doing not much more than listening, and didn't have it in her to argue or complain about Drew. She nodded instead, figuring she'd eventually use some of the same energy she'd used with Holly yesterday to get Drew to understand she needed to step it up.

"I decided to order mini sticky buns. Typically, we avoid anything that might yank out a denture—" Carol was cut off by a warbling sound that sent a shiver down Allison's spine.

"What is *that*?" she asked, looking around for an answer.

"That is not good," Carol said quietly, closing the binder. "Stay put, doll. I'll be right back."

Allison watched as Carol hustled out of the atrium, looking both ways before entering the hallway. Seconds passed and the warble ended, replaced by a series of beeps. Paranoia gripped her. Was it hurricane season? She had no idea. She looked around, realizing she and Carol had been alone in the atrium. If it was hurricane season and that was some kind of weather alarm, surely Carol wouldn't have left her here to fend for her hurricane virgin self. Or would she?

Allison stood up and walked briskly to the door. The hallway was empty, and oddly so. There was almost always a resident or a staff member roaming about. She sucked in a breath and crept along the side of the hall, keeping her back to the wall. She was obviously not well versed in hurricanes but was pretty sure the slightly overcast day wasn't that foreboding. She also had no idea where the safest place to be for a hurricane was, so as she shuffled down the still empty hallway, she cursed Carol— lightly, with humor and no real malice—for leaving her behind in what was clearly a state of emergency.

Except maybe it wasn't. The closer Allison got to the front of the building, the less she felt like she'd wandered into an episode of *Fallout*. She heard voices and none of them sounded panicked. When she rounded the corner and spotted the desk at the main entrance, she breathed a sigh of relief. People, and quite a few of them, including Carol. All staff, though. Not a resident to be seen.

Carol spotted her and gave a visible "tsking." Allison shrugged and walked over to her.

"I thought it was a hurricane warning or something," she said, stopping a foot away from Carol. "And you left me in a room literally made of glass."

"It's just a little emergency," Carol said. "That's the sound for all residents to either skedaddle back to their rooms, or stay put where they are."

Before Allison could ask why such a system was even in place, she got her answer. Through the sliding glass doors came two paramedics with a gurney. One of the head nurses of the Dunes met them, speaking quickly as they all jogged toward the eastern side of the facility. Their voices were too low for Allison to catch anything said, but a shiver ran through her nonetheless.

It came with the territory, of course. But she had a feeling no one here ever got used to it.

A commotion at the front doors pulled Allison's attention from her unpleasantly realistic thoughts. Someone came through the doors, a rush of harried energy cushioning each step. Allison blinked once, then twice. She thought about waving her hand in front of her eyes, certain that what she was seeing was impossible, but there was no escaping the vision of Drew.

Drew, in a navy polo shirt tucked cleanly into navy BDU pants. Drew, who looked official in a way Allison could not compute. That was not her work outfit. That was not any outfit Allison had seen her in, and it looked too uniform-y to be anything but...a uniform.

Allison had never known herself to have a uniform fetish, but in the most catastrophic of ways, Drew's hotness shot up about 78% right before her eyes.

Not the time, she thought, cheeks heating at the indecency of lusting after Drew during an emergency situation. Unfortunately, her brain decided that was an excellent time to float the word "role-play" through her mind, and Allison found herself biting down on her lower lip, wondering what the fuck had come over her, and *how*.

Drew had already disappeared down the hallway, following the ghostly footsteps of the paramedics. Allison breathed in slowly, trying to compartmentalize the variety of thoughts and feelings bouncing within her. Drew was... Drew was untouchable. A salty ice block. And if Allison were to ever consider getting involved with a woman again (she still wasn't sold on the idea that she wanted to), she had learned she needed someone the opposite of icy.

Of course, none of this mattered, since Drew had made it perfectly clear she wouldn't even entertain Allison buying her a drink, let alone asking her out.

Noise rose around her, thankfully pulling Allison from her insipid and useless train of tangled thoughts. The paramedics had returned and though they were no longer jogging, they were positioned in such a way that it was impossible to see who was on the gurney. Once they were through the doors, a collective sigh of relief wound its way through the people hovering around the desk. Carol finished her conversation with a male nurse and walked back over to Allison.

"Next time," she said, reprimand slipping through her voice, "you stay where you are." She sighed, the tension visibly leaving her body. "It was a false alarm, thankfully."

"Was it June?" Allison asked quietly.

"Oh, no. No, no, no." Carol shook her head and placed both hands on the counter. "June is just fine, doll. It was a woman down the hall from her. Bless her heart, I can't remember her name, and I should because she's a fall risk and we get these calls at least every other week, and..."

Allison tuned out, certain Carol would go on for a while, but more importantly, Drew was coming back down the hall.

Slower now, head hanging, eyes seeming to track each labored step she took.

There was a sullen heaviness clipped to her shoulders, a shade darker than the usual gloom that tended to invisibly weigh her down. Allison expected relief, knowing that June was okay, but instead, Drew was layered with visibly warring emotions. Again, the stark contrast from her usually unreadable expression was jarring and did not help Allison's determination to not want to…to…oh, she didn't know. Be there for Drew? Talk to her about something other than renovations? Give her a safe space she had a feeling Drew had never had before?

"Let her go," Carol said in a quiet voice Allison hadn't known she could achieve. "She'll be okay. In the meantime, you and I have more work to do." She watched as Drew left the building. "She'll need a little time, but then you get right back on her, you hear me?"

The phrasing didn't help Allison's struggle to confine Drew to a "Can't Touch This" zone in her mind, and she let a giggle slip at the notion of being on top of Drew.

Regrettably so, as Carol had the hearing abilities of a dolphin. "What are you giggling about?" She shook her head, but was smiling. "You know what, forget I asked. Let's go, doll. I'm the only one who knows what kinds of snacks are approved for our choking hazard residents."

CHAPTER TWELVE

Two great blue herons stalked back and forth on the patch of scrubby sand between the newly replaced deck and the Mandalay Channel. Drew watched them with the kind of curiosity that came from living in Clearwater Beach for one's entire life, which is to say: not much at all. They were likely looking for dinner, but in a perfunctorily lazy way that Drew could relate to.

She should eat. The thought swung in her mind, amplified by the slow growl of her stomach. She had eaten breakfast, or at least eaten something during the morning hours, but those had passed long ago, and lunch had been swept away by work issues. Dinner had blinked at her an hour or so ago, but she hadn't moved from her deck since she'd come home, ripped off her work clothes, and collapsed into her favorite papasan chair.

The day itself hadn't been terrible. It was business as usual: putting out some fires, haggling suppliers, calming clients. That wasn't the problem at all.

It was the incessant emotional hangover that clung to her like a second skin.

The moment she'd walked into the fire station yesterday, she'd had an unsettled feeling. It happened sometimes when she took on an extra volunteer shift, but it usually dissipated after the first call. And, living and serving in a community that had a high number of elderly residents, there was always a first call.

Drew had barely gotten settled when she'd realized that a call had come in and two of her pals were readying to respond. She didn't hesitate to join them, especially since it was for a person in distress, not a fire (in other words, an "easier" call). When they pulled into Sunset Dunes and saw the ambulance, the driver, Patrick, was ready to turn around and head back to the station. Drew had bolted from the truck, a sick feeling of dread building brick by brick in her stomach.

It wasn't June. She had realized that as soon as she hit the corner and stopped twenty feet from June's apartment. But the blanket of worry, of shivering panic, had yet to shrug itself off.

She couldn't shake it. If she lost June... No.

It was inevitable, Drew knew that. She simply preferred to avoid thinking about it.

Her stomach growled again and Drew closed her eyes, trying to pull up a mental image of what her refrigerator held. Nothing impressive. A shame, since eating would likely make her feel better, fill some of the empty agitation.

Speaking of agitation... Drew opened her eyes and glared out at the water. Allison. She'd made the mistake (not that she'd had a choice, seeing as her construction team needed her input on the damn former kitchen, which was a sinkhole of problems) of stopping by the building on Eldorado Avenue that morning, and she'd almost executed her escape when Allison, just coming in, met her at the door.

She'd looked unfairly cute, dressed in slouchy jeans and a T-shirt that had seen better days. Her hair was mostly pulled back, but blond strands framed her face, which was flushed with exertion. A painfully good look for Allison, as it turned out, and as Drew had tried like hell to ignore.

"We need to meet up," Allison had said. "This Winter Wonderfest isn't going to get planned on its own."

Drew had nodded. Allison had unknowingly caught her in a weak moment, a moment fueled by a desire to do everything she could to make the rest of June's life as excellent as possible. So, yeah. She would step it up with the planning.

For June's sake.

If Allison had been surprised by the lack of an argument or even a sideways shitty comment, she hadn't shown it. She suggested that evening, Drew nodded again. She mentioned The Hideout, Drew shrugged and said, "That's fine." The only thing they hadn't cemented before Drew made her escape was a time to meet, and that misstep was allowing her to sit on her damn dock and pretend she didn't have to stick to the promises she'd made without actually, technically, agreeing to anything. Not with words, anyway.

She could not go. She could pull a Classic Drew and ditch Allison.

Her stomach growled again, this time sounding more like an irate gurgle, and Drew pressed her hand against it.

Well. At least The Hideout had food.

The moment Drew walked into The Hideout and locked eyes with Allison, she knew she'd made a mistake.

It wasn't that she didn't want to be there. The problem was that she kind of *did*, and she didn't *want* to want to be there. Nor did she want to like the way Allison's cheeks flushed just the tiniest bit when she saw Drew, or the way her eyes lit up with a devastating kind of delight.

"You came," Allison said, then seemed to catch herself. She blinked and the enthusiastic energy nearly disappeared, replaced by a stoic expression that still leaked a bit of happiness—maybe some surprise, too. "You're here. Good. We need to get started on these activities."

Drew hid a smile, easy to do beneath the shadow of her beat-up Phillies hat. As she slid onto the stool next to Allison—and points to her for grabbing the two seats by the Megatouch, though Drew probably wouldn't get a chance to beat her own erotic high score tonight—she slipped her phone out of her pocket and cued up two obnoxious Christmas songs on the bar's Touch Tunes.

She side-eyed the plastic bag on the bar top. "What's that?"

"That's our activity," Allison said, tapping the bag. "But I just got here and I'm starving, so it needs to wait. Are you hungry?"

Oh, she so wanted not to be hungry, because now this little "let's work on our planning thing" situation was becoming something too similar to a date.

Instead of answering, Drew motioned to Bartleby, who came over right away.

"Hey there, Drew. The usual?"

"Yeah." She nodded in Allison's direction. "Her, too."

"Oh," Allison said, not doing a great job at hiding her confusion. "So you do come here often."

"Often?" Bartleby, the world's most ineffective bartender, threw his head back and laughed. "Honey, Drew practically lived here for a while. I don't think she's made herself dinner in fifteen years."

"That's not true," she argued. "I cook."

Bartleby waved her off. "What can I get for ya?" He nodded when Allison gave her order, then lumbered back to the kitchen to deliver it.

"Does it take long for food to come out?"

Drew shook her head. She looked at the Megatouch with longing, missing its silent fun.

"Okay," Allison continued. "I don't care if you don't talk, but I need to know if we have time to do the activity before the food comes out."

"Can't we start it and pause if we have to?"

"She speaks." Allison smiled, then swallowed it. "We could. I guess." She paused, then angled herself on her stool so she was facing Drew. "Why were you in that outfit yesterday? At the Dunes?"

Thanks to growing up with five siblings, Drew was ace at keeping up with multiple conversations, even when they came from the same person. "We can wait till after we eat. I'm a volunteer firefighter."

She didn't look at Allison because, frankly, she was tired of the gape that came with the admission. She did side-eye her a bit, just to check. When she realized Allison's mouth was shut, Drew looked at her full-on.

"You own your own renovation business, and you're a volunteer firefighter?"

Drew nodded. She wanted to peel her glare off Allison's eyes, but they were so damn beautiful.

"What don't you do?"

"Relationships." The word spat out on its own, the product of years of rehearsal. Drew waited to see a change in Allison's expression, but there wasn't so much as a flicker of disappointment. Interesting.

"Understandable," was all she said.

Drew didn't love the silence that fell upon them. She felt like it was her fault, since Allison always seemed ready for conversation. "I don't have to wear a uniform," she explained, kicking the rung on her stool. "But I think it's sloppy to show up in whatever. So that's why I was wearing that."

"It was a nice outfit," Allison said carefully. "It fits your role. I guess. I don't really understand what a volunteer firefighter does, to be honest."

"Same thing as a regular firefighter, just on a lower scale." Drew reconsidered. "Or not really. I can do everything they do."

"I know this is going to sound stupid, but…There wasn't a fire."

She didn't need to say more; Drew had explained this more times than she could count. "It's not stupid," she said, surprising herself with her able reassurance. "We're first responders. It's the rule: you hear the call, you respond. We're all trained to handle basic medical emergencies."

Allison nodded, leaning forward as Bartleby placed their food on the bar. "That makes sense. Thanks for explaining it and not making me feel like an idiot."

Something rough chafed deep inside Drew, a fully unusual desire to ruin whoever had made this woman feel like an idiot. She picked up her loaded hot dog and took an enormous bite, hoping that would sink the unfamiliar and unwanted sensation.

"That looks good," Allison remarked.

"It is," Drew said around her bite. "The Hideout is famous for their loaded hot dogs. The secret is the mac and cheese."

"My mom used to make mac and cheese and hot dogs every Friday night." Allison got a faraway look on her face as she picked up her chicken Caesar wrap. "And baked beans. But I never thought to put the mac and cheese on the hot dog. Only the beans."

Drew made sure to chew and swallow before responding this time. "You realize that doesn't make sense, right?"

"I had mustard on the hot dog," Allison explained. "Mac and cheese with mustard? No thank you."

Drew shrugged as she took another bite. Her hot dog was loaded indeed: mac and cheese, crushed potato chips, barbecue sauce, and—wait a minute. She inspected it. No crunchy onions?

Bartleby chose that moment to swing by and refill their water glasses; it was only then that Drew realized Allison wasn't drinking a beer.

"Hey," Drew said, gesturing to her hot dog. "Missing something?"

"Nan thought you could use the night off from 'em." Bartleby shrugged innocently, then winked. The problem was he had heavy eyelids so his winks always got a little stuck on their way back up.

Drew glared at him and the implication. She wanted her damn onions, but she'd devoured three-quarters of the hot dog, so it wasn't worth it now. She ate the house-made potato chips with equal greed and hunger, stopping only when her plate was spotless.

She realized belatedly that she was technically eating with someone. And that someone was only halfway through her dinner. You know, like a normal person consuming food.

Drew thought it was rude and uncomfortable to talk to someone while they were eating, so she let her eyes drift around the bar. It was like a second home to her, or maybe a third, because she probably spent more time at the Dunes than she did at The Hideout. Whatever the case, she loved this bar. It was rare that someone new showed up; the cast of characters was not unlike *Cheers*, a show her dad had watched religiously when she was growing up. With Bartleby at the helm and his wife, Nan, in the kitchen, everyone was always taken care of like family.

Down at the other end of the bar, Ivy was sitting with Kato, her dog. Idly, Drew wondered when Tommy would stumble in. Watching them do their song and dance once a week never got old.

"That was really good," Allison said, pushing her plate away. Drew eyed the remaining potato chips, but kept her hands wrapped around her water glass.

"Bartleby's wife is the cook," she offered. Friendly conversation. That's all.

Allison laughed, then stopped when she saw Drew's serious expression. "Bartleby?"

Drew nodded in the direction of the bartender, who was playing a round of pinochle with the three old guys who sat in the middle of the bar every Friday night.

"That's his real name?"

"As real as the Scrivener."

"Okay, hang on." Allison leaned back to take in more of Drew, or at least that's how it seemed, and the seeming made Drew squirm, but not altogether uncomfortably, which ultimately made her…uncomfortable. "That's total nerd humor."

"What, because I'm a dumb carpenter who sometimes puts out fires or administers CPR, I don't know how to read?"

"No," Allison said, her voice stern. And Drew liked it. A little too much. She busied herself with selecting a new song for the Touch Tunes. Seemed like a prime moment for The Waitresses with "Christmas Wrapping." "Wait, you're a carpenter?"

Drew dipped her head. Dammit, she had to stop accidentally peeling back the iron layers she preferred to keep wrapped tightly around herself. "By trade, yeah. I do a lot of stuff. But that's what I focused on."

"In trade school," Allison finished.

"Yes, *in trade school*," Drew mocked.

"I do not sound like that."

Drew snorted. "You absolutely do. And for the record, I took Honors English in high school, so I read all the insipid classics that nerds get their panties in wads over."

Allison laughed. "Can you never say that again? Please?"

"What, you have an aversion to *panties*?"

"The word, yes. The—" Allison stopped herself, her round cheeks reddening with words unspoken. "Anyway."

"New topic," Drew said. A smile was pushing at her lips, but she wasn't ready to admit to the greater world that she was A) feeling better than she had when she'd walked into the bar, and B) actually enjoying being in the presence of a woman who was attractive and funny and—

And nothing. *Nothing. Absolutely not, Drew. Hard no.*

"Okay." Allison hesitated, picking at a splintered piece of wood on the bar's edge. "So, should we talk about the other day?"

The words rang with an expectation Drew could not live up to. It was enough to flip the switch she'd been half-heartedly batting at. "We're not friends," she said, her voice flat and even.

A smile—small enough to miss, sly enough to hit its mark—touched the corners of Allison's mouth. "Yeah, I gathered that by the look on your face when she walked in."

Several voices pinged in Drew's head: June's, telling her she needed to be kinder; Celeste's, suggesting Drew make an effort to make more friends, because who knows who those friends know, and blah blah blah, find a girlfriend, you reclusive loser; her sixth-grade teacher's, firmly explaining that Drew needed to find a way to be less abrupt and give people a chance. They were overlapping and annoying but not as loud as New Kids on the Block beginning to rap-sing their way through "Funky, Funky Xmas."

"No," Drew said, measuring the pace of her words so she wasn't abrupt but still managed not to give Allison a chance. She knew what (well, who) Allison was referring to, but couldn't resist the opportunity to build a boundary. "You and I. We're not friends."

CHAPTER THIRTEEN

It shouldn't have stung, at least not the way it pierced like a recently sharpened knife sliding into the hollow of Allison's throat, but it did. She'd been doing her best not to show her truth, the shimmer of a stupid crush that she was rapidly falling into. And she thought she'd done a damn good job.

Now, here was Drew, laying her flat with crisp, wintry words.

And Allison hadn't even been talking about them. Not that there was a "them" of any sort. She wanted to know what the hell that weird interaction with Holly had been about.

But Drew had closed up, a barrier erected around her that flickered with hazard lights brighter than the Christmas lights strung along the bar. Allison had pushed through such hazards too many times in her past (read: The List) and had learned all the lessons the hard way.

"Can we just"—Drew motioned to the bag on the bar—"do what we came here to do?"

"Yeah. Let's do that." Allison pulled the bag toward her, then paused. "Did you bring anything?"

"Uh, no." Drew's tone implied that Allison should have known that. She seemed to reconsider her attitude, then said, "I mean. I have an idea."

"An idea is a start. Tell me."

It was the first time Allison had seen a dip of confidence in Drew. And it was subtle, highly missable if someone wasn't paying too much attention. Her dark-brown eyes softened as though a veil of vulnerability had slipped over them. And her eyebrows, thick and every bit as dark as her hair, pulled together, drawing a tiny wrinkle between them. As quickly as the gentle expression appeared, it melted away, features settling back into the nonchalant cockiness Allison had become familiar with.

"So." Drew paused, clearing her throat, then taking a sip of water. Stalling, probably. Allison wanted to give her the benefit of the doubt and believe that she wasn't leaving all of this planning up to her, but the longer this pause went on, the heavier her doubt became.

Just as Allison was reaching for the bag she'd brought so they could blast through this terrible awkward imbalance, Drew reached out and put a hand on her wrist. Allison nearly jerked away. She would have, if Drew hadn't done so first.

"My idea," Drew said, resting both hands on her lap, her right hand rubbing her left as though Allison's skin had burned and blistered her, "is the Reindeer Antler Game."

"The Reindeer Antler Game," Allison repeated. She hadn't come across that one in her searches. "Can you demonstrate it? Now?"

"Uh, no. I don't have the supplies." Drew smiled. "But I can explain it. Ready?"

"Been ready."

"Okay." She stood up and shook her hands out, causing Allison to smile despite her waning annoyance. "All we need is a lot of balloons, at least eight for each team, and one pair of pantyhose per team."

"You've already lost my bid," Allison said, shaking her head. "I refuse to purchase the latter."

"Oh my God, what is your deal with *panties*?" Drew tried to affect a British accent but failed miserably, somehow making the word even more repulsive.

"It's a disgusting word!"

"Worse than moist?"

Allison rolled her eyes. "I used to hate that word, but my friends tormented me with it, so I've built up immunity."

"And no one tortured you with panties?"

The two looked at each other, both refusing to crack a gay, panty-loving smile. Drew could have won an Academy Award for her unaffected performance. Allison, on the other hand, worried her attempt at trying not to give in to the queer camaraderie was causing her to look more "Here's Johnny!" then she was comfortable with.

"Never," Allison said through gritted teeth. "You?"

"My lawyer has forbidden me to answer questions about panties," Drew said seriously. "Now, could I please return to the explanation of the Reindeer Antler Game?"

Allison nodded, and with that, Drew was off.

"Okay. Each team, like I said, gets the supplies. First, they blow up the balloons. As many as they can. They don't have to be huge, because they're getting stuffed into the pantyhose."

"Again," Allison interrupted, "you've lost my bid."

"Let me finish. We're getting to the good part."

"There is no good part when pantyhose"—the word whispered out like a dirty secret—"are involved, Drew."

"Aha!" Drew grinned. "You said it. Progress."

Allison rolled her eyes and gestured for Drew to continue. She wasn't sure what to make of the speed with which her feelings toward Drew ricocheted back and forth. One minute she wanted to walk out of The Hideout and never see her again, and the next, she wanted to do everything she could to hear Drew's laugh. She was maddening, that was clear. But beneath the "walking salt lick," as Carol so appropriately stated, there was someone who wasn't all salt burn. Drew had a sense of humor buried deep within her. And Allison knew she cared for her grandmother. So, she had a heart.

The problem was that Drew, in all her salty complexity, was making Allison remember that she, too, had a heart.

A heart she desperately wanted to board up.

"So, like I said, the blown-up balloons get stuffed into the legs of the pantyhose." Oh, that did it—the worn, splintered boards arrived at the foot of Allison's heart, ready to be nailed in if Drew kept saying that fucking word. "And then, this is the best part. Ready?"

"Still ready."

Drew looked like she had just opened the Christmas present her eight-year-old self had been dying to receive. "The team picks one person. And that person sits down. And the rest of the team has to put the pantyhose, you know, the waist part? They put that part around the top of the person's head." She spread her arms out to show her invisible antler success. "Bam. Reindeer antlers, à la the hose of panties."

Mmhmm, yup, there went the boards, hammered into place with a flourish, never to have their nails pried off.

"Too far?" But she was grinning wickedly.

"There exists no measure of distance for how too far you just went," Allison said. "But can we discuss the practicality of this activity for a sec?"

Drew sat back down, nodding. "Hit me."

Oh, that was a little tempting, too. Allison mentally batted down her seesawing emotions. "Remind me where this activity is taking place."

"Winter Wonderfest," Drew said slowly, enunciating every syllable.

"*Where*," Allison prompted.

Drew blinked at her, eyes dimming with confusion. "The Dunes?"

Allison motioned for her to keep going.

"Sunset Dunes? What? What are you trying to get me to say?"

"Who lives at Sunset Dunes?"

"My grandmother." Pride sparked in Drew's voice, her eyes once again brimming with life.

It was a step in the right direction, though woefully narrow. "And your grandmother is…"

"Amazing. You've met her."

"Yes. She's lovely and wonderful. And she has great hair. But, Drew, come on. You know what I'm getting at."

"She sure does," Bartleby interjected from behind the bar. "Stop bein' a little puss, Drew."

Drew held up her hand to deflect Bartleby's reprimand. "Okay. Fine. An assisted living facility for seniors." She shrugged. "Failing to see your point."

"My point," Allison said, "is lung capacity."

Drew tilted her head, taking Allison in. The look made some of those damn boards quiver and Allison was none too pleased about it. "Oh, I get it. You think because they're old, they can't blow up balloons. Wow. Didn't peg you for an ageist, Allison."

"I am not an ageist," she hissed, glancing around to ensure no one had heard the slander. Bartleby laughed and walked down to Ivy, who was starting to look impatient. Tommy still hadn't arrived. "I'm being *practical. Thoughtful.*"

"Two things I'm not?"

She heard the tease in Drew's tone but didn't feel like volleying back to her. This whole night was becoming too confusing. "I didn't say that. I just don't love the idea of having a room full of seniors huffing and puffing their precious breaths into spheres of latex."

"Fine, but you gotta admit, the image of them with the pantyhose antlers would be worth it."

"Enough!" Allison shouted. She ducked her head once she realized how her voice carried across the bar. She motioned at Drew, not sure what she wanted, but Drew responded by whipping out her phone and cuing up "Do They Know It's Christmas?" which, honestly, Allison liked.

"Sorry," Drew said after a few blessed seconds of silence between them. "I will refrain from using the word for the rest of the night."

"Thank you." Allison grabbed the plastic bag and reached inside. "Now—"

"We could," Drew said, amusement lingering in her voice, "rent a helium tank for the balloons. That would add an extra level of entertainment."

Images of seniors inhaling helium from balloons caused Allison to shake her head, but Drew's hand hovering above her shoulder stopped her midshake.

"Just think about it, okay?"

"Fine." As Allison shifted so too did Drew's hand, falling away from its almost-touch. Allison resumed her retrieval of the supplies and laid them on the bar. "For now, let's try something more practical. All we need to do is create a festive tree."

"With pipe cleaners?" Drew said, fisting the furry sticks. "Weird but okay. Why not just say a Christmas tree?"

"Nondenominational," Allison reminded her.

"Or secular," Drew murmured.

"Semantics. Here." Allison passed her a pack of colorful pipe cleaners. "For decorations."

Drew nodded, then spread out an array of pipe cleaners, touching each one as she thought. Allison wasted no time brainstorming and leapt into her project. The vision began to come to her as she bent and wrapped the pipe cleaners. She'd never been the star student in art class but she should have received an honorable mention for trying with enthusiasm.

As they worked, Drew fell quiet once again, making Allison wonder if she'd daydreamed their entire previous exchange. Being around Drew was not unlike being trapped in a pinball machine. One lucky bounce and the playfield world lit up, but one errant strike with a flipper and it was back into the trough, ready to be rolled into the shooter lane once again. One day maybe Allison would figure out the right bounce off the slingshots, the one that could keep Drew talking.

"Look at this! Arts and crafts at the bar!"

Both women turned when Tommy, sans hat but donning a Marlins T-shirt, came up behind them. Allison swiveled her head to catch Ivy's immediate reaction, and sure enough, her face lit up with incalculable glee before falling into a look filled with boredom. Allison smirked. Whatever game those two played, it had to be good to keep doing it as often as Drew had implied.

"You want in?" Drew held out pipe cleaners to Tommy.

"Nah, nah. Wouldn't wanna wow you with my talents." Tommy clapped Drew on the back before meandering down the bar. He looked back, once at Allison, then focused on Drew. "Hey, she's cute. Nice job, Kingsley."

Kingsley. Allison paused her creative task, trying to remember where she'd heard that name before. It nagged in the back of her brain, but nothing was connecting. She brushed it off and avoided looking at Drew's reaction to the comment, but couldn't help but laugh when she saw the middle finger fly up in Tommy's direction. He guffawed in response then took his place a measurable distance from Ivy, barely glancing her way before ordering a Miller Lite.

Bartleby dropped off the draught, then swung down the bar and leaned over to say something to Drew. Allison missed it but she caught the smile and snort response from Drew, who pressed a few times on her phone. Allison groaned when the music jingled into the bar. This song would haunt her for days.

"Oh for Christ's sake," Tommy bellowed. Clearly this was not his first beer of the night. "Nobody wants a damn hippopotamus for Christmas."

"I do," Ivy said, her voice a tightrope between dreamy and demanding.

"Of course you do. You want everything for Christmas." Tommy shook his head. "You know they use their tails to spread their shit around?"

Ivy looked aghast. She clutched her dog, who was donning elf ears tonight, close to her chest. His fluffy paws pressed against her chin. "Tommy, don't be foul."

"I ain't being foul. Just speakin' the truth."

"Gonna be a nasty one tonight," Drew said under her breath.

"Those two?"

Drew nodded. "We probably want to wrap this up and get out of here before it starts."

Allison dared a look down the bar. Tommy and Ivy were glaring at each other. Where the flirting was hiding, she had no idea, but she also didn't want to find out.

"Done," Drew said, holding up her tree.

Allison had to admit brainstorming had paid off. Drew had executed a nearly perfect outline of a Christmas tree. She'd used red pipe cleaners to string from one side to the other, and crafted little yellow balls to hang from the red lines.

Wait. It looked familiar. Allison scanned the bar, eyes landing on the red-and-gold Christmas tree.

"Nice inspiration," she noted. "But seriously, that's really good."

"Thanks. Yours is too."

Allison held it up for both of them to inspect. She'd tried to make a 3-D tree and it was almost good. She'd stuck with yellow and white "decorations," layering them around the tree. Not her best effort, but not too bad for a first shot.

"It could use some fine-tuning."

Drew rolled her eyes. "Didn't peg you for a perfectionist."

Was she? Allison would have to overthink that later.

"This'll work," Drew added, beginning to clean up. "For Wonderfest."

"I think so. It's easy enough but has room for creativity."

"We'll have to have Band-Aids on hand," Drew said. "The ends of those pipes are sharp." She handed Allison the bag and stood up.

"Wait, I didn't pay."

"You're good. I have a running tab."

Allison bit her lip. This was *not* a date. Not even close. "Thank you."

"No problem."

Drew had a few words with Bartleby before they left. Allison caught something about cutting Tommy off after one more drink. They made it a few steps from the bar before Drew looked over her shoulder, sharing a moment with the Megatouch.

"Do you want to stay and play?" Allison said, half joking, half hoping.

Drew smiled and hitched her shoulders up. "I'm good. But thanks."

They made it outside without hearing more of Tommy and Ivy's ill-fated flirting. Allison took a deep breath, marveling not for the last time how crazy it was that it was December 6th and she wasn't bundled up or inhaling cold, snowy air.

"Listen. Wait." Drew held out her arm, her fingers centimeters from Allison's, not daring to come closer. "About earlier."

Allison, jarred from her weather thoughts, startled. Earlier... Oh. Right. The blunt comment to end all blunt comments. "It's fine."

"I should explain." There was a note of something in Drew's voice that Allison couldn't place. "I don't—this isn't something I do."

Allison looked at Drew, her features glowing under the halo of the streetlight. It wasn't fair, how quietly attractive she was and how utterly impenetrable her walls were. "What? Christmas activities in a dive bar with one of your clients?"

The word hit its mark and Drew winced. "Okay, that's fair."

Allison turned to leave but this time Drew's fingers did make contact with her arm. They grasped, firmly enough to send the message of "I don't know how to tell you I need you to stay here for a minute," but lightly enough to shock a ripple through Allison's nerve endings.

"About what I said. Us not being friends."

"I heard you, Drew. Message received, loud and clear." A familiar—unpleasantly so—wave crested within Allison, splashing old debris right into her mouth. "I fully understand that we have a working relationship, nothing more."

It was then that Allison realized Drew's fingers were still wrapped around her arm because they squeezed. She shut her eyes against the traitorous sensation that wandered its way down her arm, leaving the tips of her fingers tingling.

"It's not that," Drew said quietly. "It's not you. It's me."

"Oh, now we're waltzing directly into cliché-land," Allison bit out. She hated that this conversation was about to erase the truth: that they'd just had a fun night together. "Spare me, okay?" She tried to pull her arm out of that confusing grasp but Drew held on.

"I'll let you go once you stop and just let me talk."

Oh. That hit square in the center of Allison's chest, yanking a breath from her with a gasp.

"It's me," Drew continued, thankfully oblivious to Allison's reaction. "I have this thing with being friends with lesbians. I can't do it." She laughed, or more like choke-laughed. "I'll spare you the long and stupid explanation and sum it up with this. Every time I become friends with a lesbian, it ends up being a problem."

Allison was dying, *dying* to interject something like, "Oh, poor you, all these women falling in love with you," but she held back. She was too surprised and thrilled that Drew was speaking in long, explanatory sentences to be an ass about it.

Drew's thumb, clearly driven by a mind of its own, pressed into the sensitive skin on the inside of Allison's bicep. "I can't tell you how many times I've been friends with lesbian couples and one of them gets all insecure and conjures up this ridiculous bullshit that her partner and I are having an affair, or at least secretly into each other. And it's never, ever been true." At that, Drew dropped Allison's arm like it was aflame. "So, yeah. I don't have friendships with lesbians."

The night air, dotted with distant traffic and pops of noise from The Hideout, swayed around them. Allison was reluctant to break the tender truce strung up between them like a wire coated with wool. It wouldn't snap, of that she was suddenly certain, but it could still cut. And with the wrong step, the inconsiderate push, it would cut deeply.

"Anyway. That's me. Not you."

Allison considered walking away. It was an easy out, but she was tired of unfinished business. She really, really did not want to add Drew to The List. In any capacity.

"I hear you," she said carefully. "And I respect your... decisions."

"But?"

"No but."

Drew sighed. "There's always a but."

"Okay, here's a but. But I'm single. So, your little theory doesn't hold weight here."

Tension waved over Drew's features. "Holly," she said bluntly.

"No," Allison said immediately. "That's not a thing. Totally single here."

Drew looked skyward. "Yeah," was all she said.

As Allison opened her mouth to reassure—and she couldn't fathom why she was doing that—Drew cut her off before a single word could escape.

"And that's its own problem." Drew shook her head. "I just can't, okay? I'll see you later."

Allison watched her go, something that was beginning to feel like a trend—Drew walking away, Allison in the background, rebuffed with questions held hostage in her mouth.

"Fine," she said to Drew's retreating form. "We're not friends."

CHAPTER FOURTEEN

"Thanks for coming in, girlfriend," Carol said as she sashayed down the hallway toward the atrium. Allison breathed a silent thank-you to the goddesses of Sunset Dunes, grateful that they were keeping her away from the cafe. "I got to talking to these ladies about Wonderfest, and they just had to get their busybody noses involved."

Reflexively, Allison started to comment on the mixed metaphor—a busybody automatically has their nose in everything—but decided to let it go. She was getting used to the quirks of Carol's speech and happily kept her giggles to herself.

"I thought everyone already had tasks assigned to them," Allison said, trying to keep up with the changes that seemed to saunter onto the scene every day.

"Yes and no." Carol held the door to the atrium open for her. "Once these two found out they weren't on the entertainment committee, they demanded to meet with someone who was." She held out an arm, stopping Allison in her tracks. "They're here," she said in a low voice. "Get ready, doll."

Seated at the edge of the atrium in the seats best arranged for everyone else's viewing pleasure sat two of the most glamorous older women Allison had ever seen. They were dressed to the nines, to a place beyond the nines if such a place existed, and held themselves with posture befitting royalty.

One of the women looked up, her eyelids heavy beneath caked-on mascara, and smiled widely. It seemed genuine. Maybe a little chaotic with the bright-pink lipstick, but nice enough.

"Sharks bite silently," Carol whispered conspiratorially as she led Allison to the table.

"Well, hello! This must be Allison. It is so very nice to meet you, honey. Please do sit down with us." Ms. Bright Pink Lipstick gestured to the chair to her right and Allison obediently sat down.

"Now would you look at her," the other woman said, leaning forward to get a better look. "She's got his eyes, Blanche."

Ms. Bright Pink Lipstick—Blanche, apparently—grabbed Allison's chin, turning her face for a thorough examination. Her eyes were a watery blue but filled with what looked like kindness. "She does! Oh, she does. Eyes of the ocean, I always said."

"*I* always said," the other woman protested. "*You* said his eyes looked like the brightest umbrella on the beach."

"What a ridiculous thing to say, Dorothy!"

Dorothy, eyes bright and dry behind a large pair of gold-rimmed glasses, snickered. "No more ridiculous than thinking he preferred you over me."

Before a rebuttal could be lobbed across the table, Carol stepped in, obviously well-versed in dealing with these two. "Now, ladies, let's get along for the sake of planning, shall we?"

"We get along just fine," Blanche said, a sliver of ice floating in her tone. "And we'll get down to business shortly enough. But first, Miss Allison, inquiring minds want to know. Just what did your granddaddy tell you about me?"

Oh, fuck. So that's what this was: her grandfather's lothario reputation haunting her from beyond the grave. As if she hadn't had to hear enough about it from her grandmother, may she rest in the most restful peace, when she was a kid.

"Well—"

"Dorothy Davis," the aforementioned said. "That's the name I'm sure you heard old Mack yammer on about!"

"Come now, Dorothy. Which one of us took every afternoon coffee with him?" Blanche batted her eyelashes so wildly that Allison worried they would either permanently stick together or fly off.

"Only because you penciled yourself in months in advance." Dorothy patted the sides of her intricate ice-white updo as she looked at Allison. "Your granddaddy had a social calendar taped outside his room. You should see the names on there!" She leaned in. "But you'll see two written more than any others."

"*One*," Blanche said. "Mine."

"Might I remind you that Mack gave me this the week before left us?" Dorothy reached into her blouse and held up a large ring on a dainty chain.

"Hey!" Allison said, leaning in to get a closer look. "That's his class ring."

Dorothy wasted no time in tucking the ring back into her wrinkled cleavage. "You can have it when I die, honey."

Bewildered, Allison looked at Carol, who simply shook her head.

"Gave it to you?" Blanche threw her head back and laughed, not a single red-orange curl moving as she did. "More like you stole it while he slept!"

"Ladies, ladies!" Carol held up both hands. "That's quite enough. I'm sure Mack loved both of you equally. But he's not here to defend himself, so it might do you good to let it go."

Blanche waved Carol off with a nicely manicured hand. "Let bygones be bygones, because by God, he's gone."

Both Blanche and Dorothy laughed, the competitive tension between them put away for another day. Carol blew out a breath of relief as Allison continued looking between the two women.

She'd known from an early age that her grandfather was a man who refused to be tied down to a single woman. His tendencies seemed to be genetically passed down to Allison's mom, who had only been married long enough to have Allison and then her brother two years later. All her mom would say about Allison's father was that "he meant well." Apparently, "meaning well" meant that her dad only ever existed on the periphery of her life. Instead, her father figures came in the form of her mother's boyfriends, a new one every handful of years. At some point, her mother had stopped dating altogether, and now lived on her own, seeming to enjoy life without romantic entanglements.

And yet, there was Allison, doomed to desire the kind of love and romance she hadn't witnessed anyone in her family have. Maybe she, too, was genetically predisposed to be unable to hold down a steady relationship.

A morbid thought, especially on the heels of her time with Drew two nights ago. They hadn't spoken since—why would they?—and Allison felt strangely adrift.

Carol tapped her on the arm with a pen, bringing her back to the table. She widened her eyes and tilted her head in Dorothy's direction. Allison looked and knew instantly that she'd missed something.

"I'm sorry," she said, stalling for an excuse. "I was thinking about drinks."

"Aren't we all!" Blanche exclaimed. "Oh, how I love champagne. Bartender, bring me a French 75!"

"Blanche, please. We're not at the Palm Beach Country Club," Carol said, and Blanche's disappointment was evident. Carol winked at Allison. "Dorothy was just saying that she thinks you have your grandfather's charm along with his eyes."

Allison fought the urge to laugh. Charm? Hardly. "Oh, no. I don't think that got passed down to me." She stared out the windows of the atrium. "I haven't exactly been lucky in love."

Carol rested her hand on Allison's shoulder. "It just hasn't been your time yet, girlfriend. It will be."

"Surely you have a line of young men clamoring after you!" Dorothy said.

"She sure doesn't have that," Carol intoned.

This time Allison did laugh. "It's true. I don't. Wouldn't want that anyway."

It took Blanche a second, but she caught the softball Allison tossed to midfield. "Oh, a lesbian! How absolutely darling!"

"A what?" Dorothy said. "She's a lesbian? Oh, we love lesbians. Do you know Drew?"

Allison bit the inside of her cheek, then said, "Sure do."

"I bet Drew is head over heels in love with you!" Blanche clapped excitedly. "Oh, Dorothy, isn't this wonderful? We'll have our own little Sunset Dunes lesbian couple!"

"What about Jeanine and Rosie?" Dorothy said. "Don't they do lesbian together?"

"Yes, but they're *old*," Blanche said. "These two are young and gorgeous!"

Dorothy scoffed. "I don't think Jeanine and Rosie would take kindly to you suggesting they're not gorgeous."

"Okay, ladies, can we please talk about food and drinks?" Carol waved her hands at both women. "You wanted so badly to be a part of this planning. So let's focus now, all right?"

Dorothy and Blanche sighed in sync, the glory of their speeding gossip taxi hitting a roadblock in the form of a no-nonsense old lady wearing an Adidas tracksuit and sneakers.

"Good, thank you." Carol opened the binder, which she'd decided to hold on to because Allison apparently wasn't trustworthy enough. "Here's the list of food we came up with."

Murmurs of "ooh" and "scrumptious!" filled the table as Blanche and Dorothy pored over the list. They made a few suggestions that Carol jotted down while Allison sat back, taking it all in. That sideways comment about Drew being in love with her had yanked one of the boards clear off her heart. It wasn't true, Allison knew that, but the potential of it was starting to feel not impossible.

Which meant, in Allison's world, it was completely impossible.

"Now, drinks." Carol placed both hands on the table. "Ladies, we all know what happened three years ago."

Solemnity stole over the group, except for Allison, who was chomping at the bit to hear the Dunes gossip.

"May he rest in peace," Blanche said softly.

"Someone died at Winter Wonderfest?" Allison said.

"No, no." Carol shot Blanche a look. "Harry Westfield smuggled in some hooch and got Della McCarthy very, very drunk. She tipped off her chair and broke her wrist."

"And Harry was exiled," Dorothy added. "Far, far away. Bless his soul."

"Good Lord," Carol grumbled. "He was asked to leave," she clarified. "And now lives a mere two miles away in another community."

"And I'm sure he's having a delightful time with all those other careless people."

Dorothy nodded. "Maybe we should move down there, Blanche!"

"And destroy our reputation here?" Blanche held a hand to her heart. "I dare not think so!"

"So, drinks," Carol said, bringing the gals back again. "We'll have our standard sherbet punch."

Dorothy clapped while Blanche rolled her eyes. Allison merely grinned.

"And then I'm stumped," Carol admitted. "All my drink ideas have alcohol in them."

"Can't you just"—Dorothy swirled her hand in the air—"leave the alcohol out?"

"I don't think it's that easy."

"It's not quite that easy," Allison said, finally feeling like she had something to contribute. "Sometimes you have to add other ingredients to get the full effect of a mocktail."

"A what-tail?" Blanche narrowed her eyes at Allison. "I don't want my cocktails without the cock, honey."

Dorothy and Carol gasped, the former clapping both hands over her mouth. Blanche dissolved into laughter, as though she'd been holding on to that joke for decades.

"Mocktails just mock the cock," Allison said and instantly regretted it. Blanche was laughing so hard she could barely catch her breath, and Carol looked like she was going to fall out of her chair. Dorothy still had her hands over her mouth but the corners of a smile were protruding from behind them.

"So to speak," Allison added with a grin. "A good mocktail replicates the flavor of a cocktail so well that you barely notice the lack of alcohol."

"I can't say that I've ever had one," Dorothy said. "The mock, that is. The cock, I've—"

"Please don't," Carol said, swiftly cutting her off and hopefully ending the cock-talk. "Allison, do you think you could whip up some of these mocktails for the event?"

She was nodding before Carol finished her question. Having worked as a bartender for several years prior to opening Perk, Allison had mixology experience under her belt. And she'd been a damn good bartender, too. There was something thrilling about twisting all the right ingredients into one drink and seeing the pleasure the finished product provided the customer. Sure, she'd done that with coffee, but with alcohol—or without, since she'd made a few of those in her day too—it was just different.

Wait. Hang on.

The lightbulb didn't just go off in Allison's head, it lit up so forcefully that light blazed through her entire brain, all her synapses and neurons finally tuning in to what she should have known all along.

She wasn't here to open another damn coffee shop, the business a dime a dozen and one she'd perfected years ago. No, she was here to do something she'd never done before. Something that definitely wasn't already here in Clearwater Beach.

And as luck would have it, she already had the perfect place to do it.

All the chatter earlier in the day about her grandfather had summoned an uncharacteristic sense of nostalgia in Allison. She realized she hadn't talked to her mom in far too long and so, with the sun setting dramatically over the barely visible waves of the Gulf, Allison sat on the beach and called her.

"Is it really you?"

Allison laughed, instantly warmed by the sound of her mom's voice. "None other."

"And what did I do to get so lucky?"

"I don't know, had sex with some guy you married then divorced, then raised me on your own?"

Patricia Bradley laughed, a deep, resonant sound that rang of childhood memories. "You've got such a way with words, Al. How are you? Are you sitting on the beach right now?"

"You know it. And it's beautiful."

"I should come visit. Maybe after the holidays."

It must have been strange for a parent to say that instead of "let's get together over the holidays," but Allison had left home at eighteen and never come back. For the Bradleys, long-distance familial love was just the way it was, holidays included.

"You'd have to stay in a hotel," Allison warned. "My place only has room for me."

"Yeah, you sent me pictures. It's so small! I don't think I could do it. Do you still like it?"

"I do, yeah. It works for me." Allison stretched her legs out in front of her. "So, I have news. Or an update, I guess."

"You decided to keep the place."

She smiled. "I did. Mom, it's perfect. Really. And the location is incredible."

"I know, Al. I remember it."

That was news to Allison. "Hang on, what? When were you ever at the sandwich shop?"

"Oh, a long, long time ago. Dad flew me down when I was in high school, over Easter break. Guess he was going through one of those guilty periods." For all his philandering, Mack only had one child, Allison's mom. It was impressive given his relationship record. Both Allison and her grandmother suspected he'd gotten a vasectomy on one of his "business trips" before he officially left his wife. "He made me work the whole week," she said through her laughter. "But I didn't care because I got to be with him."

It was rare that Patricia shared happy memories of her childhood, and Allison clung to this one like a rescue raft. Too, it filled a tiny hole inside of her, a worry that accepting the incredible if not ludicrous gift of a building in Clearwater Beach was somehow hurtful to her mom, considering the gift came from *her* father who had acted about as much like a father as Allison's had.

"I've already started renovations," she said. "And I was dead set on a coffee shop. Like, Perk the Second."

"Of course you were. Are there any good coffee shops around there?"

Allison grinned. She and her mom didn't have much in common, but an appreciation for *good* coffee shops was at the top of their list. And in fact, just the previous day, Allison had found one tucked away on a side street, a little less than a mile from her rental. Knowing it existed helped push her away from what she knew and into something that she kinda knew but that would still be a new challenge for her.

"I found one," she said. "And it is really good. There's also the usual suspects."

"Dunkin' and Starbucks," Patricia monotoned. "Blech. So no Perk the Second?"

"Nope. I'm going in a completely different direction."

"A sandwich shop revival?"

"God, no. The mechanics of that are overwhelming."

"You're not much of a foodie anyway. Much more of a drinkie." She laughed at her own weird joke.

"You're right. I'm a drinkie. And that's why I'm opening a mocktail bar."

Patricia was quiet for a moment. Then, "A what?"

"A mocktail bar," Allison repeated. "They're really trendy right now. Well, mocktails are. I don't know of any bars that are completely alcohol-free, but why can't I be the first?"

"Interesting. You think that'll pull business?"

A daunting question Allison could not answer. "I don't know," she admitted. "But I keep meeting people"—Drew at the bar with her glass of water flashed in her mind—"who don't drink. It's a whole lifestyle thing."

"Not just for alcoholics anymore, huh?" A touchy subject, one they could just barely joke about, since one of Patricia's ex-boyfriends had a more powerful relationship with alcohol than he'd had with her.

"Nope. And there are all these zero-proof liquors out now." The more she talked about it, the more excited she felt—and the more secure. "So you really get the essence of the cocktail, but it's a sober experience."

"I don't know, Al. It feels a little risky, but I think this is the perfect opportunity for you to take a risk."

It was, and Allison felt more confident about this decision than she'd felt about anything in a long, long time.

"Now that you've got that all settled," Patricia went on, "tell me about your new social life. Meet anyone exciting?"

Again, Drew popped into her mind. Allison shook her out. Too complicated, or maybe not complicated enough. Too inexplicable. Or maybe too easy to explain. She sighed.

"I've met a few people," she settled on. "Emery and Burke are coming to visit soon, so that'll be good."

"You sound good, Al. Better than you have in a long time."

Allison nodded and smiled, digging her toes into the cooling sand. "I think so, too."

CHAPTER FIFTEEN

The faster Drew walked, the faster her sister walked. She was tempted to break into a jog but fought the urge, knowing Celeste would take the opportunity to sprint and then she'd win the unspoken race and Drew would be annoyed.

"I'm in heels," Celeste complained, throwing her elbow into Drew's ribs. There was more power behind the movement than Drew expected and she bounced into one of the many blow-up snow globes lining the sidewalk. Celeste snickered and tried to get ahead but failed, the bounce sending Drew further into the lead.

"So?"

"*So*, maybe you could slow down."

"Can't keep up?" Drew sped up for a few steps.

"God you're annoying. Why did I agree to come with you?"

Drew stopped, causing Celeste to teeter dangerously as she tried to stop in line with her older sister. Older by eleven months, that is. And every one counted.

"You didn't agree because I didn't ask," Drew said. "You invited yourself."

"Because for some reason I have to invite myself to come see *my* grandmother," Celeste huffed. "It's like you think you own her."

"It's hard being the favorite." Drew resumed walking, this time at a normal pace.

Celeste, ever unwilling to lose anything, sped past her, jogging in her heels like she wore them every day to run three miles. She flashed a smile and the middle finger as she reached the door first.

"You might be the favorite but I'll always be the fastest." Celeste graciously held the door open for Drew who mouthed a full sentence of uncouth words in her direction as she stepped into the Dunes.

Of all her siblings, Celeste was the only one Drew had a relationship with. And while that relationship was built upon a deep desire for each of them to outdo the other in any possible way, it was also bolstered with genuine love and care for each other. Celeste had won the whole "get married to an upstanding citizen and have four gorgeous, disturbingly talented children" thing, but Drew swore up and down she had never entered that competition to begin with. Fortunately, Pete was a good guy and Drew didn't hate being around him, so she was relieved Celeste hadn't thrown herself into a marriage just to win that lopsided game.

Celeste could have the standard, predictable wins of life. Drew was holding out for the ultimate win: Creating a more lasting and more heartfelt legacy with Southern Magnolia than Kingsley Properties could ever dream of achieving.

A lofty goal? Sure. But the impossibility of it only served to drive Drew harder and with stronger determination.

Meanwhile, Celeste continued working for Kingsley Properties in a role neither of them could define. Pete, as all the spouses did—Drew had a hunch that "you will work for the family business" was etched into all the prenups—also worked for Kingsley Properties. His role was quite definable: The Tile

Guy. His skills were so impressive that Drew had used him in her own home, but under the brother-in-law role and rule, not officially through the business.

"Lead the way," Celeste said as she adjusted her kelly-green shift dress.

"You don't even know where her place is." Drew stood with her hands on her hips, irritation rolling off her in choppy waves.

"It's been a while," Celeste admitted. "Come on, Drew. Don't be a prick about it, okay?"

Any other sibling would have received a tongue-lashing, but Celeste knew she was the favorite. *Drew's* favorite, that is. Not June's.

Drew led the way to the west wing, toward June's apartment. It still chafed her that her grandmother, simply because she relied on a cane to walk, was annexed to the west wing. But on the flip side, more help was available there if anything ever did happen and Drew wasn't there to—

To what? Save the damn day? She shook her head as they approached June's door.

"Put your hands over your ears," she directed Celeste.

"What? Why?"

"Just do it."

Celeste glared at her and did as requested, though purposely not holding her hands tightly enough to block out sound.

Drew ignored her insolence and rapped out her special knock. Moments later, the door swung open and their grandmother beamed at them.

"I knew it was you," June said, warming Drew's heart. "Oh! And you brought a special guest! How lucky am I."

Celeste looked between June and Drew, not missing the soft sarcasm in June's voice. "Okay, you two have been spending way too much time together. Hello to you too, Gram." She bent down and kissed June's cheek. "Isn't it so nice of Drew to allow me to come see you?"

"She's a gem, that Drew. Come in, come in."

The siblings followed their grandmother into her apartment, elbowing each other as they walked. They settled in the sunroom, which was really just a small alcove off the living area that held a comfortable loveseat and a sturdy armchair that June eased into.

"Oh, I should have offered you something to drink," June said.

Celeste practically leapt from the loveseat where Drew had been slowly stretching out to the point of nearly knocking her off anyway. "I'll get it!"

Drew didn't wait for her to be out of earshot before snarking at June. "She acts like she owns the place."

"Shut up, asshole!"

June shook her head, but she was smiling. "Let her feel important, Drew."

"I heard that!"

June dissolved into giggles and Drew laughed along. She loved little more than bonding with her grandmother by making fun of everyone else in their family.

"While she's gone," June whispered, "give me updates."

Drew quietly and quickly filled June in on how her business was doing. Obviously her family knew what she did, but it was a taboo subject since it often challenged, if not directly opposed, what Kingsley Properties prided itself on. As Drew rambled on about Allison's project, she noticed her grandmother's expression changing.

"What?" she asked, stopping in the middle of a bland dissertation on drywall. "Why do you have that face?"

"Oh, no reason!" But June was a terrible if dedicated liar, and everyone knew it.

"What's going on? What's Gram lying about now?" Celeste handed a glass of iced tea to June before sitting down so close to Drew she was practically on her lap.

"Get off of me, you skank." Drew shoved Celeste, who toppled over into the other side of the loveseat.

"Takes a skank to know a skank," Celeste said, blowing her sister a kiss. She adjusted her dress and took on an entirely professional appearance. "Now. Gram? Telling tales again, I hear?"

"No, no. I haven't told a single lie today."

Both Drew and Celeste laughed, knowing that was impossible. June, mockingly offended, pointed a crooked finger at Drew.

"Go ahead, Drew. Tell her."

"Tell her what? That you had a weird look on your face and tried to say it meant nothing but it always means something?"

Celeste nodded, her expression serious. "Always something."

"Drew knows what it means." June sipped her iced tea.

"What's she talking about?" Celeste said through a large smile that was built upon a foundation of gritted teeth.

Drew had a feeling she knew exactly what her nosy-ass grandmother was inferring with that look, but if she was wrong, she'd be mortified for saying what was on the tip of her tongue.

"Oh, she won't say it out loud," June said, winking at Drew. "But I will. Your sister has a *love interest*."

"Oh!" Celeste clapped. "Tell me everything!"

"She's lying," Drew said loudly. "The biggest lie of the day, I'd bet."

"Oh, I'm not lying. You two are the talk of the Dunes, you know."

Celeste spun to look at her sister. "You've brought her here?"

"No! God. Stop, both of you." Drew raked her hands through her hair, nerves rising and falling like a short-circuiting elevator. "It's not like that. At all. In any way imaginable."

"I don't know about that." June leaned toward Celeste. "The ladies are all abuzz about it."

"What ladies?" Drew exclaimed.

"Calm down," Celeste said, patting Drew's knee, which she tried but failed to yank out of reach due to the miniature measurements of the loveseat. Celeste dug her nails into the skin on either side of Drew's kneecap. "What are you going to do? Find them and cut out their gossiping tongues?"

"Someone should."

"She needs to embrace it," June said to Celeste. "Allison is a lovely woman. Her grandfather used to live here, you know. And they have the same exact eyes."

Those were two facts that Drew hadn't known before, and suddenly, Allison's connection to Carol and her being dragged into the Winter Wonderfest planning made a lot more sense. Sense Drew hadn't been previously seeking, if she was being honest. For some odd reason, she'd taken the whole thing in stride.

Which set quite the alarm bell suddenly blaring through her brain.

Drew Kingsley did not "take things in stride." This was… unprecedented. Concerning. Insane, even.

And fucking terrifying.

"I think it would be lovely for Drew to find love," June went on. "And I would be thrilled to see it."

"Wouldn't we all." Celeste held up her iced tea and June leaned in to clink their glasses together.

"Not me," Drew mumbled. She dug herself deeper into the corner of the loveseat, crossing her arms like the petulant child she often reverted to in Celeste's presence.

"You know I treasure the time we spend together, Drew." June gave her a look filled with adoration. "But you need to remember I won't be here forever."

"What, are you planning on moving?" Drew joked, but it fell flat on her tongue.

"No, I'm talking about death. I will die. Sooner rather than later at my age. Who knows when! Could be in five minutes."

"Jesus, Gram," Celeste muttered. "Talk about a buzzkill."

"It's just life, Celeste. We all come and go. It's quite lovely when you think about it."

Celeste looked at Drew, who merely shook her head. She'd heard this lecture before. Once June started, there was no stopping her.

Sure enough, despite Celeste's attempts to distract their grandmother with pictures of her kids (which June admired, then said, "They'll die someday, too," causing Celeste to gasp then shriek with laughter), June continued on with her death-talk. She'd grown quite fond of it recently, Drew noticed. She'd truly perfected some of the finer points.

When June reached the part about her hopeful heavenly rekindling of a highly erotic lifestyle with an old boyfriend, Drew stood up and walked into the kitchen. She had that part, unfortunately, memorized. But it was time for Celeste to be tortured by it, so it could haunt her dreams as well.

Drew scanned the countertops. Perfect. Her grandmother hadn't let her down, not that she ever had. Drew grabbed the pack of Oreos and waited until she was certain the BDSM discussion had ended. When she returned to the sunroom, however, she realized she was off by a few surprise seconds. She heard the word "restraints" and saw that June was glowing with excitement and Celeste looked a little too interested.

"How about a palate cleanser?" Drew announced, holding up the Oreos.

Celeste fanned herself. Her cheeks were flushed in a way that made Drew want to vomit. "Oreos. Great idea. Gimme."

"What happened to you?"

Celeste avoided eye contact with her sister, simply holding out a hand for a cookie, which Drew pushed back. "I think it's best we don't ever talk about it."

"You come back soon," June said to Celeste. "Without Drew."

"Hey!"

Celeste waved her off then resumed waving toward herself. The exposed skin of her chest was hot pink. "Let it be, big sister. Let it be."

So she did, because the alternative promised to be one of the most revolting things she would ever hear in her life. Drew rummaged through her messenger bag and held up a Santa beard.

"Oh! Are we playing dress-up?"

Drew shot a look of horror toward her grandmother. "Absolutely not. Put this on."

June did as instructed, though she shot a look at Celeste that Drew did not appreciate. "Now what? Are you taking my picture?"

"No," Drew said, opening the Oreos. She slapped Celeste's reextended hand away. "We're just going to have a little bit of fun. With a snack."

"Gram just told me about a lot of fun she had with her snack back in the day, and—"

"Celeste, I beg of you, shut the fuck up."

"Drew! Watch your mouth!"

She gaped at her grandmother, who was smiling. "Me? You're the one who—"

Celeste interrupted with a hearty cackle. "I can't believe I've been missing out on this for all these years. You don't get to hog Gram anymore, Drew."

"Whatever. She's free property."

June wiggled her eyebrows. "That sounds se—"

"Anyway!" Drew bellowed. The other two settled, though Celeste continued to giggle. "I'm going to put this cookie on your forehead. And you're going to somehow get it into your mouth—"

"That's what he said," June said deviously, the disgust of the phrase levied by the thick white beard shaking on her chin as she laughed.

Drew threw up her hands. "Are you quite finished?"

"Yeah, yeah, tell me what to do with the cookie."

Celeste snorted from behind them. "I think Drew's the one who can tell us what to do with a cookie."

Drew jammed an Oreo in her mouth for the sake of stuffing down every insult she had up and ready to go. She wouldn't let June see it. Nope. She'd fire them all off at Celeste the moment they stepped out of the Dunes.

"We're sorry, Drew." June glared at Celeste until she nodded and repeated the words. "Give me a cookie."

Drew waited, making sure she really was settled, then gently tilted June's head back and placed an Oreo on her forehead. She stepped back to watch.

"What kind of occupational therapy is this?" Celeste mumbled, snatching an Oreo before Drew could smack her hand away.

"The fun kind," Drew said.

They both watched silently as June wiggled and stretched her facial muscles. Sure enough, the Oreo slid down her face. When it slipped to the side, both grandkids gasped, but June rallied and turned her head so the Oreo was level once again. It was around that time that Celeste erupted into uncontrollable giggles, and Drew found herself fighting like hell not to be drawn into the never-ending bout of laughter. June was not laughing. No, she was focused and steadfast, working that Oreo down her face like she'd been doing it for years. Just when Drew was sure the cookie was going to fall to its floor-death, June maneuvered a quick twist of her face and just like that, she had an Oreo in her mouth.

Drew and Celeste clapped as June happily chewed her prize.

"That was impressive," Drew said. "What do you think? Is it a keeper?"

"A keeper for what?"

"Winter Wonderfest."

June leveled her granddaughter with a steely stare. "Drew Alondra Kingsley."

"Ooh," Celeste whispered. "The trifecta."

"What?" Drew said. "What did I do?"

"You've ruined a special surprise, that's what you did!" June pouted. "I'm not your guinea pig. You're supposed to be working with Allison on these things."

"Ooh, Allison," Celeste sang.

"Shut *up*." Drew turned to June. "We are. I know you like Oreos so I thought you'd want to help with this one."

June gave her a look that she'd been perfecting for all of Drew's life. She knew exactly what her grandmother was saying, and in response, she nodded. No more tests here at the Dunes. She would get in touch with Allison. Soon.

"Heard," was all Drew said.

"Good."

"So, Gram," Celeste began. "Quick question. What if this Allison person isn't as into Drew as the ladies think she is?"

"Drop it," Drew warned.

June's eyes sparkled. "I don't think that's something we have to worry about, dear."

"Okay, but it's *Drew*. She's, you know, so *Drew*."

"At least I'm not so fucking *Celeste*."

"Girls, you'll have plenty of time to be at each others' throats when you leave here. Give me just another moment of peace with you."

That shut them up. Drew couldn't resist kicking Celeste on the side of her calf, though.

"Allison is a very kind, warm person," June said, aiming her words at Drew. "I can tell she has a good heart."

"Okay, but we don't know if she likes Drew, right?"

"Like we can't know what your husband sees in you?" Drew fired off.

Celeste stuck out her ample chest. "Oh, I think we know."

"What can we ever truly know about the heart?" June sighed, ignoring their childish antics while curling her fingers around the arms of her chair. "What will be will be. And if Allison is too foolish to realize what's standing right in front of her, well, like I always say, let sinking ships—"

"Scrape the bottom of the ocean," Drew and Celeste finished in unison. They looked at each other and grinned, for once not caring who spoke louder.

CHAPTER SIXTEEN

"No," Drew said firmly. She was in her office at Southern Magnolia's headquarters, arguing over the phone with a contractor yet again. "I specifically said no subway tiles. That includes in the showers. Not. Happening."

She dropped her forehead against her palm as the contractor rattled on and on about pricing and the client's budget. Drew shook her head and stayed silent, letting him get his fight out of his system. The client had a budget that could stand to purchase something other than those godforsaken white subway tiles. Drew hated them so much she was considering putting a clause in her contracts that forbade her clients from requesting them.

"Drew," Kelly said, leaning into the office. "Your dad's here."

"Yeah, right."

Kelly pushed her glasses up her nose, the thick gold hoops in her ears bouncing with the movement. "Would I joke about that?"

"No," Drew said warily. She held the phone out from her ear.

"Oh, shit, you're actually on the phone?"

"I'm muted. It's the contractor assigned to the Harbor Bluffs project."

Kelly grimaced. "The one you didn't want to hire?"

"Yep."

"Okay, well, hurry up because your dad's here and he looks like he doesn't want to be sitting around waiting for your ass."

"Shocking," Drew mumbled. She unmuted herself and delivered her repetitive message to the contractor, whose name she couldn't remember: no subway tiles. Period. No more discussion, goodbye.

She hung up and stood up, surveying her office. It was casual but effective, exactly how she needed and liked it. But it was nothing fancy, nothing that would impress her father, who was the king of wanting to be impressed. Drew's shoulders sagged as she half-heartedly straightened a pile of invoices that needed to be filed.

Hopefully her dad was enjoying the comforting and inviting ambience of the main office area. Drew and Kelly had worked hard on that, meaning Kelly had told Drew what it needed to be and Drew, for once, had listened and executed as told. The end result was a gorgeous, open area. The walls were the palest of pinks, almost white, but with a tinted warmth that gathered and held all the natural light flooding in from the floor-to-ceiling windows at the front of the building. Kelly had chosen the art, all from local artists, including a stunning seascape oil painting Bartleby had given them for free. That was Drew's favorite, the old yellow-and-orange surfboard that had been pristinely restored and leaned against the wall near the door in second place behind it.

When Drew walked out into the main area, she hated herself for feeling an instant tightness in her stomach when she set eyes on her father. Dressed in a dark-gray suit, he looked entirely out of place in the chill environment. It should have made Drew smile. Instead, it made her feel incompetent.

"Dad," she said, purposely not using a question mark.

"Hello, Drew." Greg Kingsley stood and sent his daughter a charming smile. "How are you?"

"Busy. What brings you to this side of town?" The words shot out like bullets from an automatic pistol, and Drew heard June's voice in her head, a gentle suggestion that sounded like a demand, telling her to try harder with her family.

Too late. Drew crossed her arms over her chest and waited to hear what brilliant response her father had today.

"To see you," he said simply. "Got a few minutes for me?"

She was knocked off-kilter by his demeanor, but dared not show it outwardly. "Yeah. Sure. Come on back."

He followed her through the office, neither of them making any conversation. She held her office door open for him, leaving it ajar after he entered. He settled in one of the chairs across from Drew's desk, blatantly looking around her office.

"You've done a nice job with this place."

The comment landed, even if it was barbed with invisible daggers. Southern Magnolia's building was a former law office, one that was notorious for representing the less-than-savory citizens of the greater Clearwater area. To say she'd done a "nice job" was a massive understatement, and everyone in town knew it.

"Thanks. So. What's up?"

Greg smiled, but it didn't reach his eyes. Not for the first time, Drew wondered how exactly he had been born of her sweet, if mischievous, grandmother. She could never find any similarities between them. "I really did just stop by to say hello, Drew. Is that a crime?"

"No, but it's highly unusual."

He sighed, pressing his hands down his thighs, smoothing wrinkles that had never existed. "I know we have our differences, but I am your father." He looked at her and just for a flicker, she could see June in his eyes. It was disorienting. "Tell me how business is going."

Drew swallowed, a thorny mass suddenly bobbing in her throat. "You really want to know?"

"Do I want to know if my only child who chose to strike out on her own instead of being a part of a thriving family business is doing well?" He raised both eyebrows, feigning disbelief. "Yes, Drew. I want to know."

Fine. She would tell him. And she did, giving him a verbal bulleted list of the past few months of her working life. She avoided hard specifics, preferring to keep details like locations to herself. The last thing she wanted was for Kingsley Properties to storm into one of Southern Magnolia's recent jobs and convince the client that they didn't *really* want to maintain the original beauty of their home. It was illogical, probably, but it was a fear Drew couldn't shake.

"You've been busy," Greg commented when she trailed off. "I'm glad you're seeing success."

She bristled at that statement. There was a compliment in it, but it was soured by his tone and the carefully chosen phrasing.

"And what about Harbor Bluffs?"

Drew's head snapped up. "What about it?" she fired back, needing a moment to get her bearings. She certainly hadn't told him she'd landed that project. In fact, the only people who knew were Kelly and Cam, plus that dimwit contractor.

Greg crossed one leg over the other, the picture of nonchalance as his mere presence attacked each nerve linked to Drew's spine, one by one, slowly and efficiently. "I heard through the grapevine that you acquired their lucrative townhome project. I was surprised to hear that, but quite proud, Drew. So tell me, how's it going?"

She wanted to believe this inquisition was coming from a place of fatherly pride, she truly did, but the history between Drew and her father was complicated. Every time she'd put her trust in him, it had backfired on her. She decided to settle for the truth, but again, no specifics.

"I contracted out for that project."

Greg raised his eyebrows. "You did, did you? I'm surprised."

"Why? It's too big for my usual crew to take on. Besides it's—" Drew cut herself off. They both knew what it was—a massive, literally, departure from Drew's usual business. She stuck to houses and small businesses right there in Clearwater Beach, rarely venturing back over to the mainland. But when the offer for a twenty-townhouse development landed on her desk, begging for her design input, Drew couldn't say no. She loved the Harbor Bluffs project, loved that the owners wanted to revitalize the old Florida charm rather than throw up a pod of uninspired, monochromatic tombs. That was her whole thing, keeping old Florida design alive, and the thought of saying no just because it was an enormous undertaking wasn't something she'd considered. She wanted her imprint on that project.

"Anyway," Drew said, aiming to change the subject. "How's business?"

Greg tilted his head from side to side. "The usual. Can't complain."

She knew he'd leave her office and go check in at Kingsley Properties' sprawling hub over the bridge in downtown Clearwater before heading off for a round of golf. Of the many things that agitated Drew about her family's business, that sat at the top of the list. Not her dad's penchant for golf. Whatever, he was of that age, plus he lived in Florida and could golf year-round. No, it was the whole housing your business's headquarters outside of the area you claimed to primarily service. It sat wrong with Drew, who prided herself on keeping Southern Magnolia right in the center of Clearwater Beach...even if the building had a reputation that could never be erased.

"Well, I need to get going." He stood up and shook out each pant leg. "Oh, one more thing, Drew."

She clenched her teeth, preparing for battle. She'd heard that phrase at least once a week while growing up and it never, never preceded anything good.

"I hope you've put more thought into quitting your other *gig*." He stressed the word, the single syllable conveying his opinion so profoundly it felt like a third person had entered the room.

Not for the first time, Drew considered shutting down Magnolia and enlisting in firefighter academy. Knowing it would likely kick her off any part of the will she might still be clinging to was nearly impetus enough. But knowing her dad and his utter disdain for "service workers," as he called them, it was more likely that she'd be disowned.

"I haven't," Drew said lightly. "And I'm not going to. Bye, Dad. Thanks for stopping by."

Drew's home was her sanctuary, and every loving detail she'd put into restoring it showed that. The interior was a juxtaposition of clean lines and comfortable curves, muted colors brushing against bold but small statement pieces. And no clutter. Zero clutter. Not even a magazine or an errant candle sat out.

She hated open-concept homes (she'd heard too many tales of fire ripping through those giant spaces from her firefighter buddies), so there were enough walls up to both separate rooms and keep the flow moving. She'd spent two full years planning before she so much as knocked down a wall and the wait had been worth it. The end result was a cocoon welcoming her home at the end of each day.

Usually, the steady and warm environment of her home decompressed her quickly. Today was the exception. Drew was restless, irritated. She'd let her dad get under her skin enough to knock her off balance. But it wasn't just his voice rattling in her brain. It was June's, too. June telling her to give her family—her dad in particular—a chance. To try. To remember that her grandmother wouldn't be around forever, and when she went, the rest of the family was all Drew had.

Drew flopped down on her sofa, eyes aimed at the ceiling fan spinning lazily above her. She had Celeste, at least. And she got along with her other siblings, even if it was on a superficial level. And her mom. She adored her mom.

Her dad was the perennial thorn in her side. Drew imagined one day she'd either yank him out, or he'd be pushed out by her skin rejecting him.

She turned her head and looked at her phone, sitting innocently on the coffee table. June's voice wasn't only blabbering on about her family.

With a sigh that sounded more like a groan, Drew picked up her phone and opened her texts. Slowly, as though the effort itself may kill her, she typed out a text and hit send. Half of her hoped she wouldn't get a response. No, easily seven-eighths of her.

Not even fifteen seconds passed before a response buzzed in. This time, Drew did groan. She peered at the text with one eye. Shit.

She sat up, brushing her hair off her face. No, she didn't want to go to The Hideout. She wasn't in the mood for that crowd, and if she went in, all she'd want to do was play on the Megatouch. With another sigh, Drew looked around her living room. She was about to break one of her cardinal rules, and she waited for the drop of despair to settle in her chest.

It didn't come. Fine. It would in a little while. She shot off a response, then got up and pretended to clean up around the house. There was, as always, nothing to clean up. But the mindless action felt good anyway.

A thumbs-up response buzzed back on her phone and Drew again waited for the despair's arrival. Still nothing. She wrinkled her brow. Something was amiss.

When her doorbell rang, Drew nodded, welcoming the despair with open arms. She paused at the door, her hand on the knob. She felt fine. She blinked, patted herself down. Was she sick? Maybe.

Drew flung open the door to find Allison standing on her front porch. Now, *now*, the despair would come! With a fury! Drew smiled then dropped it, not wanting to mislead Allison. Yes, she was feeling something. Finally! Okay, there it was, creeping up, swirling through her belly, and—

Oh, fuck. Drew's eyes widened and she took a step back into her foyer. That was not despair. That was something she absolutely did not want to feel. Ever.

"Hey?" Allison said, sensing the internal crisis punching its way through Drew's nervous system. "You good?"

"Yeah." Drew coughed. "Great. Come in."

"I didn't realize you live, like, a block away from me." Allison stepped into the house and looked around. "Oh, whoa. This is…"

"Not what it looks like from the outside?" Drew finished, her panic replaced by satisfaction.

"Not at all. It looks"—she looked at Drew, apology in her expression—"kinda...dilapidated? Outside, I mean. Definitely not inside."

Drew puffed with pride. "Yeah, that's on purpose. The outside needs some work, but I haven't decided what I want to do yet. I like that it looks a little rundown. Makes this a nice surprise."

"You designed this," Allison stated as though she knew it was true.

Drew nodded. "And did most of the work."

She watched Allison take in the main living areas. Again, pride swelled. Drew so rarely had anyone in her home; seeing someone appreciate her hard work was far more satisfying than she'd imagined it would be. Maybe she should invite some siblings over. Like, two of them. Maybe.

"This is beautiful, Drew."

And just like that, it was too much. Drew held her hand inches from the small of Allison's back, allowing herself only one brief thought of what it might feel like if she went ahead and closed the distance, and gestured her toward the kitchen with her free hand. She'd set out supplies for the activity on her butcher block countertop. Using both hands to avoid any further temptations to touch, she grabbed the sleeve of plastic cups and moved them out onto the deck.

"Holy shit," Allison breathed as they stepped out into the cooling evening air. She looked at Drew. "Do you actually live here? Or did you rent this place to impress me?"

Drew balked at the implication, but, to her surprise, quickly realized she didn't hate the implication. But she didn't need to impress Allison. On any level.

"I live here," she said as she began stacking the cups in formation. "I've lived here for eight years. The house was a foreclosure and my—" She caught herself, though she didn't understand why she didn't want Allison to know who her family was. "I knew I could make it into the perfect house."

"Were you going to flip it?"

She glared at Allison, who smiled innocently. "No. I don't do that." She was tempted to go off on a rant about the flipping business, but that would out her DNA connection to the area's most well-known flippers, and again, she just didn't want to go there tonight.

"Drew," Allison said.

Drew looked up, half-expecting her to be staring out at the boat that bobbed gently in the bay. The boat that was snugly attached to Drew's dock. Bringing Allison into her home, showing her all these sides of herself, wasn't her best idea. She knew that. But it also didn't feel wrong.

But Allison was looking at the cups, lined up in perfect formation. "I thought we were going to practice a Winter Wonderfest activity."

"We are," Drew said, brandishing a packet of red, gold, and silver round bells. "This is Jingle Bell Toss."

"This is *beer pong*."

"No, it's *Jingle Bell Toss*," Drew said, holding up the bells. "Wait. I'm forgetting something."

She walked around to Allison's end of the table and pulled out the bucket of sand from beneath it. She carefully filled each cup with less than an inch of sand, then kicked the bucket out of the way. Before she returned to her end of the table, she dropped two bells into Allison's hand, doing everything in her power not to let her fingers graze the skin of her palm.

She hadn't forgotten the way Allison's arm had felt a few nights ago. Nor had she figured out why she'd impulsively touched her. Drew didn't touch. She was not a toucher. That moment, outside The Hideout, was so uncharacteristically her that she'd done everything she could to avoid figuring out why she wasn't freaking out about—

"I get it. The residents can't have alcohol." Allison nodded, rolling the bells in her hand. "And we're at the beach, hence the sand. And of course, the bells." She held one up and shook it, sending a tinny ringing over the table. "Well played, Drew. But it's still beer pong."

"Do you want beer?"

Allison looked surprised by the question. "Uh. No, I'm good."

Drew nodded. She hadn't gone out of her way to stop at Publix and grab a six-pack of a local IPA that she knew Allison had been drinking that one night at The Hideout, then stored it in her fridge where no other alcohol had ever hung out.

No. She definitely hadn't done that.

"Okay, so you know the rules."

Allison started laughing. "Yeah, but I just realized bells don't bounce. I'm going to have to adjust my form."

Drew gaped at her. "You're a *bouncer*?" She whispered the word like a sin.

"Should've pegged you for being an arc shot." Allison shook her head. "All right. Let's do this."

They played silently for a while, each determined to win. Drew liked Allison's competitiveness, and she liked that she wasn't an asshole about it. She was casual but determined. Two excellent qualities, especially when working together.

Drew shook her head, missing an easy shot. Fine. She could admit that she liked Allison as a human being. Absolutely nothing wrong with that. She just had to keep her wits about her and stop thinking she was attractive. Or, okay, she could think she was attractive. Also fine. But she absolutely could not give this woman the impression that she was capable of being anything more than a…

A what, Drew? Like, really. What? You already told her you don't have lesbian friends.

Drew shook off the self-admonishment. She had a game of Jingle Bell Toss to win. She could examine herself to death later, once this veritable stranger who felt like anything but was gone.

"That was close," Allison said a bit later. "I guess I'm more of an arc shot than I thought."

"You adapted," Drew said simply. She looked up at the sky. The clouds were scattered but the moon shone brightly, and stars poked out through every open space they could find.

"It must be nice, living on the water."

"I love it," Drew said, surprising herself with the sincerity in her voice. "It's peaceful."

"Did you grow up on the water?"

One earnest answer to Allison's casual attempts to get to know her was enough for one night. She shook her head (a partial lie) and began dumping the sand back into the bucket. "We could do one more before you go."

Allison moved right along with her and Drew was thankful she didn't pin her to the wall (metaphorically, of course) and took Drew's avoidance in stride. "Two in one night? I'm impressed."

"Yeah, well, I wanted to do things that don't involve heavy breathing."

Allison laughed as she watched Drew make two stacks of eighteen cups. "The residents will appreciate that. I think. Actually, I'm not sure anymore. They're wilder than I thought."

Drew flashed back to her grandmother's comment about the rumor at the Dunes, the one about her and Allison being romantically linked. "What makes you say that?"

"I spent some time with Dorothy and Blanche a few days ago."

Drew stopped her. "Say no more. That tells me everything I need to know." Those damn horny hags and their obsession with gossip—Drew knew immediately the saucy little rumor had come directly from their over-lipsticked mouths.

"So what's this one?"

Again, Allison took her in stride, not pressing or even questioning her comment. Drew accidentally awarded her a few points. Again, something to obsess over later.

"Oh Christmas Tree." Drew shot her a look. "And no, we're not giving it a secular name."

"Fine by me."

She talked Allison through the instructions and pulled out her phone, opening the timer app. "And it's timed," she added. "We each get a minute."

Allison pushed her hair behind her ears and assumed some kind of take-off position. Drew tried not to smile but failed.

"I assume you're going first?"

That got her a wicked grin in response. "I usually do," Allison said slyly.

Noted. Drew shook her head and pressed the timer. "Go."

Allison moved quickly and carefully. As the rules decreed, she kept one hand behind her back. The form of her pyramid was not as precise as Drew would ensure hers was, but overall, it wasn't bad, and she ably stacked all thirty-six cups right before the minute expired.

"Nice," Allison said, stepping back from the table. "I like this one."

"Good." Drew leaned over to start restacking the cups for her turn but miscalculated how close she was to the table and jammed her hip right into it. They both watched Allison's pyramid tumble to the deck floor.

It's not like the cups were treasured items, or even breakable. But the speed with which Allison and Drew both dropped to their knees to collect them would have implied otherwise.

And it was there, on their hands and knees on Drew's deck, that they found themselves precariously close to doing the very thing Drew had only moments ago thought might not be the worst thing she could do.

It was the air. It had to be the air. It was thin and hopeful, ribboned with the moonlight but easily broken through. The bay splashed gently, its quiet persistence cushioning the silence around them. It begged romance, that air, that moment.

Drew froze, her lips parted and far too close to Allison's. "Don't fall for me."

If Allison was thrown by the blurt, she didn't show it. Instead, she scoffed, "Why would I?"

Drew glared at her. "You have the look."

Allison sighed, and even Drew, steeled in her armor of self-protection, could recognize the truth of the sound, layered as it was with echoes of pent-up hurt and the delicate battle cry of unspoken fear.

"I should go," Allison mumbled, getting to her feet. But she didn't leave. She bent down and picked up a few cups.

"You don't have to." Drew shook her head. "The cups, I mean. Leave them."

"It's okay." She continued picking them up until the only ones remaining were scattered around Drew, who had yet to get up. "Should I see myself out?"

Drew stood, giving a silent answer as she led Allison back through the house. At the front door, Allison gave her a questioning look, then simply said, "See you around," and disappeared into the night.

Drew closed the door and pressed both hands against it, stepping back and pushing all her weight against it. Regret, an unfamiliar emotion, stung the inside of her mouth, causing her lips to feel swollen with a kiss she'd only allow herself to dream of.

CHAPTER SEVENTEEN

Allison broke into a jog the moment she caught sight of that familiar messy bun. There was no other like it, the way it sat like a damn cake decoration atop Emery's head. She would know, since she'd been following it around since they'd met during their freshman year at Oregon State University.

It was wild to think that they'd known each other for all this time, through wrong turns and dead ends, and now here they were, with their lives finally together.

Fine, okay. Emery had her life together. And Allison, as usual, was working on it. But this time—she felt it, she really did—this time, she was doing what she was meant to be doing. She finally felt like she fit into the world she was building.

And now she could share that with her best friend, the one who had stuck by her (and given her the harsh truth more times than was necessary to count) through all of the wrong turns and dead ends.

"It's you!" Emery dropped her carry-on and pulled Allison into a hug. "Hi, hi, hi. Oh my God, I'm so happy to see you."

"Me too, Em. Me too." Allison squeezed extra tight before turning to Emery's wife. "Oh, hey there, hot stuff."

Burke Calloway pulled Allison toward her, giving her a quick but warm hug. "She didn't stop talking about you the entire flight," she murmured close to Allison's ear.

"Yeah, well, someday you'll realize *I'm* the most important woman in her life."

"Come on, we both know we'll forever be in line behind her mom."

Allison rolled her eyes. "I only accept that because I love Emery's mom."

Emery looked between them. "Should I ask why you're talking about my mom?"

"Nope!" Allison picked up Emery's carry-on, pushing Burke's arm away when she tried to take it, and led them to baggage claim. "You guys hungry?"

"Starved." Emery grabbed Burke's hand, then dropped it. "Wait. Can I do that here?"

"We're in Florida, my love," Burke said softly, just loud enough for their party of three to hear. "Maybe wait till we're in the car."

"Fucking Florida," Emery grumbled. "I can't believe you're living here, Allison. Don't you feel like you have to hide?"

She mulled over the question while they waited for the bags. "Honestly, no. And you shouldn't either." She shrugged, thinking of sitting at The Hideout, then her conversations with the ladies at Sunset Dunes. "I think it's more of a government issue here than it is an everyday concern."

"So…you're staying?"

"I am." Allison gave Emery a toothy grin. "I'm happy here. I know, I'm as shocked as anyone else. But for right now, it…it feels right, Em."

"Good," Burke said, touching Allison lightly on the back. "I know she's been waiting a long time to hear you say something like that."

"Haven't we all," Allison muttered.

After a long lunch at a local brewery, Allison drove them to the beachfront hotel where Emery and Burke had booked a suite. She dropped them off so they could check in, shower, and change. Emery had started to complain about the "airplane ick" and both Allison and Burke knew it wouldn't stop until she showered and put on clean clothes. For someone who flew a lot for work, Emery was a surprisingly high maintenance traveler.

Allison left the hotel and headed to her building. Her business. Okay, she really had to name it, because she was tired of not knowing what to call it. Now that she'd settled on the premise, she was hoping the name would come to her in an equally blinding shot of inspiration, but so far, it was dead air in her brain. She had managed to find a good selection of zero-proof liquors, though, and had done a shopping trip specifically for ingredients. What better way to announce her future business to her friends than by showing them exactly what her place (okay, again, she needed a name, and *stat*) would offer?

When she pulled up, she barely paid attention to the trucks parked nearby. It was late afternoon on Friday. Whatever crew was working would be knocking off shortly. Allison walked a little faster, realizing she might be able to see some new walls up.

She was not prepared, however, for new walls *and* fresh paint. Allison gasped as she walked through the door, spinning slowly to take it all in. Nine days. Only nine days had passed since Drew's first demo crew had arrived, and every wall was repaired or replaced and covered with a base coat of white paint. Maybe it wasn't much, but to Allison, it was huge.

"Looks good, huh?"

She startled. She hadn't gotten June's comment about Drew not doing much active work on jobsites out of her head. But here she was. Again. Working on an active jobsite. *Allison's* jobsite.

"It looks amazing," she said, glad her voice was even. "I can't believe how quickly this is coming together."

"Look where you're standing."

Allison, not yet having turned around to see Drew, glanced at the floor. She gasped again, this time pressing her hand against her heart. Her floors were in. Those gorgeous luxury vinyl tiles that mimicked the look of real, dark hardwood. They shone in the late afternoon light flowing through the wall of windows. Allison could have squealed with delight.

"I can't believe this," she repeated, still staring at the floor. Then, confusion pricked at her and she turned, slowly, to look at Drew. A mistake, as Drew was leaning against the doorframe of the kitchen-turned-office (well, future office; as far as Allison knew, it was still a total shithole of despair). If Allison had been wowed by Drew's chill but authoritative volunteer firefighter outfit, she was damn near overwhelmed by Drew in ripped jeans, worn-in work boots, a plain white T-shirt with the sleeves rolled a few times to expose—oh, shit—arm muscles Allison had not previously registered, and…no. Really? Fuck, no.

A toolbelt.

A toolbelt, wrapped casually around Drew's narrow hips. Tools clinging to it like there was nowhere else they'd rather be (Allison could not blame those tools). Just enough stains on the toolbelt to suggest a life well lived, one filled with hard work, sweat, and success.

"You can pick your jaw up off the floor now."

"Fuck off," Allison fired back, doing as she was told.

Drew laughed, still leaning, still looking like the hottest fucking carpenter who had ever walked the lesbian earth. And her hair. Oh, come on. Her shaggy dark-brown hair was *sweaty*. It was messy, chunked in pieces over her eyes, other parts swept back over her ears. Unfair. This was all completely unfair.

"Never seen a woman in a toolbelt before?"

"I hate you."

She laughed again, finally standing upright in the doorframe. Unhelpfully, Drew crossed her arms over her chest, bringing Allison's eyes right to the spot(s) over her strong, flexed arms. Her black sports bra dotted through the sweat stains on Drew's shirt, and Allison, yes, she was going to pass out.

"I think that's the first lie you've told me."

Allison turned, giving her back to Drew, hoping she would enjoy the eyeful of shapely ass Allison had to offer. "Yeah, well. Remember it."

"I will." There was shuffling, and Allison steeled herself for the possibility of Drew coming closer. "So you like the floors?"

"They're perfect." She paused, listening to Drew move around behind her. "And maybe this is a stupid question, but should they be in already? I mean, there's more paint work to do."

"Yeah, I know. I'm not worried. These floors are extremely durable, and we'll be sure to cover them when we do the final color."

Allison nodded. Her body chilled then abruptly overheated as Drew came and stood next to her. She was too close. This was, suddenly, out of nowhere, too unpredictable, bordering on unsafe, or maybe just terrible. How that had happened, Allison had no idea—unless those damn old ladies at the Dunes had put a hex on them with their little comment about Drew being in love with her.

She wasn't. Allison knew that.

But the other night, with those stupid plastic cups on the ground between them... That moment *had* existed. Allison was sure of it.

Tentatively, with a gauzy film of protection wrapped around her, Allison angled her head to look at Drew.

She hadn't seen Drew for two days, or less than—whatever amount of time had passed between the moment she was certain Drew was going to kiss her and the moment of now, when Drew was looking at her like not kissing her had been the best and worst decision of her life.

Allison's breath caught and she couldn't help but to lower her eyes to Drew's lips. They were parted again, just as they had been two nights ago. When she pulled her glance back to Drew's eyes, a shot of electricity bolted through her. That was new. *That* hadn't been there two nights ago.

Neither of them moved until a banging from the back of the building spooked them, causing both to take abnormally large steps away from each other.

"Toilets," Drew mumbled before adjusting her tool belt and sauntering in the direction of the bathrooms.

"What the fuck is going on," Allison breathed in her absence, raising her fingers to her lips. She had (mostly) written the other night off under the romantic guise of the starry night. It would have been too easy to kiss then. And now, okay, now... Well, okay. The excitement of the progress! Yeah, that. Definitely a reason to almost kiss the owner of the company who was handling your business's renovations and had made it very clear she wasn't going to be friends with you.

Allison blew out a frustrated breath and headed back to her car for the grocery bags. She'd never almost-kissed someone and then felt a tangible blast of electric chemistry shoot between them. That was energy, pure and simple. Attraction, energy, yearning, desire. It was all there.

With fucking Drew.

On Allison's third and final trip from her car to the building, she realized one of the work trucks had left, leaving one behind. She sucked in a breath as she walked inside. Maybe Drew had left. That would be fitting.

But no, there she was, packing up tools. She looked up as Allison entered then dropped her eyes back to her task.

"Planning a party?"

Allison placed the last bag on the floor. "No. My best friend and her wife are here for a couple of days, so they're coming to see the space. I thought I'd give them a taste of what's to come."

Drew straightened and pressed Allison with a "and how are you going to do that?" expression.

"I decided what I'm doing with the space," she added, wanting to roll her eyes but keeping them steady, locked on Drew, taking in every nuance of her body language, which she'd realized tended to give more information than her face.

"And that is..."

"A mocktail bar."

Yup. Expressionless, just as Allison expected. But there was a shift in her posture, a melting of sorts. The tiniest drop of her hunched shoulders. "A mocktail bar," Drew repeated.

"That's what I said." More than ready to detach from the confusing and intense eye contact, Allison began setting up. She opened the folding table she'd borrowed from Carol, then set about unloading her grocery bags.

"I thought you…" Drew cut herself off. "Never mind. I'll get out of your way."

"You thought what?"

"Nothing. Now that you've made a decision, I'll let Cam know so you can select the furnishings with him." Drew looked around the space. "You'll need a bar."

"I know."

Drew shook her head, but she was smiling. "Of course you do. And I'm sure you already know where you want it set up."

"Yeah, I do."

"Good."

"Great."

"Goodbye."

"Drew—"

But she was gone, moving out the front door with a speed that definitely did not mimic her usual saunter. Allison kicked the leg of the table, regretting it when her glass bottles of zero-proof liquor wobbled angrily.

Drew's opinion did not matter. Not one bit. Allison nodded once, then cracked her knuckles. She would mocktail the shit out of this place and let Drew Kingsley see exactly what she was missing.

"I love it!" Emery exclaimed, holding up her glass. "I cannot believe there's no alcohol in here. It tastes just like tequila."

Allison leaned back on one of the blankets she'd thrown over the new floors. She hated to cover them, but since she didn't have any furniture yet, she, Emery, and Burke were forced to share mocktails on the floor. The least she could do was pad them with a couple of blankets—again, borrowed from Carol.

"Not one bit. But it tastes exactly like a paloma, right?"

"Totally." Emery took another sip. "Maybe one of the best palomas I've ever had." She turned to Burke, who was peering inside the cup, inspecting the drink like it was the most interesting thing she'd seen all week. "Did you know Allison was a bartender before Perk?"

Burke cocked an eyebrow but didn't take her eyes from her drink. "I didn't. College?"

Allison shook her head. "No. Well, wait. I did bartend for a while my senior year. But this was after college, when I moved back to Oregon." She and Emery exchanged a look. "The first and last time I moved across the country for what I thought was love."

"Hang on," Burke said. "You went to college in Oregon, then moved to where?"

"To New Jersey, just for a few years."

"Then she came to visit me in Portland," Emery said, "and my dumb ass introduced her to Sidney, and—"

"*My* dumb ass thought she was the love of my life, so I left Jersey and came back to Portland. And stayed."

"And got your heart broken," Emery said, a bit too joyfully.

"Repeatedly," Allison added. "And now, I'm back on the east coast."

"Where you belong." Emery grinned at her before turning to gaze at her wife. "Where we all belong, apparently."

"Anyway," Allison said, bringing them back to the subject at hand. "The first job I found when I moved to Portland was as a bartender in one of their infamous live music bars. I stayed there for a couple of months, then the owner offered me a job at one of his other bars, which was way more upscale. That's where I truly learned the art of mixology." She dropped the fake posh accent and continued, "I worked there for a couple of years, then met Neil."

"Her co-owner at Perk," Emery interjected.

"I was tired of the bar scene. The idea of a coffee shop sounded so peaceful and chill." She laughed. "And except for the morning rushes, it was."

"And now…" Emery prompted. "You're returning to your roots."

Allison studied her glass. She hadn't thought of it that way. But Emery was right, in a way. Mixology was something Allison had loved, and the sense of comfort that had come over her when she made her decision… She was definitely returning to something that felt right.

"Do you have a name yet?"

"No, and literally no ideas to speak of." Allison set her glass down and got to her feet, ready to make their second drink. "Feel free to brainstorm for me."

As she mixed up a batch of nonalcoholic Sultans of Sling, Allison wove in and out of conversation with Emery and Burke. When their talk turned to all things New York City, she floated off for a moment, entertaining the strange, unbidden thought of Drew sitting on the floor with them. Her stomach fluttered in response and Allison shoved that sensation far away.

If Drew wanted to kiss her, she would have. She'd had two perfect opportunities in the last forty-eight hours, and she'd taken neither of them. Message received, done and done.

Allison threw back her shoulders and walked back over to the blankets, pitcher in hand. "Ready to be dazzled?"

CHAPTER EIGHTEEN

Drew stepped out her front door, paused, looked around her ragged front lawn, and debated stepping right back inside. It wasn't the lawn that was a deterrent, though Allison's comments from her visit a few days ago had pushed "do something slightly better with the front landscaping" higher on her list. It was the keys in her hand and the task that sat ahead of her, beckoning with something too similar to…happiness.

The breath that shoved itself through Drew's lungs and out her mouth was one filled with trapped feelings that she knew no longer served a purpose. They'd done their work, cementing that spectacular and razor-blade-edged wall around her for years. Too many years, maybe, but Drew had stopped counting at some point, choosing instead to keep track of the one-night stands she'd accumulated (current count: three in five years— okay, fine, so she knew the years, too).

She looked at her keys. She could walk to the beach from her house in five minutes at a normal clip, seven or eight if she meandered, three-ish if she speed-walked. Which meant the reverse was true, too, and if she needed to sprint home, she very well could.

But the truck provided not only an escape, but also a silly armor. If she had to leave the beach at a moment's notice—say, if she got too close or looked at Allison's stupid pretty mouth again—the truck was her knight in shining armor and could move fast while walling her up from the dangerous air that was sure to follow her mad dash off the sand.

Drew leaned against her front door, well aware of how ridiculous she was being.

It was just that, after all those years and all those tired promises she'd made to herself, she didn't understand how in the world this random-ass woman from across the fucking country had shown up and made Drew want to kiss her.

And not, like, just one kiss. Or just one night's worth of kisses.

Decision made, Drew stalked over to her truck, got in, and drove (slowly) to the destination. Allison had given her explicit directions, which was absurd on so many levels, but Drew had taken the late-evening text in stride. Yes, she would meet Allison at the beach late morning on a Saturday to practice whatever godforsaken sand-infested Winter Wonderfest activity she had lined up for them. No, she would not ask questions, nor would she put up a fight. After all, it was all in the name of Winter Wonderfest, and if Drew did one thing right that holiday season, it was giving her grandmother the best Winter Wonderfest she had ever seen.

From what June said, the bar was pretty low, but that didn't deter Drew.

She parked near the intersection of Eldorado and Mango, as instructed. She sat in her truck for a moment, luxuriating in the silence that would dissipate as soon as she found Allison on the beach. The only sound that disrupted the quiet was Drew cracking her knuckles, a habit she'd long ago given up on trying to kick.

"Just go," she said aloud. She didn't want to be late, nor did she want to prolong the activity session. Drew's Saturdays were usually spent catching up on managerial work things that she put off during the week, visiting June, and working a few volunteer shifts at the firehouse. Sometimes she hung out at the firehouse even if she didn't have a shift. That had, at some point, become her only real method of socialization and she wasn't mad about it.

When Drew stepped off the sidewalk and onto the sand, she paused to kick off her shoes. Living in Florida and within walking distance of the beach was something she did not take for granted. Nothing calmed her like the feeling of sand between her toes and the low and slow waves glittering across the expanse of the Gulf.

She spotted Allison quickly, a feat considering the number of people hanging out under the sunny sky. The temperature wasn't budging from sixty-eight degrees, but the sun was showing off, not allowing a cloud to stand in its way. If Drew closed her eyes and kept her sweatshirt on, she could pretend it was balmy.

"I can't believe you're wearing a sweatshirt." Allison gawked in disbelief as Drew came up and stood in front of her.

"It's not hot," Drew pointed out.

"It's almost seventy degrees. That's practically hot."

She smiled and dropped her shoes next to the blanket Allison had spread out. "Says the northerner."

"The northerner turned Pacific Northwesterner turned Floridian," Allison corrected. But she grinned as she shrugged. "Okay, so I'm not used to not being bundled up in a parka and a beanie."

"No scarf?"

She shook her head, pausing to tuck blond strands behind her ears. "Too itchy. So," she said, looking at Drew with a bit of hesitation in her expression, "I may have recruited help for this test run."

Drew nodded immediately. She didn't need to know more than that—Allison's social life was her business—but if Holly Althouse walked up to them, Drew would indeed sprint to her truck and speed away, never to return.

"My friends—I mentioned them yesterday?"

Oh, right. That made more sense. Relieved, Drew nodded again.

"I was telling them what we're doing and they offered to help today." Allison looked skyward for a moment before lowering her gaze back to Drew. Her eyes matched the ocean, and it was impossible for Drew to look away even during that little reprieve. "The more the merrier, right?"

"Is that a Winter Wonderfest pun?"

"If you want it to be." Allison turned away, busying herself with organizing items on the blanket. "Gimme a sec and I'll get you a drink."

Drew almost turned her down, but their brief conversation from the previous night echoed in her mind. The mocktail bar. She'd thought Allison was kidding at first. And part of her wanted her to be kidding, because it seemed so far-fetched, so idealistically nonprofitable that Drew was—oh, Christ.

She was worried for Allison and her success.

Drew clenched her jaw, focusing her gaze on the ocean. She had half a mind to walk toward it and plunge in, if only to rid herself of this weird, unpredictable, and uninvited feelings-shit that had blasted itself into her mind and possibly other places she was not yet willing to visit. (Fine, she knew it wasn't just her mind, because her mind had the thoughts, and the thoughts knuckle-balled their way right down her throat, into her chest, and knocked at the steel trapdoor of her heart. But she was ignoring that, thank you very much.)

"Here."

Drew blinked and came back to the moment. Allison was holding out a red Solo cup.

"No alcohol," she added before kneeling in the sand to pour three more cups from a plastic pitcher that had almost definitely been borrowed from Carol's kitchen. The gentle reminder— the casual remembering of Drew's nondrinking habits—thrust into her as the most nonlethal rounded edges of a double-edged sword.

Surreptitiously, Drew sniffed the contents of the cup. Her nose picked up on tomato, and lots of it. She inspected the interior, tipping the cup back and forth to see what all was going on. It was a lot of ice and a pink-orange liquid.

"It usually has a sugared rim," Allison said, standing back up. "But—oh, they're here."

Good enough reason to wait to try the mysterious fluid. Drew looked up and saw two women just a few feet away. Their hands were interlocked and both wore serene smiles that looked like they were permanently, and happily, etched onto their mouths. The couple presented with a calmness that was both enviable and reassuring. Drew, to her surprise, felt instantly relaxed as they came to a stop in front of her and Allison.

Allison threw Drew a look, something that could have been a warning to be on good behavior—and how dare she know Drew so well—before making introductions. "Drew, this is Emery, my best friend since college. And Burke."

The woman with a pile of brown hair tucked into a messy bun atop her head inflated her serene smile into one that was much livelier. "Drew, as in Southern Magnolia Drew?"

"The one and only." Drew shook her hand. "Nice to meet you."

"You, too. This is my wife, Burke." Emery winked at Allison. "She likes to leave that part out."

"I don't *like* to," Allison rebuffed. "I just assume people know when they see the rings."

Drew had assumed, having indeed seen the rings. But she also appreciated Emery taking every opportunity (she imagined, anyway, given that quick introduction) to refer to Burke as her wife. Drew saw no possession in it, only love.

She nearly gagged on her own thoughts. "Nice to meet you as well," she said as she shook Burke's hand. "Do you live around here?"

"No, we're up in New York. Brooklyn at the moment," Burke said.

"We're also transplants from Oregon." Emery wrapped her arm around her wife's waist. Again, not possessive, Drew noted.

Just clearly full of love. She almost thought she could melt a little, being around these two.

"Here," Allison said, wiggling into the conversation. She shot Drew another indecipherable look. "A new drink."

Both Emery and Burke reacted the same way Drew had, going full detective mode with the strange and unnamed substance. "This looks interesting," Emery murmured.

"It's unlike anything you've ever had before." The confidence in Allison's voice was radiant and adorable. Drew angled her ear toward the water, wishing for pounding waves to drown out the (warm, inviting) sound. "You can think of it as an Italian Bloody Mary."

Drew caught Burke making a face that was the polar opposite of excited, but she switched back to that serene expression before Allison caught it.

"I know you don't like them," she said to Burke. "But try it. For me."

"We should cheers," Emery said, holding out her cup. Everyone followed suit, and the usually bright word was shrouded in uncertainty. Allison just rolled her eyes.

Drew's first sip was… Well, it was interesting. She definitely caught the Italian Bloody Mary comparison, and she didn't hate it. She took a bigger sip, swishing the liquid around her mouth in a terribly uncouth manner, but she caught Emery doing the same, and Emery nearly spit hers out with laughter but managed to keep it together.

"Okay, someone say something. I can handle criticism."

"It's unique!" Emery said, taking on the role of bubbly cheerleader. "You're right, it is absolutely unlike anything I've had before."

"Is there basil in here?" Burke asked, swishing the liquid around the cup.

"Yup! Well, basil sugar." Allison looked between Drew and her friends. "I'm getting the sense no one likes it."

"I think I do," Drew said. "Emphasis on *think*."

Allison rolled her eyes. "Okay. Fine. You can all *think* about it while we do this snowperson thing."

Emery started laughing. "Wait, wait. Is this like the antler game you made us do last night?"

The speed with which Drew's head whipped in Allison's direction would have been immeasurable by science. "You had them do the reindeer antler game?"

Allison's cheeks were flushed. "I may have."

"With the pantyhose?"

Emery laughed harder. "The pantyhose, yes. And she hated every moment of it."

Drew continued gawking at Allison as Burke went on. "She touched them. I couldn't believe it. She wouldn't say the word though. Emery, what did she keep calling them?"

Nearly doubled over, Emery managed to say, "The fabric leg traps."

"The balloons wouldn't go in," Allison said defiantly. "I kept having to let air out of them and then I had to—I had to—*touch* them," she finished in a tortured whisper.

"Oh, don't get your panties in a wad over it," Emery said, still laughing.

Drew turned to Allison and jerked her thumb toward Emery. "I like her."

"Yeah," Allison said, looking between them. "I was afraid of that."

Drew was doing her best to turn her gawk into a serious expression as she ignored Allison's little comment, but she knew she was failing expertly. "I'm proud of you for taking this step toward overcoming your fear," she said solemnly, but a laugh choked out at the end.

"Whatever. We did it, and we are *not* doing it at Wonderfest." Allison put her hands on her hips, a move that pulled Drew's attention to a feature she hadn't spent enough time observing. Allison was curvy in, yes, all the right ways. And those hips... Those hips. Drew tried to cover her slow swallow with a clearing of her throat but that backfired and she exploded into a coughing fit.

Burke hit Drew on the back a few times, a motion harder than a pat but softer than a whack. "You good?"

Drew nodded, clearing her throat again. She took a long sip of the mocktail and shivered as the acidity prickled her throat. "Never better." She was surprised to see her cup was nearly empty. Since Allison was busy explaining the activity to Emery, Drew subtly poured herself more. As she was replacing the pitcher in the cooler, she looked up and found Allison watching her. A soft, surprised smile lit up her face.

Drew flexed every muscle in her body to ward off the warm shiver that cascaded through her.

"So you and Drew are partners?"

Allison darted her eyes over to Emery. "What? No."

"We're—"

But Emery cut Drew off. "For the game. Activity. Snow thing." She gestured toward the blanket. "The thing we're doing now."

"Oh," Allison said, looking between Emery and Drew. "I figured you and I would partner up and Drew and Burke could work together."

"I think you and Drew should work together," Burke said, picking up a roll of toilet paper. Wait. Toilet paper? What the hell was Allison planning here? "Good for the team building and all."

"Yes." Emery nodded emphatically. "So true. You two have more work to do, and this will definitely help bring you closer."

Allison nodded, avoiding Drew's eyes. "Yeah. Okay. Drew, come here."

And she did. Happily, if forced to admit it, but she never would. She stood in front of Allison as Burke stood in front of Emery.

"What do I have to do?" Drew asked, looking down at the array of items on the blanket. She clocked a few, like a plaid scarf and a hat that looked like an old-timey detective would wear while driving an Alvis through London.

"Stand there and be cute," Emery said, smiling. "And Allison will make you even cuter."

It was possible Drew was blushing. Or maybe just hot from the idea of having a scarf wrapped around her neck when she was already accidentally overheating in her sweatshirt.

"The sun is hot," she muttered as Allison approached her with a roll of toilet paper. She narrowed her eyes. "What's happening?"

"You might want to take your sweatshirt off. For competitive purposes."

Drew obliged, catching the way Allison watched her every movement. "Now what?"

"Now," Allison said, poking at her phone. "I set a timer and we kick their asses. Go!" she shouted at Emery.

Drew stood stock still as Allison began circling her, winding—or rather, unwinding—the toilet paper around her body. She started at Drew's shoulders and got four rounds around before pausing.

"Were you a swimmer?"

"No."

"You have swimmer's shoulders," Allison said, resuming her toilet-papering. "Hold out your right arm."

"Is that a good thing?" Oh, if Drew could have cursed herself out loud for saying that, she would have. But, you know, making good impressions on the friends and all. Not that she had a reason to. But still.

"It's a…Yeah," Allison finished. She wasn't moving as fast as Drew had expected her to, given the whole competitive burst. "Your arms are heavy."

"Muscles," Drew retorted. "Comes with the territory."

Allison's response was a noise, not a word. She finished wrapping Drew's right arm and ripped the paper, tucking the end into Drew's new paper sleeve. She moved to the other side and began wrapping Drew's left arm.

"Is that arm heavy too?"

She laughed. "A little less heavy."

"Makes sense. Right-handed."

"Not ambidextrous?"

"No." Drew tried to catch Allison's eye but she was focused on the toilet paper. "Are you?"

"Maybe a little." Her words carried on a gentle sea breeze, and it was definitely the breeze that sent a wild, lingering chill through Drew's body. Not the words.

Left arm complete, Allison moved back to Drew's torso. She stepped back to assess the situation, then seemed to come to a conclusion. She began wrapping again but stopped circling Drew's body. Instead, she stood closer and as she wrapped, she kept her arms on either side of Drew, passing the roll from right to left as she wrapped her chest, stomach, and hips.

"You can breathe," she whispered as she completed another pass.

Drew, not having realized she'd stopped, took a staggered breath. Allison's closeness had kicked off an impassioned battle in long quieted areas of her body. She had to get out of the war with her wits safely contained within her, so she looked over to Emery and Burke. They were laughing through the wrapping, Burke giving little pointers that Emery refused to adhere to. Drew watched them as they worked, trying to focus on everything but the feeling of Allison carefully wrapping her entire body with toilet paper.

She was at Drew's legs now, wrapping her right one. Her fingers moved quickly around Drew's thigh, not lingering, and Drew allowed herself a quick exhale of relief. The left leg went even faster, and soon Allison popped up, her face millimeters from Drew's.

"That's…That's it for the wrapping," Allison said, her words landing directly on Drew's lips like miniature airplanes weighed down with yearning.

"Okay," Drew said simply. She watched as Allison dragged her gaze from her eyes to her mouth.

"Okay," Allison repeated. "Well. There's more."

"Of course there is."

Some of the light flickered out of Allison's oceanic eyes, and Drew could have kicked herself. She would have, probably, if she wasn't wrapped from shoulders to toes in toilet paper from

Costco. It was for the best, though. She swore it was. Allison did not want to get involved with Drew; she would figure that out soon enough.

A hat dropped onto Drew's head. The old-timey detective one, she hoped. A dark-green scarf was wound around her neck, perhaps a bit tighter than warranted, but she didn't make a sound. Allison lifted her arms to slide on oversized mittens.

"Snowmen don't have hands," Drew said.

"This one does."

"I know I'm from Florida, but I'm pretty sure they just have sticks for arms."

Allison folded her arms over her chest. "Why do you think I wrapped your arms?"

"To make them look like they're covered in snow?"

She tapped her foot against the sand. "I should have brought branches. Dammit."

"We're not taking branches into the Dunes."

"Why not? It's authentic."

Drew rolled her eyes as Allison taped big black circles down her chest. She ably avoided any near misses of…sensitive regions, and Drew avoided pointing that out. "Do you really want a bunch of elderly people wielding branches as arms?"

"Well, as you've pointed out," Allison said, stepping back to take in her creation, "snowpeople don't have arms, so they wouldn't be covered in snow, therefore the wrapping of the arms is pointless."

"But fun," Emery piped in.

Allison and Drew looked over at Burke. "Jesus," Drew said. "She made you a snowperson who escaped from the psych ward."

Sure enough, Emery had wrapped Burke from head to toe, pinning her arms to her sides and her legs together in a TP straightjacket.

"What?" Emery said, setting a top hat on Burke's head. "I took some creative liberties."

"I'm not enjoying this," Burke said. "There's a round two, right? So I can give back what my lovely wife has so thoughtfully gifted me?"

"Maybe. Open up," Allison said to Drew. When she did, Allison slid a pipe into her mouth. "Perfect."

"I can still talk," Drew said around the pipe. Damn, she missed her arms.

Allison snorted. "Because you talk so much without a pipe in your mouth?"

"I use my words sparingly but meaningfully."

"So I've noticed." Allison stood in front of Drew, eyeing her. Her serious gaze roved up and down Drew's papery body.

The look traveled to pliable, unprotected parts of Drew's body and she closed her eyes, trying to ward off the intrusion. She wanted to run, or at least walk away, but she was bound by toilet paper and her mouth, free, took advantage of the moment.

"Is there something you're waiting for me to say?"

The words surprised them both, Drew stumbling to take a step backward, and Allison's head snapping up to see the finely wound toilet paper gracelessly ripping right off of Drew's left leg.

"We won!" Emery exclaimed, holding up a hand to high-five Burke, who glared at her. "Oops. Sorry, babe."

Drew leaned over and carefully pulled the ripped toilet paper from her leg. When she straightened, hands full of flimsy paper, she offered the wreckage to Allison. "Sorry," she said, meaning it.

"It's fine."

But her tone, her body language, the very air between them said otherwise.

CHAPTER NINETEEN

The sound of drills from the former kitchen was familiar and comforting, lulling Drew's cranky brain into the shade of peace as she lounged on the scaffolding and gazed up at the ceiling. Her predilection for construction sounds was probably born from some early childhood memory that she could no longer grasp. Her grandfather, as in June's husband, had owned a local construction company and Drew had hazy memories of tagging along to jobsites. It had been June's wish that Drew's dad would take over the company, and he had...only to turn it into Kingsley Properties, the reigning royalty of all things renovations and real estate in southwestern Florida.

Drew had no desire to usurp her family's company. She saw no benefit to it; she had her success, and her family had theirs. In the twelve years that Drew had owned and operated Southern Magnolia, she'd watched her business flourish right along with Kingsley Properties. It was possible she took business from Jacqueline Smith and her cute/obnoxious little operation, but Drew wasn't worried about that.

Despite all the irritation her family provided by simply existing (no one's fault, just life as the near middle child in a family overrun with kids and grandkids), she wanted their business to remain profitable. After all, she couldn't support her fourteen and counting nieces and nephews if Kingsley Properties was run into the ground. She doubted that would happen, though, since Afton was the head of finances, and he was Mensa-level when it came to numbers and money.

Drew's phone buzzed in her pocket with the triple-vibration that was assigned to all members of her family. She considered ignoring the text, but curiosity got the best of her, as it usually did when it came to the Kingsleys.

As soon as she saw it was a new sibling group text, she slid the notification option to "hide alerts." Before she put her phone back, she checked to make sure it wasn't anything important. As usual, it wasn't. Just Celeste and Mae discussing possible Christmas presents for their mom. Drew squinted. Natasha, their oldest sister, wasn't on the thread. Weird. She might be curious enough to side-text Celeste later for the drama, because Drew was certain there was some.

"Whoa."

Drew rolled her head to the side and saw Allison, who had just walked through the front door, which was currently a gaping hole since the dumbass installers hadn't brought the correct hardware. "Don't worry. It'll be on within an hour."

"Not that," Allison said. "You. Up high."

She grinned, a little excited at the prospect of fucking with Allison, who appeared to have some sensitivity toward heights. "I nearly fell asleep up here. Could have rolled right off."

Allison winced. "Could you not? I'd prefer not to have a ghost haunting my brand-new business."

"Yeah, fine. It's too early in the game for that." Drew sat up, swinging her legs over the scaffolding, which was just a couple of two-by-fours propped up on a bright-yellow rolling platform. She continued grinning as some of the color drained from Allison's face. "Can you hear the boards creaking?" She knocked on one. "They feel kinda bouncy today."

"No," Allison said, taking a step back. "I'm sure they're perfectly steady."

"I don't know. They could snap at any moment."

"You could get down?" Oh, so she could ask questions. And there was no denying the cute factor in that specific question.

Drew shook her head, then pointed to the beams a few feet from her head. "Can't. Got some staining to do. Boss's orders and all."

"You're the boss."

Drew scoffed. "The boss of the property. You."

Allison shook her head. "Actually, I think the beams are fine. They're good. No stain necessary."

Drew angled her head, causing a dangerous lean in her posture. She held in a laugh when Allison gasped. "I think they'll look great with a refresh. It won't take me long. Besides, I already sanded them and now they need to be stained." She reached for the can, which was naturally just out of reach. With a sigh, Drew hopped onto all fours in a swift movement she had maybe four years left to use before her body decided it wasn't up for that anymore. This time the boards did creak and bounce with just enough oomph to make the can of stain jump.

"Drew!"

She laughed as she righted herself and the paint can. "I'm fine. I do this all the time."

"I can't watch this shit," Allison mumbled before walking back out of the building.

"You'll be back," Drew said to the empty room. She popped open the can and got to work.

Allison stayed away longer than Drew expected. By the time she returned, the beams were stained and the new front door was installed. Having packed the scaffolding back into her truck, Drew was milling about the space, taking measurements Cam had requested.

"Nice to see you on the ground again," Allison said. She looked up at the beams warily, then broke into a smile. The elation on her face was enough to trip wires in Drew's nervous system, forcing her to turn her back. "Okay. That was worth the mild heart attack."

"Thought you'd like them." Drew bit the inside of her cheek and told herself not to turn around. "How'd it go with Cam?"

"Good. Wait. How'd you know that's where I went?"

Drew did turn around then, feeling less vulnerable now that she'd swatted away that moderately flirty comment with work talk. "He texted me when you left."

"Oh." One side of Allison's mouth curved up. Drew appreciated the look; there was something about Allison's personality, a natural collision of mischief and sincerity, that was pulling her in like a moth to the flame. The only reason she wasn't sprinting full speed from it was because the serious imp in her recognized the impish sincerity in Allison.

"So you guys are, what? Tracking me now? Or was Cam warning you that I was coming back so you better get your ass off that scaffolding?"

She didn't want to smile because, son of a bitch, Drew could not keep almost-flirting with and almost-kissing this woman. Yes, she was well aware that she'd nearly kissed Allison twice now. Twice. The Drew of twenty, even ten, years ago, wouldn't have missed that opportunity twice. But this Drew, the Drew that carried a poignant weight of distrust and bitterness, didn't see them as missed opportunities. She saw them as moments of weakness that had been triumphed by her strength and resolve to never, ever let someone close to her heart again.

The problem was that Allison wasn't doing anything to get close to her heart. She was simply existing. Being herself. Holding up a damn mirror of what could be as she continued moving forward at a pace Drew could match if she chose to.

She lagged behind, a step or ten depending on the day. But she stayed on the same course, never veering from it, hence the big, bold feeling stretching between her ribs, getting stretchier yet stronger each time she came face-to-face with Allison.

"He sent me measurements," Drew said. She tried to look away from Allison, who was wearing baggy light-tan cargo pants and an army-green T-shirt with a pocket right over—well, the spot where shirt pockets went. Precisely where Drew needed to stop aiming her eyes. "And now that you're here, we can talk about where you want the bar."

"I already know." Allison walked a few steps closer. She reached out, put her hands on Drew's shoulders, and spun her around. "Right there. Can you picture it?"

Drew stayed still, every nonthinking part of her yearning to stay in that moment for as long as possible. Allison's hands were warm on her shoulders, her touch comforting and suggestive all at once. Her body wasn't quite pressed against Drew's back, but the closeness was intimated, enough to wake up the sleepier parts of Drew. And her voice, just a whisper from Drew's ear. She inhaled, a mix of lemon and something earthy filling her nose.

"Yup," she said quietly.

"It won't be big."

"I saw the measurements."

Allison laughed, the air from it tickling Drew's neck. She hadn't taken her hands off her shoulders yet. "Right, I forgot. Do you think it's a good size?"

"I do." Drew stepped away, needing space to get a damn grip. "And you'll have the back bar, too."

"Yes. It'll work." Allison spun around, taking in her space. "It's going to be small, but I like that. It's more intimate. Plus there's not a crazy huge market out there for a mocktail bar, so I'm sure I won't be bursting at the seams with customers."

"You never know." Drew nodded at the last of her crew as they left. They were making great progress in the old kitchen, but Allison needed to figure out what she was doing with it, and soon. "Have you thought more about that extra space?"

"Not really."

"Could you?"

Allison nodded. Her excitement seemed to flush out of her, leaving a quiet, contemplative woman behind.

"I thought you'd be more excited about the progress," Drew said, doing her best not to sound confrontational. She tended to be too pushy when people were like this, or so her sisters had repeatedly told her.

"I am." Allison looked around then laughed. "There's nowhere to sit."

It was the simplest and truest thing Drew had heard all day. They only had the floor. Not even a paint can to perch on or a toolbox to drop onto.

"Outside," Drew said, gesturing to the old chairs and single, weather-beaten table. "If you want."

"Yeah. Okay."

Drew followed Allison outside and waited till she sat, taking the seat across from her. They were quiet for a moment and Drew fumbled for a way to get back to the conversation she'd thought they were at the brink of.

"I am excited," Allison said, and Drew nodded, relieved. "Really. But it's a little overwhelming, knowing that I'm going to be running my own business way sooner than I anticipated."

"We could slow down."

"No, don't do that." Allison leaned back and crossed one leg over the other. "It's weird, you know? I'm in this position where I don't have to rush to open. I can take my time and make sure everything is exactly how I want it before I ever take in a single customer."

"That's a nice benefit."

"It is." She eyed Drew. "You do realize that every time we talk like this, I'm the only one really talking?"

"Well, you talk a lot."

Allison rolled her eyes. "And you don't talk enough."

Dangerous territory, but Allison didn't know that. Drew rolled some sentences around in her mouth before choosing, "I talk sometimes."

"You could talk more. To me."

"Like Holly?"

"Well, that was a leap." Allison folded her hands in her lap. "Do we need to clear the air on her?"

There was an implication there, one Drew saw, admired, and filed away. "Sure."

Allison gestured toward Drew. "You first."

"You dated her."

"That's not news," Allison said. There was no emotion in her voice, no indication that Holly had meant anything to her. "Yeah, I did. I had just moved here and I was...I was lonely. I guess." She took a deep breath and blew it out slowly. "For most of my time in Portland, I had a relationship that never became what I thought it would eventually become. I dated kind of obsessively when that ended, then I hit a long stretch of being single. It was a good thing. But then I moved here and I knew absolutely no one, and being single felt like a massive strike against me." She shook her head, looking away from Drew. "I know that sounds stupid."

"It doesn't."

Allison went on as though she hadn't heard. "I met Holly the literal second day I was here. It wasn't fate or anything like that. It was loneliness, pure and simple. And she seemed easy." She grimaced and looked back at Drew then. "I don't mean it that way. I thought her personality was easy."

"When did you realize you were wrong?"

She laughed and Drew smiled at the sound. "Pretty quickly. But I kept dating her. Again, loneliness. Emery—" Allison paused and Drew nodded, understanding the best friend reference. "Emery used to tell me that I operate from lonely. I make decisions based on how lonely I am, or because I think doing something—"

"Or someone," Drew couldn't help but interject.

"Gross, but okay, maybe this time, yes." Allison shuddered and Drew was thankful for it. "Anyway. Sometimes I think something or someone is going to cure the loneliness."

"It's not that easy." She did her best to keep her tone light, but this conversation was spinning into something much deeper than Drew had expected.

"Not at all. And since ending things with Holly, which only lasted, like, a month for the record, I've realized that it's okay to be lonely. Because it's not, like, the focus of my personality." Allison bit her bottom lip. "I was not prepared to have a therapy session this afternoon, Drew. But honestly, moving here at my age, and knowing no one...It's been a bigger challenge than I thought it would be. Uprooting your life as a single adult is freeing and lonely. Not always in a bad way, though."

"My grandmother always tells me there's a big difference between being lonely and being alone."

Allison studied her, eyes bright in the late afternoon sun. "I like that. I should change my wording then, huh? I'm alone, not lonely."

"Well, I don't know. You're probably lonely and alone."

"You're such an asshole."

Drew laughed. "I know."

"But I keep coming back for more."

The air between them stilled, laden with the unwritten letters of gentle, unexpected love. The envelopes were thick and unsealed, spilling out phrases of what could be, invisible ink scrawled over torn pages.

Drew had absolutely no idea what to say or do, so she froze in her incredibly uncomfortable chair, waiting for Allison to take the lead.

"Did you date her?"

Not quite the lead Drew had expected, but she wasn't surprised this was finally coming up. The whiplash from one blooming topic back to one that should rot off and die was a bit much, however.

"Holly? No. Never."

"Really? Then why does she make it seem like you did?"

"You're basing that off of one interaction," Drew said patiently.

"Uh, yeah, one interaction where she stomped into *my* building because she saw *your* truck outside and completely changed her entire persona the moment you walked out of her line of vision." Allison looked very proud of herself. "So I'll ask again. Did you date her?"

"Never."

"You're sure?"

"Could not be surer."

"Then—"

"Okay. Stop. You want the truth?"

"Obviously, yes." Now Allison looked vaguely alarmed. Good. Served her right for pushing this ridiculous topic.

"Fine." Drew leaned forward, resting her elbows on her knees. "I've known Holly since we were old enough to hit the bars, which is nineteen down here. She has always had a reputation." She held up a hand. "I'm not lumping you in with that, so don't get all weird about it. I'm just stating the facts." Hand dropped, intentionally casual posture resumed. "Holly has been hitting on me since the moment she found out my last name, which, if you're looking for specifics, was when I was twenty-four. Understand that prior to knowing my last name, she never hit on me. Ever. I'm not her type." A pointed look at Allison, who smiled as though it was a compliment, which, fine, maybe it was. "The thing is, she made it absolutely clear from the first time she invited me back to her place that she was not looking for casual with me."

"You don't strike me as the casual type, anyway."

"I'm not." A bit of a lie, considering those three one-night stands, but she had her reasons for that, and it would never happen again. "I don't do casual. Dating, sex, friendships. Nothing about me is casual."

"Okay. I'm trying to stay with you here. She didn't want casual and you don't do casual, so…Match made in heaven?"

Allison's naivety was very cute. Truly. "Did you miss the part about my last name?"

"No. I mean, I forgot, I guess. But I don't get why that's important here."

"Kingsley," Drew said slowly.

"I know," Allison said, just as slowly.

Huh. Maybe she hadn't put it together. "Remember when I asked you what other companies were coming in to do estimates?"

"Sort of." She shrugged. "My memory's kind of shit, honestly."

"Clearly. Allow me to remind you. You had Jacqueline Smith come in."

"Oh, yeah, I remember her. That neon-green van was wild." Allison perked up. "Oh! You two knew each other. I remember now." She wrinkled her nose. "Are you related to her?"

"No, thank God. Fierce competitors."

"Oh," Allison said, nodding. "You slept with her."

"I did not!" But Allison was laughing, clearly pleased with her ability to get under Drew's skin. "Never did, never will. But that's beside the point. The last company, Allison. You really don't remember?"

She held up both hands in surrender. "I truly do not."

Drew sighed, annoyed that she had to spell it out. "It was Kingsley Properties."

"Was it?" Allison tilted her head to the side. "Yeah, that sounds familiar."

Drew waited for her to make the connection, but the neurons were obviously not firing with any urgency in the brain across the table. "Does it sound familiar because I just reminded you that it's also my last name?"

The neurons flickered and fully took a snack break before finally relaying understanding. "Wait. Is Kingsley Properties your family?"

"Yes. My entire family."

"Huh. And you have your own company?"

Drew gritted her teeth. She'd have to get into this at some point, but she just didn't feel like it right then. "Correct. Clearly."

Allison swirled her finger in a circle. "And this comes back to Holly, how exactly?"

At this point, Drew felt the only thing to do was be as blunt as possible. "Holly told me she wanted to marry me—"

"Well damn, that's bold."

"Stop interrupting and let me finish this stupid story," Drew grumbled.

"I've only interrupted once," Allison said. "Maybe if you talked faster—"

"She wanted to marry me because she wanted to marry into the Kingsley family," Drew blurted. "It had absolutely nothing to do with me. I don't think she even likes me as a person. She just wanted to get in with my family."

Allison stared at her. Then, finally, "I'm sorry, did she tell you this on your first date? Because that's super bold."

"Allison, stay with me." Drew leaned closer, a difficult feat considering the table between them. "We never even went on a date. This was a singular conversation one night when we ran into each other at a bar in Tampa. It was one conversation that became her fucking rallying cry every time she saw me after that, and I would swear on my life she put a tracker on my truck because she was everywhere. Still is." The image of Holly waltzing into Allison's building still chafed at Drew. "We never went on a date. Why the fuck would I go out with someone who literally told me she only wanted to be with me so she could work for my family?"

Allison was quiet again, taking it in. Drew watched the emotions flicker over her face and dropped her shoulders in relief when disgust blared bright and bold over Allison's features.

"That's horrific," she said, her voice tense. "I'm really sorry she did that to you."

Struck by words no one had ever said before, Drew felt concrete crumble around her heart. Her entire family thought the Holly thing was alternately funny or an exaggeration. June gave her some sympathy but usually told Drew to take it as a compliment. She'd confided in no one else until this moment. And for Allison, not quite a friend but no longer a stranger, to give Drew empathy and an apology she did not have to give... It was more than she knew what to do with.

She stood up and brushed imaginary dirt off her work jeans, which were...always dirty. "I should go."

Allison, ever the go with Drew's annoying and abrupt flow persona, also stood. "Yeah, of course. I've kept you long enough. You probably have work things to do."

"Yeah," Drew said noncommittally as they walked inside. "And you probably want to spend some time here, to get a feel for what kind of furniture you want."

"Right." Allison's voice was warm, and Drew was half-tempted to slide right into it, knowing she'd land softly. "I should do that."

Drew paused at the door—the new door, a double black steel French door that was going to integrate seamlessly with what Cam had shared about Allison's design intentions—and waited for Allison to say something, anything, to make her stay.

But silence fell around them, the unsealed envelopes releasing half-written letters, only for them to sweep over the floor, untouched and unread.

CHAPTER TWENTY

"Well, I have to say, this sounds risqué." Blanche patted her curls, which looked exactly the same as when Allison last saw her. She idly wondered about the amount of hairspray used in the Dunes' on-site salon. "And I do like risqué."

"We know," Dorothy deadpanned. "I can just imagine the group you'll commandeer to be on your team for this activity. Won't be a lady in sight!"

"Now I can't do that. People will talk!" Blanche leaned back in her chair. "I'll invite a mousy gal or two to balance it out."

"You do realize that there's no actual physical contact in the activity," Allison said patiently. She'd been going over the rules for Candy Cane Hook 'Em for the last ten minutes, and each time she thought she had the women on track, they detoured into something that was barely connected to the activity. It was a marvel. Or maybe mild dementia.

"That's your version, sweetheart. We like to bend the rules around here." Blanche wiggled her dark-red eyebrows (painted on, and well, Allison had to admit) at Dorothy, who giggled like a schoolgirl.

"Okay but the candy canes—"

"We heard you," Dorothy said, patting Allison's arm. Her fingertips were calloused from decades at the sewing machine. She'd shown Allison some of her designs and they were impressive. Dorothy was surprisingly modest about her success, so much so that Allison had to get it out of Carol that she'd been a costume designer for Broadway. She even had an award tucked away somewhere in her apartment. Allison, a secret lover of musicals, was determined to find it and use it as leverage to get Dorothy to spill all her glorious Broadway stories. "We're old ladies. We need to find fun wherever we can."

"Don't let them steamroll you, girlfriend." Carol sat down at the table with them, shooting glares at Dorothy and Blanche. "This is your event. They don't get to make the rules."

"Nonsense! It's *our* livelihood!" Blanche pouted and Allison grinned, seeing the reflection of a young woman who was endlessly spoiled by her traveling businessman father and only had to throw on the pout to get her way.

"I promise the game will be fun," Carol said. "Which one are they pestering you about?"

"Candy Cane Hookers!" Dorothy said delightedly. "Oh, it's going to be so much fun. We get to wear little fancy outfits and everything!"

"That is not at all what I said." Allison shook her head. "Hook 'Em. Not hookers."

"Oh, I don't know. I think you should change the name." Blanche picked up a wrapped candy cane and twirled it around like she was conducting a grand orchestra. Or leading a parade. Yeah, that was more likely. "Hookers draw quite the crowd around here."

The three other women at the table gasped. Blanche merely laughed, still twirling the candy cane. Allison was dying to ask questions but smart enough to realize she didn't truly want to hear any answers.

Before she could slip and ask one anyway, she was saved by people entering the atrium; the old biddies swiveled their heads to size up the new company. Allison took the opportunity to begin cleaning up the candy canes, and as she did, she noticed that Dorothy had used them to create a crude, if childish, outline of a penis. She swept those away immediately.

"Well look who's here," Blanche said. She had the courtesy to drop her voice so it didn't echo around the room. "Someone must have sensed your presence, Miss Allison."

"She could have made more of an effort with that outfit," Dorothy grumbled.

Allison looked down at her jeans and long-sleeved shirt. She thought she looked fine. Besides, who would she be—

"Not you," Dorothy hissed, smacking Allison's arm with more force than was necessary. "Your paramour."

"My *what*?" Allison turned to see what—oh. Right. She should have known.

Drew had come into the atrium with June and…two people who kind of resembled Drew? But not really? Whatever the case, Drew looked perfectly fine. Or maybe it was accurate to say that she looked like she almost always looked. It seemed that Drew wore work clothes even when she wasn't working, which was endearing. It made Allison feel like Drew was always at the ready for any renovation type snafu that she might encounter while she was out and about, enjoying her day.

However, it was midday on Tuesday. So, in all likelihood, Drew was working. Which made her worn-in jeans with a couple of rips that were the product of actual wear and tear and the faded black T-shirt splattered with paint all the more reasonable.

And all the more attractive.

Allison turned before she could make eye contact with Drew. She didn't need to give Dorothy and Blanche any more fuel for their little gossip campfire. By the looks on their faces, though, they were ready to douse that precious, dainty fire with gasoline.

"I love new love," Blanche breathed, fanning herself despite the pleasantly cool temperature of the room.

"There's no love to speak of," Allison said. "You're imagining things."

"Oh, let us have our excitement! Besides, we've been around much longer than you have, pretty girl. We know things."

"Yes," Blanche said, nodding and still fanning herself. "We *know* things."

"You two know as much about love as a doorknob knows about being turned." Carol paused, rethinking her statement. "Now hang on, that's not—"

"Why, I think she just inferred that we're *loose ladies*," Blanche said haughtily.

Dorothy waved a hand in Blanche's direction. "Don't go pretending you're offended by that. We all know the truth about you."

"I, for one, don't need to know the sordid details of your previous love lives," Allison said, standing up. "As always, it's been a delight. But I need to get going."

"Sit down," Dorothy said through clenched teeth and a vibrant smile. Her lipstick was perfectly applied but it was a shade of red no one over twenty-five should ever wear, and the overall effect was frightening enough for Allison to drop right back into her chair. "Your paramour is approaching."

"Ladies," Drew said as she came to a stop next to Allison. "What's with all this?" She pointed to the candy canes, which had made it into a pile but not back into the bag.

"It's nothing," Allison said quickly, opening her tote bag and swiping the candy canes in. "Just running an idea by them."

"She has such wonderful ideas. Always dazzling us with her creativity, this lovely girl." Blanche had stopped fanning herself, thankfully. She patted her curls again. "Won't you sit down with us?"

"She's here with her family," Carol said. "What brought your siblings in?"

Drew shoved her hands into her pockets, angling herself so her back was to her grandmother and the man and woman she'd come in with. "Guilt, most likely." She looked like she wanted to say more but held back, flicking her eyes at Allison and giving her a small nod.

Not small enough, as Dorothy pounced on the gesture like a dog in heat. "Allison was just telling us how much she loves working with you. I do wonder if you'll keep seeing each other after Winter Wonderfest."

Allison died a bit in her chair, but Drew swept in with the easy, and rational, rescue. "We will. Until her renovations are done, at least."

At least. The words had no right to slip into a nook of Allison's brain and root themselves there, swaying in the breezes of maybe and could be.

She was maybe getting a little tired of could be. Drew was... Well, she was a challenge. But something kept telling Allison that she was worth it. She didn't even know what that meant, not yet, but the fact that she wanted to find out was enough reason to keep slowly chipping away at the fortress of self-protection Drew had surrounded herself with.

"Oh, Blanche, we better hustle." Dorothy stood up, a slow process and one she refused help with. "We have a shuffleboard double date in ten minutes."

"That's right! I almost forgot." Blanche, on the other hand, sprung from her chair like a spry but aged gymnast. "We mustn't keep the boys waiting."

"Lovely to see you, Drew. Just think, the next time you see us, we'll be so dolled up, you might not recognize us!"

"One can always spot a maneater," Blanche said blithely.

"Blanche!" Carol exclaimed.

"It's fine, Carol. She's just jealous. As usual."

"I am bursting with excitement to see what you two have come up with for Winter Wonderfest." Blanche squeezed Drew's upper arm. "Just think! We only have to wait four more days!"

Panic seized Allison's throat. How had that happened? Everything was moving so quickly in her life, moments and events blasting past with careless speed, hurtling toward unavoidable endings.

"Oh! One thing," Dorothy said. "Blanche and I thought it might be a grand idea to invite some of the gentlemen from Serenity Springs."

"Absolutely not," Carol said. "That is not happening. Certainly not this late in the game."

"Oh, come now. There's something about large parties. They're so intimate. At small parties there isn't any privacy," Blanche said dreamily.

"All right, F. Scott Fitzgerald, run off and play your shuffleboard."

"You are simply no fun," Blanche huffed. "Come on, Dorothy. Let's go show those boys what we're made of."

With air-kisses, the two women hobbled off to their shuffleboard date. Drew, however, hovered next to the table.

"Sit down already," Carol said, pushing out an empty chair. "You're making me nervous, standing there."

Drew sat down next to Allison and a sigh escaped as she did. Allison looked closer, seeing dark circles under her eyes that hadn't been there when she'd seen her less than twenty-four hours ago. So many mysteries surrounded this woman who had wormed her way into Allison's daily thoughts and daydreams. She was tired of wondering. She was ready for answers.

"Is that your brother and sister?" she asked.

Drew nodded. "Yeah. The two oldest."

"I don't think I've ever seen Derek here," Carol remarked.

"June's not feeling well."

"Ah." Carol nodded. "The guilt. Got it."

"How many siblings do you have?" Allison saw the opening and took it. She was determined to know more about Drew. All her obsessing was driving her crazy, and she knew it was because she lacked knowledge. The more she knew, the better she could arrange her growing attraction. Or smash it with a sledgehammer.

"Drew's one of six," Carol said. "She's right there in the third spot in the lineup."

"So kind of a middle child."

"Close enough," Drew said, glancing over at June. Just as quickly, she darted an annoyed look at Allison. "Don't try to analyze me. I don't have middle child syndrome."

Allison held up both hands. "Wouldn't dream of it. Just trying to learn more about you."

"Why?" The word shot out like a tired but angry bullet, knowing it had to do its job but not fully dedicated to doing a good one.

"Because that's what people do," Allison said slowly. "They get to know each other."

The dramatic flair Drew employed to roll her eyes would have impressed even the most critical of Broadway casting agents. "Not this again."

"Stop it," Carol snapped, whacking Drew's shoulder with the Winter Wonderfest binder, which, frankly, had to hurt. "I've had enough of you trying to be Ms. Not So Nice Guy. It's old, Drew. Knock it off."

To Allison's surprise, Drew stopped rolling her eyes, and when she looked at Allison, some of that protective grit had washed away.

"Fine. What do you want to know?"

"Everything," Allison said, the word leaping off her teetering internal balance beam and landing with arms stretched toward the ceiling.

Carol swept in, saving the moment and Allison from disintegrating on the spot. "Start with the family stuff, Drew. She deserves to know." She stood up and gave Allison a small smile. "I'll go check in with June."

Neither Drew nor Allison made a move or a sound as Carol walked away. They remained silent as Carol suggested that June show Derek and whoever the sister was the exciting shuffleboard court. Not a word escaped as Drew's family left with Carol, no one but June, with a wave, acknowledging their departure.

Alone and tucked into the cocoon of silence, Drew finally spoke. "My family is a lot. There's a lot of us and—" She sighed, pressing her hands into her thighs. "Remember what we were talking about yesterday?"

Every word, yes, but Allison merely nodded.

"The part about being lonely or being alone." Drew's dark-brown eyes, ringed with flecks of gold, shone as she looked at

Allison. "I was never alone. When you have two brothers and three sisters and a mom who's kind of a helicopter but also really involved with the family business, there's always someone watching you. But I was always, always lonely."

"But you had June," Allison said, the pieces of Drew's puzzle beginning to click together.

"Exactly." Her eyes shone brighter at the mention of June. "I always had my grandmother. So now you know why I'm here all the time."

"She's where you feel most at home."

Drew opened her mouth then shut it before mumbling, "Yeah. I never thought of it that way. But yeah. That's it."

"So then the whole family business thing…" Allison wanted to stay on the emotional tracks with Drew but she was wary to do so, assuming the train could derail if it hit the slightest dent in the steel.

"Is complicated." Drew pushed her hands through her dark hair, some strands falling back against her forehead. "Or maybe it's not. Maybe I make it more complicated than it is."

"I doubt that."

Drew just looked at her, her eyes communicating her suspicion.

Allison shrugged. "I don't know you, Drew. You make it pretty hard to allow for that to happen. But"—she pushed her fingertips against the side of Drew's leg, warding off her sure to come protests—"one thing I do know is that you leave no room for complication in your life."

"You're not wrong about that."

"Kinda makes you wonder what else I'm not wrong about, doesn't it?"

"Nope." Drew smiled, though, softening the word. "As for the businesses, let's just say my family and I don't see eye to eye."

"But you run the same kind of business?"

"No. Well, yes. Technically." Drew glanced at her watch. Then, having made a decision, she looked directly at Allison. "What are you doing today?"

"I'll probably go into the bar—"

"Oh, we're calling it a *bar* now, are we?"

She shot Drew a look filled with irritation. "Isn't that better than saying 'the building' all the time? Call it what it is, right?"

"What it *will* be," Drew corrected. "And no, you're not going into *the bar*."

"I'm sorry, are you banning me from my own property?"

"Today, yes." Drew stood, motioning for Allison to do the same. "My guys are working on that side room today and it's going to be too loud for you to do any creative thinking."

"I'll have walls?"

"Yes, you'll have walls. And a floor, hopefully." Drew snapped her fingers. "And completed bathrooms."

"And running water?"

"Tomorrow."

Allison smiled, warmth spreading through her. She prided herself on being an independent woman who got shit done, but damn if there wasn't something reassuringly magical about letting someone else—a very sexy and competent someone else—take the lead on things.

"Since you can't go into *the bar*—"

"Stop doing that."

"Never." Drew grinned and Allison's entire body shot to alert. A very pleasant, tempting alert. "So you're not busy, right?"

"Presumptuous, but correct."

"Good. Come with me."

"And where exactly are we going?" But she was already following Drew through the halls. It didn't matter the destination; Allison was on board, having thrust her ticket at the conductor without hesitation.

"I want to show you the difference between me and my family." Drew held the front door open for her, then headed toward her truck. "You said you want to know everything, right?"

"I did."

"Well, we gotta start somewhere."

CHAPTER TWENTY-ONE

This was not how Drew had thought her Tuesday would go. She'd gotten a call from her mom early that morning, casually mentioning that June had called her dad at six a.m. and hadn't been making much sense. Greg Kingsley, naturally, batted the responsibility off to his wife, who volleyed it to Drew. Somewhere in the middle, however, the two oldest Kingsley children had been drawn into the drama, hence their unusual appearance at Sunset Dunes.

Drew could generally handle Natasha, but Derek was a mini version of their father and therefore not exactly palatable. He was a control freak, too, and had stormed into the Dunes with some wild agenda to get June evaluated for a laundry list of potential medical concerns. Natasha was his clueless sidekick, there to look good and attempt to keep Derek level-headed. When they'd shown up, Drew had already assessed the situation. June was fine. Maybe a little more confused than normal, but she was ninety-six and bound to have foggy moments.

Still, Drew had agreed to have her meet with her doctor as soon as possible. It's not that she didn't care about June's health; on the flip side, she cared a whole damn lot and maybe preferred to live in denial that anything could be wrong and therefore tried to not get any diagnoses that could remind her that June was not immortal.

It had been a relief, then, to walk into the atrium with her family and see Allison. Drew wasn't sure what to call the feeling that came over her in that moment, but she knew it was a good one. That was enough. For now.

And when faced with opening up to Allison—something she'd been entertaining for a couple weeks but couldn't find the right internal knob to turn—she'd jumped on the opportunity to get out of the Dunes and reset. It would be easier to show Allison what she meant when it came to her family.

As Drew drove down Mandalay Avenue, leaving the Dunes and their respective neighborhoods behind, she stole little looks over at Allison, who looked perfectly at home in Drew's less than glamorous truck. She'd been meaning to buy a separate truck for all things nonwork, but considering her life was pretty much all work, it didn't seem necessary. Now, though… She looked at Allison again, taking in the curves of her face and the three tiny silver hoops lining her ear. Her blond hair was pulled back into a ponytail, but her hair wasn't long enough to all reach the hair tie, so some strands brushed against her face.

Maybe it was time to buy a truck befitting someone who had a social life.

They'd been riding in comfortable silence for several blocks when Drew cleared her throat. "Have you explored much of the area since you've been here?"

"Not really," Allison said, still looking out the half-open window. "I've driven around and I went to a really good Mexican place in North Redington Beach."

"Burrito Social?"

"Yes. So good. You've been there?"

Drew laughed. "Yeah. I thought I was the only person who'd drive that far just for a good plate of tacos."

"Listen," Allison said, turning to Drew. "One thing you need to know about me is that I take food very seriously, and I will absolutely drive that far for one meal."

Three points to Allison. Not that Drew was keeping track of that. Was she? That hadn't been part of her plan, which wasn't a plan at all, more like a to-do list where items kept getting scratched out and renamed in a new column. Over and over again, no sense to it.

Much like feelings, which Drew plainly avoided, and—

"But I haven't explored much of Clearwater Beach, which I guess sounds weird."

Another point in the pro column: Allison's ability to interrupt Drew's thoughts just when they started to go places she wasn't ready to explore.

"It's not weird," Drew said, turning left onto Bayside Drive. "You've been busy."

"Something like that," Allison murmured. "Definitely haven't been down this street."

"Welcome to the very spot of the battle between Kingsley Properties and Southern Magnolia."

"I don't see any body parts strewn about."

"You sound disappointed."

"Well," Allison said, "you used the word 'battle,' which made me think I'd get to see some swords and blood."

"Think of it more as a real estate battle."

She contorted her face and still managed to look cute. "That sounds kind of boring, Drew. No offense."

"Does it help to know that many a heart has been stabbed right through on these very streets?"

"Well, yeah, but why clean up the blood?"

Drew shook her head as she pulled into a driveway at the tip of the peninsula. "Real estate, Allison. Who's gonna buy a home that's splattered in blood from an ancient family grudge?"

"Ooh, okay, this is starting to sound like *Romeo and Juliet*. Who are you? Mercutio?"

"No." Drew put the truck in park and hopped out. "Let's go," she called back to Allison.

"Wait, I take that back. You're definitely more Tybalt." Allison jogged to catch up.

"Are you serious? Tybalt?" Drew paused at the front door and glared at Allison, who wore a pretty smirk that Drew had half a mind to kiss right off her lips. "He was a total asshole. No control over his temper. Never thought before he acted. I am the polar opposite of Tybalt."

"Those are valid points. I'll take them into consideration as I reassign your role."

"This is my life, not a Shakespearean drama," Drew said. She keyed in the code and opened the front door. "Get in here before you whip out a dagger and scare the neighbors."

But Allison stood firmly on the front steps. "Are we breaking and entering? I'm not really in a place to get arrested, Drew. Starting a new business and all that. It wouldn't look good."

"Get in here." Drew grabbed Allison's arm and pulled her in, shutting the door behind them.

"Tragedy, by the way." Allison folded her arms over her chest. "Not a drama."

"Are you done?"

"Quite, Benvolio."

She didn't dignify that with a response. (And honestly, if she had to be a character in *Romeo and Juliet*, Benvolio wasn't a bad choice. While Drew didn't necessarily see herself as the peacemaker—June would make a great Benvolio; no, hang on, she'd have to be Mercutio, what with her racy past—she could see how technically she was the least dramatic of the family. That had to count for something.)

"Welcome to Hibiscus Hideaway." Drew didn't move, giving Allison the opportunity to look around before she started the grand tour.

"Again, you're sure we're not breaking and entering? This is…stunning. Someone very rich lives here, right?"

"No one lives here."

"Then how—"

"I own it," Drew said, as simply as she would say she preferred ketchup over mustard on her burgers.

Allison gawked at her and quickly reined it in, though surprise still illuminated her features. "You own this? Wait, sorry, I don't mean that to sound—shit, okay. I know your business is profitable; I mean, I've seen your house." She squinted. "Hang on. Was that even your house? Is *this* your house?"

"That's my house that I live in," Drew said as she led them through the foyer. "And this is the house that I bought so that my family's company couldn't abuse its worth. Let me show you around."

And so she did, guiding Allison through the spacious downstairs. It was decadent in its style, furnishings Drew never would have chosen but she could admit Kingsley Properties had done an impeccable job with renovations. Drew preferred a clean but laid-back style. This house was anything but laid-back. There was way too much stainless steel for one kitchen, and the dreaded subway tile danced across the backsplash. The main living room held furniture that looked terribly uncomfortable, including a chaise lounge that Drew knew cost ten thousand dollars. Absurd, really, even if it was the only comfortable piece of furniture in the room.

She led Allison upstairs and they poked through the bedrooms, three of them, each with an en suite that was nearly half the size of the bedrooms. The primary bedroom had a closet that made Allison swoon.

Back downstairs, Drew pointed out the office, family room, and dining room. The office was the only room that felt livable to Drew, and as they left that space, she made some mental notes of improvements she could make to her office at Southern Magnolia headquarters.

"And back here," Drew said, gesturing to the wall of glass doors in the family room, "is the deck that caused my dad and my brother to actually go to battle."

"Yeah? Any blood stains?"

"No, but somewhere along the railing is a nail that sticks out. It's a little fuck you from Van."

"Van? Like the thing soccer moms drive?"

Drew snorted. "Yeah, and also my younger brother who specializes in building decks and docks."

"Show me?"

Drew swallowed. Two little words had no business creating a tidal wave of arousal in her body. And the question mark, the punctuation Allison so infrequently used, coasted over the wave, creating an aftershock of need.

She opened the doors in response, following Allison onto the deck. It took Drew just a minute to find the offending nail, and Allison laughed heartily.

"That could hurt," she remarked, gliding her hand over it.

"Yeah, but it's too classic Kingsley bullshit to fix."

Allison leaned against the railing, her elbows resting atop as she looked out over Clearwater Bay. "The view is lovely. The whole house is, really." She angled her face toward Drew, meeting her eyes. "Tell me the story."

That period jumped right onto the wave next to the question mark. They rode it all the way in, causing ripples through Drew's body.

She was fucked. Utterly fucked.

Only one way to avoid the fuckage, and that was: talking about her family. "My dad bought this house after it was damaged in a storm. Seems noble, but I knew his intentions. And he proved me right like he always does. They repaired and renovated it, decorated it to the extreme, as you noticed." Allison nodded. "And then I expected them to sell it. They did put it on the market but the asking price was insane. So it sat for a while."

"And you bought it?"

Drew shook her head. "Well, yeah. I did. But first they took it off the market and listed it as a rental." She gestured to the houses on either side of them. "You see how close those properties are. Could you imagine paying millions of dollars for a gorgeous home right on the water, only to have every damn night disrupted by a cluster of ignorant partiers ruining this home?"

"That's a very narrow perspective of people who rent homes," Allison said. "As a reminder, I'm currently a renter."

"I know. Sorry. But that's not the main point of why I bought it."

"Care to share that point?"

"I was getting there," Drew said. "My point is, greed. My sister showed me the numbers for renting this place. It made me sick. So I had her convince them to give it another go on the market with a lower price point. My dad agreed and I bought it."

"And they know you're the buyer?"

Drew looked down, a smile curving her mouth upward. "No. We worked around that. Don't ask how."

Allison shifted so she was leaning against the railing, facing Drew, who immediately looked out at the water. "I won't. But I will ask what your intentions are. I mean, you're not living here and you're not renting it. What's your plan?"

"I'm going to hang on to it until the market flips. Then I'll sell it at a criminally low price, ultimately lose money in the process, and rest easy knowing that someone who can afford it for what it's worth finally has it."

"Okay, Robin Hood."

Drew shrugged. "If the tights fit."

"Until then…no one can have it?"

"Right. But more importantly, it can't be used as a rental and continue to feed my family's greed." She took a steadying breath. "Kingsley Properties does it all: buying, selling, renovating, tearing down, flipping, renting, selling out. It's why they've worked themselves into a multimillion-dollar status." Drew paused, waiting for the usual response when she revealed this detail. Allison simply gestured for her to continue. Another point for her. Usually that was the moment that people admonished Drew for striking out on her own instead of absorbing her family's money. Or, you know, informed them they would like to marry Drew simply to join the Kingsley legacy.

"Look, every company wants to be successful. I do not fault my family for that," she continued.

"But you fault them for how they do it."

Drew didn't know if she was that obvious (scratch that—she *knew* she was not an obvious person) or if Allison was that intuitive. Or maybe she just paid attention. Or excelled at reading between the lines.

"Yeah." Drew pressed her palms against the railing and looked out over the water. "They have worked very hard to destroy some of Clearwater Beach's history. Mostly homes, but some commercial properties, too. I don't care much about that part. There are a lot of commercial properties that need a boost around here. It's the homes that bother me. There's such rich history here and the old homes are beautiful. They need work, but they don't need to be torn down."

Allison was nodding. "Like your house. Your other house, I mean."

"Exactly. My dad would have razed the land and built a monstrosity in its place."

"Like your neighbor's house."

"You noticed?"

"Of course I noticed." Allison peered at Drew in disbelief. "No offense, but the outside of your house looks like a swamp child next to its beauty pageant big sister."

"I'm going to fix it," Drew said. "But keep its charm."

"So let me get this straight. You won't work for your family's business because you don't agree with their renovation philosophy."

Drew shrugged, tilting her head from side to side. "That's a simplified version of a much longer vendetta, but yeah. Essentially."

"And you created your business to counter the damage that Kingsley Properties inflicts."

"Pretty much. Yes."

"And I'm guessing that causes some strife within your family."

Nail: head: hammered. "Yep."

Allison brushed against Drew as she turned to face the water. The touch was short enough to seem casual but its reverberation within Drew was anything but. "You'll tell me more when you're ready."

It was that very confidence that continued to shock Drew. At first glance, Allison did not present herself as someone who held the wealth of confidence she continued to demonstrate. It was a mystery Drew found she didn't want to solve. She wanted to appreciate it, repeatedly. As often as possible.

"I like your philosophy," Allison continued. "And I hope that what I'm creating in the building that was so graciously left to me by my philandering grandfather is something you'll be proud of." She stopped abruptly. "Or like. Just like. Appreciate, I guess. Not hate."

The sound of the bay lapping against the docks was soothing but Drew was beginning to feel incapable of being soothed.

Every time they spoke, Allison threw her a curveball that Drew could not hit. She could only catch it and hold it to her chest, her fingers tight and reluctant to let go. She didn't know how Allison did it, and did it so well with so little information about Drew. This person was nothing like anyone Drew had ever known. She wasn't even sure Allison was real. She couldn't be.

Drew poked Allison's arm.

"What are you doing?"

"Making sure you're real."

Allison gave her that half-smile Drew had grown to adore. "I promise I'm real, Drew."

But Drew wasn't sure, and the only way to be sure was to wrap one hand around Allison's hip, gently pulling her closer as her other hand cupped her chin. She held her there, suspended in the moment they'd neared twice before. Allison's eyes, luminous and alert, held steady on Drew's.

"I just need to make sure," Drew said softly before dipping her chin and hovering the most infinitesimal distance from Allison's mouth.

"Please do," came her response, and it was just what Drew needed to reassure herself it was okay to finally close the distance.

Allison's lips were soft, commanding, and a seamless match for Drew's. The kiss itself was hotter than it had any right to be, a fully stoked fire born of a slow burn spanning weeks that felt like years. Drew pulled Allison's lower lip between her teeth, sinking into the groan that echoed from her throat.

"I like your mouth," she whispered.

Allison's response was to deepen the kiss. When her tongue brushed against Drew's lips, she shuddered, dropping her hand from Allison's chin to her hip. She held Allison's body tightly against her own, doing everything in her weakened power to keep her hands from roaming.

But she could not stop kissing Allison. That simmering confidence poured out through each pass of Allison's tongue, each movement of her lips. She was a fucking masterful kisser and Drew couldn't believe she'd waited so long to indulge.

It was Allison who pulled back first, mischief sparkling in her eyes. "What will the neighbors say?"

"Don't care." Drew leaned back in to reignite the kiss. Allison allowed it, her fingers skimming over Drew's back.

Drew could have stayed there all night, doing nothing more than kissing this woman who had come out of nowhere from clear across the country and slowly but patiently dug her heels in so deep that Drew could not move past her. She'd wondered if the curious feelings would translate into actual chemistry and now, yes, she had her answer. Admittedly, it was nearing the point of being overwhelming. Her body was single-minded in its desires, but Drew's mind was starting to light up with fireflies of warning.

When Drew pulled away, she moved her hand back to Allison's chin, tilting it so they were looking into each other's eyes. The height difference was just enough to allow for it and Drew found that she liked that very much.

"So there's that," Allison said. Her lips were full and ripe with kissing. A tempting fruit if there ever was one.

What Drew wanted and what Drew needed collided within her, digging their fingernails into the moment. They could stay. She owned the damn house, after all. But Drew needed to go.

"Come on," Drew said, tugging Allison's hand. "I'll take you back."

CHAPTER TWENTY-TWO

"Heads-up, kid."

Drew looked up just in time to see she was about to be decapitated. She ducked as she stepped to the side, preferring not to die quite yet.

The crew working at the Harbor Bluffs jobsite was... different. It was composed of a group of heavy-duty construction guys that Drew rarely used, mostly because she rarely had jobs that required heavy-duty construction type things. They leaned toward the construction guy stereotype but fortunately, Drew hadn't had any issues with them. Except for a couple of close calls with decapitation, that is.

Considering she'd kissed Allison last night then dropped her off at Sunset Dunes and driven off to bury her head under her pillow and scream, maybe she should opt for the decapitation.

Drew scanned the site, looking for something to do. She had no reason to be there. She'd met with the construction lead at eight a.m. for a whole ten minutes. Updated and confident in the progress of the project, Drew should have left and driven over the bridge, back to the beach town she loved with her whole heart, three hours ago. But she didn't want to go back there. Or she did, but she wasn't ready.

She walked around the razed ground slowly and carefully, mindful not only of more decapitation attempts but also of where she was stepping, since it had rained overnight and there were surprise mud pits every couple of feet. The skies had been heavy when she'd dropped Allison off at the Dunes. The silence in her truck was heavier, but not in a dangerous or foreboding way.

Allison had watched Drew carefully, seeming to understand that any abrupt movement would cause her to flee. When it became clear neither of them knew what to say, Allison thanked her for showing her a different side of town, said she'd see her soon, and left.

That was it. She just…left.

Drew was relieved and she hated to admit it. She was also impressed and appreciative of how Allison was handling her. It wasn't comfortable to do so but Drew could admit—and would, eventually, she believed—that she wasn't easy. She had her reasons. Tucked into her dark, silent corners were the fragments of her past, stacked one on top of the other, ready to tumble over and scatter across the floor so that someone could sweep them up and finally, finally throw them away.

Maybe Allison would be that person. Drew wasn't sure. Yet. She also wasn't sure which was worse: the almost-kisses that left them in a tidal pool of wonder, or the very, very real kiss that was a towering swell of far more than simple attraction and chemistry.

"That's enough," she said aloud. She stalked over to the skeleton of the first townhome, certain she could find a distracting task inside.

Starving and a little dehydrated, Drew finally left Harbor Bluffs around three o'clock and headed toward The Hideout. Nothing would cure her hunger like a loaded hot dog, and it was Wednesday, which meant it was the chef's choice. Nan had a few misses, but mostly hits on Wednesdays. And Drew was her more than willing guinea pig every week.

"Drew!" Bartleby greeted her enthusiastically as she settled onto her usual stool. "Haven't seen you for a few days."

A glass of ice water appeared in front of her and she took a few long sips before nodding her thanks.

"We don't usually see ya in the middle of the day, kid."

Drew's head jerked up, trying to place the familiar voice. It was the right place but the wrong time of day, and the wrong area of the bar. She squinted in the dim light; there sat Tommy Marlins (Allison's use of the nickname had rubbed off on Drew) all the way at the other end of the bar, right next to Ivy. His arm was wrapped protectively around her shoulders. Both were haloed by the Christmas lights hanging above them and the overall effect was disorienting but lovely.

"Likewise," she retorted. Her brain was trying to make sense of the scene. She'd always assumed Tommy and Ivy were... involved. Like in a bully romance flirtation situation (something she'd unwillingly learned about via Celeste, who devoured those books and loved to tell Drew about them). Not an actual *relationship*.

Tommy laughed heartily and Ivy sent Drew a sweet, caring smile. "My wife and I have lunch here every day," he said, then leaned over and kissed Ivy's temple.

Drew's internal world tilted and she looked at Bartleby for confirmation. He nodded and shrugged, as if to say, "Stranger things happen."

"Is this a new marital union?" Drew couldn't help but ask.

"Oh, sweetie, we're going on twenty-five years."

At that, Drew nearly choked to death on her water.

"I told ya she hadn't figured it out," Tommy said, nuzzling Ivy's ear.

Recovered, Drew shot them accusatory looks. "So this thing you two do almost every night in here. It's a farce?"

"Oh, I wouldn't call it a farce." Ivy still had that serene smile floating on her face. Drew had never seen her so...so happy. "I suppose you could say it's how we keep our marriage lively."

"Okay, ew, no thank you." Drew shook her head and tapped on the Megatouch. She glanced up at Bartleby. "Could I please have the chef's special hot dog and absolutely no more information about those two people at the end of the bar?"

"You got it, Drew." It wasn't until Bartleby scurried off to the kitchen that Drew realized she'd made a critical error and was now alone with Tommy and Ivy, husband and wife, affectionate and loving.

"Where's your friend today?"

Drew tried to ignore the question but, though cynical and introverted, she wasn't rude. "Not here," she said. Perhaps not her best amelioration.

Ivy giggled. *Giggled.* Drew understood it was not in her best interest to look up and see why. She focused instead on the naked woman sprawled across a dark-pink chaise lounge that screamed *porn*. Huh. Bright-purple thong on the left side of the screen, pale-purple thong on the right. Bingo.

"She seems nice, Drew." This came from Bartleby, normally Drew's ally. She'd have to reconsider that label.

"She's perfectly nice," she mumbled. More than nice.

"You thinkin' about given' her a shot?"

Oh, for fuck's sake. Had Drew's life really lowered to the point where she looked like she needed Tommy Fucking Marlins giving her dating advice?

"I'm removing myself from this conversation," she said loudly, reaching for her phone. She knew how to piss him off and shut him up. In seconds, John Denver was warbling the opening words of "Please Daddy," begging said daddy to not get drunk this Christmas.

"Oh, hon, remember when we used to play this song for the kids?" Tommy Marlins was bopping his head along to the strum of the guitar. Drew could not believe it.

"The kids used to play this song for *you*," Ivy amended, and they both burst into laughter.

Briefly, Drew thought of Allison. She'd had enough exposure to Tommy and Ivy that even she wouldn't believe the surreal scene Drew was being forced to watch.

"He has a point, Drew." Bartleby stood in front of her, wrapping and unwrapping a towel around his hand. "Allison sure does seem nice. You could do with a nice girl. And she sure seems to like you. Maybe think about it?"

Saved by the ding of the kitchen's bell. Bartleby gave a shrug before he went off to retrieve her hot dog. She stared down the Megatouch while she waited.

A nice girl. If only it were that simple.

"Here you go," Bartleby said, sliding the basket onto the bar in front of Drew. "Nan says she made this for you special."

Drew smiled as she investigated the masterpiece before her. Not only was there mac and cheese, and the good, breadcrumb-topped kind that Nan specialized in, there was also a layer of jalapenos topped with the crispy onions Drew dreamt about. When she took her first bite, her eyes widened. No. She held the hot dog out. Yes. Doritos lined the bottom of the roll. Incredible choice.

"She let you have the onions because you're here by yourself."

"Thank her for me," Drew said around a mouthful of food.

"She thinks so too," Bartleby said, almost sounding sorry for bringing it up again. "Nan, I mean. She thinks you and Allison have a nice energy together."

It was a very Nan thing to say. And it was sweet, too. For Drew's Hideout pals and anyone else who thought they knew Drew, it seemed simple: Drew + Allison + nice energy = romantic success!

For Drew, it was worlds away from being that simple.

In their defense, they didn't know. No one did. Well, one person did, but Drew tried to forget about that. It was too embarrassing to repeat, too humiliating to relive over and over again, knowing the story would then exist in memories that did not belong to Drew.

And maybe she was exaggerating other peoples' abilities and desires to remember things. But plain and simple, Drew had been made a fool of, and if she could erase that trembling, sunken feeling, she would, right along with the staggered heartbeats that had made her believe it was real.

It—she—had arrived clear out of the blue. But she wasn't a stranger; she and Drew had circled each other for years at jobsites because she was an interior designer. A very popular one at that. Suddenly—truly, it had happened suddenly—there she was, talking to Drew, and the desire to be as close to her as possible hit Drew like the sheets of drywall she'd been carrying not ten minutes before.

The designer was a few months out of a long-term relationship and Drew knew, she *knew*, it wasn't long enough. But her heart and her gut said otherwise, and she leaned in, wanting to believe the timing was right. It was kismet. It was beautiful. It was a sea of calm in a world of chaos. It was everything Drew had thought a real, growing, mature attraction and connection could be. And because Drew was a quiet romantic beneath a cactus veneer of cynicism, she cracked open her ribs and spoke only with her heart. Every word, paragraph, and essay: ribboned with nothing but vulnerable adoration and respect.

In the end, it was all handed back to her. That timing was a real bitch and there was no escaping the fact that the other woman, a name she wouldn't ever speak, was not as ready as she'd wanted to be. The heart's past is dabbled with pits of quicksand, and Drew could only stand on firm ground, watching the woman she knew she would one day love get sucked right back into the place she'd proclaimed she was never returning to.

It may not seem like much. It happens, of course: hearts break every day. But for Drew, the loss of that relationship dug right into a fissure she'd spent years sealing up, only to have it scratched open in the same shape by a hand that knew why the original crack existed. It was a curious pain, one layered and flecked with disbelief and disappointment. It trailed Drew everywhere she went and there were days where all she wanted was for someone to steal the state she was in, never to return it.

Once the angst settled and Drew saw more clearly, she had no choice but to accept that she was the fixer. The one who swooped in with all the good feelings and words, all the validation and genuine respect and *like* for another human being. All the love, given in unspoken ways before the three words ever hit the air. It had happened too many times with too many ex-girlfriends to be a coincidence, and normally Drew would forgive, but this one had come riding on the tails of her extensive battle with healing, and this time... She just couldn't.

Oh, she forgave the interior designer. But she couldn't forgive herself.

The only way to step out of the pattern was to forge new territory. Drew understood that for her, that meant no relationships, ever again. The risk was too high for her pliable, easily dented heart. Better to keep it contained in a glass cage and forget about it.

Drew chewed the last of her hot dog and concentrated on the image on the screen, cracking a smile at the eighties perm that rippled over the woman's bare shoulders. Some things were certainly better left in the past.

But Allison.

When she'd first met Allison, she gave off the energy of a project that needed fixing. It was a damn siren call. As much as Drew felt herself being yanked in, she also felt the stubborn and tired stomp of her past heartbreaks. She didn't want to fix anymore. She didn't want to be the Band-Aid that got slapped on to staunch the blood from someone else's cuts, only to get yanked off when something better came around, whether that was the comfort of the past or the dazzle of a *new* new beginning.

So she'd tried like hell to put a stop to the yanking. And she was successful. But Allison kept showing up on a different path, and Drew kept trailing behind her.

Now that she'd spent more time with Allison and learned that her confidence was real and not a cover-up for the wounds Drew was too familiar with, she'd decided maybe she could let a wall or two down. Gently and with purpose. It was a start and in order to keep going, Drew had needed more information.

So she'd kissed her.

And the results were valid. Meaningful. Surprising, if she were honest. She wasn't about to divulge any of that to anyone here at The Hideout, or anyone in general.

She wanted to kiss Allison again.

The hot dog had done its work, filling one hole of hunger. Drew completed the round of photo hunt and rushed through the next scene, purposely making mistakes. Her game ended and she left The Hideout.

She had work to do.

As luck would have it, Allison's car was not parked outside the bar. Drew debated moving on to another project then realized it was the perfect time to work on the pain in the ass old kitchen. Without Allison there to kiss or distract her, she could make good headway.

For the first time, the front door was locked. Drew smiled, seeing that as a step in an excellent direction. It also meant no one from her crew was here, which was surprising. She checked her watch. Or maybe not; it was nearing six o'clock. She'd completely lost track of time, probably because she hadn't stuck to a schedule.

Drew hadn't been in yesterday and when she stepped into the side room/old kitchen, she was taken by surprise. All the dirty work had been completed. The walls and floors were installed and everything looked fresh and new. No one would ever guess the state of disrepair the room had been in the first time Drew toured the space. She ran her hand along the walls. Base coat, check. Allison would have to pick a color.

A little emotion dug its nails into Drew's heart. Part of her wanted to do something special for Allison, make this space into something she could use every day and be comfortable in. It wasn't something Drew did as a standard for all her projects. No, she'd accepted (only a couple of days ago, but who was counting) that this project was different.

There was a commotion of laughter from the main space. Drew stood at alert, immediately recognizing both laughs. There was absolutely no reason for the alert to transform into jealousy, but she'd given up trying to control her emotions long ago. The best she could do was contain it as she walked out of the side room and into the main space.

CHAPTER TWENTY-THREE

"Hey," Allison said, seeing Drew come out of her future office. "I thought that was your truck outside."

She hoped with every fiber of hope she'd ever had within her that her voice didn't give away the vibrant but languid rush of nerves that coursed through her at the sight of Drew. She looked tired and Allison yearned—when exactly she'd begun yearning, she didn't know, but she didn't have time to analyze that right then—to wrap her arms around her and hold her, nudge Drew's head onto her shoulder and let her rest.

There was something else in Drew's expression, something she appeared to be trying to hide. Allison clocked it, though. After all, she had years of experience with that particular feeling.

"Cam and I are conducting an experiment," Allison said easily. She wanted nothing more than to put Drew's unease at rest. She thought it might be her personal old pal jealousy, and there was no way Allison was going to let that fucker interject itself into a situation where it would never belong.

Slow down, she told herself. Words like "never" were too strong to use at this juncture. She would not get ahead of herself and damage what she felt in her bones was going to be a very, very good thing with Drew.

"Allison had a really great idea," Cam said, his voice mellow and soothing. It was then that Drew's emotions seemed to level out. Allison let out a breath she hadn't realized had lodged itself in her lungs. "We were discussing furniture over at the office and she thought we should come over here and check out the evening lighting."

"So we brought some samples."

On cue, Cam presented the box he'd been carrying. "We're seeking ambience."

"I get it," Drew said. "It's a good idea. I'll leave you to it."

"No, wait." Allison paused. "Stay," she added, figuring easy truth was the way to go.

"Yeah, we could use your expertise," Cam said. He began placing pieces of wood around the room, then looked toward the ceiling. "I didn't even think about lighting."

All three of them looked up at the beams and angled ceilings. Allison, again, admired the job Drew had done staining the beams. They were glowing darkly beneath the freshly painted pristine white ceilings, which were composed of wooden slats, giving a beachy but classy vibe to the place.

"Lighting," Allison repeated. "Add that to the list, Cam."

"I have some lights in my truck."

Both Cam and Allison looked at Drew, but no one looked surprised. A random selection of lights in Drew's work truck seemed entirely appropriate, and very Drew indeed.

"I'll help," Cam offered, and the two walked out the front doors.

In their brief absence, Allison took a moment to breathe. She scrubbed her hands over her face. She hadn't expected to see Drew here, in—she really needed to come up with a name for her place. When she'd gone over to Southern Magnolia's headquarters, she'd half-expected to run into Drew there, but

Cam had informed her immediately that Drew was on a jobsite over in "land Clearwater," which Allison found hilarious.

She'd been so careful with Drew the night before. All she'd wanted to do was throw herself over the midsection of the front seat of Drew's truck and kiss her until their lips chapped. But she'd felt the shift in Drew and had instead left without a single kiss goodbye. And it killed her to do so. Because all she wanted, now, was to kiss Drew and feel the incredible, sensual, familiar sizzle of *finally*.

Allison kept getting stuck on that word. Not finally, though that one stuck a little too. Familiar. It wasn't that kissing Drew felt like kissing anyone from her past. It was more of a relief, a familiarity, a sense of coming home. The word and its feeling sent chills throughout Allison's body that quickly melted into the most sensational yet calm arousal she'd ever experienced.

Drew was foreign territory that Allison knew with certainty she should have been exploring all along.

Alas, timing and life. She shrugged it off the best she could while she waited for Cam and Drew to come back inside. Had Allison met Drew even one year ago, they wouldn't have been able to connect the way they were slowly connecting now. She knew that, believed it, and treasured the understanding of it. It was also why she was okay going as slowly as Drew needed to.

If, of course, she could get Drew to talk to her about any of this.

Allison peered inside the side room/future office and smiled. Fresh and clean, ready to become what it was always meant to be. She tried but couldn't avoid the cheesy-ass analogy as she thought, *just like my heart.*

"Be cheesy," she said into her future office. "You fucking deserve it."

The three of them stood around the space, all with their arms crossed to enhance their pensive intensity, eyes skipping from one sample to the next. Allison hated all of them but was reticent to say so. She and Cam had spent a good amount of time picking out the potential stains for the long, wooden tables

Allison had selected. She'd loved them all in the lighting of Southern Magnolia's office, but here, they all looked drab. Kind of formidable. Way, way too dark.

"It's not good," Drew said, breaking the thick silence.

Both Cam and Allison dropped their arms to their sides, then laughed at the matching expressions of relief on their faces.

"You see the problem?" Drew continued, looking at Cam.

"Yep." Cam pointed to the ceiling. "I was pushing her to match the stain of the beams."

"Too matchy-matchy," Drew said. "You want something lighter." That seemed to be directed to Allison, though the eye contact was lacking.

"Good, because I hate all of these." Allison began collecting the samples. "And I think I saw the stain I liked in another sample."

"The one I immediately set aside and told you wouldn't work?" Cam grimaced.

"That's the one."

"While you're both here," Drew said, crossing the room to the spot Allison had designated for the bar. "Care to enlighten me on any decisions you've made about the biggest and most important piece in the space?"

Cam took the samples from Allison, freeing her to walk over to Drew. She pulled out her phone and swiped through her pictures until she landed on the one she'd pulled from Pinterest just that morning. "I was thinking something like this. It's light and bright, and I think it'll tie everything together."

Drew pushed Allison's phone back toward her. "No."

She took a step back, surprised by the quick denial. "It's my bar, Drew."

"Yeah, I know that." She walked a few paces away then stopped, her back to Allison.

Dumbfounded and a little hurt, Allison glanced over at Cam, who shook his head and mouthed, "Wait."

So she did. The tense silence ticked into a full minute before Drew turned around.

"I'm going to say something," she said in a tone that gave nothing away, "and I don't think anyone in this room is going to like it."

Cam made a noise that sounded like he was being strangled by a ghost. Allison looked between the two of them, trying to figure out what was happening, stomach sinking further with every pivot of her head.

Drew brushed her knuckles over her chin and only then did she look Allison directly in the eye. "We picked the wrong flooring."

Allison looked down. She loved the floors. They were pretty and durable and…and…oh.

"Oh, shit," she said aloud. "These are coffee shop floors."

"No," Cam said, the word a moan laden with grief.

"She's right." Allison scuffed her shoe against the lovely luxury vinyl tile. "It has to go."

Cam, his eyes wild, shook his head with violence and passion. "It can't. I won't let it happen."

"It's her bar, Cam," Drew said lightly. "And after looking at the picture she just showed me, there's only one option for flooring."

"Concrete," Allison said. "I didn't even think of it before."

"Of course you didn't. You had coffee shop brain, not trendy and chill mocktail bar brain when you were looking at flooring options."

She blushed at that, Drew's first positive recognition of what Allison was planning to bring to town.

"And," Drew continued, pointing to the floors, "we floated them."

"So we can reuse them." Cam raised a silent fist in the air. "Success. Okay. I'm on board now."

"But your idea for the bar is still a no."

Allison couldn't help but stomp her foot, just once, on the soon-to-be-gone floor. "Drew. Hello? My bar, my decisions."

"And once you see the concrete flooring, you'll see exactly why white subway tile layered over a bar will look absolutely hideous."

"Oh, Allison," Cam said quickly. "No. No white subway tile. It's a phantom clause in all Southern Magnolia contracts."

Drew pointed at Cam. "He is correct."

"Besides, you're starting to clash designs," Cam went on. "For a space like this, you want to streamline and have the design be the backdrop, you know? Your customers will create the environment. Stick with your ideas for light and bright, but make it more natural…"

"So…maybe soothing colors? Muted." Allison nodded, beginning to see it. It was a different vision than what she'd set out to create but she got it now: she'd been stuck in coffee shop brain. Mocktail bar brain was a completely different vibe, the very vibe she'd been chasing since she left Portland.

"What you can do behind the bar is put up some ceramic stone that echoes the trash tile look but gives a much more refined visual. And let's consider installing an L-shaped bar since you have the corner to work with."

"I like that," Allison murmured, watching Drew move around her bar like she owned the place. Everything she said was clicking into place in Allison's head, and her excitement was beginning to grow much more authentic. Drew, apparently, was the key to a whole lot of excitement for Allison. She squirmed with the thought, briefly sinking into the memory of Drew's full lips against hers.

"It'll look great against the light wood of the bar and the more natural wood stains for the tables." Drew did a double take back at Allison. "Stop me if I'm saying too much."

"No," she said quickly. "Keep going. This is great."

"Told ya to wait," Cam said delightedly. "Drew's visions always come together. Sometimes they're even better than mine."

Drew blushed, the first splash of color on her cheeks Allison got to witness. "If we do a muted olive concrete pour," she said, "it'll pull together all your wood tones right along with the ceramic tiles. And over here." She moved to the wall opposite the entrance. The bathrooms were tucked into the corner and the wall itself was windowless. "You could do something other than paint. Maybe—"

"Shiplap," Allison breathed, seeing it.

"Shiplap," Cam and Drew echoed in unison, Cam's tone more obviously enthusiastic than Drew's.

"So as far as paint," Allison said, getting into it, "we only have to worry about the area where the bar ends and my office begins, plus that extra wall space there. And the wall with the front door, plus the little areas on the window-wall."

"Exactly. But don't go crazy with the color." Drew eyed her and Allison did not miss the flirtatious sparkle in her eyes.

"No, I'm over color. I'm feeling the whites and creams and natural, light woods."

"Some gold accents would be killer," Cam said thoughtfully.

"Yes! Gold. Oh my God. Yes." Allison could have clapped. She could finally see what the space could be; she hadn't realized that's what had been missing, the piece preventing her from truly being excited for her new venture.

Drew, however, groaned. "Nice going, Cam. Next she's going to want a shit ton of plants."

Cam and Allison gaped at her. "That was always the plan," Allison said haughtily. "Plants bring so much life to a space."

Instead of arguing, Drew stalked across the space between them, grabbed Allison's shoulders, and spun her around. They stood like that, Drew's body so close that Allison could feel the faint rub of her breasts on her back, both looking out the wall of windows. Allison accidentally, though not entirely, stumbled so their bodies closed what little distance had been between them. Drew's tiny exhale was very, very satisfying.

"Might I remind you," she said, her voice low and dangerous, cutting through that satisfaction with a fell swoop and leaving hot desire in its wake, "that we are at the beach. There are no plants out on that sand."

"Dune grass," Allison whispered. She angled her head so Drew's chin brushed against her neck. Another satisfying exhale, though this one only stoked the fire. The sensation of

Drew's nipples hardening against her back sent the flames into an uproar. "I think that qualifies as a plant."

Drew's fingertips pressed into Allison's shoulders, powerful bursts of pressure that wound right into the blazing heat of her untethered desire. "I don't like plants."

"It's not your bar."

A quiet laugh, its breathy tendrils curling around Allison's ear. "Let me rephrase that. I don't like plants in places where I'm going to eat. Or drink, as it is."

"Oh," Allison said sweetly. She rolled her shoulders so her back arched into Drew's breasts. "You're planning on coming to my bar?"

"I've considered it." Allison inhaled sharply. Drew had pushed her hips into Allison and the bodily connection was almost too much to handle. Slowly, her fingers released their sensual grip and slid down Allison's arms, gliding effortlessly over the chills they raised.

"Cam," Allison squeaked out. "Cam is here."

"He left. I gave him the signal."

At that, Allison turned around—both to see if it was true that Cam was gone, and to give Drew a disconcerting look. Cam, in fact, was gone, and Drew received the look with a sly smile.

"You have a *signal*?"

"Yeah." She had the grace to look a bit embarrassed. Her hands, though, had slipped from Allison's arms when she spun around. They found their way to her hips, gripping just as tightly as they had on her shoulders. "We use it when I need to have a one-on-one come to Jesus with a client."

"Is that what this is?" Allison leaned in, brushing her lips against Drew's but not kissing her. "Are you going to lecture me until I agree to leave plants out of my design plan?"

"No." Drew's voice was thick, even in the resonance of such a small, impactful word. "This is—"

Her words vanished, the need for action overtaking conversation. The kiss was lightning on a heady and humid summer night, thunder rolling across a cloud-smeared sky. It was rain, torrential and steady, saturating and soaking.

It was the most heavenly of storms. Drew's mouth was commanding but gentle. Allison tumbled into the rhythm of her movements, gasping as Drew parted her lips with a forceful swipe of her tongue. There was no doubt in Allison's mind that this woman was going to absolutely destroy her in bed—destroy her in all the best, reviving, comforting, exhilarating ways.

She knew with sudden, startling certainty that she would love this woman.

The awareness pushed through Allison, filling her with a want that could not be stilled. She slipped her hands beneath Drew's T-shirt, stroking her sides, brushing her thumbs over her stomach. The kiss deepened, all the notice Allison needed to keep her hands wandering up the stretch of Drew's torso, just skimming the underside of her bra, and—

"Not now," Drew said, the words choppy with her short breaths. "Not here. Not like this."

Allison took the moment to inhale a good, long breath. "That's a lot of not."

"Just for now," she said, pressing her lips against Allison's once again.

Allison cupped Drew's face with her hands, wanting to press both fast-forward and pause. There was something about kissing Drew that made her feel like she was sinking into the softest era of her life. She could stay there endlessly, not caring for air to breathe as long as Drew's mouth continued to lavish hers.

"Not forever," Drew said, hitting pause with her lips still touching Allison's. "Okay? Just for now."

The record of love songs in Allison's head screeched to a grating halt. Those were not the words she wanted to hear. She pulled away so there was space between their mouths. Now she could see Drew clearly, see the desire rippling over every feature on her face.

Understanding slowly dawned. "Meaning eventually?"

Drew cocked her head. Allison could practically see the wheels turning. "Yes. I know I don't say much, but…I thought it was obvious…" She sighed. "I'm not good at this part, Allison."

"You don't have to be. Just tell me this isn't casual."

At that, Drew laughed. She reached out and pulled Allison in, holding her close. "I told you nothing about me is casual."

"I know. I just wanted to make sure I'm not the exception to the rule."

Drew was quiet for a moment. "I think you're going to be the exception to many of my rules. But not that one."

Allison had questions, many, but not a single answer was needed in that moment. No, all she needed right then was to kiss Drew until her lips simply could not take any more kissing.

And, she thought as Drew tilted her chin up and captured her lips once again, she'd happily keep kissing her beyond that point.

CHAPTER TWENTY-FOUR

The first shimmers of the sunrise hit the bay with a delicate splash. All the birds were out, herons, egrets, and pelicans milling about at the water's edge. Others were tucked away in the palm trees dotting the grassy backyards butting against the sand, singing and chirping to each other.

At the ripe old age of forty-four, Drew was just beginning to embrace her midlife bird-watching habits. She'd never paid much attention to them prior to slipping into her forties. After all, it was Florida and birds were everywhere, all the time. But now, as she danced the line of becoming *middle-aged*, she was finding that she kind of liked the feathered creatures. They were elegant and singular in their tasks. That, and the ability to fly away was an enviable power.

Drew leaned back in her chaise and crossed one ankle over the other. The analogy was not lost on her; as of late, she'd begun to see that she, too, had the power to fly away.

She'd done it again two nights ago. And she had yet to forgive herself for it.

Kissing Allison, right there in the space they were both invested in (Drew more so than she could admit even to herself), had not been her plan. Yes, she'd spent most of Wednesday thinking about kissing her, but there was a sanctity to Allison's future bar, a pureness that Drew didn't want to infiltrate with her wanton desires.

She snorted. When she'd crossed the line into mass media romance lingo, she didn't know. But there was something about the magnetic, chemical pull she felt toward Allison that made her feel utterly wanton.

And when she kissed her again, when she dropped her self-imposed, prisonlike boundaries and allowed herself to feel shit she hadn't felt since the interior designer, she panicked. She'd hidden it by diving into that kiss, by not allowing space for conversation or questions. They'd have to talk eventually, Drew was well aware of that and not, by nature, an avoidant communicator.

She was simply terrified. Of feeling. Of wanting. Of needing. Of removing herself from the lonely jail she'd stuffed herself into after presenting her heart to someone she thought would cherish it, only to have it mailed back to her with "return to sender" heartlessly stamped on the envelope.

A pure white heron, a coastal Florida treasure, sailed down from the sky and stuck its landing in the shallow edge of the bay. It began a slow wade around the area, eyes on the water, ready to find breakfast.

The stalking is what brought Drew's other issue to mind. She dropped her head against the back of the chaise. Holly. God, she hated Holly. She always had. Drew prided herself on her ability to feel energy that others gave off. Admittedly, it was sometimes overwhelming, hence her preference for hermitage. It was also very difficult to handle in business situations, especially when she wanted to please a client but could not get past the shit energy they were giving off.

Holly was a black hole of horrible energy. Drew had sensed it immediately and known to stay as far away from her as possible. It helped that Holly's overall personality was nothing that Drew found attractive, romantically or platonically. Her persistence, however, and absurdly bold proclamation of intending to woo Drew into marriage so she could join the Kingsley empire… Literally, undeniably, hands down the most disgusting thing Drew knew Holly to have ever done. Turning down her nonproposal was a no-brainer.

But Allison. Drew gazed out at the snowy-white heron, who was preparing to snag an unsuspecting fish. Allison had been that fish. Drew empathized with her cross-country move and knowing no one, and damn if Holly wasn't a beacon of good times and entertainment. So it made sense that Allison had been snapped up into Holly's beak.

It was the fact that she'd continued to date her that rubbed Drew the wrong way. It made her a little ill, to be honest. Not that she was the gold medal winner of Great Past Dating Decisions. It's just… It was *Holly*.

On the plus side, Allison had ended it before… Before what, exactly? Before the attraction between her and Drew flickered into existence? Or before she'd gotten in too deep?

It didn't matter. Drew pushed herself off the chaise and headed inside. The past was the past. She could let that go as long as Holly stayed away from both of them. An unlikely scenario, but a girl could hope. After all these years and Drew's continued denials, Holly hadn't given up on trying to worm her way into the Kingsley family by way of marital bli—hell. Drew had to believe that under that bravado was an inkling of actual attraction, maybe even feelings. And if Holly saw that Drew was off the market, hopefully for good, maybe she would finally give up.

Drew smirked as she walked into her bedroom's en suite and stripped off her shorts and T-shirt. She did not hate the idea of Holly seeing her and Allison together. Not one bit.

"Tell me again what happened."

June turned her face away from Drew, refusing to meet her eyes. "There's nothing to tell. Everything is just fine, Drew."

Her continued denial was not helping the growing ball of panic in Drew's gut. When she'd arrived at the Dunes, she'd found June alone in the atrium. It wasn't unusual; her grandmother, like Drew, enjoyed her solitude from time to time. What bothered her was that when she approached June, she hadn't seen any bit of recognition in her grandmother's face. It was blank. June had said hello, sounding like herself, but hadn't used Drew's name. She'd invited Drew to sit with her and began telling a story that made absolutely no sense. For a moment, Drew thought June was retelling a dream. Then, through the jagged sentences and dreamy phrases, she put some pieces together and realized it was a story from when June was in high school and dating the all-star pitcher of the baseball team. But she was telling it in a way that made Drew the star of the story, not herself, still without identifying Drew as the person sitting with her.

It had shaken Drew, and all she could do was wait June out. So she did. The story went on and on, and about four minutes in, June seemed to snap out of whatever memorial reverie she'd tumbled into. Her eyes cleared, her expression righted itself, and she looked right into Drew's eyes and said, "Oh, Drew! I was hoping to see you today."

Doing everything in her power to remain calm, Drew had conducted an off-the-cuff medical interview (which she had training in, thanks to her volunteer firefighter experience). June had brushed off every single question. No, she hadn't fallen. No, she hadn't hit her head. No, she wasn't tired. Yes, she'd eaten. Yes, she'd taken her pills. Yes, she could still recite from memory the full address of the home she'd lived in for over fifty years.

Now they were at an impasse. Drew didn't want to continue needling her grandmother, but she didn't know what else to do, let alone how to feel. And June was utterly irritated with Drew's inquisition. She seemed fine, all things considered. Throughout the interview, she hadn't slipped once. Her mental faculties were clear and present, fully functioning.

So she'd spaced out. Gone back for a visit to her younger years and threaded her favorite grandchild into the memory. No big deal.

Drew knew, though, it would become a big deal.

"What's in that bag?" June asked, giving Drew the stink eye. "Don't tell me you came here to do exactly what I told you not to do here."

Drew nudged the bag under the table with her foot. "Of course not. I thought maybe some of your friends would help me. I wouldn't dream of spoiling another surprise for you."

"You can't lie to me, Drew Kingsley. I used to wipe your ass, you know."

"Please. You had the au pair do that."

June giggled, another flash of her teenage self, unable to deny the truth. It was Kingsley lore: Every time Greg and Yolanda had another child, the former-youngest got shipped off to June, who was armed and ready with a nanny. She probably hadn't changed a single Kingsley grandchild's diaper.

"Hello, Drew!" The trill was familiar, and Drew steeled herself for the inquisition that was likely coming her way. Karma was quick on its feet that day.

"Oh, June, you didn't tell us you had company!" Without an invitation, Dorothy settled herself into one of the chairs at the table. Blanche was a few steps behind her, a bit slower than normal.

"My bones!" she exclaimed as she sat. Or, really, hovered slowly until the chair somehow met her butt. "It must be the weather. I'm terribly achy today."

"Blanche, please. Everyone knows you didn't sleep in your apartment last night."

June gasped loudly. Drew stifled a laugh, then wished Allison was there, knowing she'd enjoy this round of Dunes gossip.

"Blanche! You didn't!"

Her curls did look a bit dented. "The rumors are true," she said loudly, as though addressing her court. "I stayed with Edward last night. Oh, did we have fun!"

June, over being scandalized and clearly interested in the details, leaned forward. "Edward! I didn't think he had it in him anymore!"

"Excuse me?" Drew blurted. The images teetering in her mind were, in a word, horrific.

June ignored her. "He and I had a few dates some time ago. I never spent the night. We didn't need that much time."

Dorothy screeched with delight. Drew was busy preparing for her imminent death right there in the atrium of Sunset Dunes.

"Well, he certainly still has *something* in him," Blanche said proudly. "He did mention you, June."

Silence skittered across the table. Drew, revived and ready to pounce if this elderly hussy dared to besmirch her grandmother's (admittedly, also slutty) name, waited. Dorothy sat ramrod straight in her chair, eyes darting from Blanche to June.

"Did he now?" Points to June for sounding as uninterested as possible.

"He did." Blanche stroked the pearl necklace that hung around her neck. "He thought perhaps the three of us could spend some time together."

"Oh for fuck's sake," Drew said, nearly jumping out of her chair. "I'm leaving."

"No, sit, sit!" Dorothy cried. "You can't leave me alone for this!"

"Both of you calm down. And Drew, sit down." She obeyed her grandmother's command without a second thought, knowing she'd get whacked with her cane if she didn't. June pressed her hand to the button at the top of her pink cardigan. "Blanche and I will discuss this another time. Drew, why don't you get out whatever you have in that bag?"

It was a dirty trick and Drew knew it, but she obliged. The fact was, she wanted to run through this activity and figured this was her best audience.

"Where's your girlfriend?" Blanche asked bluntly, then winked at June.

"She is not," Drew said, plunking three pairs of winter gloves onto the table, "my girlfriend."

"The stars are aligning, Drew," Dorothy said, her voice a sweet melody. "We all see the sparks flying between you two."

She imagined they did but was not about to give them the satisfaction of agreeing.

"I like Allison," June said, pulling on a pair of gloves. "And I think Allison likes you."

"But does Drew like Allison?"

"Have you seen the way she looks at her?" Dorothy said, answering Blanche's question. "The sparks! They're more on fire than you and Edward were last night."

"This morning," Blanche deadpanned, and the three old ladies erupted into laughter, sounding like Macbeth's witches around the fire, concocting some kind of love spell.

Drew didn't need it. She knew, with certainty, that if she stayed the course she was stumbling onto, she would fall in love with Allison all on her own.

"Can we please stop the sex talk and play the game?" she said.

The ladies continued to titter but made an attempt to look like they were paying attention as Drew went over the rules for North Pole Pop. As much as she knew she and Allison would have had fun trialing this one, she needed to be sure their participants could do it.

"This does look like a challenge." Blanche clapped her hands, seeming to enjoy the glove-muffled sound. "I don't think I've ever worn winter gloves in my life!"

"They're scratchy," Dorothy complained. "And I can't get a hold of this damn balloon." Sure enough, the balloon Drew had handed her shot out of her hands for the third time.

"That's kind of the point," Drew said around the half-filled balloon protruding from her mouth.

"My, my, my. Your granddaughter's got some strong lungs, June."

Drew paused in her blowing to flip Blanche the bird. Wrong move, as the ladies dissolved into girlish laughter once again.

The game called for ten balloons per person, but Drew stopped at five each, both because she felt that would be enough and because she was a bit lightheaded. She guided Blanche and Dorothy to separate tables, each with five balloons. Once everyone was settled with a balloon between their gloved hands, Drew set the timer for one minute and stood back to watch.

It was a shit show, just as she'd imagined and hoped. They had to pop as many balloons as possible with their hands, but maintaining a grip on the latex while wearing gloves was proving to be difficult. It was a fine occupational therapy activity, that was for sure. And it was entertaining the hell out of Drew, so she mentally checked it off as a success.

In the end, Blanche won, having popped three balloons. Drew suspected she'd found a way to poke one of her sharp nails through a tiny hole in the glove, but she allowed Blanche her victory. June had popped two, and Dorothy, for reasons she could not explain, had popped a grand total of zero.

"Now that's two games I know about," June said, huffing.

"And Winter Wonderfest is tomorrow!" Blanche exclaimed. "Are you meaning to tell us that you're not prepared?"

Drew smiled as her insides wiggled with nerves. "No, we're prepared."

"I heard that." Dorothy wore a cocky grin, quite proud of her aged hearing skills. "You said *we*."

"I did," Drew said slowly. "Because Allison and I have been working on this together. As a team."

"A team of two." Blanche winked again, the effect of which was a little disconcerting and not at all sexy or playful. "That spells love."

"Oh, leave her alone." Finally, June came in to defend her. "If Drew wants to love Allison, she will. And I know my granddaughter," she said proudly. "If we keep nagging her about it, she'll tuck tail and run in the other direction."

Drew stopped listening at that point, focusing instead on cleaning up. The ladies continued to dissect and plan her love life, not realizing that Drew already knew she had zero control over whether or not she was going to love Allison.

CHAPTER TWENTY-FIVE

It's not that Drew hadn't realized that Winter Wonderfest was *the very next day*. She knew. Totally knew. It was at the forefront of her mind at all times, absolutely, never left, right there next to all her other Pressing Responsibilities that couldn't be trusted to linger in the recesses of her mind.

It *was* possible she hadn't put the days of the week together and remembered that Saturday came immediately after Friday, and seeing as it was Friday and had been all day, there were now less than twenty-four hours till showtime.

In Drew's feeble defense, she'd had a few other things on her mind that week.

When she left the Dunes, she sent Allison a long text about making sure they had everything ready to go for tomorrow. As they'd practiced and added activities, Allison had been going out to get whatever materials they needed, and handing her receipts over to Carol for reimbursement. So, realistically, the only thing that wasn't ready to go was likely the very activity Drew had discovered at the last moment. She could run out right then and get the materials if need be, but she wanted to check with Allison first to make sure there weren't other loose ends she needed to grab.

Allison didn't reply right away, which was a thing Drew assumed she did. The vaguely hollow feeling settling in Drew's gut did not please her one bit. She didn't want to be a nag and text Allison again, so she waited a while, sitting in her truck in the parking lot of Sunset Dunes. Minutes ticked by, adding up to a full ten. The hollow feeling had expanded, breaking invisible boundaries and taking up as much space as it desired. Drew cursed into the growing darkness of her truck, then headed to the one place that always prevented her from thinking.

The firehouse, only a half mile from Drew's home, was quiet when she arrived. She wandered around inside, doing her usual equipment checks. Eventually she ran into a group of guys back in the kitchen. She declined their offer of dinner, though her stomach was beginning to rumble. Instead, she made her way back through the firehouse and stepped outside into the evening air.

It had been overcast all day and the low-hanging air matched Drew's mood. Allison still hadn't replied. It wasn't a big deal, but it bothered her all the same. She liked consistent communication. And yes, she understood the irony of that, considering she needed to have a conversation with Allison about the kissing. The very kissing that was turning Drew into someone who craved kissing. The hot and warm, satisfying and beckoning kissing that felt like no kissing Drew had ever experienced before.

"I figured I'd find you here."

Drew, having been focused on the dirty concrete sidewalk under her feet, snapped her head up. "Really? Of all the places, this is where you came to find me?"

Cam shrugged. "I know your patterns, Drew. Haven't you figured that out yet?"

They'd been friends since high school, back when they played on the same soccer team, and coworkers since Drew had started Southern Magnolia. Cam was the only person in Drew's life who could slip past her boundaries. Drew wasn't sure if that was because she allowed it, or because Cam had that way about him. He'd always been incredibly insightful, picking up on things Drew was years away from admitting to herself. But the best thing about Cam was that he waited for Drew to catch up.

"You're doing that thing again," Cam said, squatting next to her, then sitting down on the concrete. "Your avoidy thing."

Scratch that. Cam *used* to have this great thing about him where he waited for Drew to catch up.

"I am not."

"Oh, really?" Cam kicked her shoe. "Then why didn't you show your face at Allison's place today?"

"I didn't need to." It was true. Thursday morning, Drew had deployed a crew to remove the flooring and prep the subfloor for a concrete pour. She didn't need to be there for that, nor did she need to check in today to see the progress.

"Just like you haven't needed to be there all those other days when you were there?"

Drew rolled her eyes and rested her head against the brick behind her. "How are the floors, Cam?"

"Fine. Great. They're going to look amazing." He kicked her shoe again. "But you're avoiding the main point here."

After a deep inhale and slow, steady exhale, Drew said, "I needed to not be there for a day. Or two, I guess."

Now Cam waited, doing the thing that Cam did so well. He'd honed it when he was away at college, coming back not only with facial hair but also with a communicative skill set that both impressed and annoyed her.

"I don't know about this, Cam," Drew said quietly. She avoided looking over at the one person she considered a good, true friend—yet a person who only knew what Drew allowed him to know. "You know what I'm talking about, right?"

"A certain blond woman with incredibly gorgeous sea-blue eyes and unearthly amounts of patience for you? Yep. Sure do."

She couldn't help but smile at the accuracy. "There's so much I don't know about her." She bit her lower lip, surprised that she'd opened up so quickly. That tended to happen around Cam, which was why Drew limited their alone time together.

"That's kind of the whole point of dating someone. You get to know them along the way."

"You've forgotten that I've done that. A few times. And I somehow always missed the parts that should have jumped up and told me to walk away."

Cam cast a sidelong look at her. "That's kind of the whole point of dating, Drew," he repeated. "Figuring it out, figuring someone out, figuring out how you work with someone else along the way. That's the only way you'll know if someone is the right fit for you."

Drew sat in the silence between them. The reason she wasn't married, something she did actually want, was because she had a merry-go-round of rusted, dented relationships spinning around the creaky circle of her dimly lit past. She hadn't thought all of them would be forever. But there were two that stuck out, two that she sometimes still wondered about and beat herself up over.

"Oh," Cam said, his tone gentle. They both knew his next words could send Drew running. "The designer."

Drew grunted in response.

"Yeah, that one was rough. Are you going to tell Allison about her?"

That startled her out of caveman response mode. "Are you serious? Why would I do that?"

Cam gestured at her like it was the most obvious answer. "Because it had a big impact on you. It still does. I see it. I mean, I know you're as over her as you can be, but she left an impact."

"She left a fucking gash."

"And you're not bleeding anymore," he said soothingly. "If you were, you would have never kissed Allison."

Drew glared at Cam. "I didn't kiss her."

"Liar."

"She told you?"

Cam grinned. "No, but you just did. And, hello, the attraction between you two is so obvious. Why do you think I bolted the other night?"

"Because I gave you the signal," Drew said.

"Okay, yeah, you did. But I was gonna go before that happened. I could feel something coming the moment you two laid eyes on each other. You don't look at anyone else the way you look at her. Actually, I've never seen you look at anyone the way you look at her. Not even the designer."

It was a punch, but soft enough that none of Drew's internal organs were affected. After wrestling with her brain for a while and deciding against informing Cam that their first kiss had happened before that night, she said, "I didn't tell you because I don't want you to have to see me deal with another failure."

"Drew." Cam slung his arm around her shoulders. "Think positively, my friend."

"I hate you."

Cam laughed but kept his arm around her. "I know. But the thing is—"

"I don't want to fix her," Drew said, letting the agonizing truth out. "I can't handle that again. I've been with too many women who were broken and then I came in and gave them everything they said they were waiting for, only to have it be a fucking Band-Aid that they ripped off and discarded. Not it. Me. I was the Band-Aid that got trashed." She avoided Cam's eyes as she went on. "I don't want to do all the getting to know you shit and the dating shit and fall for her only to have her get up and walk away because she wants her past back." She felt a cold shiver race through her body. She may not be bleeding anymore, but that gash was certainly still there. "I can't do that again, Cam. I can't."

"But you don't know that that's what would happen. I met the designer. Remember? You two had an intense connection. And it just wasn't the right time for her." Cam, casual as ever, as though he wasn't peeling back the corners of Drew's skin and exposing her pain to the evening light, popped a piece of gum into his mouth. "Maybe what you and Allison have right now isn't as intense as that was, but it's definitely something. Maybe it's the something you need. And, I know you know this, but Allison is different."

"She's got a past, too," Drew mumbled as the fisted grip on her argument began to loosen.

"We all do. And are you listening to yourself? Maybe Allison's afraid of having to fix you."

"I don't need to be fixed." Each word snapped like a rubber band around a rolled-up newspaper.

Cam kicked Drew for the third time. "Again. Are you listening to yourself?" At Drew's grunt, he went on. "Remember when I dated that chef?"

Another grunt, but this one was full of despair. "The worst."

"Well, yeah. But I lived. Anyway. Remember what happened after that?"

Drew thought for a moment. Cam was very chatty about his love life, but it was difficult for Drew to keep track of. "Was it the woman who works on yachts?"

"Yes! Andrea." Despite that relationship having ended, Cam still sounded dreamy when he said her name. "She and I started dating knowing that we both had stuff to work on. And we did, independently. But then we realized that we were also healing together."

"This sounds like a Hallmark movie that never aired because it was too fucking cheesy to show to the masses."

"It was cheesy." Cam tilted his head back and looked up at the impenetrable dark-blue sky. "But it was also amazing while it lasted. She's coming to visit in a couple months, by the way."

"Cut to the point."

"My point is, we all have shit, Drew. And the best of us own our shit. And by owning it, we stumble right into the people who own their shit, too. That's where all the best healing takes place. Even if it doesn't last."

Drew shook her head. "If it doesn't last, it adds another gash and bleeds out over all the healing that was done together."

"Sometimes. But if you don't try, you'll never know if it'll help heal or scratch open an old wound…" Cam trailed off, darting a quick look at Drew. "Um, I think my lecture just shot itself in the foot."

"Ya think?" Drew pushed off the ground and stretched when she stood. She touched her pocket, thinking she'd felt her phone vibrate. "This is why I don't talk about this stuff. There's no clear answer."

Cam jumped to his feet, the image of irritatingly youthful energy at the ripe age of forty-four. "That's the beauty of it, Drew. The beauty is in the trying. The experience. The maybes and what-ifs and could-bes."

Figuring it was a phantom vibration, Drew waited a moment before pulling her phone out of her pocket. Nope. Not a phantom. Allison had finally responded with a succession of five texts, a mixture of apologies for taking so long to reply and a rambling explanation of her conversation with Carol about last-minute Winter Wonderfest prep.

"Tell Allison I said hi," Cam said, beginning to walk off.

Drew looked up, squinting in disbelief at his back. "How'd you know it was her?"

"I can read you like a book, Drew." Cam turned briefly and shot her a winning smile. "Even when most of your pages are written in invisible ink."

With that, Cam disappeared into the night. Before Drew could send a second reply to Allison, her phone buzzed in her hand. She steadied herself. Their first phone conversation. Okay. She could do this. No problem.

"Hey," she said as casually as possible.

"I am so sorry," Allison said immediately. "I was busy with Carol at the Dunes and I didn't even consider that you were going out and getting last-minute stuff."

"It's okay. Not a big deal at all." Drew hesitated, slow understanding dawning on her. She hadn't pressured Allison about not texting her back. This response was strong enough to spotlight the truth for Drew: Here was a wound, shining bright with tender new skin stretching over it. Allison wasn't even trying to hide it. Or maybe she couldn't.

Okay. Communication stuff. Drew could definitely help heal that wound.

She smiled despite the small whir of nerves in her gut. "Do you need me to grab anything? I haven't gone to the store yet."

Allison was quiet for a moment. Again, Drew registered the tension coming from the other side of the phone but knew it wasn't about her. She puffed up, proud of herself. And, okay, maybe grateful for Cam and his impeccable timing with a little bro-therapy chat.

"Actually, yeah, if you don't mind. I don't think we have enough mini pompoms for the snow shovel activity. Carol thinks we do, I disagree. So if you can grab another bag or two, that would be awesome."

"You got it."

"Thank you." Allison's voice was lighter, as though a weight had shifted within her. "I heard through the Dunes grapevine that you added another activity today."

Drew grinned and leaned against the wall of the firehouse. "Were the ladies gossiping about my visit?"

"Oh my God, they wouldn't shut up about it. I know Blanche gives off that 'I love men so much' vibe, but I think she has a crush on you."

"Respectfully, Allison, that's the most heinous thing you've said to me in the short time we've known each other."

She laughed, and when she calmed said, "It really hasn't been long, has it?"

"No." Drew scuffed her shoe against the concrete. "Not long at all."

"And yet…" Allison trailed off, but she didn't need to finish her thought. It, much like the front of the firehouse, was lit up like a Broadway marquee.

"I can't believe Wonderfest is tomorrow," Drew said. She shut her eyes, annoyed that she couldn't keep up with that almost-flirt that would have led them right to where they needed to go. Not yet. But soon.

Allison took the redirection in stride, forever one of Drew's favorite things about her. "Right? Everything is happening so quickly."

And there they were, right back to the fork in the road Drew had detoured them away from.

She blinked up at the night sky, wondering about healing and old gashes and scabs and wounds, matters of the heart she knew too well.

"Maybe after the festivities," Allison said, her voice confident with an undertone of vulnerability that Drew recognized instantly, "we can do something together not involving winter activities or my future bar's renovations."

Drew grinned. She didn't believe in perfect people, but she did believe in perfect moments. And right there, in the middle of one, she knew to belt herself in and gently tap the gas instead of slamming on the brakes.

"Yeah," Drew said, trying to sound casual but for the first time not caring if she failed at it. "Let's do that."

CHAPTER TWENTY-SIX

Allison turned back and forth, trying to see all angles of herself in the mirror in her bedroom. It had only occurred to her that morning, when she woke up at the unsightly ass crack of dawn, that she needed an outfit for Winter Wonderfest. The dress code, according to Blanche and Dorothy, was "to the nines." Allison didn't feel the need to go to that extreme, especially considering she was there more as a facilitator than a guest, but she did want to look good.

Of course she did. She'd finally gotten Drew to agree to go on a date with her.

She smiled at her reflection as their conversation replayed in her mind. Drew was tough, Allison understood that. But she was quite experienced in being patient with tough women. The difference, finally, was that Drew wasn't being tough for the sake of being tough. It wasn't an image or a facade, or even a way to challenge someone to attempt to break down walls that served very little actual purpose.

No, Allison understood a mutual wound when she saw one. She didn't know the specifics and didn't need to. She wanted to, sometimes. But in her experience, digging up the old bones of past relationships when entering a new one wasn't the most promising or appetizing recipe for success. Some things deserved a sliver of light, while others were best left in terminal darkness.

Speaking of darkness... Allison stopped moving around and looked over at her bedside table. She hadn't opened that drawer in a couple of weeks. She was both proud of that and a little unsettled over it. It's not that she wanted to see that lengthy reminder of all her mistakes. It was more that she couldn't believe she hadn't had to add to it.

Yet.

The word trudged through her. She shook her head and opened the drawer, pulling out The List. She didn't want "yet" to be in her vocabulary, at least not in this regard. True, she didn't know what would come—if anything—with Drew, but either way, she didn't want Drew's name to ever be in this tortured packet of papers.

They had time. There was no rush. Allison let the truth of those statements pour over her. She was going to stay right here in Clearwater Beach, open her mocktail bar, and continue volunteering at Sunset Dunes. Everything could unfold as slowly as it needed to. Despite Drew not having said that aloud, Allison knew it was likely her truth. She was okay with slow. Nothing good in Allison's life had ever come from rushing or making quick decisions (see: The List).

What she did need to know was—no, she knew. Allison sat on the edge of her bed, running her fingers over her duvet. Drew had said it herself: She didn't do casual. There wasn't a need to read between the lines. When Drew was ready to talk, Allison would be ready to listen.

Funny, she'd never realized how patient she was until she was being patient for the right reasons.

With one last glance, Allison folded up The List and slid it back into the drawer. She lingered for a moment, feeling the anxiety of hope chafing against a lifetime of disappointment, then shut the drawer.

Before she could return to the mirror to obsess for five more minutes over her outfit, there was a knock at her door. Allison's silly little heart jumped, wondering if maybe Drew had surprised her and come to pick her up. As she moved through the tiny home, however, she saw a familiar head of hair through the front windows that definitely did not belong to Drew.

"Hi, girlfriend!" Carol waved from the front porch. "You almost ready?"

"Almost," Allison said, opening the door and letting Carol in. "Oh, I love your outfit! Excellent choice."

Carol had gotten the memo to "dress to the nines." In a black, sparkly sleeveless jumpsuit with wide-legged pants, she looked effortlessly chic. Thanks to years of gardening, she still had toned upper arms and a constant Floridian tan.

"Let me get a good look at you," Carol said, stepping back to assess Allison's outfit. "Well, well, well. You're going to knock that curmudgeon right off her grumpy feet."

Allison rolled her eyes, though the thought of impressing Drew did give her a little thrill.

She looked down at her white pants (something she never would have worn back in Portland) and deep-blue V-neck dolman blouse. She'd picked it because it felt wintry and still true to Florida. And, sticking to her roots, she'd decided on a pair of white slip-on Vans; there was no way she was going to wear anything fancy or uncomfortable on her feet, no matter Blanche's expectations.

"I was going for comfortable but classy," Allison said.

"You've succeeded." Carol's eyes sparkled and Allison wasn't sure if it was the cataract surgery effect or excitement over the upcoming evening. "Now let's go see what those old gals pulled out of their ancient closets."

All things considered, the "grand hall" at Sunset Dunes was in good shape for the event that was set to begin in just one hour's time. Carol's design team, a group of ladies Allison had not yet met, had put together a lovely setup. Round tables were covered with simple white tablecloths, and centerpieces made of blue and white sparkly snowflakes sat on each table. The chairs even had slip covers of a deep navy blue. When Carol caught sight of that, she grumbled, "They blew the damn budget."

The rest of the hall—perhaps not grand, but definitely large enough to house the entire population of Sunset Dunes and then some—was awash with… Well, a lot of silver. Allison walked around, trying to figure out the theme or artistic concept. There were some disco balls and strings of silver stars. Giant silver sprays had been fastened into each corner, giving off a firework vibe that, like the disco balls, didn't quite coincide with the wintry theme. Along one wall was a black sheet edged with hanging silver decorations. Allison smiled, realizing it was a backdrop for photos. The design team really had thought of it all.

After taking in the scene, Allison went to work. She and Drew had decided on eight activity stations, including one for the Reindeer Antler Game. Setting up was a breeze since Allison had been storing the supplies right there at the Dunes as she bought them. She lugged the items out from beneath the tables (tables that were covered with, inexplicably, blazing yellow tablecloths) and went about setting up each station. She nodded appreciatively when she noticed the laminated instructions.

"Which one will you work?" Carol asked as she buzzed past, arms full of giant cotton balls.

Allison watched as Carol spilled her armload onto an empty table near the photo station. "What is that?"

"They wanted snowballs," she said nonchalantly. "And so, they shall have snowballs."

"Amazing," Allison murmured. "I think I'm going to go between Candy Cane Hook 'Em and Snow Shovel."

Carol put her hands on her hips and fixed Allison with a steely glare. "You're not going to let them have any fun, are you?"

Surprised, Allison raised her eyebrows. "Of course I am."

"Then why," Carol said, walking toward her, hands still fixed on her hips, "are you going to position yourself at the two activities that involve mouth-stuff?"

The term "mouth-stuff" coming out of a seventy-eight-year-old woman's mouth made Allison want to perish on the spot. "Hold on. Every time we met, you were trying to get them to control themselves!"

"That was then," she whispered loudly. "This is their night, girlfriend. We have to let them live a little."

Allison shuddered. "I don't have to watch, do I?"

"Of course not. You and Drew just make sure the stations are running smoothly." Carol eyed her, the steel returning to her expression. "And it's about time you stop denying that something is happening between you two. You don't have to tell me a word of it, but don't you keep pretending it's nothing."

Properly admonished, Allison could only nod. She'd be delighted to tell Carol what was going on. Just as soon as she and Drew figured that out.

Speak of the devil. Allison blinked, making sure her vision wasn't blurred. Drew was here. And gorgeous.

She stopped in the doorway of the hall, looking around as though no one was watching her. But Allison knew Drew knew she was watching, and a tremor of pleasure ripped through her.

Black was certainly Drew's color. The pants she wore looked like they'd been sewn specifically for her body, hugging her muscular thighs and tapering over her slim (but still muscular in their own way) calves. A black button-up was tucked neatly into the pants and the top two buttons were undone, allowing a small but promising glimpse of the smooth, tan skin of her chest. Allison's eyes begrudgingly traveled up. For once, Drew's hair wasn't hanging in her face. She'd used some kind of product to give it a little extra oomph, and pieces were tucked behind her ears, revealing an expression that Allison felt herself being pulled across the room to.

"Go say hi," Carol said from behind her. "Don't keep her waiting."

Allison moved as though on a silken cloud, step after step carrying her closer to Drew. She didn't stop until she was inches away and fully under the heavy cloak of Drew's gaze.

"Hi," Drew said, keeping her eyes steady on Allison's. "I'm here."

"You're here," Allison repeated. "And you look incredible."

A flush, almost shy in its appearance, spread over Drew's cheeks. "Thank you." Now she looked Allison up and down, a grin pinching the corners of her mouth as she did. "So do you."

The moment was broken, more like busted straight through, by the appearance of Dorothy and Blanche behind Drew. They were already giggling as they took no pains to disguise the fact that they were staring at Allison and Drew.

"Ladies, it's not time yet!" Carol called from across the hall. "Go gossip somewhere else for another fifteen minutes."

"Fifteen minutes?" Allison turned. "Shit. Okay." She turned back to Drew. "We have work to do."

And as though it was the easiest choice she'd ever made, Drew stepped fully into the room and fell in step with Allison.

Twenty minutes later, the hall was filled with Dunes residents. There was plenty of gasping and laughing as they tottered around the space, checking each other out. Most of the women were, in fact, dressed to the nines, but not a single one could compete with Dorothy.

Allison suspected she had some old costumes stored away in her apartment from her costume designer days and could see her jokingly wearing one to Winter Wonderfest, but she hadn't expected Dorothy to show up in a floor-length gown that she had sewn just a few months ago. It was stunning, a deep black fabric bejeweled with tiny crystals that shimmered with every step she took. Her ice-white hair was perfectly tucked into an elaborate updo and her make-up complimented her sophisticated look. Allison was awed by her, and even more determined to find the award she *knew* was stowed in her apartment somewhere so she could use it as an opening to get all the stories possible out of Dorothy.

Blanche, not to be outdone, was decked out in an upsettingly short silver sheath dress. Her curls were immovable and her make-up was, as always, over the top, but somehow befitting the outfit and the general atmosphere. She was a walking party herself, the belle of the ball, full of conversion and laughter.

The older ladies were gorgeous, June included, but Allison couldn't keep her eyes off of Drew. They'd agreed to stay near the activity tables in case anyone had questions or problems, but Drew was having a hard time leaving June's side. Allison saw the creases of worry around Drew's eyes and wished she could smooth them away.

"She sure does clean up nice."

Allison smiled, recognizing the voice. "That she does."

Dorothy nudged her. "I have something for you."

She turned to see Dorothy holding her grandfather's class ring in her hand. "Go on, take it. It belongs to you."

Torn, Allison hesitated before plucking the ring from the old woman's calloused hand. "Are you sure? I know you two meant a lot to each other."

A smile blazed across Dorothy's face. "I know we did, too. But he would want you to have the ring, honey. I'm sure of it."

A surprise swell of emotion hit Allison square in the chest. She missed her grandfather every day but tried not to dwell in the sadness. It was a thing she did, organizing feelings into boxes in her mind and leaving them to be covered in dust until they tumbled off in an earthquake of unexpected emotion. Her mind flashed to The List, and the important notation that read a little something like: "You can't run from grief, you fucking idiot." Clearly, she couldn't strike that off yet.

"Thank you," she said quietly, hoping Dorothy could hear her above the music. "This means a lot to me."

"Well, it means a lot to all of us that you and Drew did all of this for us." Dorothy looked around the room. "My grandkids would never take time out of their lives to help plan a party for a bunch of old-heads."

Allison shook her head, not sure she'd heard correctly, partly because of the surprise of Dorothy's statement, and also because she'd caught Drew's eye from across the room. She wasn't quite so unreadable tonight, and Allison felt every lingering second of Drew's gaze as it took her in from head to toe. "Hang on," she said, reluctantly tearing her eyes from Drew. "You have grandkids?"

"Six." Dorothy looked at her and cupped the side of her face. "But that's a long, not so happy story for another day, honey. Let's enjoy ourselves tonight, okay?"

Allison could only nod, and Dorothy patted her face once before moving off toward the group at the Candy Cane Hook 'Em table. She threw a devious look over her shoulder as she sauntered up to join the activity.

Though it was tempting to watch Dorothy maneuver a candy cane between her false teeth, Allison had better things to view. She stood still as she covertly looked around the room. It didn't take long for her eyes to locate Drew. She was chatting with a few men, the picture of nonchalance and entirely at ease right there in a sea of dentures and canes. It took a few seconds before Drew angled her head to catch a glimpse of Allison, and when she did, she smirked.

Fine. Allison didn't mind being caught staring. Not one bit.

She sent a coy smile back to Drew, counting the minutes till she could kiss that smirk right off her gorgeous face.

CHAPTER TWENTY-SEVEN

Large gatherings and Drew had always had a complicated relationship. On the one hand, being around so many people who expected small talk and quick jokes was overwhelming. And on the other, the more people, the easier it was to disappear in the seams.

Growing up a Kingsley had thrown Drew into more large gatherings, even some outright galas, than she could count. They'd been easier when she was younger because people expected less of her. Once she hit her late teens and stumbled into her early twenties, every gathering came with pressure to perform. Pressure to be the best. And when word traveled that Drew was doing the unthinkable and not joining the family business, she suddenly had many, many people expecting her to offer an explanation.

Tonight, though, Drew felt no pressure. Very few eyes were on her; aside from the handful of waitstaff floating around with trays of food, she and Allison were the youngest people in the room by at least forty years. No one wanted anything from her.

It was freeing. Hell, June didn't even want her hovering—June's word, not Drew's—because she wanted to enjoy her evening.

She'd done her due diligence, however, and made the rounds with June on her arm. It was mostly to calm Drew's nerves about her grandmother's new talent of fading out in the middle of conversations. Fortunately, she was alert tonight, on point with retorts and sharp cuts in conversation. Drew was blessed with the discomfort of watching June flirt, and it was at that point she decided to let her grandmother go. There were some things Drew did not need to be a part of, and June's seduction was at the top of the list.

As Drew moved between the reindeer antler activity table and the bar (nothing alcoholic, just a wide variety of juices, seltzers, and the requisite sherbet punch bowl), she kept her eyes peeled for Allison. Last Drew had seen her, she was laughing with a group of people at the Candy Cane Hook 'Em table. She'd been sparkling, and not just because of the disco ball swinging above her head. Drew had taken the opportunity to walk past her and press her hand against the small of Allison's back, making it seem as though she was inspecting the game when all she wanted was to touch her. Allison hadn't moved, hadn't given any inclination that she'd even felt the touch— and then she'd reached back and stroked the outside of Drew's thigh, right before Drew moved along.

That touch was still lingering on her leg.

"Looking for me?"

Drew's body reacted before her mouth could. She paused, making sure her voice wouldn't give away her instant arousal, then said, "And what if I was?"

A warm body brushed against her arm and Drew nearly leaned into it before remembering where she was and how many eyes were guaranteed to be on them. "I'd say good, you should be."

She smiled and shoved her hands into her pockets. It had been a long time since she'd been around someone and had a difficult time not touching them. It was the most pleasurable pain. "Looks like everything's a hit."

Allison nodded, scanning the room. While she looked away, Drew stared at her. She still didn't understand when it had happened, when she'd stopped seeing Allison as a stranger and started seeing her as someone she actually wanted to be around. Like, *really* wanted to be around.

"I'd say so. Unsurprisingly, the mouth games are the biggest hits."

Drew coughed. "The what?"

"The mouth games. The ones over there." Allison pointed to a table where two old men gripped candy canes in their mouths, wiggling their furry eyebrows at the ladies standing with them. The next table over, Blanche was standing with a plastic spoon in her hand. Her lipstick, a bold and dark red, was smeared on the end of the spoon, and she looked to be arguing with the bald man standing with her. He was holding out one hand and there were a few mini pompoms on the floor between them.

"Is he…?" Allison reeled back, cringing. "Oh, God. No. He's holding *his teeth* in his hand."

Drew mirrored her cringe. "I don't think I want more information."

"You don't," Allison said simply. "But you know what you do want?"

Another zap of arousal shot through her. This woman was going to kill her before they could even make it past kissing. "Tell me."

Drew would love to say her sultry tone was accidental, but when she saw the effect it had on Allison, she knew it had come out of her for a reason.

"Jesus," Allison said, fanning herself. The casual innocence of the gesture broke a grin across Drew's face.

Allison turned to her, their mouths close but not touching. Those ocean-blue eyes tracked Drew's eyes, then glanced down at her waiting mouth, only to sweep back up and meet her eyes again. A cocky smile sat crooked and tempting on Allison's lips. "Everything," she said softly, ten letters piling up on Drew's lips like a multicar fender bender.

"Might I remind you," Drew said, "that we are standing in the middle of the grand hall at Sunset Dunes, surrounded by a horde of elderly folk who would probably have heart attacks if either of us moved even a centimeter closer."

"I am very aware of this."

"And," she went on, unable to break eye contact with Allison, "when you say things like that to me, I hope you know that I am writing it down in my brain and I will hold you to it."

That did it. Drew watched the gulp bounce in Allison's throat. She kept her smile as steady as possible as Allison took a step back, letting air pillow between them.

"And I," Allison said, her confidence billowing, "will hold *you* to *that*."

"I'd expect nothing less from you."

Allison nodded and quickly looked away. Drew allowed herself a moment of wild grinning. She still wasn't sure Allison was real. She'd have to check again. And soon.

"Now," Allison said suddenly, turning back to Drew, the picture of calmness. "There is something that you want right now."

Drew flexed her quadriceps, not allowing her knees to buckle.

"Come with me," Allison continued, gesturing for Drew to follow her.

And follow her she did. At that moment, Drew would have followed Allison anywhere. It was new and confusing, an untethered sensation that left her feeling solid and steady. She suspected everything with Allison would be that way, a strange and beautiful quilt of paradox.

"Oh, Allison, your drink is delicious!" Dorothy waved her half-empty glass toward them. "You wouldn't even know there's no alcohol!"

"I'm so glad you like it. Oh, perfect timing." Allison stopped as a waiter approached them, then took two glasses off his tray. "Thank you. Here," she said, handing one to Drew. "Try it."

Drew took a sip, and it wasn't even a tentative sip. After all, she'd loved that weird basil tomato drink Allison had brought to the beach. She had full confidence that all of her mocktails were going to knock it out of Citizens Bank Park.

"Oh, that's good," Drew said, taking another sip. "Blood orange?"

"Did the giant orange slice give it away?"

"Maybe." She held the glass up, inspecting the liquid. "It kind of tastes like alcohol."

"That's the point, Drew." Allison's eyes sparkled. "There's alcohol-free rosé in it."

Another sip went down easily. Yeah, Allison was going to have a successful business. Drew held the glass to her lips, trying to hide the proud smile that was bursting at the seams of her mouth.

But Allison didn't see it; she'd gotten pulled into a conversation with some men who certainly were not blind. Drew took advantage of the moment and stepped back to breathe.

Just a day ago, she'd been worried about falling into the patterns of her past. And today, she was standing here, already feeling things that should be so far down the line on the feelings timeline. Drew, as a rule, did not rush. She didn't leap. But Allison was challenging everything she thought she knew about herself.

It didn't make sense. None of it. That wiggle of uncertainty wormed through Drew's stomach, but on its tail was Cam's voice, reminding her that the whole point of dating is getting to know someone, to see if they fit.

"You okay?"

Drew blinked at Allison. She ushered away the ping-pong match swatting back and forth inside her. She didn't want to mess this up. She didn't want to get hurt, but she also didn't want to miss out on something potentially amazing.

"I'm better than okay," Drew said.

Allison grinned. She reached over and gently squeezed Drew's bare forearm. The touch vibrated and settled her, all at once.

"Good," she said. "Me too."

"Can you believe it?" Carol exclaimed, plopping into a chair. "I knew we should have searched them before they came in."

Allison and Drew exchanged a look, both trying not to laugh.

"Someone could have gotten hurt!" Carol went on. "I just can't believe these old hags. The audacity!"

"Okay, but no one got hurt," Allison said. "Everyone is perfectly okay."

Carol grumbled something unintelligible. Allison looked to Drew for reassurance.

"It was just one little airplane bottle of vodka," Drew said. She leaned back in her chair and propped her feet up on another. "And only two people drank it."

"Honestly, I'm surprised there wasn't more brought in. I thought for sure Blanche would find a way to get a bottle of champagne in here."

"Oh, don't think she didn't try, girlfriend. I'm sure she's drinking a gallon of it in her room right now."

"Hang on," Allison said, holding up a hand. "They can have alcohol in their apartments but they can't have any at facility functions?"

"Weird, but true," Drew confirmed.

"Well, I hope she's chugging a French 75 right now. She deserves one."

Carol shot Allison a look. "Are you gonna help her get up off the floor after she falls?"

Allison shrugged. "If she puts me on her Life Alert, sure."

Drew couldn't stop the laugh that bubbled up inside of her, even if it meant being on the receiving end of a dirty look from Carol.

"All right, you two go on. Get out of here." Carol stood and looked around the room. "It's late. We can clean up tomorrow."

Drew practically jumped to her feet. She'd been waiting to be released for the last thirty-three minutes, but had respectfully sat through the debriefing she hadn't known would take place.

"You're sure?" Allison stood as well. She looked exhausted. "It's only eleven."

"Only?" Carol sputtered. "Listen, doll, I don't know what kind of hours you keep back there in that tiny home, but I am sound asleep by nine-thirty p.m. without fail. If you two want to stay and clean up, be my guest."

"We don't," Drew said bluntly.

"I didn't think so." Carol smirked. "Go have some fun. We'll meet here tomorrow at noon."

She shuffled out of the room, leaving Drew and Allison in a sea of Winter Wonderfest debris. Drew could see the wheels turning in Allison's head, and knew—

"We should start cleaning now," she said, confirming Drew's suspicions.

"Maybe. But we're not going to." Drew nodded toward the exit door, which led to a pathway that would deliver them to the beach. "Come on."

Without a word, Allison followed. Once outside, they both took off their shoes before walking down the path toward the Gulf. The night around them was quiet and still. No breeze, no clouds. The sky was an endless carpet of stars.

"Do you ever get used to how beautiful it is here?" Allison asked as they began walking along the water's edge.

"No." Drew, under the protective shield of night, reached over and took Allison's hand as they walked. She was rewarded with the gentlest squeeze.

"I like that, actually. It's like, every day you're reminded of the beauty."

"If you're lucky."

"Oh, I thought cynical Drew had taken the night off."

She laughed at that, knowing it would never be the case. "Nope. She sometimes gets distracted, though."

"I can handle that."

Water splashed over Drew's bare feet and she nodded. "Yeah, I think you can."

They walked in silence for some time, their hands clasped tightly together. Thoughts scattered in and out of Drew's mind, words she wanted to plug into sentences, phrases that wouldn't make the cut. She didn't know where to start, and certainly hadn't a clue how to end. But she wanted to bridge the silence between them. She wanted to take the leap.

Drew cleared her throat. An auspicious beginning. "So, us."

Another hand squeeze. "About that."

"About that," Drew echoed. "I'm not great at this part."

"Is anyone?"

That was a good point. Drew was sure someone out there was. But it obviously wasn't either one of them. Fine. They could be not great together.

"I like you," she said, deciding to go with the simplest truth. "And I know that there's so much we don't know about each other. But I like what I know so far."

"That's a good start. I like what I know about you, too. So far."

Drew smirked, but it fell quickly. She had no idea what to say next. All the fears she'd expressed to herself and to Cam snowballed through her mind. She was, right there in the balmy Floridian night, frozen.

"Maybe that's all we need right now," Allison said, swooping in to save the day. "We can go slow."

Perfect, and exactly what Drew needed to hear. Now that she could feel her limbs again, she nodded. "Take it day by day."

"Yes. But to be clear, we're dating, right? Which means we're not dating anyone else?"

"Is that what you want?"

That earned her a kick of water. Deserved, she knew.

"Not if you're going to be an ass about it."

There it was. That dangerous pocket-sized spark that Allison carried with her and launched at Drew with ease. God, she loved that.

She stopped and pulled Allison toward her, wasting no time in threading her fingers through her hair and eliminating the distance between their mouths. It was their third kiss and Drew was stunned to realize it was even better than the previous two. Maybe it was the growing comfort with each other, or the natural way their lips fit together. It could have been the night itself, bursting with romance: ankle-deep in the warm Gulf of Mexico with a starry blanket hanging far above them.

It was possible that it was just because it was them. Together.

"I know there's a lot we have to learn," Allison said when she pulled back. "But for the record, I already know that I really, really like kissing you."

"That's a mutual feeling."

She was grateful that Allison laughed, though it came with a light slap on her butt. "I do need to know one thing before we go any further," Allison said.

"I'm listening."

"I know you don't talk much." There, again, was the confident tone holding the underbelly of vulnerability. Drew could stand to learn something about that. She hoped Allison would teach her. "Do you talk about the important stuff? Feelings? Future plans? Conflict?"

Drew reached up and smoothed Allison's flyaway hairs off her face. She hoped the action would convey more than she worried her words could. "I do." She took a deep breath, knowing she was heading directly into unknown territory: a relationship with a mature, emotionally available woman. "You might have to push me a little bit. At first."

She watched as Allison mulled that over. Drew had a sudden and uneasy feeling it wasn't new territory for her. But she couldn't change the truth of what she'd said.

"Just at first?" Allison finally said, looking at Drew.

"I have a feeling," Drew said, pulling Allison in close, "that once you crack me open and get me talking, I'm not going to shut up."

Allison smiled and tapped on Drew's heart. "I bet she's holding a lot in."

"More than a lot."

"Well," Allison said, "I think we're going to find out just how much is in there."

Drew wanted to say something but found there were no words befitting a response. Instead, she leaned in and kissed Allison again, hoping that would translate a strand from her heart.

CHAPTER TWENTY-EIGHT

"I just don't see the point in taking down the decorations when it's still December."

"Because they're in the way, Yolanda." Greg's voice had that low, firm tone of Drew's childhood. "Let's start with the family room."

Yolanda gasped dramatically, leaning against the kitchen island. Drew rolled her eyes and continued putting food in a leftover container. She wanted no part of this argument.

"But Christmas is the highlight of my year! Give me one more week, Greg."

To Drew's surprise, her dad hesitated. Maybe he was getting soft in his advancing age. The idea nearly made Drew laugh out loud. Greg Kingsley would be a force to reckon with even after he died.

"Fine. On one condition." He smiled at his wife, who was giving him a demure look that was nausea-inducing for her children. "No more Christmas music."

This time, not only did Yolanda gasp, but so too did Celeste and Natasha, who were lingering in the kitchen. Yolanda would listen to Christmas music year-round if she could (and they all knew she did when she was alone in her car). She usually played it in the house until mid-January, when Greg slyly removed the CDs from the multidisc player that was an ancient relic but still well loved and used in the Kingsley home.

"I don't like this arrangement," Yolanda said. She tapped her long nails on the marble countertop. "Drew? Help me."

Drew shook her head. "You're on your own."

"She'll be out of here as soon as she finishes jamming a week's worth of food into that container," Celeste said.

"You're not staying?"

Normally, Drew would fall for that sticky sweet pouting voice her mom put on specifically because she knew it snagged Drew in her crosshairs of guilt. But Christmas was over. Well over, in fact, considering it was the thirtieth and Drew had spent entirely too much time with her family over the past week.

She wasn't sure if it was June's casual nagging about needing to give her family more chances, or maybe it was Allison having made a sudden decision to spend the holiday with her mom in Georgia. Likely a combination of both; Drew made the effort with her family, and it was easier to do so without the distraction of knowing she could spend time with Allison.

Which is not to say that the family time had been without ego clashes and uncomfortably stern conversations. Drew had abruptly left her parents' house a total of three times due to her oldest brother being a controlling asshole and her dad being, well, her dad.

When Drew wasn't with her family, she'd been working. Specifically, she'd been spending as much time as possible at Allison's bar. Even she couldn't believe how quickly it was coming together. She wanted to slow down and savor the experience, make sure everything was perfect, but she also wanted to see the business open and flourish with Allison at the helm.

Drew smiled to herself as she snapped the container shut. In a weird way, being around her family for the last week had softened her. It tended to do the opposite because she stalked around the spacious rooms with her guard up as high as possible. But something was shifting within her. She'd imagined Allison sitting at Christmas dinner with her and had not felt nauseous or panicked by the thought. She'd felt calm, assured. Ready.

She felt ready.

Drew blinked, annoyed at the warm emotions trying to escape her eyeballs. If she shed even a single tear in front of her sisters and her parents, she would never hear the end of it. As casually as possible, she wiped the corner of one eye with her sleeve. There. That would have to be enough.

Just as Drew opened her mouth to bid her farewells, the entire downstairs of the house exploded with Paul McCartney's voice. Emotional moment gone, Drew laughed beneath the lyrics of "Wonderful Christmastime." Her dad *hated* that song.

"I'm out of here," Drew said, giving Celeste a quick hug. Celeste, in turn, pinched the back of Drew's neck. "Asshole."

"Goodbye, my baby," Yolanda said, coming back into the room. Drew hadn't even noticed she'd left, but that explained the eardrum-bursting concert coming through the downstairs speakers. "You promised me lunch soon. Don't forget."

"I won't, Mamá." Drew hugged her extra tight.

At the front door, she paused, looking for her dad. He was nowhere in sight, and while the right thing to do was to go find him, Drew knew it wouldn't make a difference if she did. Instead, she called out, "Bye, Dad," and left without waiting for his response.

After stopping at home to drop off the leftovers (which, for the record, Drew never missed out on. Yolanda leaned hard into her half-Cuban roots and always had a whole roasted pig for Christmas dinner along with black beans and rice), Drew drove the short distance to Allison's bar.

She walked up the freshly fixed front steps and unlocked the front door. A smile lit her face instantly. She couldn't believe the transformation—not only from the beginning, but also from the time Allison had finally envisioned her, well, vision.

The concrete floors were a faded olive, a perfectly neutral color for whatever design changes Allison would make over the years. With the lighting installed, the room shone with inviting warmth. The bar had gone in just a few days ago—Allison had yet to see it—and the light wood stain was the perfect buffer between floor and ceiling. There weren't any stools yet, but they would be there by the week's end. She'd had to pull some strings for that.

Drew walked through the space, taking in the big picture. The bar-height tables could seat six. Again, no stools; again, a favor called in. The shiplap was hung and perfectly worn-in. In the space near the bathrooms, Allison had opted for a "cozy spot," as she called it. Four armchairs had arrived over the weekend and were staged in the area with a round coffee table. Drew wasn't sure exactly what layout Allison was envisioning, but she had to admit that the coziness brought something special to the bar.

She brushed her fingers over the smooth, natural wood-stained tables as she moved back past the bar and into the office. After a moment's hesitation out of pure nerves, she opened the door and poked her head in.

It was perfect. Well, she thought it was; she could only hope that Allison would, too.

No one would ever know that space had been a nearly rotted out kitchen. Everything had been replaced, and the walls were painted a deep sage green that beautifully complemented the recycled dark wood luxury tile floors. Drew wasn't about to make furniture purchases without Allison's input, so she'd had Celeste pull her own strings and loan her staging furniture.

Drew cast her eyes over to the loveseat that sat against the outside wall. She was hoping, quite selfishly, that Allison would spring for something similar.

An hour or so later, Drew was wiping off the last of the grout on the ceramic tiles behind the bar. She was very pleased with it, if she had to say so herself. More importantly, she was sure Allison would like it, too.

Normally a fan of silence, the quiet had scratched its anxious, overthinking way under Drew's skin and she was forced to bring in the portable speaker from her truck. The time away from Allison had been fine, completely fine. They'd texted and talked on the phone a couple of times. Normal, easy stuff. Their reunion was pacing at the forefront of Drew's mind, however, and she found herself uncharacteristically nervous. The silence had to go. She'd cycled through music options until she landed on an old playlist, one she'd made during a rare moment of feeling hopeful about love. Seemed appropriate, hopefully not a jinx, so she put it on while working.

She was so into the music that she missed the sound of the front door opening, but definitely heard it close. When she looked up, she was treated with the image of Allison standing in the doorway, gazing around the space in awe.

Not wanting to break the first-look moment, Drew put her sponge down and simply watched her. It had been one thing for Drew to walk in and see the incredible progress of a week's work, but to see Allison seeing it… It did something to Drew. Something she found she liked, and wanted to feel more of.

Something she truthfully hadn't expected she would ever feel, or even like to feel.

"I can't believe it," Allison finally said. "How did this happen?"

"Magic."

She spun around and grinned at Drew. "You'll never give away your secrets, will you?"

"There are no secrets." She moved from behind the bar and stepped closer. Suddenly nervous after not having seen her for a week, Drew faltered, unsure if a hug or a kiss or just a wave was her best bet. Allison chose for her, wrapping her arms around Drew's waist. When she leaned back, she smiled up at Drew until the message was clear as day. Drew pressed her lips against Allison's, sighing with relief.

"Hi," Allison said, her lips still moving against Drew's.

"Hey."

With a final kiss, Allison moved away and walked around the space. "I'm seriously blown away, Drew. This is so much better than I imagined it could be."

"You realize you're complimenting yourself, right?"

Allison laughed and it was then that Drew saw the miniscule change in her. She seemed freer, lighter. It was alluring, and not for the first time, Drew felt herself being pulled in.

"Kind of, yeah. But none of this would have happened without you." She stopped at the accordion doors and turned to face Drew. "We make a pretty good team. We should capitalize on that."

Before speaking, Drew weighed her options. She could go serious, flirty, or sarcastic and knew Allison would come along on whatever path she chose.

Drew crossed her arms, having decided. Call it a test, because it may very well be, but she couldn't resist. "Okay, Holly."

The range of expressions that curtained over Allison's face was impressive. Drew was having a hard time keeping a straight face, and when Allison stomped over to grab her and kiss her, she knew she'd made the right choice.

"For the record," Allison said, shoving Drew back after kissing the life out of her, "I have no interest in joining your family business."

"Thank God."

"And also, for the record," she continued, "if you *ever* call me that name again, I'll…I'll…I'll go back to her."

Drew laughed so hard she hurt her throat. "That's more punishment for you than it is for me."

"Then we'd both suffer." Allison shrugged. "Seems fair."

"Okay, big shot." Drew grabbed her hand and pulled her toward the office door. "Before you get too far ahead of yourself, I want you to see something."

"Wait." Allison tugged on Drew's hand, stopping her. "If there's a bunch of people hiding in there to jump out and surprise me, you need to tell me right now. I. Do. Not. Do. Surprises."

"Noted. And no. There's no one in there." Drew pushed open the door and nudged Allison inside. "The furniture's not permanent, but I wanted you to see what it could look like."

"Drew." The word was breathy and slow, intoxicating. Allison walked into the room and took in every inch of it. When she looked down at the floors, she tossed Drew a grin. "I really do love these floors."

"I know," Drew said quietly. She still didn't know exactly what it was about this woman—likely never would, and probably for the best—but she was having an incredibly hard time not grabbing her and throwing her onto the loveseat.

As though Allison could read her mind, she sent a devilish look in Drew's direction as she stood in front of the loveseat. "Interesting addition," she noted. "Is this for me to take naps?"

"No." The word, singular in its meaning but studded with weeks of tension and building desire, scratched Drew's throat. She moved across the small space and grabbed Allison, kissing her with a ferocity she'd never felt before.

Allison gripped Drew's hips, yanking her closer. Their kiss deepened, moving from explorative to possessive. Drew spun them around and sat down on the loveseat, pulling Allison onto her lap. The mood shifted instantly, slowing and filling with need.

Allison squeezed Drew with her thighs as she rocked slowly back and forth, building a heat that Drew feared would never be extinguished. She was starting to lose control and while she knew she could safely do so, she wasn't ready for that. Not yet.

So when Allison reached up with both hands and went to place them on Drew's shoulders, Drew grabbed her wrists and stopped the movement. Allison gasped, then recovered by giving her a knowing, sly look.

"Too much?" Drew asked between staggered breaths.

"Not at all."

"Good."

With Allison's hands secured, Drew was ready to submit to every pinprick of desire coating her body. She struggled to take a deep breath as she wrapped her fingers around both of Allison's wrists (a bonus of having big hands and dating someone with tiny wrists), freeing one of her own hands to touch. When she lifted her hand with Allison's wrists enclosed in it, Allison's back arched, drawing a ragged breath from deep within Drew.

She didn't know where to begin. She wanted everything, all at once, everywhere and always. The tips of her fingers grazed the skin of Allison's neck, dipping into the hollow between her collarbones. Allison's chest rose and fell as Drew traced the line of her V-neck shirt, leaning in to allow her tongue to follow the path her fingers had blazed.

"I need you," Allison whispered. Her blue eyes were dark and soulful, rimmed with naked vulnerability.

With effort, Drew swallowed. Years ago, those words would have sent her running. But now, it was the only thing she wanted to hear.

"Come home with me."

CHAPTER TWENTY-NINE

Never had Allison been so thankful for living in a small town. She'd been ready to combust just from straddling Drew in her office. Had the drive to Drew's house been more than five minutes, she absolutely would have had to either pull over and take a succession of deep breaths, or demand that they stay right where they were and do the damn thing already.

As it was, they were speed walking into Drew's house within minutes of leaving the bar. Drew unlocked the front door with one hand, grabbing Allison's hand with her other and pulling her into the dark house. Before Allison could eke out a word or even form an idea, she was pushed against the shut front door and Drew's mouth was on her, all consuming.

Drew took her in, kissing her mouth, her jaw, her neck. Allison's knees weakened with each swipe of Drew's tongue. She kept her hands to herself, though it about killed her. She was dying to touch but understood this had to go Drew's way.

And, honestly, she was more than happy to oblige.

"Bedroom," Drew said, abruptly removing her mouth from Allison's collarbone.

"Lead the way."

That earned her a quiet laugh. Drew flicked on a few lights as she walked through the house. Allison didn't waste time looking around. There would be plenty of time for that later. Right now, she needed to get into Drew's bedroom and get them both out of their clothes.

Drew shut the bedroom door behind them. A single bedside lamp was on, casting the room with a sensual glow. Allison looked over at the king-sized bed then back at Drew.

"Tell me where you want me," she said, purposely keeping her voice low and confident.

Drew closed her eyes briefly—Allison made a note to use that tone more often—then opened them, her hands instantly roaming all over Allison's body. Moments later, Allison was standing naked before Drew. She felt nothing but deep arousal and comfort, the two sensations colliding and intertwining.

"You are stunning," Drew said, her eyes roaming freely over Allison's body. "And I am going to devour you."

Allison's heart fell to the side, then picked itself up and began sprinting. She waited, knowing Drew would take the lead. And so she did, taking off her own jeans and long sleeved T-shirt but keeping on her sports bra and boy shorts. She backed Allison up till the back of her knees hit the edge of the bed, then gently pushed her so she was lying down.

"Up there," Drew said.

Allison moved into the indicated position, never taking her eyes off Drew. The darkness in her eyes was glittery and full of intent. Never had Allison felt so wanted in her life.

And then, Drew was on top of her. Her body hovered over Allison's as their furious kissing ignited once again. Allison wanted, needed, to feel Drew against her. She dared one hand to brush against Drew's side and immediately, the kiss was broken. Drew's hand encased Allison's, reaching over to grab her other hand for good measure. In a flash, Allison's arms were above her head on the pillow, her wrists pinned down by Drew's hand.

"I'm going to trust you," Drew said. Her deep-brown eyes were glowing. "If you move your hands, I will tie them down."

Allison gasped, certain she was about to explode right then and there, without any touching at all. She nodded.

"Good girl," Drew whispered. Satisfied with Allison's groan-sigh response, Drew's mouth returned to hers, biting and sucking her bottom lip.

Before Allison could lavish Drew's bottom lip with the same favors, Drew's mouth disappeared. She sighed then jerked as Drew's teeth clamped over her nipple. Teeth, then lips, then teeth, then lips. The seesaw of sensuality rocked Allison's body right along with her mind. Drew snaked her hand over Allison's other breast, stroking the skin around her nipple until Allison was absolutely certain she was going to scream for Drew to touch her fucking nipple already.

And right there at her breaking point, Drew kissed her way across Allison's chest. The sudden shift from carnal intensity to sweet, soft touches settled low in Allison's belly, sending a singular message to her brain.

She was going to soak the bed.

As Drew began to ravish Allison's other nipple with that same incredibly pleasurable pain, she swept her hand over Allison's hips. The touch skittered over her stomach, creating another implosion of contrast between the feelings coming from Drew's mouth and those coming from her hand. Allison was vibrating on the bed. Her legs were already shaking and Drew wasn't anywhere near—

Oh, fuck.

It happened quickly, without pretense or warning. Drew's fingers slid over her arousal, brushing against the places Allison needed her touch. Her clit was throbbing and she was certain Drew could feel that as her thumb skated over it. Allison gasped, the sound coming from deep within her, and arched her back as Drew effortlessly slid two fingers inside of her.

"You're so wet," Drew said, her voice surprisingly calm. Or not so surprisingly, considering what Allison was in the midst of learning about her. "Do you want me to fuck you?"

"Yes," she nearly yelled. She bit the inside of her cheek and when she spoke again, her words were measured and cool. "Yes. Please."

Drew said something but it was lost in the cacophony of Allison's response to her sliding another finger inside.

"You can take it." Again, that low, in control voice. That alone could undo Allison.

She could take it. And she did. Happily. Allison tried to keep her vocalizations to a minimum, but it was no use. Simply put, Drew knew how to fuck a woman. Her fingers curled and thrusted, slowed and sped up, finally settling into a rhythm that caused Allison to call out so loudly her voice cracked. All too soon, she shook as her body gave in.

"Beautiful," Drew murmured. Her fingers hadn't slid all the way out before her mouth settled over Allison's clit. The instant of dual pleasure nearly shoved Allison right over the edge again, but when Drew began slow, purposeful strokes over her clit, she used both hands to hold Allison's thighs apart, providing a shuddering relief before she sank into the singular and luxurious feeling of Drew's mouth.

Drew had said she was going to devour her, and devour her she did. Allison could only stare at the ceiling, mouth gaping, as Drew's lips and tongue brought her closer and closer. She held out for as long as she could, clinging to the fuzzy but vibrantly alive moments right before she hit her limit and came, hard and fast.

Her hips rolled and her legs jerked, neither movement stilling much as Drew slowly moved up the bed and laid next to her. Her hand fell on Allison's stomach, fingers fanned out. She propped her head up on her hand and looked down at Allison.

She reached up and touched Drew's cheek. "You look so serious."

"I need to know that was okay," Drew said. A flicker of insecurity made its way into her expression. "I…You have this effect on me. I should have checked in earlier, I know—"

"Hey," Allison said, leaning up to kiss her. "I would have stopped you if I didn't like it."

"Promise?"

"Promise." Allison pointed to the sheets beneath her. "Besides, I think there's evidence that I really fucking liked everything about what just happened."

Drew laughed, insecurity gone. "I'm not sleeping in that."

"Well neither am I."

Allison was pretty sure Drew had a rebuttal waiting to launch, but she wasn't interested in hearing it at that time. She pulled her in and kissed her, finally sinking her teeth into Drew's bottom lip. The grunt she received in return was well worth the wait.

A thought occurred to Allison and she paused the kiss. "Drew."

"Yeah?" Her hand had moved from Allison's stomach and was cupping one of her breasts, her thumb lazily rubbing her nipple.

"I can…You know. Right?"

Drew cocked her head. Allison knew she knew what she was asking without the words, and she readied herself for the gameplay.

"You can do lots of things, Allison."

She quirked her eyebrow. "To you."

"Oh, *that's* what you meant." Drew scooped her up and rolled them over so Allison was on top. "What would you like to do to me?"

The list was long, and the night was young. But there was one thing Allison had a hunch they both needed.

"Turn over," she said, moving off Drew.

Drew raised both eyebrows but obliged without argument. Lying on her stomach, her head nestled in the pillows, she was the picture of vulnerability, and Allison knew that as much as she hated it, she felt safe in it.

Allison straddled Drew's hips, drifting her fingers over her back. Drew's tanned skin highlighted each sculpted muscle, their flexed lines and firm curves begging for Allison's touch. She lowered herself, nipples grazing against Drew's skin. She moved her hands under Drew's bra and pushed it up until it was over her head. She wanted her mouth on Drew's breasts more than anything, but that could wait till later. Right now, she needed this.

With her own breasts pressing against Drew's back, Allison reached around and slid her hands between Drew's chest and the bed, both women gasping when her fingertips found Drew's nipples. She rolled them between her fingers, arching herself harder against Drew. As Drew's muffled grunts grew louder, Allison lowered her mouth to the tender space where Drew's neck met her shoulder and bit.

"Oh, fuck," Drew said, her voice muffled by the pillow. "How did you—"

"Shh," Allison said, biting again. She bit her way down Drew's muscular back, her hands moving with her. She shifted off Drew once again and slowly pulled her boy shorts down, exposing an absolutely incredible ass.

Allison nudged her way between Drew's legs, spreading them just enough so she could kneel between them. Drew's breathing was growing more and more rapid by the second. She would question herself for years to come, how it was that she knew precisely how to fuck Drew that first time, but in that moment, all Allison saw was *finally*.

"Get on your knees," she said quietly. Drew did, her back a downward slide to her neck. She cradled her head in her crossed, flexed arms.

Allison ran her hands over Drew's ass, her own heartbeat accelerating. By the time she pushed into Drew from behind, she was nearly at the brink again herself.

Hearing Drew's uninhibited pleasure, however, was going to push her over. Allison squeezed her thighs together, keeping her own desire simmering as she fucked Drew slow and hard. With each push, Drew arched back to meet her. They moved in sync, like they'd been fucking for decades, and when Drew growled out a shuddering orgasm, Allison gritted her teeth, trying to keep her own at bay.

She didn't have to wait long. Drew, needing no time to recover or languish, flipped over and grabbed Allison, sitting up and pulling her onto her lap just as she had back at the bar. This time, there were no barriers and Drew was deep inside her in a flash.

The noise that came out of Allison was not one she had ever made before. She wasn't even sure where it had come from. The feeling of being filled by Drew was otherworldly, and she was so turned on that she was just thrusts away from breaking open yet again.

"Did you like fucking me?" Drew's words were somehow hotter than her fingers, which felt like a sensuous fire inside of Allison, thrumming and spreading with each curled thrust.

"God, yes."

Drew reached up with her free hand and held the back of Allison's neck. "This is just the beginning."

Emotion smashed into unbridled pleasure, and Allison came hard, flowing out over Drew's lap. She laughed through her tears, the intensity having crashed through any barriers she'd tried to uphold.

"You okay?" Drew's fingers caught her tears. The gentleness shimmied right up against the potency of every other touch they'd shared in that bed, bookending what Allison knew would be the most read pages of their story.

"Yes. Sorry. That was…That was a lot."

"I know. Come here." Limbs untangled, they laid down on the bed, Allison resting her head on Drew's chest. She draped her leg over Drew's and wrapped her arm around her waist. They settled into the comfort of being together, time passing without either noticing. The quiet was reassuring and calm, and after a while, Allison was contemplating falling asleep.

"Not bad for our first time," Drew remarked, and Allison burst into laughter, both tears and tiredness gone.

"We did good," she agreed.

Drew smoothed Allison's hair off her face. "Are you hungry?"

"Oh my God, I'm starving."

"Good. Give me five minutes, then meet me on the deck."

CHAPTER THIRTY

Drew had just finished setting up a late-night picnic on her back deck when Allison padded out. She glanced up and her heart trip-hopped at the sight of her. She'd found a pair of Drew's sweatpants and put her own T-shirt back on. Barefoot and messy-haired, Allison gave a shy smile as she sat down at the table.

"Rooting through my drawers already, I see."

"I don't waste any time, Drew." The shy smile widened into something more confident. Drew wasn't sure which she liked more.

"Clearly." Drew sat down and pointed to the items on the table. "Leftovers, courtesy of my mother. I'd say she cooked it but she never does."

"Your mom doesn't cook?"

Drew shrugged as she dished some roast pork onto Allison's plate. "She did when I was a kid. But when she got busier with the family business, we got a chef."

Allison gaped at her. "You're telling me you grew up with a *chef*?"

"Partly, yes." Drew took advantage of Allison's open mouth and forked warmed-up rice and black beans into it. "Chew and swallow, please."

She did as requested, shooting Drew a patronizing look in the process. "You enjoy ordering me around."

The should-be-a-question-but-definitely-purposely-a-statement sent a delicious chill down Drew's spine. It was those exact moments in conversation over the past month that had made her think she and Allison would be wickedly compatible in bed, and now she had proof. So much proof that she was certain neither one of them would be getting much sleep that night. Or possibly (hopefully) ever again.

"Yes. Now eat. You'll need your energy."

Allison leaned over and kissed Drew on the cheek. "I like you."

"So I've noticed."

"God, you're annoying."

Drew smiled around her mouthful of food.

"But I think that's why I like you," Allison continued. "You're definitely not like anyone I've ever known. And that's a good thing."

It was the most relatable thing Allison had said in Drew's presence. So far, anyway. And as much as Drew wanted to echo the sentiment, she found herself pulling into the quiet spaces within her. She felt she was straddling a finely dotted line and worried about leaning too far in either direction.

They ate in silence for a while, the night doing its cloaked, clandestine work around them. When Drew finished, she pushed her plate away and sat back, staring out over the water. The peace of her home was something she treasured, and it was not lost on her how easily Allison fit right into the landscape. She felt no need to entertain or impress her (well, maybe a *little* of the latter). It felt right to have Allison beside her, comfortable and safe.

Allison snuck her hand over onto Drew's lap and Drew tucked her own hand around it.

"So," Drew said.

"Uh-oh. That's a foreboding beginning."

"It's not. At least I don't think it is." Drew brushed her fingers over the back of Allison's hand. "You want me to talk."

"Yes, when you want to talk."

Drew nodded. "First of all, I like seeing you in my clothing. Second, I like the way it feels, having you here with me. Third, I'm very much looking forward to fucking you again."

"I'm loving this list."

"Fourth," and here Drew hesitated. The first part was easy. This part, not so much. Arguments and worries overlapped in her tired brain. She didn't need to say anything more right then and there—she knew that and believed Allison would listen whenever she chose to talk—but she felt compelled to.

"Fourth," Allison picked up, "you don't do casual, so I should stop worrying that this was just sex."

Drew twisted so she could meet Allison's eyes. "That wasn't number four."

"What number was it, then?"

"Like, ten."

Allison's eyes widened and a smile threatened the corners of her mouth. "Oh. Okay. I didn't realize this was a long list."

Drew shrugged. There was no way she could act careless anymore with Allison, but she could be a little petulant just for fun. "It could be very short if that's your way of telling me you'd rather fuck and run."

Allison's silence stirred a quivering worry deep within. Drew peered at her, waiting for a sharp retort.

"Drew." An auspicious start. "There is not a single cell in my body that wants to run."

Relief unspooled through Drew's body, relaxing her limbs and loosening that anxious grip on her brain. She hadn't realized until Allison responded that her own stupid joke could backfire tremendously, but it was also—she was remiss to admit this, even to herself—a test.

"Look. I know you have a wall around your heart. And don't even try to argue with me because I've seen it since the very first time I saw you."

Drew couldn't protest the truth, so she didn't bother. She listened, waiting to see what all Allison had learned about her simply by watching.

"I get it," Allison continued. "Before I moved here, I had a fortress around my heart."

"With a moat?"

"Yes. Definitely a moat."

"And sharks in the moat?"

Allison wrinkled her nose. "Okay, no, it's just water. Without sea life."

Drew hummed with disappointment. "Shame. I've got sharks. And razor blades on the walls."

"That's a lot, Drew."

"After you have your heart crushed enough times by people who make you believe they want the same things you did, you'll add sharks. And razor blades. You would add everything you could so you didn't ever have to take the risk of being open and vulnerable for people who said that's what they wanted but couldn't actually handle it." Drew stopped herself before more came tumbling out. She desperately did not want to go there, not now. Someday, maybe. But not now.

Allison waited to make sure she was done before saying, with all the gentleness a woman like her could possess, "Do you want to talk about it?"

"And be the cliché lesbian couple who spends hours talking about their past relationships? No thank you."

"Oh, we're a couple now?"

She had no fight left in her. Drew released Allison's hand so she could hold her face between her hands, and kissed her slowly. Her body, not having come too far down from the wicked heights of arousal, perked up. Yeah, this conversation would need to be short.

"Yes," Drew said at the end of the kiss. "I still want to go slow, but I figured we could go slow together. Officially. If that's okay with you." She knew it was contradictory, but the idea of going slow was something she needed to hold on to for a bit longer.

"Way more than okay." Allison pushed Drew's hair off her forehead. "And you don't have to talk about it—ever, but especially right now—but if you do, I will always listen. Even if it makes us a cliché." She paused before saying, "If there's anything you need from me to, I don't know, help with that wall, tell me. Okay?"

Yet again, Drew was struck with the belief that Allison was not, nor could she be, real. But there was her hand, on Drew's thigh. And there were her eyes, serene and thoughtful under the dark sky and glowing string lights hanging above the deck.

"You being you helps," Drew said. "Just keep doing that."

"That," Allison said confidently, "I can totally do."

And that was enough talking for the night. Drew stood and cleared the table, telling Allison to stay and enjoy the cooling night air while she cleaned up. In the solitude of her kitchen, Drew went through the motions of rinsing off dishes and putting them in the dishwasher. She packed up the rest of the leftovers, already looking forward to having them tomorrow, and put them back in the refrigerator. Then she stood, her palms pressed into the edge of the counter of the island. Her head hung low, hair falling into her eyes.

That was not at all what she'd intended to say. It was too early to bare those particular skeletons to Allison, especially less than an hour after they'd had crazy intense sex. She wanted to do this right. Dipping into her past like that… Drew didn't want to be that person. If she could swipe an eraser over everything that had gone wrong in her romantic past, she would, just so she wouldn't have any scars to bare to this incredible woman who had walked into her life from all the way across the country.

Allison didn't need to see the shards and crumbles. But they were a part of Drew. Unavoidable, really. She thumped her hand on the island. It was too soon. She'd said too much.

Caught up in her self-admonishment, she didn't hear the sliding glass door open and close. It wasn't until Allison slowly and gently wrapped her arms around Drew from behind that she even realized she'd come inside.

"Is this okay?" At Drew's nod, Allison tightened her hold. "Did I upset you?"

She shook her head, not trusting her damn mouth. Apparently, Allison possessed some annoying-ass quality that made Drew want to talk freely and openly about all the shit that made her into who she was right then and there in her perfectly designed and appointed kitchen. The last time Drew had felt like she could be that open, she'd dove in and come back out (or was ejected, more accurately) with gashes lining her knees and heart alike.

She knew Allison wasn't the interior designer. She knew Allison wasn't anything like her past. The very fact that she'd known to come inside, known to hold Drew just as she was—delicately but firmly—Allison just knew her. It made no sense at all but there was no denying it anymore.

Drew relaxed in Allison's arms, rubbing her hand. "I don't want to get hurt again."

"And I don't want to add you to The List." Allison made a weird noise right when her sentence ended.

Drew creased her brows. "What's the list?"

"Nothing," she said hurriedly, then seemed to reconsider when Drew turned in her arms and gave her a curious look. "It's not nothing. It's just this thing that I have. I'm sure I'll end up showing you eventually, and be completely mortified the whole time, but whatever. It's part of who I am."

"Well now I'm very curious."

"Mmm, yeah, well, stay curious."

That feisty attitude was never not going to be a turn on for Drew. With little effort, she picked Allison up and swung her over her shoulder, grinning when Allison gasp-squealed.

"Volunteer firefighter," she said by way of explanation.

"I'm here for it. Hose me down, baby."

Drew stopped short in the hallway. "Allison."

"Yeah, no, that was awful. It won't happen again. Carry on."

With a playful swat to Allison's firm ass, Drew did just that.

EPILOGUE

Six months later

Living in Florida during winter had been blissful. Allison found she didn't miss the snow and ice that had perpetuated the majority of her lifetime further up the east coast, and then over on the west coast. Instead, she luxuriated in long walks on the beach in the middle of January, and a Valentine's weekend spent in the Keys. She wasn't even sure she still had a winter coat.

Now, in the middle of June, Allison had some regrets about moving to a southern beach town. Only one regret, truly, and it wasn't even a regret, just a distinct dislike for steady hot, humid weather that only broke briefly for a nearly daily afternoon thunderstorm.

She liked the storms, though. She liked them quite a bit.

What she was ill prepared for, despite Drew repeatedly telling her to get ready for the shift, was the influx of people the moment temperatures started spiking. First came the snowbirds, most arriving in late January. Then there was the spring break rush, which staggered throughout March and into the beginning of April. After that, swarms of people came and went every week. The beach got packed, then emptied for a day or two. Clearwater Beach was a revolving door of visitors.

It wasn't all bad, though. While she preferred the slightly sleepy nature of her winter beach town, the steady turnover of tourists was a boon for Fizz. It turned out there was quite a market for a mocktail bar after all, and she never let Drew forget it.

Thursdays were notoriously extra busy, and this one was no exception. Allison had opened the bar at one p.m. and no more than one table had been empty since. It was a stiflingly hot day, so few people wanted to sit outside. Even with the umbrellas Cam had found, if there wasn't a breeze out there, it was simply not a nice place to sit and enjoy a mocktail. At least not until the sun went down.

On the flip side, the tables right by the accordion doors were the first to fill. Allison watched her newest server, Drew's niece Ashley, move gracefully between the tables. She missed having the windows open but was not about to steam herself and her customers out of the perfectly cooled space.

The clink of glasses at the bar drew her attention in that direction. She'd spent the off season being the bartender and hadn't wanted to give up her favorite job, but when business began to pick up, she'd had to hire another set of capable drink-making hands.

Allison walked over behind the bar and stepped in to help Scarlett with the ticket Ashley had just dropped off.

"Thanks," Scarlett said as she reached for the Juniper Berry Blush. "These Floradoras were a great addition to the summer menu. Everyone wants them."

"I think it's the ridiculous name." Allison poured lime juice and raspberry syrup into the four glasses lined up. "They're nothing fancy at all. Plus, they taste like cranberry ginger ale to me."

"My nana loves it. She has one in her hand every time I visit her."

Allison smiled down at the glasses. That was fitting, since the Floradora drink was named after a Broadway show.

Scarlett, Dorothy's youngest grandchild, had moved to Land Clearwater (some of Drew's verbiage had rubbed off on Allison despite her attempts not to allow that to happen) back in March. Allison had gotten many, many stories about Dorothy's time designing costumes on Broadway but still hadn't gotten all the family lore. Scarlett, too, was very closed off about her family drama, but she was making a concerted effort to spend as much time as possible with her grandmother, and she won endless points in Allison's book for that. Plus, Scarlett being around had brought a new life to Dorothy, who was happier every time Allison saw her.

It was a matter of convenience that Scarlett had been bartending for a couple years and was more than happy to come work with Allison.

"Hey," Ashley said as she leaned over the bar. "I know the passion fruit mojito is off the menu, but do we still have the puree?"

"I think there's enough left for a drink, maybe two." Allison squatted down and checked the mini fridge under the bar. "Yup." She stood up, container in hand. "Two max. Use it up."

Scarlet went to work and Ashley bounced off to inform two very happy customers that they could enjoy the very last passion fruit mojitos of the season. There would be a new mojito as soon as Allison figured out what flavor combination would best suit the second half of the summer.

She paused at the end of the bar, surveying the space she had watched be brought back to life after having been abandoned for years. No matter the weather or her mood, every time she stepped into Fizz, she felt a jolt of elation, knowing she was right where she belonged.

"Busy day."

Speaking of being where she belonged. Allison ended her visual tour on Drew, who was standing near the bar. "It's June in Clearwater Beach, and wouldn't you know, the people love a mocktail."

"Never doubted that for a second."

Allison laughed and reached out for Drew. "Liar. Come here."

Once they were tucked into the closed-door privacy of her office, Allison pressed Drew against the door and kissed her. The passion between them was every bit as sweltering as it had been the first night they'd given in to, to use Drew's favorite wording, their wanton desires. While the sex was unerringly hot, it was everything else that kept Allison hooked. She gave Drew all the space and patience she needed and little by little, Drew had begun to open up. It hadn't taken long at all for her walls to splinter and fall, board by rotten board, to the ground.

And Drew, though adamantly against fixing, was effortlessly healing wounds Allison hadn't even known still existed. She wasn't doing anything in particular; she was just being Drew. Allison credited it all to that familiar feeling between them, the sense that this is where they had always belonged. It was a peculiar feeling, one she couldn't define, but it continued to grow the more they got to know each other and gave them both a soft place to land.

All of that combined made it difficult for them to want to spend time apart, but the rest of their lives took care of that for them. Their schedules had conflicted lately, with Drew managing a big project on the opposite end of town and Allison working steadily at Fizz. They had a standing date night at The Hideout on Wednesdays so Drew would never miss any of Nan's experimental hot dogs, but it was only Tuesday, and they hadn't seen each other since Saturday morning.

"I don't like this not seeing you every day thing," Allison said. She slid her hands around Drew and grabbed her ass.

Drew dropped her mouth to Allison's neck and kissed a line to her throat. "We're going slow, remember?"

It was a running joke, and likely had been since the first time they'd made the proclamation. Perhaps the only slow thing about their relationship was that it had been six months and they hadn't moved in together. Yet.

Slow felt like torture in that moment as Allison's body responded to Drew's alternating kisses and nips on her throat.

"Are you finally going to fuck me on that loveseat?" she asked, breathless against her will.

"You wish." Drew pulled back and grinned.

"Yeah, I do."

That tone still worked on Drew, and Allison imagined it always would. She watched as Drew's features pulled together into concentrated desire. Just when she thought she would finally get that loveseat fuck, a knock on the office door jolted them both out of their near seduction.

Drew stepped out of the way and Allison yanked the door open to find Ashley standing there, a single sheet of paper in her hand.

"Oh, hey, Aunt Drew. I didn't see you come in." She handed the paper to Allison. "Another resume came in. I didn't want to lose it or spill something on it out there."

"Thanks, Ash." Allison placed the resume on her desk. She wasn't hiring anyone else at the moment, but a little reserve never hurt.

"You going to your sister's soccer game tomorrow?" Drew asked. She was lounging on the loveseat, legs and arms spread like she owned the place. It was obnoxiously sexy.

"Yup! See you there?"

"Probably. Unless your mom pisses me off."

"Yeah, okay, Drew." Ashley rolled her eyes before turning and strutting back to her customers. They all knew it was bullshit; Drew never missed a game, even when Natasha was being an asshole to her, which was, admittedly, often.

Allison looked forlornly at the open door, knowing even if she closed it, she wouldn't get her dream of a loveseat fuck today. Oh well. Another time.

She snapped her fingers as she looked back at Drew. "I almost forgot. I found something today."

"Oh yeah?"

"Oh yeah?" Allison mocked. She gestured for Drew to come over to the corner behind her desk. No sense in letting her sit there looking all fuckable when no fucking was going to be taking place. "Look familiar?

Drew's grin lit up the room. "It took you this long to find it?"

"It's not like it's in the most obvious place."

She squatted down to inspect her artistry. "Oh, I like the frame you put around it."

After discovering the protruding nail, Allison had dug in her desk to find her favorite Washi tape. It was yellow and printed with pink martini glasses. She'd outlined the nail in a square of the tape, forever framing Drew's territory-claiming gift.

"I know you won't take it out, so I figured I might as well dress it up."

Drew looked up at her, an adorable mix of adoration and amusement on her face. "I know I'm the handy one in this relationship, but you could remove it. If you wanted to." She straightened and came face-to-face with Allison.

"No, I don't want to remove it. I'm happy being stuck with it."

"Good." Drew leaned in and kissed her thoroughly. "I have to go."

"Tell June I said hi."

"Always do." She brushed her thumb over Allison's cheek. "Can I see you tonight?"

"I'm not out of here until eleven."

"I'll wait up."

Allison shook her head, laughing. "We both know you'll be sound asleep."

"So wake me up." Drew brushed her lips against Allison's, not permitting a full kiss. "See you later."

She left, both of them knowing Allison would in fact come over after she closed the bar, and she would absolutely wake Drew up.

Later, when the bar was full with the predinner crowd, Allison stepped outside for fresh air. Clouds had moved in, blocking the sun as it swung lower in the sky. But the air was still overly warm and thick with the promise of a nighttime storm.

Allison looked back through the window wall, feeling a deep sense of satisfaction and belonging. She no longer hesitated to call Clearwater "home." Staying here had never officially been her plan, but she could see now that it was always meant to happen, and happen right when it did.

She'd never say she'd moved across the country to find love. Sure, she'd been lonely and heartsick over failed relationships, but the potential of new love wasn't what encouraged her to pack up and leave. She'd come to start fresh, to discover truths about herself she'd buried long ago because she didn't think they'd ever have space to see the light. They were out now, bold and bright, never to be shadowed in darkness again. She'd never felt more comfortable in her own skin. Or more at peace with who she was and who she was becoming. And she knew she could not have grown this much had she remained in the place that was determined to keep her still and stagnant.

Seagulls squawked overhead and Allison ducked. She'd confided in Drew about the great shit event when she'd first moved to town, and after Drew had managed to breathe after her bout of laughter, she'd told Allison that being shat upon by a bird was an omen of good things to come. Figuring those good things had arrived in the form of Fizz and Drew, Allison kept her head down as the birds flocked over her. She wasn't in the market for any more poop produced prosperity.

Maybe it was luck (not from the bird crap), maybe it was divine timing. Whatever the case, Allison had no reservations about how much her life had changed. She'd spent years hoping for it, and now she treated every day as a gift.

As it turned out, she didn't need her list of mistakes to guide her into the life she'd dreamed of living. All she needed was a chance to begin again.

Bella Books, Inc.
Happy Endings Live Here
P.O. Box 10543
Tallahassee, FL 32302
Phone: (850) 576-2370
www.BellaBooks.com

More Titles from Bella Books

Hunter's Revenge – Gerri Hill
978-1-64247-447-3 | 276 pgs | paperback: $18.95 | eBook: $9.99
Tori Hunter is back! Don't miss this final chapter in the acclaimed Tori Hunter series.

Integrity – E. J. Noyes
978-1-64247-465-7 | 228 pgs | paperback: $19.95 | eBook: $9.99
It was supposed to be an ordinary workday...

The Order – TJ O'Shea
978-1-64247-378-0 | 396 pgs | paperback: $19.95 | eBook: $9.99
For two women the battle between new love and old loyalty may prove more dangerous than the war they're trying to survive.

Under the Stars with You – Jaime Clevenger
978-1-64247-439-8 | 302 pgs | paperback: $19.95 | eBook: $9.99
Sometimes believing in love is the first step. And sometimes it's all about trusting the stars.

The Missing Piece – Kat Jackson
978-1-64247-445-9 | 250 pgs | paperback: $18.95 | eBook: $9.99
Renee's world collides with possibility and the past, setting off a tidal wave of changes she could have never predicted.

An Acquired Taste – Cheri Ritz
978-1-64247-462-6 | 206 pgs | paperback: $17.95 | eBook: $9.99
Can Elle and Ashley stand the heat in the *Celebrity Cook Off* kitchen?